SKIRTING DISASTER

Kay Keppler

SKIRTING DISASTER

Acknowledgments

Many thanks to Beth Barany, Patricia Simpson, Jilly Wood, and Anne Victory, who did their best to help me make this book the best it could be. And a special shoutout to that unknown participant in the writers workshop, who, when asked what the young woman in the poodle skirt might do for a living, said, "Maybe she works for the CIA."

Chapter 1

Phoebe Renfrew sat at the scarred picnic table in the one-room office and hoped to high heaven that she knew what she was doing. Did she really want to be a private investigator? Two months ago she had an important job that she liked and had worked years to get. The CIA wasn't perfect, but she'd used her brain to solve problems and, she hoped, help her country. She had a regular income. She wore suits to work. She had *benefits*.

That was before. Before the CIA suspended her. Before Las Vegas.

And before Chase Bonaventure.

She looked around at the fresh paint on the walls of the tiny office, her fingers clenched under the table, and wondered if she'd snag her tights on the picnic bench. One thing was for sure: she wasn't at the CIA anymore.

"I'm glad you're here, because a case came in and I could use your help," said Dave Greenaway, the ex-cop she'd worked with when she first arrived in Vegas. Now retired from the LVPD, Dave had opened a private investigator's office so he could, as he said, accept only the cases he wanted—preferably just the boring ones. "That is, if you still want to do this. It's not too late to back out."

Did she want to back out? The CIA had lifted her suspension, so she could return to work—and a big part of her wanted to. But the CIA was back in Langley, Virginia, and

Chase was here in Las Vegas, Nevada.

She had six months to make up her mind. If she stayed, she wanted employment that used her skills. And that's where Dave Greenaway came in.

"Case?" she asked, stalling for time. "You have a case already?"

"Yeah," Dave said. "From your boyfriend. Vandalism at the car factory."

"*What?* What happened? He didn't say anything about it this morning."

Dave shrugged. "That's probably because he didn't know about it then. Last night somebody went into a secured parking area out there and damaged a bunch of cars that were supposed to be part of a fancy demonstration or conference or something—"

"Oh no! Not the Cars of the Future expo?"

"That's it." Dave nodded. "See? This is helpful. You got the inside scoop on everything."

"Not quite everything," Phoebe said. "How bad is the damage?"

"Bad enough that they can't be repaired and sent to the expo. All the cars in that lot were spray-painted, pounded with something—probably a tire iron, maybe a rock—windshields and windows broken."

Phoebe closed her eyes, feeling sick. Everyone had worked for weeks getting all the new models ready for the expo five days from now. If they had nothing to take to the expo, not only was the time, money, and effort wasted, but they couldn't get reviewed by the websites and magazines, wouldn't make any sales. The company's bottom line would take a huge hit. Maybe wipe them out.

She blinked. "Wait a second," she said. "Why did Chase call you? Why not the police?"

Dave let a hint of a smile cross his impassive features. "He called me because he thought I still *was* the police. He didn't know that today was the first day of operations for Western Private Investigations. I guess his girlfriend didn't tell him that."

"Who's that?" she said. "What girlfriend? Because I'm sitting right here."

"You mean you're *not* dating Las Vegas's most prominent citizen?"

"Dave, you're confusing me. I thought *you* were Las Vegas's most prominent citizen."

Dave laughed. "Touché. Yeah, Bonaventure is chasing me in the popularity polls. So anyway, I told him to call the cops."

"And did he?"

"He did. They went out there and said there wasn't much they could do. He filed a report. They dusted for prints. I put in a call to a buddy in the department, and I got the impression that the evidence collection was more a courtesy than anything else. Not that they won't run the prints, but they probably won't find anything definitive. Lots of people at the plant worked on the cars, so any prints they find won't mean much. It's basically a dead end."

"So then Chase called you back, and *you* said—"

"I might not be able to find out who damaged the cars. Probably won't be able to if the cops can't. But this little episode demonstrates that Venture Automotive needs a lot more security now. They're getting to be a big operation. They got assets to protect."

Phoebe hadn't been positive that working for Dave Greenaway would be a good idea. But now that Chase's business—and his hopes and dreams—were on the line, she had to help if she could. "So where do you see me in this?"

"Basically, I need a warm body, and you're right here already," Dave said, dispelling any notion she might have had that special skills were required.

"And I'm warm." Phoebe tried not to feel deflated. "Good to know."

Greenaway flashed a grin. "If this job turns out to be bigger than some stupid-ass kids messing with Vegas's most prominent citizen, I'll probably have to hire another couple of investigators no matter what you decide to do long-term with the CIA."

"Okay." Phoebe nodded. "Stupid-ass kids, huh? You think that's who did it?"

"No," Dave said, surprising her. "But anything's possible."

"Why don't you think it's kids?"

"I went out there to look at it. The fence is nine, ten feet high, topped with razor wire. So not that easy to get over, and there's no sign that anybody did. Wire's intact, not bent, and they didn't cut through it. Gate to the street wasn't tampered with. But there's two doors from the building right out to the lot. I think somebody strolled out there, banged up the cars, went back in, punched out, and went home. Unless Bonaventure is handing out keys to all and sundry, I think it has to be an inside job."

"An inside job? Chase will freak."

"You are correct. He is, as you say, quite concerned. And that's where you have an edge. You know everybody out there."

"Well, I know some people. They've been hiring like crazy to ramp up production. They got all that investor money, you know."

"I do know—largely because of you, is my understanding. Okay, you won't know all the new hires, but you have a reason to be there. People will talk to you because they'll think you have an ear to the top. Which they won't be wrong about."

"You're killing me here, Dave. But I guess we'll find out if people will talk to me. Where do we start?"

"We'll take a drive out there. Check out the damage. Assess what they need for security. But before we go, there's a few things we have to get out of the way if you plan to work here, even temporarily. First is pay."

Let it be enough to retire my CIA school loan. She'd accepted three hundred thousand dollars from the agency for her college education and follow-up training. That debt would be forgiven if she worked there for six more years— but if she didn't return, she'd have to pay all the money back.

"Fifteen bucks an hour right now," Dave said. "As we

grow, you'll get more. Assuming you stick around."

"Okay." Fifteen bucks an hour was about half of what she'd need to earn every year for the next thirty or forty years to pay back her school loan. It wasn't nearly enough to pay off the loan. It was barely enough to pay rent.

But hey. It was a start.

"Now, about this job," Dave said. "It isn't what you're used to. Even if this were the biggest PI agency west of the Mississippi, which it sure as hell isn't, it still isn't the CIA. You'd be giving up a lot if you quit there. And you have a lot of work ahead of you if you're serious about becoming a PI."

Phoebe nodded. "I'm not afraid of the work, and I want to give it my best shot. Are you okay with a six-month commitment? The CIA gave me that long to decide if I want to go back or not."

"Sure, that works," Dave said. "Anybody else I hired would be provisional anyway. We'll call it a probationary period. You won't need to start weapons training right away, but—"

"Weapons training?"

"Yes," Dave said, an implacable glint in his eye. "Required for the PI license."

At one time she'd used a pink collapsible umbrella for a weapon, but Dave probably wouldn't be on board with that idea.

"Weapons training." She swallowed hard. "Check."

"The CIA didn't give you weapons training?"

"No. The CIA is about intelligence gathering, not law enforcement. I'm a language analyst. We wear suits and sit in cubicle farms and read stuff. No weapons required."

"Unbelievable what the government is coming to. Okay. Moving on. You might need to do surveillance for this gig. You'll have to use your own car, and—"

"Wait." Phoebe swallowed again. Dave wasn't going to like this, either. "You didn't know? I don't have a car. Or even a driver's license."

Dave shook his head. "I didn't know. No license. Of

course not. Just because everybody over the age of sixteen in the United States has a license, and their biggest wish is to have their own wheels."

Phoebe didn't think it would help to tell him she got around on her bicycle. He probably thought she'd ridden it there for the exercise.

He sighed. "Can you get a license and a car? You can't do surveillance otherwise."

"I'm working on the license. I got my learner's permit. Chase took me out practice driving last week, and Sanjay is taking me again tomorrow."

"Sanjay—your friend with the taxi, right? A professional driver. Okay, that's good. The sooner all that happens, the better." He frowned, drumming his fingers on the scarred picnic table. Evidently the bad news was still coming.

"Here's the part that might be the hardest for you. Before you can get a license as a PI, assuming you want to do that after six months, you need to put in two thousand hours of supervised work with somebody who does have a license. That's me. Think you can handle that?"

"No problem," Phoebe said. Of course, Dave knew that she'd been in trouble with the CIA for—well, *insubordination* was probably too strong a word for what she'd done. But maybe she'd overextended her authority a little bit that one time.

"I'm asking because what I know of you demonstrates that you don't take orders that well."

"I can take orders!" Phoebe felt indignant. She could learn, anyway. She was learning everything else for this job.

Dave sat there, looking at her with those assessing eyes. *Oh, for Pete's sake.*

"The secretary of state would have been *kidnapped* if I hadn't acted. And nobody, not the CIA, or the FBI, or even the cops—no offense, Dave—would do anything. And who knows what would have happened to her?"

"I was thinking about the Empire State Building."

Oh. Yeah. The Empire State Building. The screwup that had caused the CIA to suspend her in the first place. Cops,

SEALs, SWAT, tanks, robots, and drones had rolled in big time when she said a terrorist threat on the iconic landmark was imminent. Except then nothing had happened.

That had been a bad day. Really, really bad.

"Well, yeah, okay," Phoebe said, conceding the point. "It would have been better if more experienced personnel had been there to evaluate my decisions. But still, I wasn't all wrong."

"Everything worked out," Dave said. "But I want you to remember that our resources are more limited here. In this office, you've got only me for backup. And the cops, of course, should any situation come to that, which it better not. There won't be SEALs and SWAT teams at your beck and call. *This isn't the CIA.*"

Phoebe clenched her teeth. "I *know* that."

"So I don't want you to go off half-cocked," Dave said. "I don't want either of us to get killed or hurt. Not even *scratched.* I want a nice, simple, retirement gig here. I want to do background checks. Quiet divorce work. Maybe follow up on a couple of missing-person reports. I want desk work. Got that?"

"Sure." Phoebe shifted on the hard picnic bench. "Desk work."

"We're gonna go out to Venture Automotive and talk to Bonaventure and assess their vulnerabilities and install some security measures, and nobody's gonna get involved in shootings or kidnappings, is that understood?"

"Understood," Phoebe said, rolling back her shoulders.

"Two thousand hours is one year of full-time work," Dave said. "For one year, if you really want to become a PI, you do what I say. After that, when you get your PI license— *if* you get it—you can do what you want, I don't care. I'll do the background checks; you can go after the shooters. Until then, we're not doing anything dangerous. I had a bellyful of dangerous when I was with the cops, and I'm done with it. Got that?"

"Sure," Phoebe said. "Safety first. Got it."

"Are you *positive*? Because I don't want to get started

on this and then have my license pulled because you can't follow the rules."

She leaned forward. "Dave, I don't know if I have what it takes to be a PI, but I will work as hard as I can and do my best for you. I worked at the CIA because I wanted to help protect citizens, just like you did as a cop. And being a PI falls right in with that. I know that I have a lot to learn and working here will be different than working at the CIA, but that's good! It'll be a whole new angle, and I'll learn a lot from you. And now that your first case is for Venture Automotive, I've got a personal stake in it. You know I'll go the extra mile."

"Okay. Well, we'll see. As long as you go the extra mile at the designated speed limit."

Phoebe grinned.

Dave didn't smile back. "One more thing."

What else could he say? He'd all but told her that her preparation was substandard and she didn't have the personality to be a PI. Maybe working for Dave hadn't been such a great idea. The CIA was looking better all the time. Or maybe bagging groceries. She could serve the public bagging groceries, too.

"What you did for the secretary of state—foiling that kidnapping," he said. "For a person with no police training, you got the job done, pretty much by yourself. The instinct you showed—you can't teach that. You'll be an asset here right from the start, and if you decide to become a PI, you'll be good at it."

That was the nicest thing anyone had ever said to her. She beamed at him, feeling a rush of pleasure.

"Thank you," she said. "I'll do my best not to let you down."

"I know," Dave said. "Because for some strange reason, you might rather be the number-two PI in a two-person office than work for the CIA."

"Call me crazy," Phoebe said, "but I think this might be more fun."

"And that's what I'm afraid of."

"Also, you don't intend to waterboard anybody."

Dave looked revolted. "Hell, no. And I thought the CIA didn't do that anymore."

Phoebe shrugged. "They don't. Of course not."

Dave assessed her again with those all-knowing eyes. She smiled back. She hadn't been part of the clandestine operations at the CIA, but she'd learned a few things even so.

"Any questions about all this?" he asked finally.

"Nope. I'm ready to roll." Phoebe slapped the rough edge of the picnic table. "But we have to do something about this piece of junk right away. No self-respecting client will believe it's a conference table. They'll be expecting us to serve hot dogs and lemonade."

"They'll be disappointed then," Dave said. "So if you're ready, let's head out. You drive. Don't kill us on the way."

By the time they got out to the plant, Phoebe was a nervous wreck. Chase had taken her out driving only once so far with her learner's permit, so she had a decent excuse for being terrified of the fast, aggressive driving she encountered on most of the wide, multilane streets of Las Vegas. But they'd gotten out here in one piece. Pretty much. She parked in the nearly empty visitors lot with a sigh of relief and got out on shaky legs.

"That could have gone a little more smoothly," Dave said, bending over to examine the underside of his car. "Bumping over the curb like back there is hell on a transmission. I hope nothing happened to my oil pan."

"I'm sorry, Dave. That truck got so *close*. I didn't realize how sensitive the wheel was. Take the repairs out of my paycheck, okay?" And there went any hope she could make a payment on her school loan.

Dave shrugged, standing up. "Learning to drive just takes practice. Get Bonaventure to take you out driving more often. Hell, he's got a factory full of cars. You could wreck one a day and not run out of vehicles."

"Thanks for that visual, Dave."

He snorted and led them around to the side of the

building. "Let's check out that parking lot before we go in."

Phoebe was familiar with the lot—they'd used the space that butted up against the building as a staging area for a car rally Venture Automotive had sponsored a few weeks ago. Since then, Chase had enclosed the area, partly to keep the demonstration models separate and secure while they got ready for the expo. That plan clearly hadn't worked.

Who would want to damage Chase's business? He was a hero in this town. The former star quarterback for the Las Vegas Rattlesnakes had led the team to three Super Bowl titles. And when his football career ended after a bad hit wrecked his knee, he'd engineered the swift turnaround of an unprofitable electric-car company, creating a couple hundred new jobs while he was at it.

She'd fallen hard for him, which made her nervous. If she quit the CIA and stayed in Vegas working for Dave because that's where Chase was, she'd spend the rest of her life paying off her school loan and upending the professional goals she'd set for herself since high school. Not only that, she'd be replicating her mother's life pattern of following every guy who crooked his finger at her because she thought that he was the guy who'd be the icing on her particular cake. In her mother's case, her particular fruitcake.

In her case, devil's food.

Thinking about Chase made her hungry for him, sending every rational concept straight out of her head. And that made her worry that she might have more in common with her mother than a shared gene pool. Brenda could fall for a guy in a span of days or even hours and move in with him, sometimes quitting her job and giving up everything else, including her daughter, convinced that the new guy was The One. Eventually she'd discover that he wasn't, and she'd move out again. The upshot was a lifetime of financial and emotional insecurity for both herself and Phoebe.

Phoebe had vowed that she'd never be like her mother, living paycheck to paycheck, believing that this next guy was the ticket to a secure and happy life. Phoebe believed that happiness came from within, and security came from hard work and planning. That's how she'd gotten to college in the first place. And because Brenda didn't believe in college and couldn't afford to pay for it if she did, Phoebe had grabbed the opportunity the CIA offered.

That decision had been easy.

What was less clear was how her relationship with Chase—so far, very short term—was different from her mother's relationships with her own short-term boyfriends. She would *not* repeat her mother's mistakes.

"Check it out," Dave said. They'd walked around to the side of the plant and were facing the fenced-in enclosure.

Phoebe inspected at the nine-foot chain-link fence topped by razor wire. A gate wide enough to allow the cars to drive out to the street was securely locked. Whoever had damaged the cars hadn't come through that unless they'd had a key. Two doors led from the building into the lot—one large enough to drive a car through, so that probably led to the production area inside. The other was a smaller, people-sized door next to it.

The fence, as well as the gate, appeared untouched, the mesh unbroken, the razor wire sharp and round. Within the enclosure, a dozen cars, all of them badly damaged, were parked in the shade of the building. The cars were splashed in layers of multicolored paint, their fenders and hoods dented and even ripped. Open doors revealed shredded and stained upholstery and smashed dashboards. Windows and windshields were broken, and glass littered the ground.

The place was a disaster zone. Chase must be devastated. And angry.

"Wow," Phoebe said, gazing at the destruction. "It's even worse than I imagined."

"Whoever did this took some time with it. Doesn't really look like kids, does it? It looks like somebody's got a hard-on for—who would you say this is targeted at?"

"The company." Phoebe checked off on her fingers. "Or somebody who works for the company—Chase, probably, or somebody else. Maybe even the technology—you know, some oil tycoon who hates electric cars. You're training me,

Dave!"

"I'm brainstorming with you. Who are some likely suspects?"

"Okay." Phoebe felt energized. "Enemies of the company—other car manufacturers, electric or gas, who don't want the competition. Organizations who want to re-zone this area for something else, like a casino or condominiums. Can't have a manufacturer in the area then. Also, maybe car dealerships for some reason? Maybe they're getting kickbacks from other companies and Chase wouldn't buy in? Or—"

"You can stop there," Dave said. "Good ideas. Our job will be to check those out, see if any of them have legs. Offhand, though, I think this is personal, somebody who's got it in for Bonaventure himself, or maybe whatever Bonaventure does."

"Chase would be an obvious target because he's so well known," Phoebe said. "Everywhere we go in town, he's stopped by lots of people. His list of enemies could be huge—I mean, a Steelers fan could have done this."

"Yeah, did you see that playoff game last season? Jesus, that pass to Dan Freer. Unbelievable. So, right, all those fans would hate him."

"You think it was a Steelers fan who did this?"

"Nope. Whatever his beef is, I think the guy who did this has a more specific bitch against Bonaventure."

"Has to be a guy, right?" Phoebe said. "Whoever pounded those cars needed a lot of strength. Check out that fender. It's peeled back from the frame."

"Yeah, I'd say it's a guy. Or even a couple of guys. Bonaventure said nobody works nights—there's no security guard on duty—so they could have taken their time."

They stood back and surveyed the scene. The lot itself was large and paved, and the fence had been erected at the edge of the pavement.

"No security cameras out here," Phoebe observed. "I don't suppose there are any marks in the dirt?"

"Like tire tracks, you mean?" Dave said. "You might be

watching too much TV."

"Tire tracks, or, I don't know, little holes in the ground where a ladder went up next to the fence. Something."

"Unlikely. Ground's too hard and dry to see anything."

"So now what?" Phoebe asked.

"We'll take another look around, although we're probably duplicating what the cops did. But we're here. Might as well be thorough."

They walked back along the perimeter of the fence without seeing anything that would give them an idea about the perpetrators.

"I've had enough," Dave said. "Let's go talk to the boss." He headed toward the front door.

Talking to Chase always seemed like a good idea to Phoebe. They entered the air-conditioned lobby and greeted Megan, the receptionist, who sent them up to Chase's office on the mezzanine.

"You think it's an inside job," Chase said after they'd all settled down with ice water. "And it might be a vendetta against me personally." His eyes focused on Phoebe.

She felt a little flutter in her heart. Chase Bonaventure was smart, full of energy and ideas, and willing to listen to other people. And when he listened, he was right there, one hundred percent, giving you his full attention, taking you seriously. And he was so gorgeous with that dark hair that didn't stay put, those beautiful gray eyes. She couldn't hold it against him that he was rich, either, because he didn't act like a snob. Even though his house was ridiculous.

When she was with him, all six foot four of beautifully athletic man with a bad knee, she wanted to melt. *Would* melt if she wasn't careful.

Phoebe nodded, taking a sip of water. "It seems likely, yes. Inside job, might be personal."

"What makes you think so?" he asked.

She glanced at Dave, but he nodded at her to proceed. "There's no indication anyone forced their way through that fence from the outside," she said. "That's the main reason. Somebody either had a key to get through the gate from the street, or somebody entered the lot from inside the building."

"Who's got keys to that gate?" Dave asked.

Chase leaned back and shoved his hands through his hair. "Megan at reception. Kristin, my assistant. My foreman. The supply-chain guy—he inventories stuff coming in and deliveries going out. His assistant. Maybe some others. Kristin has a list. I trust them implicitly."

Dave nodded. "All those people been with you a long time?"

"The supply-chain guy and his assistant are fairly new, but they both came with great references."

"We'll look into those folks, eliminate them from consideration, if nothing else."

Phoebe made a note on her laptop. "I'll get a list. So if the vandals didn't get in through a lost or copied key, it was an inside job. You've recently made a lot of new hires to ramp up production. Maybe somebody has a problem."

"Could be a new employee," Dave said. "Could also be a long-term employee who has a grudge, wants you to fail."

"I can't imagine how anyone who worked here would do all that damage," Chase said. "Everybody across the board has put in one hundred and ten percent for the expo."

"Well, somebody doesn't like you," Dave said. "You or the company."

Chase sighed. "Evidently not."

"Like I told you on the phone, we probably won't be able to find the culprit," Dave said. "But if we beef up your security, we can stop future sabotage. Or make it very hard to do without getting caught."

"That's something anyway," Chase said.

"And let me say right now, there's a fast and easy first step you can take to protect your property: if you suspect someone, fire them. You don't have to be able to prove in court that they committed a crime."

Chase nodded. "Good point. Okay. I don't want to fire anyone without cause. But I'll do what I have to do to protect the company and the people who work here."

"That's a bridge we can cross later," Dave said. "Right

now our main focus will be addressing your vulnerabilities, making your cars as safe as possible."

"I wish we'd had this conversation a week ago." Chase rubbed his eyes, and Phoebe felt his weariness from where she sat. "Our plans for the expo are shot. And besides losing our exhibition vehicles, everyone is demoralized. We can get past this, I think, but we can't afford too many hits. Not if we want to grow. We don't have enough resources to compensate for more losses like this."

"Let's get a tour of the plant," Dave said, getting up from his chair. "See how everything's set up. Figure out a strategy."

Phoebe remained sitting. "Is there no way to get something to the expo?"

Dave sat down again.

"We're going to try," Chase said. "Maybe you and Dave want to stick around for the next meeting with the department heads and Kristin. We're brainstorming, including how to protect the plans."

"I'd like to stay," Phoebe said, glancing at Dave.

"Absolutely," Dave said. "If we see what *you're* doing, we can figure out more of what *we* should be doing."

"Plus I have an idea for the expo," Phoebe said. "I'll need Kristin to help. Wait. Maybe two ideas. Because we have to go *big*."

Kristin Seiler, Chase's no-nonsense admin, poked her head through the door.

"I'm not eavesdropping, I swear I'm not, but I heard my name," she said. "You have an idea, Phoebe? Whatever it is, let's do it."

"Oh, my god," Chase said. "This morning I was just angry about the damage. If you two have ideas to fix things, I'm angry *and* terrified."

He didn't look terrified, though. He looked interested.

"Oh, please," Phoebe said. "We'll simply be helping you with your marketing initiatives. Which need to be extensive."

"And that's what scares me."

"You know what?" Dave said. "That's exactly what *I* told her this morning."

Chase and Dave high-fived each other. Phoebe rolled her eyes as they stood up and headed downstairs to the production area.

"Honestly," she said. "You guys are worrying for nothing."

Chapter 2

A couple of hours later, Chase Bonaventure called his meeting to order. Besides Phoebe and Dave, only his most trusted department heads were included—Matt Tinkham, chief electrical engineer; Tony Minaya, software engineer; Rinsho Nakamura, foreman; and Kristin Seiler, admin. If these people were somehow involved in the sabotage, he might as well give up the company, because they'd helped him build it from the start. But they weren't involved. They all looked too depressed, for one thing. He didn't blame them.

"The Cars of the Future expo is the biggest and best automotive trade show for new-car reveals," he told Phoebe and Dave. "Exhibiting what you have is an absolute must. We've been getting great feedback on our vehicles, and we'd hoped—expected, really—to generate buzz and take orders there. Not going at all is unthinkable. So we have to figure out how we can salvage an appearance and stop future sabotage. Dave, I believe, has some ideas about that."

Dave nodded. "I do."

"Great," Chase said. "Let's talk first about what we can get done in five days for the expo, and then you can take the floor. So, everybody—ideas?"

Matt scrubbed his head with his hands. "I don't see what we can do in five days that will make an impact."

"Yeah, we worked like dogs for a month to get all the

models ready as it was." Tony slumped in his chair, his eyes closed, the picture of dejection.

"But we must do *something*," Rinsho said. "Maybe take fewer customized models? It won't be what we wanted, but we have to do what we can."

"*Exactly*." Phoebe glanced at Rinsho. "Related to that, I have a couple of thoughts."

Chase felt a surge of interest. In his experience, Phoebe's marketing ideas were always huge and usually wildly successful.

"I like thoughts," he said. "Let's hear 'em."

"I think this is where I come in," Kristin said.

"It is." Phoebe grinned at her friend.

He liked seeing those two smile. Best friends since the second they'd met, whenever they plotted, things happened.

Phoebe stretched her hands out, encompassing the group. "You want to make an impression, right? Venture Automotive is *the* up-and-coming electric-car company—up-and-coming car company, *period*. So we have to go *big*. We have to *splash*."

"Phoebe, we *can't*." Chase felt depressed and angry again. "We don't have enough time."

"Maybe there's not enough time to build a lot of cars— a lot of *fancy* cars," Phoebe said. "But we can still make a splash. What had you planned to show?"

"Six models, six colors," Rinsho said. "Thirty-six vehicles. Doesn't sound like much. But we have to reprogram the assembly line for each model. And we customized to show all the new features."

"That takes time," Tony said. "And three of the models are new. So that was more time."

"And we had a power outage for three days after that storm," Matt chimed in.

"We have to cut back," Rinsho said. "Maybe make only one car for the showroom."

"That's what I think, too," Phoebe said. "Maybe you can have a different model every day of the expo. Four cars. Is that doable?"

Rinsho, Matt, and Tony appraised each other.

Then Rinsho nodded. Took a deep breath. "Yes."

"We can do that," Tony agreed.

"Okay, then. Chase shows them to the audience, right? Not a salesperson. Because people would come just to see him." She grinned at him. "Maybe you should wear your old football jersey."

"I'm not wearing my old football jersey," he said. "I've moved on."

"Okay. Just a thought. Then you have a raffle. Require people to include their addresses and phone numbers to win. At the end of the expo, do a drawing and give the cars away. Those four."

"*Give* them away." Chase considered the idea. It would work. A giveaway of that magnitude would attract a lot of people to their expo showcase every day.

He considered his crew—Rinsho was nodding; that was good. Tony and Matt were nodding, too. *Excellent.*

"Okay," he said. "Good idea. Let's do that. Rinsho, why don't you—"

"And then I had another idea, too," Phoebe said.

"Okay," he said again. "Shoot."

"What about making a limited-edition car in an NFL theme? One car only. Paint it in the Snakes colors with the Snakes logo. And then maybe six players get out wearing different team jerseys, and you take preorders for cars with other team colors. Maybe you could do it for all the sports. Soccer or whatever. Baseball."

"Hey, I like that idea," Tony said. "Nobody else will do that, and we'd really stand out."

"Assuming we can license the logos and specific team colors," Kristin said, making a note. "I'll check into it. Maybe the teams would promote the idea if we gave them a percentage for charity. Something like that."

He liked their enthusiasm for the idea. "Thanks, Kristin. Let me know if you need help persuading Snakes management."

"Will do, Coach."

"All right," he said. "Now we have a plan. About security. Dave—"

"I thought of one other thing," Phoebe said.

Chase glanced around the table, seeing the interest in the faces of the others. Whether they could do everything she was suggesting was one thing. Right now, almost more important was the fact that these guys—the people he depended on—were feeling hopeful. But this idea would be the killer, he could feel it.

"It'll be expensive," she said.

Of course it would be.

"Go," he said.

"The expo is at the convention center," she said. "The Snakes stadium is only a couple of miles away. Maybe a ten-minute drive, tops."

"Do we want to go to the stadium?" Tony asked.

"We want the *expo attendees* to go to the stadium," Phoebe said. "The Snakes aren't playing football there yet, right? It's too early."

"The Snakes are still in training camp for the fall season, yes," Chase said.

"So we'll rent the stadium, to put on a fancy-driving show, like a halftime marching band routine, but with cars instead. Venture Automotive cars. Choreographed and driven by professional drivers."

"I love it!" Kristin said. "With fireworks! And an actual marching band! Cheerleaders!"

"Cheerleaders!" Phoebe said. "Yes! I hadn't thought of that."

"And confetti!" Kristin said. "Bobbleheads! Monogrammed key fobs! And a T-shirt cannon!"

"Wait," Matt said. "What?"

"We want to have a spectacle, in a good way—like a flashy Super Bowl halftime show, but without wardrobe malfunctions," Phoebe said. "We could get Jeff Gordon to drive for one hundred thousand dollars. People would go to see him. Evidently he's very popular."

One hundred thousand dollars? Chase almost choked.

He'd barely been able to get past the idea of renting the stadium, which—since it was the off-season—they might actually be able to do. "*Hang* on."

"Jeff Gordon?" Rinsho asked. "Who's he?"

"He drives cars and he gets a hundred grand for an appearance," Phoebe said. "I looked it up."

"Jeff Gordon is a big NASCAR driver, wins everything all the time," Matt said. "Top-of-the-line guy. Like Coach."

"But one hundred thousand dollars," Tony said.

"Yeah, too much for our purposes," Phoebe conceded, "but we can get lots of NASCAR drivers for much less, and they'd be perfect, right?"

"Right!" Kristin said. "How many drivers do we need?"

"Well, a lot," Phoebe said. "As many as we could get, right? I think we'd have to design the routine first, and then see."

"Who does that?" Kristin asked.

"I found a guy—" Phoebe started.

"*Wait one second*," Chase said. All heads turned to him. He felt like an executioner about to drown a litter of kittens.

"What?" Phoebe said.

"Too many problems," Chase said. "Too expensive. Too complicated. Why would anyone leave the expo to go there?"

"That's where you'll hold the drawing for the cars you're raffling off," Phoebe said. "People have to show up to win their free car."

"And they'll want to see famous NASCAR drivers do something neat," Kristin said. "Maybe the drivers would sign autographs."

"And take selfies," Matt ventured.

Phoebe beamed at him.

"Great idea," she said. "We'll ask them. And maybe we could have a party afterward on the field. It could be like a closing-night event."

"With a rock band?" Kristin said. "Or Beyoncé? I'd love to get Beyoncé."

"Metallica," Rinsho said.

All heads swiveled to stare at him.

"What?" he said. "They're a good band."

"I think the conference already has a closing-night event," Chase said, relieved that he could put some brakes on Phoebe and Kristin's enthusiasm for big events. Beyoncé. Metallica. Jesus, he'd be out millions for the music alone. He could be bankrupt in a week.

Unless they sold a lot of cars.

Which they might.

"I need a reality check here," he said. "Somebody tell me, is this a crazy idea?"

"No," everybody said in one voice.

"Coach, people will come," Matt said. "They'll come because you're putting it on. They'll come because they might win a car. And they'll come because they can see NASCAR drivers doing cool stuff."

"There's still one problem," Chase said. "If we can't build thirty-six cars for the expo show floor, how can we build all the cars the NASCAR drivers will be driving? It would take *weeks*."

The team deflated faster than tires running over a tack strip.

"That's the thing!" Phoebe said. "You don't have to build them."

Chase raised his eyebrows. "We don't? How do you figure?"

"Well, it's not ideal, but you've got that feedback program where you give interested employees a car to drive around, right? For testing. Measuring the diagnostics. Whatever it is that you do. My point being, the company still owns those cars. So, borrow them back for a couple of days. It'll inconvenience a lot of people, I'm sure, but—"

Rinsho brightened up. "That's it, Coach! We can do that. Lots of people would be happy to volunteer their cars for a couple of days—we'd all feel like we were doing something to help. Everybody I've talked to feels lousy about the vandalism."

"I'll donate mine," Tony said.

"Me, too," Matt said.

"And me," Rinsho added.

"Thanks, y'all." Chase was touched by their willingness to sacrifice. "I really appreciate the offer. But—"

"So we're a go," Rinsho said.

Chase gazed around at the eager, determined faces. Well, hell. It looked like they thought they could do it.

"I can't believe I'm agreeing to this. Okay, let's say this crazy, car-marching-band-spectacular-at-the-stadium plan is a go if Kristin and Phoebe can get some estimates on cost and availability by tomorrow. And if we can borrow back enough cars without causing undue hardship. If everything seems doable tomorrow, we'll map out a work schedule."

"Great!" Kristin said. "Phoebe, see me after. I mean, unless Dave needs you."

"No, feel free," Dave said, waving his hand. "Borrow my apprentice PI whenever you need her. Don't mind me."

Phoebe beamed at him. "Thank you, Dave."

Everyone laughed, even Dave.

They're not depressed anymore, Chase realized. And he wasn't, either. They were energized. They had a plan now, and goals. He could have reached across the table and kissed Phoebe for doing that. Except, of course, he couldn't. But he wanted to. Later on, when they were alone, he would. Multiple times.

"Are we ready to let Dave talk about security now?" Chase asked, getting his mind back to the meeting. "That is, if there are no more ideas for how to rework our presentation efforts at the expo."

"Well, actually," Phoebe said, "one more thing."

Everyone laughed.

"Phoebe, what else could we do after putting NASCAR drivers in a stadium with a marching band, cheerleaders, confetti, fireworks, and a T-shirt gun?" Kristin asked. "Plus Metallica, but don't tell Coach."

"Well, it's this," Phoebe said. "I don't know if this could work. Maybe it won't. But I was thinking—can we get some use out of those damaged cars?"

"What do you mean?" Chase asked.

"People have accidents and damage their cars every day," Phoebe said. And she should know—she was pretty sure she'd damaged Dave's car. It was *way* too easy to do. "Can we show how a car from Venture Automotive is better because—I don't know—it's easier or cheaper to repair? Is the finish scratch resistant? Or can anyone—say a child—remove a dented fender and put on a new one? Have a demo. People will like it if they think their car repairs will be less expensive."

The idea appealed to him. Not only could the vandalized cars pay their way, so to speak, but showing them at the expo, damaged as they were, would essentially give the finger to the perpetrator. If the jerk was an internal hire with a grudge against him, as Dave and Phoebe thought, Chase could get the upper hand on a psychological level.

"I like that idea," he said. "Rinsho, what do you think?"

"We're working on a plastic chassis," Rinsho said. "One of the damaged cars is plastic. Let me look into it."

"Okay. Phoebe? Is that it?"

"I'm done," Phoebe said.

"Anyone else?" Chase asked. "No? All right, then, moving on. Dave, any thoughts so far on security?"

"Yeah," Dave said. "First thing I'd advise—"

He was off and running. For an off-the-cuff presentation, he had a lot of good ideas. They weren't all cheap ones, but Dave was right about one thing—the vandalism had proved that Venture Automotive had a lot of assets to protect now.

And he intended to do everything he could to safeguard them.

Later that night, at Phoebe's request, Chase drove them out to the Spring Mountains to watch the sunset. He wanted to get away from the office and see the big picture, get a grip on what mattered. At ten thousand feet, the vista stretched on for miles, and the light show against the jagged peaks was spectacular, with shifting cloud patterns and colors until finally the sky faded from blue to purple to black and the stars came out and beamed down at them like they'd never quit.

"That was fantastic," Phoebe said. "Thanks for bringing me." She leaned up from where her head had been nestled against his chest, put her arms around his neck, and kissed him.

The outfit she had on—that poodle skirt he could never resist—rode up, exposing a smooth line of thigh. And the sweater she'd worn with it exposed a tantalizing strip of skin at her midriff. If he'd known Phoebe got turned on by sunsets, he'd have driven her up here weeks ago.

He shifted in the front seat to get more comfortable and winced when his bad knee hit the door handle. Well, maybe coming up here wasn't such a great idea after all. He was getting too old to make out in the front seat of a car, much less have sex in it, if things should happen to go that far. He had a giant house with fifteen bedrooms, all of them furnished with comfortable mattresses and one-thousand-thread-count sheets. He had central air and central heat, cool tile, warm rugs, and soft pillows. In his experience, women liked that kind of thing.

But Phoebe seemed to be having a pretty good time in his cramped car, and really, he was enjoying himself quite a bit, too. Call him crazy, because he wasn't that enthusiastic about risking death or even arrest by parking in a turnout on a narrow road at ten thousand feet. But when Phoebe wore that damn poodle skirt, he'd pretty much do whatever she wanted. He hoped the parking brake held.

Right now she was straddling him, and he had one hand up her sweater and the other under her skirt. Her quick, soft breath, tasting of the peppermint Tic Tac she'd had earlier, mingled with his. Her arms were braced against the back of the seat, her fingers thrust into his hair, and she kissed him rapidly, gently, on the mouth before she rose a bit on her knees and feathered her lips over his cheeks, his eyes, and his ears, her breasts mere inches from his face. Or really, in his face.

Oh yeah. Let them arrest him. So what if they fell over the edge of this cliff to their deaths? It'd be worth it.

He slipped his fingers under the elastic of her panties and heard her swift intake of breath as he stroked her softness. In fact, she was soft everywhere—her breath, her skin, her breasts, her hair, her kisses—and right now all that felt pretty fantastic.

If he was reading the situation correctly—and he thought he was—Phoebe wanted to forego the assets of his house for the more primitive accommodations of his car, which was fine with him. Variety was the spice of life, after all. So he took his time, enjoying the sensations—not just the warmth and textures of her, but the coolness of the evening air, the darkness of the sky, the hum of insects, and the danger—very muted—of the deserted road. He knew her responses well enough by now to sense when she was close to release. She'd been breathing quickly, her body tense, her eyes closed, and she'd buried her face in his neck as she clung to him. He tightened his hold on her back, touching her where she liked to be touched, and then she shuddered, gasped, and collapsed against his chest.

Shoving his knee against the door handle again.

He sucked in his breath—or maybe that was the altitude—and she noticed.

"Oh no, I hurt your knee," she said, her voice muffled against his fleece jacket. "I'm sorry." Then she looked up at him, her eyes twinkling and full of mischief. "Want me to kiss it and make it all better?"

He grinned at her, shifting her and his knee away from the door. "Forget it, *cher.* As appealing as that idea is in the abstract, there's no way you could do that comfortably or safely from where you and I are sitting."

"Speak to your SUV designers." Phoebe rubbed her hands over—and now under, thank you very much—his jacket. "The front seat of this car is too small."

"It didn't seem that small when the guys were building it. And let's not forget, we could have put down the back seats and stretched out when we got here, but some people were in too much of a hurry to get to the goal line."

"I wanted to try out the front seat." Phoebe squirmed around, trying to get into a different position. The squirming was incredible—she could do that for a couple of hours; he'd be good with it. "I read a book a while ago where the characters had sex in the front seat of a car. On the driver's side. They weren't that comfortable, either, now that I think about it, but the hero was shorter than you, so they probably weren't this cramped. We might have to put down the back seats. I'm not sure—"

She yelped as something on the middle console stuck her somewhere.

"Settle down over there," Chase said. "Maybe—"

"What do you mean, *over there?*" Phoebe said, pulling her skirt free. "I'm right here. Practically on top of you. Actually, *right* on top of you. Wait. I have an idea. Is this as far back as the seat goes?"

"Yes. Hold on. What are you doing?"

"I'm trying something. What were you guys thinking with this design? *This car's not big enough.*"

"Less than four percent of the male population is taller than six-two," Chase said, acutely aware of Phoebe's hands and where they were going. "This car is big enough"—he inhaled sharply—"for ninety-six percent"—*Christ!*—"of the male population."

"You're missing a niche market, then," Phoebe said, settling herself.

"What—" *Damn*, that felt good. Chase dropped his head back against the headrest, closed his eyes, and lost himself in the heat and softness and flair that was Phoebe. Her back was to him, her strong thighs cradling his legs and her hips flexing in the confines of the SUV. And then he stopped thinking altogether and simply held her tighter, his face against her hair, leaning into her, feeling the urgency build until a surge of energy cascaded through him.

He breathed heavily—almost panting, resting his chest against her back, his hands on her hips. Between Phoebe and the ten-thousand-foot altitude, he'd be lucky to survive the evening, small SUV or not. But if he didn't survive it, what a way to go.

"You know, if you moved in with me, we'd have all the room we could possibly want," he said. "Plus cushions."

"No can do." Phoebe's voice was languid. "Where's the adventure in that?"

"We'd be a lot more comfortable."

"I'm comfortable now."

But she squirmed around again until she could lay her cheek against his chest. But how she could say the SUV was more comfortable than his house, he didn't know.

"Is it about the house? I know you don't like the house."

"It's not that," she said. "Your house is beautiful. The pool is great. Trouble loves the backyard."

"I'm not living there because your dog likes it."

"It's a good reason. Besides, he's your dog, too. But fifteen bedrooms! Plus a million other rooms."

"The place is way too big, no question. I always meant to turn it into a hotel. I just never got around to doing anything about it."

"It would be a great hotel. Plus, the Chase Bonaventure factor."

"Hey, I've got an idea, *cher*. The house is too much? You want something smaller? I'll move in with you."

Phoebe snorted in amused horror. "You must be kidding! My entire apartment would fit in your living room with space to spare. If you lay down in *my* living room, your head would stick into the kitchen."

"We'd be cozier than two bugs in rug. I can't wait."

"Stop smiling at me," Phoebe said. "No one's moving anywhere, and that's the last I'm saying about it."

He'd been joking about moving into her place, but he'd do it if she'd agree. Mostly he wished that she'd simplify their lives—and add a whole lot more fun to everything—by moving in with him. He knew that she liked him. And he'd told her how he felt about her, too, although she clearly didn't trust his feelings for her.

She fretted about his first-and-only marriage, a six-month headlong rush to catastrophe that was over almost before it had begun. He got that. She thought he was charging too fast into a relationship with her, too—one that couldn't last longer than his marriage had. But what he had with Phoebe was completely different than what he'd had—or hadn't had—with Tracy. And how could he demonstrate the difference to Phoebe if she didn't move in with him and let him show it?

He stroked her hair, enjoying its silky softness against his fingers. "Is this about Tracy? You won't move in because of my history."

Phoebe sighed. "Yes, sort of. I just don't see how you can be so positive we'll work out when you and she got divorced in six months. You were positive then, too, I bet."

"I'd say I was more optimistic than positive. We really did get married too quickly."

"See, that's my whole point. Besides—" She sighed again, biting her lip.

He was sorry that the glow seemed to have dimmed a little, but he wanted to get this figured out, allay her fears, whatever they were. "Besides?"

Phoebe glanced at him ruefully. "Well, my mom. She set a bad example. Or maybe I should say, she set a good example of how I don't want to live my life. That would be focused entirely on the rapidly revolving door of unsuccessful boyfriends. You and I haven't known each other long enough to have a feeling that we'd work out. Or, at least, I don't. Plus, I come with all that other baggage."

"You mean your school loan? That isn't about us, you and me."

"No, but it affects my work life. My professional choices."

"If you stay here and work with Dave, if that's how you want to proceed, I told you before—I'll pay off that loan."

"No. Absolutely not." She shook her head. "That's *my* loan. *My* responsibility. I'm paying it back. Every. Single. Penny. One way or another."

And that was Phoebe. He was crazy about her in part

because she was so responsible. So determined to succeed on her own merits, even though that CIA school loan was an albatross around her neck. He'd offered weeks ago to give or even lend her the three hundred thousand she needed to pay it off, but she'd squashed that idea flatter than an eighteen-wheeler could squash an armadillo on a bayou byway. Three hundred thousand was a lot of money, but he could afford it and she couldn't. He hated how it burdened her.

"Phoebe—"

A sharp crack on the driver-side window jolted him. Phoebe shrieked, and he covered her head and pulled her down as a brilliant beam of light shot through the window and blinded him.

"Hey! You in there!" an authoritative voice said. "You can't, ah, park here."

A cop, he realized. Or a park ranger. With a big mag light. Not a confrontation he wanted, but better than a shooter, anyway. Which, knowing Phoebe's line of work, it could have been.

"Officer," he said, buzzing down the window.

Phoebe tried to scramble off his lap into the passenger seat. Not the best idea. She at least was decent. He snaked out an arm and held her where she was.

"Folks," the cop said. "This is a public road. You can't be doing this here. Driver's license, please."

Getting his wallet out of his pocket without losing Phoebe wouldn't be easy, but he hadn't been the most agile quarterback of the NFL for a decade without learning a few moves. He dug out his wallet and handed the license through the window, shifting Phoebe a little. She grunted but stayed put, which was a miracle in itself.

The cop peered at the license and then leaned through the window to peer at him fully in the face.

"Are you *Chase Bonaventure*?" he asked, his voice rising at the end. "Holy crap! You *are* Chase Bonaventure!"

"I am, officer, and I apologize for—"

"You're Chase Bonaventure! I never thought— Wait'll I tell— You know, I'll never forget that game last fall against the Steelers. You and Dan Freer—unbelievable. That pass into the end zone? Nobody else—I mean *nobody*—could have thrown that pass. Freer made it seem easy, and he must have had, what? Three defenders on him. Talk about threading the needle! I won fifty on you that day from my brother-in-law, too, the jerk."

Chase laughed. "Yeah, Freer makes a quarterback look good. I'm glad I could help you out with your brother-in-law."

"The wife and I got a nice meal out of him, so thanks for that. Yeah, the Steelers have a great reputation, and I'm not saying their quarterback's not prime when he's healthy, but they're not so tough when they're playing the Snakes!"

"We had a good game that day," Chase said, wishing that all the fans could let go of him, just like he'd had to let go of the game. Time to move on. Like off this mountaintop for starters.

"A good game! I'll say you did. One for the record. Well, I'll let you go. Parking here doesn't get you a ticket, but you can't— Well, you can't. Sorry about that."

"No problem, Officer. We got carried away with the sunset."

"Would it be—" The cop's voice sounded uncertain. "Could I ask you for an autograph?"

"Of course. Who should I make it out to?"

Phoebe leaned over and rummaged around in the glove box, eventually finding some kind of empty envelope and pen. She thrust them at him.

The cop's face brightened. "Hey, thanks! I'm Mike. Mike Janda."

Mike, Chase wrote. *Thanks for a great evening. Chase Bonaventure.* He handed the envelope to the cop, who read it and grinned, stepping back from the window.

"Nice car," the cop said. "I'm pulling for Venture Automotive. You always gave it one hundred percent on the field, and I bet you'll do that with the company, too. My next car, that's what I'm buying, I told the wife. Something from Venture Automotive."

"I appreciate that," Chase said. The cop seemed like a nice enough guy, but Chase was more than ready for him to take off.

Now that the cop and his flashlight had stepped away from the window, Phoebe slid off his lap. Chase adjusted his jeans and fleece jacket and started the car. He pulled out of the turnout, waving to the cop as he headed down the narrow mountain road.

"Did you see what just happened?" Phoebe said, leaning forward to straighten out her own clothes—the poodle skirt that always turned him on and that tight, short sweater. Also a very nice item.

"Well, I think so," Chase said. "Because I was right there and all."

"I mean," Phoebe said, "that that cop said he was going to buy a car because you own the company. *You*, Chase Bonaventure, former football player."

"Yeess. And? Where are you going with this?" He negotiated a tight turn, not willing to take his eyes off the road and plunge them over the mountainside at this point.

"You're naming the car models with football terminology, right?" Phoebe said. "Snap, Rush, Kick—like that. If you paint the cars in team colors, the naming thing will totally tie in. Call them Victory models. Like Rattlesnake Victory, or Steeler Victory, whatever. They'd sell like hotcakes, I bet you anything. You could raise a bucket for charity, and that's always worth publicizing. You'd get a lot of attention for it."

"Remind me to hire a marketing team. The thing is, Phoebe—I'm not saying we shouldn't paint a car like that for the expo, but that kind of car would probably have to be issued in a limited edition. And a guy like Mike Janda wouldn't be able to afford an expensive, limited-edition car."

"He could get one used." Phoebe settled back into the seat, turning to face him as much as the seat belt would allow.

"I'm not in the used-car business," Chase said, amused.

"Well, he let you off without writing you a ticket, so I'm not that impressed with him. Cops shouldn't let you off because you're Chase Bonaventure. Are we going for dinner now? I'm starving."

"He didn't let me off because I'm Chase Bonaventure. He let me off because it's not illegal to park in the turnouts. That's what turnouts are there for—parking. Weren't you listening?" Chase glanced over and saw her wicked grin.

"I was, but mostly I was concentrating on protecting your modesty. I mean, that's all you'd need—Mike Janda taking a selfie with you in your altogether and posting it on Instagram. The fans would love it, but I'm not sure that kind of publicity would make the investors happy."

Chase snorted. "Mike Janda and I are buds now; he'd never do that to me." He risked a stern look in her direction.

Phoebe reached out and patted his arm. "Sure, and you're not missing a niche market here with this small SUV, either. Just ask your knee."

Chase laughed. "Okay, I'll check into the Big-and-Tall SUV category. We'll name that model the Score. Happy now? So, dinner. Where do you want to go?"

Chapter 3

The next morning, still on something of a rush from the evening he'd spent with Phoebe, Chase drove to the office for a morning of meetings. With any luck, the good feeling from last night would last through the day. She'd been practically an acrobat in the front seat of his car. Maybe he could talk her into trying that again. Or better yet, something else. And he'd have to talk to R&D about her idea for bigger cars. Even in the cool light of morning-after thinking, that seemed like an idea worth further consideration.

As he entered the lobby, he saw his first appointment of the day—six men lined up on the visitor sofas. The new hires. And they were early, always a promising sign. He needed more workers to ramp up to their production goals.

"Hi, guys," he said as he approached. "Glad to see you. Come on up now, why don't you?"

Kristin was in and setting up the coffee service, he was happy to see.

"Thanks, Kristin," he said. "I'll take that in."

"Here you go, then, Coach," she said, handing him the tray.

They all trooped into Chase's small office and crowded into the small, comfortable sitting area to one side. Chase handed out coffee and took a big swallow, his first hit of the day. *Damn* that was good.

"Okay," he said, glancing at the six men. Four young or

youngish guys, two older. Two of them looking at him with curiosity, four of them looking anywhere else. Some of them scarred or heavily tattooed. All of them on parole after serving time at Ely State Prison on various felony charges.

The guys who'd be taking Venture Automotive to the next level.

He'd decided some months ago to hire ex-cons after he'd complained to the city administrator at a business meeting that he couldn't find enough workers to meet demand. *Parolees have trouble finding jobs*, the city administrator had told him. *And many are eager for work.*

Some of the department heads were uneasy about his decision, and he understood their anxieties. No one wanted to wonder if the person standing next to them would steal from them or even mug them in the parking lot. So far, they hadn't had any problems.

But he'd wondered if any of his employees with prison records had been responsible for the vandalism to the cars earmarked for the expo. He hoped not. So far, there wasn't any evidence to suggest that. And until he had proof of wrongdoing, he'd trust that the parolees needed the job as much as—or more so—than his other workers.

"Just a word on your first day," he said.

The men didn't move, didn't even blink. *Cautious*, Chase thought.

"I want you to know that I'm happy you're here. We have plans to grow the company, and we need workers who can make that happen. I want you to be part of it, to be part of the team."

A couple of the men shifted in their seats. He'd have to reevaluate the welcome speech; maybe it was too rah-rah for the older guys.

"As far as I'm concerned, any problems you've had with the law are in the past. Yesterday is old news—for the car business, too. What's important is what we all do from here on out."

All the men gazed at him now, but their faces gave nothing away.

"To get where we want the company to go, we need everyone to perform well," Chase said. "We'll do what we can to help you succeed, because we've got too much riding on you to let you fail. So tell us if something's going on with you or isn't right here at the plant. Maybe we can fix it."

One of the older men snorted. Chase smiled. *Definitely* too rah-rah for this guy.

"Seriously." He nodded directly at the guy. "You got a meeting with your parole officer in the middle of the day you can't reschedule, or a drug test you have to take, or your kid screws up at school and you gotta go down there, or you have trouble with your shift manager, or a beef with a coworker. Whatever it is, tell us and we'll get the shift covered. Or we'll arrange a meeting, talk it out, move somebody around. We can adjust, right? If we know. So don't let something fester. Don't disappear."

The men nodded, a movement so slight that if Chase hadn't been watching for it, he wouldn't have seen it.

"What's your name?" he asked the older guy who'd snorted.

"James Harrington."

"James. Okay. Where was the last place you worked?"

"My uncle had an auto body shop. Before I went inside."

"Good. Your experience will be helpful here." He turned back to the larger group. "Y'all aren't the first bunch of parolees we have working here. You probably know that some of our other employees have served time. They get together occasionally to talk, compare notes, I don't know. It's informal, a resource you can take or leave. They'll reach out to you."

Everyone nodded now. So they had known about that. Probably their parole officers had told them when they recommended that their clients apply at Venture Automotive.

"I been out for more than a year," another man said. "I haven't had no regular work in a long time."

"We haven't had a layoff since we started," Chase said, "and I'm not expecting any in the future. So the work will be steady, forty hours a week."

"I'm Ramon Valenzuela," the man said. "My mother's sick. I got two kids, too. This job will make a big difference."

"For me, too," another man said. "I'm Aquintis Jones. I got a daughter. For her an' me, I'll do my best for you."

"That's all I ask." Chase reached out and shook everyone's hand. "Welcome to Venture Automotive. Let me know if there's anything you need. As you can see, there's no door on my office, so it's always open."

"How did that go?" Kristin asked when he emerged from the meeting. The new employees had filed downstairs and entered the production area. By the end of the day he'd know which of the men were quick tempered or quick learners or quick to make friends.

"As well as can be expected. They don't trust me. I don't blame them." He wanted the newcomers to work out, both for their sake and his, but inevitably some wouldn't. Some employees didn't work out even when they didn't have a prison background.

"Next time ask on the application if they're Snakes fans. That'll reduce vandalism, for sure. And speaking of Snakes fans, Cliff Frizell is waiting for you downstairs."

Cliff Frizell was another new hire, a former teammate, a guy who'd been through a tough divorce and needed a job. He'd been the second-string—and sometimes third-string—quarterback during the years that Chase had led the Snakes to three Super Bowl wins. When he'd torn out his knee in the last Super Bowl, ending his career, he knew that Frizell had thought he'd finally get the call. Instead, the Snakes had drafted some young guy and released the aging QB.

He hadn't liked Frizell much when they were on the squad together, and he didn't want to make a practice of hiring guys he didn't much like. Still, if Cliff knew his business, he supposed he couldn't object.

Chase wasn't looking forward to this meeting—Cliff had sat on the bench the years they'd played together, and recalling that kind of history was never fun. But he still liked to meet all the new hires, although at the rate they were taking on new employees, he'd have to give that up soon. Maybe after this interview.

He went over to the mezzanine edge and surveyed the downstairs lobby.

"Cliff?" he called out. "Come on up."

The thirty-eight-year-old ex-pro backup quarterback strode up the stairs, his hand outstretched. Chase shook it.

"Chase," Frizell said. "It's been a while. This place is a lot different than the locker room, isn't it?"

"It sure is," Chase said. "Good to see you. Come on in. Have a seat."

They entered his office, and he waved to the chair across from his desk. Unlike his meeting with the parolees, whom he'd seated at the informal meeting area across the room, he wanted to keep the desk between himself and Frizell. They were still colleagues of a sort. But the relationship needed to become more boss/employee than teammates.

"I just wanted to say hello, see how you're getting on." He settled into his chair. "You've been here at Venture Automotive now, what? A couple of weeks?"

"Something like that," Cliff said, crossing his legs.

"In our playing days, I don't think I ever knew what anybody had studied when they were in college. But since then, I've found out that you have a systems design degree. That's an advantage. Eventually we want to expand to other alternative fuels as well branch out in terms of models and styles."

"Sounds great," Frizell said. "The company's going gangbusters, and Rinsho Nakamura seems like a great guy."

"It's a tough transition from football to the normal world, isn't it? It was tough for me at first."

Frizell shrugged. "When you're young, I suppose nobody ever thinks their playing days will end at some point. But you adjust. And I'm happy to get in on the ground floor here. Venture Automotive could take off like Google or Microsoft. And then we'll all be millionaires again. Makes me glad I actually went to class back in the day."

Chase smiled. "I hear that. When you talked to Kristin, did she mention our testing program? We give employees the use of a company car if they want it. We gather diagnostics data from it anonymously to analyze vehicle performance."

"I'm in," Cliff said. "She gave me the keys already."

"Great. Then I guess you're all set. Welcome to Venture Automotive."

"Thanks, Chase. I'll give it my best shot."

The two men stood and shook hands again. Chase walked him to the door, and Cliff loped down the stairs and into the production department.

Chase sure hoped they'd done the right thing hiring that guy. He glanced at Kristin. "So, you heard all that. Tell me—what did you think of him?"

Kristin pursed her lips as she thought. "He seemed all right," she said finally. "He wants to be a millionaire again pretty bad—all that talk of us being the new Google or Microsoft. Does he understand we're a car company? General Motors, or at least Tesla, is what we should aspire to, not business or consumer software. But I didn't hear him say anything that was bad, exactly."

"No." Chase frowned. "Maybe it's a holdover from football. He always seemed—I don't know—weaselly, or something. Maybe in a different setting, in a different job, things will be different."

"Weaselly? You know, Coach, you don't have to like everybody who works here. They just have to do a good job. *Then* you'll like them."

He grinned. "Let's hope you're right."

"Are you ready for the next meeting? The department heads are waiting for you in the conference room to talk about security."

"Right. I'm ready if you are."

Kristin closed her laptop and followed him down the narrow hallway to the conference room. But as he looked at the expectant faces of the four people sitting around the table, he felt the weight of his responsibilities settle around him like an evening fog.

A year ago when he'd taken over an all-but-defunct electric-car company, he'd felt as if they were on the cusp of something big. Electric vehicles would take over the market and improve the world. And he and the scrappy band of outcasts and misfits who worked for him would show all the naysayers what they could do. With their innovative designs and can-do attitude, they could stick it to Detroit and save the air at the same time. Beat the dinosaurs at their own game!

Yeah, that was before. Before the bank loan officers and international investors got involved, and certainly before the vandalism. Managing the bureaucracy and its paperwork, justifying how they spent every penny, was one thing. But with the damage, he had to spend time and money protecting the company from somebody on the inside. He hated thinking about it. He hated not trusting his own employees. He'd rather be crushed by the biggest linebacker the Steelers had on their roster. Any day of the week.

Yet here he was.

If he couldn't protect the company and its product, if he couldn't make good on his promises to his backers, hundreds of people would be thrown out of work, and his investors and bankers would lose tens of millions—hell, hundreds of millions—of dollars. All those jobs, all that investment—everyone would lose, and that failure would be on him and him alone.

And he hated to lose. He'd hated it on the field, and he hated it still.

So he'd do everything in his power—absolutely everything—to make sure that didn't happen.

"We all heard what Dave Greenaway said yesterday," he began. "Nobody likes thinking about how to protect the company from criminals, but some of his safety measures coincide with what the bank has already told us to do—starting with running background checks on all the employees."

"All the *incoming* employees," said Tony Minaya tentatively, the chief software guy. "The people we've had with us since the beginning, we know they're fine. They've been working here a while already without any trouble."

"Nope," Chase said. "We have to have paperwork on everybody. Even y'all."

"That's more than a hundred new employees right now," Rinsho protested. "And we've got another hundred hires in the works, and we'll have to hire another couple of hundred in the next few weeks to stay on schedule. And a thousand more by the end of the year. That takes too much time."

"HR can't handle it," Kristin said. "She's only one person, and I can't help. I'm swamped as it is, and I'm the paperwork queen."

"Hire another HR person or two and assistants if you need them," Chase said. "In the meantime, we'll outsource the background checks."

Kristin grinned. "To Western Private Investigations, I presume?"

Chase shrugged, but he grinned back at her. "They're already working on the security angle for us. And the two investigators have more than twenty-five years of local and federal investigations and intelligence gathering experience behind them. They've a good fit for us."

"Plus, Phoebe works there," Kristin said.

"Security-wise, she saved our bacon with the investors last month," said Matt. "I bet she and Dave figure this thing out, too. I'm glad she quit the CIA and came back."

Phoebe had indeed saved their bacon by uncovering a trio of investors who were not all they claimed to be, and while doing so, she'd averted what might have been an international disaster. He'd been incredibly proud of her.

The problem was, Phoebe hadn't quit the CIA—or the CIA hadn't quit her. If she decided that their personal relationship wasn't working—or if the gig with Dave Greenaway at Western didn't pan out—she could go back to Langley. She had six months to decide.

He wanted her to stay in Vegas. He was crazy about her. He wanted to step things up, make a bigger commitment, but she wanted to take things slow. He needed more time to show her that they were good together, that they had something they could build on and that would last.

"Speaking of the new hires," Rinsho said, getting them back on track. He browsed the bunch of résumés in his hand. "You know one of the guys, Coach—Cliff Frizell."

"Yeah. I just talked to him. You like him?"

The foreman shrugged. "He seems willing to learn. Of course, he's been playing football for the past ten years. Or warming the bench, anyway. But we can use him. Or somebody like him."

"Will his experience help you?"

"Can't hurt. The thing is, we didn't get any better prospects. We've run through the talent pool in Las Vegas for this kind of position. We'd get more candidates if we advertised nationally. But it'll cost us a lot more if we want to bring anyone in for an interview."

"Okay," Chase said. "From now on when we need somebody with specific talent, let's do that. In the meantime, give me the applications of the new hires. Until we get another HR person in here, I'll deal with Western and the background checks."

Rinsho nodded, handing over the paperwork, and everyone got up to leave.

Kristin paused at the doorway. "Phoebe hasn't decided what to do yet, has she?"

Chase sighed. "No, she hasn't."

"Make her stay. I like her. And good things happen when she's around."

"Working on it."

Kristin frowned, shaking her head. "Time's running out," she said. "Work harder."

Chase put out fires for the next couple of hours, thinking maybe it was time to hire a couple of vice presidents or a finance guy or somebody to handle some of the workload. He'd have to think about what he'd like to hand off, what he had the experience and interest to do, and what areas of the company could be improved with more expertise. He sent the employee applications to Western Private Investigations for the background checks, finalized a budget, returned email, and just before lunch, tried to call his kid sister Josie. They'd been playing phone tag for a couple of days, but she sounded persistent rather than worried, so he wasn't concerned when he didn't catch her.

Then Kristin stuck her head in his door. "I've got the Indian embassy on the phone. They're confirming your appointments on Wednesday with the Indian trade delegation and the lunch with the Indian ambassador."

The Indian embassy was sponsoring a trade conference—a weeklong series of events showcasing Indian business and culture, all geared to furthering ties between the two countries. India's electric-car industry was in its infancy, and Chase hoped to get in on the ground floor there, either with trade deals or a joint manufacturing agreement.

"Yes for everything. Ask them if I can bring Phoebe. Tell them she's our—I don't know—"

"International trade liaison?" Kristin supplied. "She speaks a zillion languages, and she knows the secretary of state. Toss that out, see if it helps you cut through red tape."

"Great, yeah, that works. She's our international trade liaison."

"Okay," Kristin said. "I'll ask."

Seconds later, she was back. "Phoebe's a go. Twelve o'clock at the Taj Palace. I put it in your calendar."

"Thanks, Kristin."

"Bring back a doggy bag, will you? The food at the Taj Palace is supposed to be spectacular."

Chase grinned at her as he reached for his phone. Now that the Indian embassy had said Phoebe could attend their events, he had to talk her into going.

"Hey, guess what?" Phoebe said when she picked up. "Dave's showing me how to do background checks. You wouldn't believe what you can find out about somebody. I'm checking you out first. *Very* interesting."

Chase paused. He could hear the laughter in her voice, so he guessed she was kidding about checking him out. Not that he had anything to hide. On the other hand, if there did happen to be a wild story out there about him, he'd like to tell her about it in his own way.

"Let me know if there's something I should explain, okay? So, would you be interested—or let me say, willing— to go to lunch with me and the Indian ambassador and about six hundred other people on Wednesday? And then to a bunch of appointments. Basically all day Wednesday."

"Oh, that's for that thing the embassy's sponsoring at the conference center, right? Yeah, I'd like to go. But we won't get these background checks done by Friday like you asked if I take the day off."

"Take another day or two then to finish the background checks. They're important, but so is this. You're part of our security team. I need you to do security."

"You need me to do a background check on the Indian ambassador?"

"I need you to assess the situation as it unfolds."

"You're the boss. Hold on, let me check with Dave."

Chase heard muffled noise in the background as Phoebe talked things over with her boss.

"Dave says I should go," she said when she came back. "And he says I don't have to check with him for every blinking thing I do that makes us look good and leads to more business. He didn't say blinking."

"Great," Chase said. "I'll send you the details."

"Can't wait. I'll meet the ambassador, practice my Hindi, *and* have a nice lunch. This gig is really working out for me."

At noon, Sanjay Agarwal got in his taxicab and drove to the airport to pick up the fare that his Auntie Lupa had commanded him to meet. He'd had to put off until tomorrow a driving lesson with Phoebe, an actual friend for whom he liked to do favors, to do this boon for his auntie, whom he barely knew. However, the appeal had come through his mother, whom he could not turn down.

The family chain of command might be distant, but it was steel-strong. Sitting pretty in Delhi, his Auntie Lupa had only to whisper in the ear of his mother—who was working very hard at her restaurant and food truck here in Las Vegas—that it would be so kind of Sanjay, and didn't Neeta always say he was the perfect son? Then his mother, to prove that he was indeed the perfect son, would entreat him to perform such actions as Auntie Lupa—or whatever other distant relations—desired.

Sanjay imagined that this organizational network also worked in reverse: that his mother could whisper to Auntie Lupa that *her* perfect child could also perform some service for herself. He didn't attempt to follow who was in the lead favor-wise, because he neither liked nor approved of such family obligations. In this particular case that was taking up his valuable time today, he failed to see how Auntie Lupa, who lived nine thousand miles away in Delhi, could reciprocate this favor. And yet, although he'd tried politely to decline the request, here he was anyway. Family duties were not something he could escape lightly.

He parked in the lot for taxis and went with his sign to the arrivals area, where he waited for passengers to come through customs and immigration. Eventually a tall, middle-aged man came by, squinting at the signs the drivers held up. He stopped before Sanjay and pointed to his sign.

"You must be for me," he said. "I am Pavel Rao."

He had a very slight paunch and fleshy jowls, and his lush, dark hair was going gray at the temples. Sanjay failed to see a family resemblance, but his family was a large one, and the gene pool had vastly expanded over the years.

"Sanjay Agarwal, at your service." Sanjay put out his hand. "You have checked baggage?"

"Yes," Pavel said, shaking hands with Sanjay. "A few suitcases, in fact."

Sanjay reined in a sigh. Retrieving, loading, and unloading baggage in the Las Vegas desert heat was never a task that he enjoyed—and this one would be without compensation, thanks to Auntie Lupa.

An hour later, the suitcases had come off the luggage carousel, and Sanjay had brought the cab around and loaded it up. He inched out into the waves of traffic leaving the airport.

"What is your destination?" he asked, following the flow of vehicles heading for freeways and side streets.

"The Oasis Pools Casino and Hotel," Pavel said. "Do you know it?"

Sanjay knew all the hotels and most of the motels, efficiencies, and vacation rentals in the Las Vegas area, and asking if he knew of a particular casino on the Strip—no matter how small and poorly maintained—was an insult to him as a professional taxicab driver.

"I do," he said, determined to be fair. Pavel was no doubt tired from his flight from New Delhi and unaware of any affront. "It is an older property, but in a good location. Auntie said you are here on business?"

"Yes." Pavel turned back from gazing out the window. "The ministry sent me here to bolster business ties to America. There's a very important conference. I have many appointments with C-level executives. I will be very busy."

"Excellent," Sanjay said, not really paying attention. He was happy that the airport was close to the Strip and many of Las Vegas's tourist establishments, including the Oasis Pools Casino and Hotel. He did not relish driving long distances with a nonpaying customer.

"I have full authority to act on the government's behalf in signing contracts," Pavel continued. "This is how much the ministers—and the prime minister himself—trust the very important work that I do."

"Ah."

"I had understood that you were in a position to help me with introductions to the people I need to meet here. Your mother told my mother that you were well acquainted with many important personages. But now I find that you are a taxi driver, so this cannot possibly be true. Your mother—Well. Obviously her judgment is clouded by her affection for her son. You can trust me not to enlighten her."

Sanjay inhaled on a count of four and exhaled on a count of eight. Twice. "Ah."

He pulled into the Oasis Pools Casino and Hotel after a

ride that felt much longer than it had been, happy that no ravine was located in the Las Vegas city center. Had this been the situation, he might have been tempted to push his passenger into it.

"Here we are," he said, shifting the taxicab into park and unbuckling his seat belt.

"This cannot be the right place." Pavel Rao gazed disdainfully at the dark exterior, chipped stonework, and tired doorman of the faded Oasis Pools. "You have brought me to the wrong hotel. This establishment is not at all what the ministry promised me. I can't stay here."

"I understand that the rooms are comfortable, although the decor could no doubt benefit from an update." Sanjay popped the trunk, waving to the doorman to bring a luggage cart. The sooner he could leave his passenger behind, the better. If Pavel wanted to go to another hotel, he could do it without him and his taxi.

"On Wednesday at eleven forty-five precisely, you must drive me to the luncheon with the Indian ambassador." Pavel got out of the cab. "It is a private meeting, and it is most important that I be punctual. Understand? The Indian ambassador must not be kept waiting."

Never. He was not this man's personal chauffeur, and he would not acquiesce to being ordered around like a dog. Furthermore, he was done driving his relations—his bragging, tiresome, and most of all, *distant* relations—for free.

"I am unfortunately tied up on Wednesday," Sanjay said, loading the luggage cart as speedily as possible. "However, I'm sure that the doorman will be able to call you a cab with no difficulty."

"My mother said I could count on you," Pavel said. "She was telling me most recently that in her weekly chats with her dearest Neeta how much Neeta depends on your kindness."

Neeta, Sanjay's mother. This was blackmail, pure and simple. If Sanjay did not do as Pavel wished, then Pavel would tell Auntie Lupa, who would in turn tell Neeta that Sanjay had failed in hospitality. And then the reproaches—

so gently spoken—would begin. After which he would most surely be searching for that centrally located ravine into which he himself could plunge.

"I can make time," he said as the concierge staff finished loading the luggage carts. He slammed down the trunk of the taxicab. "Eleven forty-five on Wednesday, I believe was the time."

Pavel escorted the luggage carts into the hotel, registered at the desk, and followed the baggage men down a dingy hallway to his room. He tipped the men a gratuity so small that he could be assured they would not respond quickly the next time he needed them, took a mineral water from the minifridge, and then sat down on the faded chair by the window and slipped off his shoes.

No question, the Oasis Pools was not a top-drawer property. Its public areas were dated and shabby, and everything in the guest accommodation was worn, faded, stained, or chipped. But he was in a suite, which was clean, spacious, and inexpensive, and the complimentary refreshments were more than adequate. Overall, he could have done a lot worse. And he was certainly accustomed to making the best of a less-than-desirable situation.

He took out his laptop and booted it up on the hotel's Wi-Fi to see if he had any further instructions about the conference. To stimulate those trade deals the ministry wanted, he would be friendly and attentive in the meetings with the Americans. And then he would take what he learned in his meetings and craft it into proposals and plans that would benefit the Indian government. And, of course, himself.

Who knew ten years ago that he would find himself on this path? When his beautiful and talented elder daughter had wanted to study medicine, she wanted to go to Harvard for the excellent education and the international experience. And she deserved that. But the fees at Harvard were astronomical. No honest commerce underminister could afford them, or even a fraction of them. The scholarship, while welcome, was nowhere near enough to pay for her schooling. So many years to become a doctor!

And so he was vulnerable when the vultures came.

Could he please tell this one when new regulations were proposed? Thank you, here is a gratuity.

Could he please tell that one when new markets will open up? Thank you, here is a gratuity.

And sometimes he himself opened the conversation— you want to demonstrate that you've met that requirement when, in fact, you have not? I require a gratuity. You want your competition to be hobbled? A gratuity, if you please.

Almost without realizing it, he'd become the ministry's conduit for commercial and industrial chicanery, helping companies bypass regulations or beat the buzzer on new legislation. Why should he not get his share? The companies he helped certainly got theirs. And in an odd way, he was aiding his country, too, by greasing the wheels that got business done, contracts awarded, and construction completed on time and almost on budget.

Not that he would ever tell his daughter how she'd managed to emerge from Harvard Medical School and her residency at Johns Hopkins and then join that prestigious private practice, all without debt. She would never know. She would do brilliant work, and now she was engaged, too, to another up-and-coming young doctor. The education, the training, the private practice, and now the brilliant marriage so soon in the future justified his actions.

However, his first daughter was not alone in her need for funds. His entire family needed much more than his official salary could provide. His second daughter was wanting now to become a lawyer, and her heart was set on Cambridge University in England. And his wife, his comfort and strength all these years, had become accustomed to the extra household money, not that she ever asked him where it came from. Probably she was too grateful for how it helped her elderly mother.

So here he was in the United States, sent to forge ties to American markets. The challenge was large and the opportunities numerous.

He finished his drink and put the bottle in the recycling bin. First he would sleep. The trip from New Delhi had lasted almost twenty-five hours, and he was tired. He needed to be rested so he could make the most of his time here. His family—and, he supposed, even his country—depended on him to do well.

Failure was not an option. But he wouldn't fail. He knew how to get what he wanted—from companies that had needs and people who had vulnerabilities. He'd always been able to turn these qualities to his advantage.

From these weaknesses, he, Pavel Rao, would wring success.

Chapter 4

On Tuesday morning, Phoebe came out of her apartment building to wait for Sanjay, who'd promised to take her out driving in his taxi before she reported to work. Right on time, a brightly painted cab boasting the Vegas Fun Fare logo pulled over to the curb.

"Hi, Sanjay," she said, climbing into the cab. "I made you some tea." She handed him a travel mug of milky black tea seasoned with cardamom, his favorite.

"Thank you, Phoebe." He took a deep swallow. "Your kindness is most appreciated."

She buckled her seat belt. "I know mornings are hard for you, so I appreciate your getting up early for me. So where are we going to practice?"

"I'm thinking the parking lot at the Town Square mall would be a suitable spot for a driving lesson. At this hour, the parking lot there cannot be crowded."

"Sounds good," Phoebe said. "Town Square mall it is. I'm ready to get started."

But by nine o'clock, Phoebe was ready to throw in the towel. "I caught those guys who wanted to kidnap the secretary of state without knowing how to drive," she grumbled, hunched over the steering wheel, every muscle tense as she inched through the mall's parking lot. "I did surveillance then."

"Yes, because we went in my taxicab and I drove,"

Sanjay said from the passenger seat, his hands clenched tightly on the dashboard. "However, to my way of thinking, as well as the thinking of the management of Vegas Fun Fare Taxicab Company, surveillance of suspicious persons by nonemployees is not an acceptable use of our taxicabs."

"You didn't complain at the time." Phoebe lurched to a stop to avoid a mother pushing a grocery cart laden with bags and a small child.

"You paid me."

"I could still pay you." Phoebe waited as the mother stepped into the pedestrian crosswalk with her burdens.

"I don't think that arrangement would satisfy management," he said. "They are opposed to getting involved with criminal elements. You can get past her now. Drive slowly. Not too closely."

Phoebe stepped on the gas, and the taxi leaped forward. The woman jumped and glared at them, planting her hands on her hips.

"Not so hard!" Sanjay said, slammed back against the seat. "Gently! No stomping!"

"I didn't stomp!" Phoebe said, stomping on the brake. Sanjay slammed forward, reaching out to catch himself on the dashboard.

"Something is wrong with the accelerator!" Phoebe said. "*And* the brake."

"Neither the accelerator nor any other part of the taxicab is malfunctioning! This lurching we are experiencing now is due entirely to driver error!"

"All the vehicles lurch in New York." Phoebe applied some pressure to the accelerator, and by a miracle, the taxi behaved. She resumed her crawl through the lot.

"We are not in New York." Sanjay glanced around. "Perhaps it is time to depart. I am thinking that the parking lot of a large mall in the hour that all the stores have opened is not the best place to practice for a novice driver with no sensitivity."

"I'm sensitive!"

"You have as yet no connection between your foot and

the controlling pedals. How should your foot feel? How much exertion should you apply to get the desired results? That is what you must learn."

"That's why we're here, Sanjay," Phoebe said. "To practice."

"Indeed, that is true. Step on the accelerator slightly and get us to that stop sign over there. Be vigilant not to hit either pedestrians or automobiles."

Phoebe took a deep breath and stepped on the accelerator. The taxi leaped forward. She backed off, but the cab didn't seem to respond.

"This is plenty fast," Sanjay said. "Go no faster. The stop sign is approaching. Apply the brake. Gently."

Phoebe took her foot off the accelerator and put it on the brake. Nothing seemed to happen.

"Step on the brake," Sanjay said.

Phoebe stepped on the brake, applying gentle pressure as Sanjay had said.

"Step on the brake," Sanjay said, more urgently this time.

"I'm stepping."

"Not hard enough! The brake! Step on the brake!"

Phoebe stepped harder.

"Now! Harder! *Now!*"

Phoebe stomped on the brake. She and Sanjay were flung forward against their seat belts, and the taxicab came to an abrupt halt mere inches from the bumper of the car ahead of them at the stop sign.

Phoebe enjoyed a moment of silence. "Are you hurt?"

"No." Sanjay straightened up and rolled his head from side to side. "Not hurt in the sense of did I break any bones in your precipitous stop. Although to exercise an excess of caution, I believe that I will schedule an appointment with my chiropractor."

Phoebe shook her head. "Now you're just messing with me."

"Did you not see the automobile?"

"I was watching the stop sign."

"You must always watch the automobiles! And the

pedestrians! And the regulating signage!"

"It's hard to watch everything and still press on the pedals correctly and watch all the gauges."

"Not that hard," Sanjay said. "Billions of people drive every day. However, luckily for you, many of them drive very badly, so even if you do not become an excellent driver, you won't be worse than any of them."

"I have to pass the test, though, Sanjay."

"You will pass it. Am I not an intrepid and resourceful taxicab driver? If I cannot teach you well enough to pass the test, who can? And if you cannot pass the test, I could speak to my cousin Samir, who works at the DMV. He can help."

She couldn't cheat on the test. If the tabloids or even the local newspapers ever found out that a friend of Chase Bonaventure had cheated on the driver's test to get her license, they'd make her screwup look bad for him. Worse, she was sure that her PI license would be jeopardized if she were caught.

And she didn't want to jeopardize that. If things worked out—if she stayed in Vegas, working for Dave—in a year she'd be a licensed PI with a decent income. Potentially, at least. In five years, she'd be the best investigator in Las Vegas. Or even west of the Mississippi. If she worked hard, she could do it.

And if nothing turned out the way she wanted—if Greenaway fired her and Chase dumped her—she could always go back to the CIA.

But Greenaway was right. She had a long way to go before she became a PI.

Starting now. She needed to get a driver's license so she could do surveillance. Or even so she could drive to the shooting range and learn how to shoot the gun she still had to buy.

Phoebe squared her shoulders.

"I can't cheat on the test, Sanjay. Can we go around the lot one more time? I want to try it again."

Chase entered the headquarters—that is, the one-room

office—of Western Private Investigations in the early afternoon and observed the laptops, paper files, and telephone that sat on the damaged picnic table. If he didn't know better, he'd think the proprietors were broke and incompetent.

Good thing he knew better.

"Nice conference table," he said.

"Told you." Phoebe glanced at Dave, who rolled his eyes and shook hands with Chase.

"Take the lawn chair," he said. "You'll be more comfortable."

"I doubt that," Chase said, but he sat down on the lawn chair, testing it to see if it would hold his weight. The two detectives joined him, both of them sitting on the bench. Dave shifted a little on the hard seat.

"Maybe if you stocked a couple of pillows," Chase said. "Give you a little padding. Trust me, padding makes a huge difference."

"Sure," Dave said. "Good thought. So, okay. About your background checks."

Chase nodded. "Kristin said you ran into some snags. What's the problem?"

"Phoebe, you did the legwork," Dave said. "Run with it."

Phoebe handed Chase a paper file and then pulled her laptop closer.

"See what we found," she said. "These guys are already working for you, right?"

Chase opened the file and nodded.

"So our report is sort of moot. If we'd gotten their names *before* you hired them, we would recommend that you not hire James Harrington and Aquintis Jones. And we're not crazy about Clifford Frizell, either."

"Jesus," Chase said. "Are you kidding me? What's the problem with Frizell? I thought he had a systems design degree."

"He does." Phoebe tapped on her keyboard and stopped when she found what she was searching for. "The problem with him is his arrest record."

"*Arrest record?* Frizell's got an arrest record?"

"He does. He was arrested for assault and battery, but the charges were dropped. So no conviction or jail time, nothing like that."

"What were the circumstances?" He never would have guessed. Frizell seemed more like a guy who'd brag or mouth off. He'd never thought of him as a guy who would take to his fists.

"He hit his wife, now his ex-wife," Phoebe said. "She decided not to press charges."

"No wonder she dumped him." To the police, maybe an assault was an assault. But to him, if Frizell had been arrested in a bar fight, well, that wouldn't have been good. But hitting his wife was unforgiveable.

"We talked to her about it," Phoebe said. "They'd been arguing about money. Evidently your guy spends a lot more than he makes."

"He's not 'my guy,'" Chase said.

"The former Mrs. Frizell says that her ex has a gambling problem. And in general, he likes to spend—cars, restaurants, jewelry. He has a Rolex. Like that. Beyond his means."

Chase didn't even know what a Rolex looked like. He himself always wore a Timex.

"Last year—his last year with the Snakes—Frizell made a million three," Phoebe said. "He got his last check in April."

Chase nodded. He knew that.

"Nancy Marlett, formerly Frizell, the ex, gets twenty-five percent of his gross salary, whatever he's earning, for child support on two kids plus another ten percent for alimony." Phoebe glanced up from her screen. "So we've got two concerns. One is the arrest record."

"You think he might beat up somebody at the plant? A woman?"

"We think he's got a short fuse," Dave said. "Does he?"

Chase thought about what he knew of Cliff. "Yes. I'd say so. You think he'd bring a gun to the plant?"

"He's got one," Dave said. "One that's registered,

anyway."

"So that's the first thing," Phoebe said. "The other concern is his money trouble. He's used to earning a lot, and even when he did earn a lot, he spent too much. How can a guy who likes money as much as he does get by on what you pay him?"

"I pay him a decent salary." Chase tried not to feel defensive. When he started out, he'd checked what other manufacturing concerns paid their employees in Las Vegas. He knew that what he offered was competitive in the industry.

"You pay him a terrific salary for an inexperienced systems designer whose degree is ten years out of date," Phoebe said. "But it's still a big drop for a guy who's used to making a million three."

Chase shrugged. "Every guy in football knows that when you hang up the cleats for the last time, you won't be making what you made in your playing days. That's what investments are for."

"And does Cliff understand about investments, too?" Phoebe asked. "Because the ex says he doesn't have any, and she says she'd know—her divorce lawyer saw to that. So what are you going to do when—I don't know—he embezzles from you? Or steals from other employees? Something like that?"

Chase exhaled. He'd hired every ex-football player who'd ever asked him for a job. Many former players had a solid work ethic and knew, better than most, the concept of going the extra mile to get the win. He liked that competitive edge. That hunger. He wanted his employees to have that.

Cliff had that desire. It was no secret that he'd spent the entire time he'd been under contract to the Snakes trying either to get Chase's job or the starting QB slot at some other franchise.

He had the desire, but not the work ethic. And truth be told, not the talent, either. Not for football, anyway. Chase would have to see how Cliff fit in at Venture Automotive. Civilian life might suit him better than the high-octane pressure of professional sports.

"Even if he doesn't steal from you, people like that can poison the atmosphere," Dave said.

That didn't seem unsurmountable to him. He already had more than two hundred people setting the tone at the factory, working hard. And Frizell was hired now. He'd let it play out, because ultimately Rinsho would be supervising him. If Rinsho wanted the guy, he could have him. If nothing else had turned up in the background check.

"Is that it on Frizell?" he asked.

"We did all the standard checks," Phoebe said. "Financial—credit checks and bankruptcy proceedings—plus education credentials. We turned up the assault and battery arrest, but there's no other criminal record. No court appearances for drug testing or sex offenses."

"Sex offenses!" Chase said. "I should hope not."

"Just saying," Dave said. "I can't recommend hiring people who have any kind of criminal record."

"That ship has sailed. I've been hiring ex-cons for quite a while now."

"So I understand," Dave said. "But you know the recidivism rates, right? Those guys are likely to commit another crime. And you don't want it to happen on your property."

He didn't, but he believed in second chances—because the whole of Venture Automotive was a second chance, after football, for himself, too.

"The ex-cons I've hired so far have all worked out, and the problem is that I need a lot more employees than I have right now if we're going to meet our production goals," he said. "At the moment I can't even staff a second and shirt shift. So I'll take what you said under advisement. But for right now, I'll stick with my current plan."

"We can't force you to follow our advice," Dave said. "But that's what you're paying us for."

"*I'll take it under advisement.* So what's wrong with the other two guys? Harrington and Jones, right?"

Phoebe nodded, shuffling her papers. "Ex-cons. Jones has multiple robbery and burglary convictions. Harrington went inside for armed robbery."

Well, he wasn't going to let them go because of that. "I hope if they have a job, some stability, they'll be fine."

"I understand giving somebody a break," Dave said. "But they come in to work on a Saturday when you're not there, you want to run the risk of getting ripped off?"

"What about since they got out?" Chase asked. "Any trouble?"

Phoebe shook her head. "No. Jones's mother is local, and she's been raising his daughter. She said that when he gets a place of his own—which he'll be able to do with the job you gave him—he wants to take the girl back. We didn't find family for Harrington. We didn't have enough time to track down anybody in two days." She raised her eyebrows at him.

He had to smile. He'd always enjoyed how she'd stood up to him. Now, in front of her new boss, she was obviously trying to be polite while letting him know what she thought.

"Everybody else seems okay?" he asked. "There's four other parolees I just took on."

"We haven't gotten to those yet," Dave said. "Other than the guys we talked about, we didn't see anything that raised flags in terms of increased risk. We still have several dozen candidates to go. You'll get those Monday."

"Thanks," Chase said. "What about plans for the security ideas you outlined yesterday?"

"Phoebe and I have been talking about what we should prioritize, given your situation," Dave said. "There's a lot you should do."

"In retrospect, I'm sure we outgrew our security setup months ago," Chase said, feeling rueful. "I think Daryl's been doing a good job with security during the day, and at night we've got the security cameras on the front door. But it clearly isn't enough." The truth was, security hadn't been a priority until the damage was done, and now he was paying the price.

"Daryl's had good training for a security guard, but he's not a plan," Dave said.

"I know that now," Chase said. "What's our plan so far?"

Phoebe settled back and tapped on her laptop. "You need both physical security—see what happened to your poor cars—and data security, to protect what's on your computers, like your designs. Whatever."

"About that," Chase said. "We don't put any manufacturing data online. None at all. It can't be accessed with the internet. Those production computers are on an altogether separate, local system. So if you're thinking computer hacking, data would have to be carried out physically, like somebody stealing a laptop. Otherwise, not gonna happen."

"Well, that's something," Dave said. "Excellent news, in fact, for the short run. So for the immediate future—what we do in the next couple of days until the expo—we can focus on physical security."

Chase nodded. "What are you thinking?"

"Until you ship those fancy cars to the convention center, you need one or two security guards to work nights," Phoebe said. "And we think we should tear down the wall that separates the production department from the warehouse you're not using. It's probably drywall, not load bearing, so—"

"What? Why tear down a wall?"

"So you can park the expo cars inside the building—not outside—when they're finished," Dave said. "Two reasons. Inside eliminates the possibility of a random attack from the outside. It's a smaller area to protect physically. And your cars will be safer from the weather, too, while you're at it."

It made sense. And that wall would need to come down anyway as they expanded production.

"Okay," Chase said. "We should get a contractor or somebody—"

"I already lined up a guy," Phoebe said. "He's going to inspect it this afternoon. Kristin's expecting him."

"Fast work," Chase said. "Good thing I approved it."

"I know!" Phoebe beamed at him. "We didn't want to lose any time."

"Next thing," Dave said. "Bodies on the ground. Short term, I know a couple of cops would like to do some extra security work. They'll cost you, but they're the best."

"I suppose you made the calls already."

"Yeah," Dave said. "We figured you'd approve it."

"I don't know why I even come to these meetings," Chase said, but he was needling them. He liked that Western was proactive, and all the steps they'd taken were good ones.

"You come for the ambience," Dave said. "And the refreshments."

"And you like us," Phoebe said. "Group hug."

"Hell, no." But Chase had to laugh. They were right, after all. He *did* like them. The ambience, though, could use improvement. And *any* refreshments would be an improvement.

"No group hug, check," Phoebe said.

"Circling back to data security for a second," Dave said. "If this expo is as successful as you're hoping, the company will be taking a big leap forward in terms of sales and personnel. And inevitably somebody will try to hack into your bank and personnel records for the cash and identify info. You need serious security software and an experienced IT security guy. At least one. For production and manufacturing data, too, if that ever goes online."

"Nick Balasco can do that," Phoebe said. "I have a call in to him."

"Nick Balasco, as in Kristin's boyfriend?"

Phoebe nodded. "One night when I had dinner over there, he said he works for Data Champion. I know that company from the CIA. They're good, and he'd work for you in a heartbeat. For free. He's a big fan."

"Okay," Chase said. "We'll interview him. Hire him if he wants to make the jump. Not for free, though."

"Immediate things: You need more external security cameras," Dave said. "Internal door locks, controlling access to different parts of the building. Employee badges."

"Fine," Chase said.

"That's everything for now," Dave said. "Other things will come up as we get started."

Phoebe grinned. "The day is still young. Dave wants to

get started on the partition removal right away—this afternoon, if that works for you? As soon as the engineer leaves."

"The sooner the better. Tony, Matt, and Rinsho are working on the replacement vehicles. We have to be ready to protect them."

"The cops said they can start tomorrow night," Dave said.

"Okay." Chase took the reports they handed him and shook hands with them both. "I'll have another fifty to a hundred names for you to check out by next week."

"Pleasure doing business," Dave said. "Drop by anytime."

"The ambience is always a draw, not to mention the refreshments," Chase said, grinning. "Phoebe, call me later, okay?"

The meeting over, Phoebe picked up her laptop and went back to her office. If she and Dave were going to Venture that afternoon for demolition, she had to get organized.

"One more thing before I forget." Dave followed her back to her teeny workspace and leaned in the door. No doubt he would have come in and sat down had there been room to have a visitor chair. But they'd had to convert a windowless closet for her office space. It had a folding chair for her to sit on and a tiny table that could hold her laptop, but nothing else.

"Bonaventure's putting some pressure on our capacity to produce," he said. "And that means we gotta ramp up, too, just like he's doing. So how's the driving coming along?"

"Sanjay took me out this morning. I drove around Town Square."

"How'd it go?"

"Fine. But I'm not quite ready for the test yet."

"Is he taking you out again?"

"He said he'd call when his taxi schedule got set up."

"Bonaventure owns a car company, as I recall. He can't take you out driving?"

"I don't ask him," Phoebe said. "He's been so busy since the company started gearing up big-time. And now he's got the pressure of the expo and rebuilding those cars."

"Here's what I don't get," Dave said. "You're okay with him giving us all his security work, which you know is a favor because he hasn't called around to any other agency, but you won't ask him to give you a driving lesson?"

"No."

"Why the hell not?"

"The work is for *us*, Dave. For Western Private Investigations. That's business. But the driving lesson is for *me*. And I'm not going to hang on him, demanding a handout like every hungry fan in town does. If he offered, okay. I'd accept. But he hasn't offered."

"I don't understand that." Dave shook his head. "You're probably the only person in this United States who won't take advantage of an acquaintance when they could. It's called *networking*. It's *legitimate*. How do you plan to get ahead in this world?"

Phoebe grinned. "I *am* networking. I'm hanging on your coat tails the whole way."

He laughed. "Well, let's make your driving a priority. Go to one of those driver ed schools. With all the work Bonaventure's giving us, you can expense it. I want you to be able to do surveillance when we need that."

"Thanks," she told her boss, touched and pleased. "I'll get something lined up."

He pushed away from the doorway. "Can't believe you never learned to drive," he said as he walked away. "Who doesn't learn to drive? And now you got a boyfriend owns a car company! That just plain looks bad."

"New York!" Phoebe called after him. "Grew up in New York! Nobody drives in New York!"

"Tell it to the hand!" he yelled back.

A short time later the engineer called Western Private Investigations to report that he'd been out to Venture Automotive, the boss himself had shown him the wall in question, and indeed, it could come down with no difficulty.

"He was nice enough to give me an autograph," the

inspector said. "Too bad about his knee. The Snakes will miss him this year."

When fans said that to Chase, he always said, *Coaches and players are working hard.* Phoebe wondered if she should say it now.

"Thanks for the call," she said. "We appreciate your quick response."

"Bill's in the mail."

Dave hired three men from the day-labor pool, rented some basic equipment and safety gear, and an hour later, they headed out to the factory.

"This is the wall that has to come down," Phoebe told the men, waving her hand at it. "Be careful! Safety first."

Phoebe and Dave handed out the equipment to the men. Everybody, including Phoebe and Dave, put on their hard hats, gloves, and safety glasses and picked up a sledgehammer. Phoebe took a step back, swung her hammer with all the force she could muster, and let it smash into the wall. The force reverberated up her arm, almost making her teeth shiver, and put a hole in the drywall. Julio took a swing and bashed a hole next to hers. Dave was next.

And then she saw the laborers nudging each other and knew that they recognized a football hero when they saw one. She turned around and saw Chase coming through the doorway. Her heart skipped a beat, like it always did when she saw him.

"Here's the big boss," she told the men, who all nodded and smiled shyly.

"Kristin said you were down here," Chase said. "I came to see how it's going. Phoebe, you shouldn't be doing this demolition. It's too heavy for you. You could hurt yourself."

Phoebe felt her blood pressure go up. *Was he kidding?*

"That's a joke, right?" She raised her arm and flexed her muscle. "See this?"

Chase wrapped an arm around her shoulders, turning her away from Dave and the crew. "Let me speak to you privately."

"Why?" Phoebe shrugged out from underneath his arm.

"Anything you want to say to me about work you should say in front of Dave."

He leaned into her, speaking directly into her ear. "No, I can't."

He steered her down the aisle and into a quiet corner. Phoebe didn't like it, but she gave up the struggle. Fine! He could say whatever was so important to say.

He dropped his arm and laced his fingers with hers. "*Cher*, sweetheart, you need to stop doing that work."

"*No*. I'm strong enough, and I don't want to look like a slacker girl to Dave and that crew. But most of all, I don't work for you! So don't tell me what to do."

"Just listen. I know you're strong, and you have the will of ten thousand. But if you insist on swinging that sledge-hammer around, Dave will feel that he has to sling one, too, and he should not be doing this work."

"What?" Phoebe glanced down the aisle, where she could see Dave in the distance. "What are you talking about?"

"I don't know what the retirement age is for the police department, but Dave was a detective for probably fifteen or twenty years. I'm sure he goes to the gym, because he looks fit. But going to the gym is not the same as doing heavy physical labor for hours on end."

Phoebe watched the demolition scene for a couple of minutes. Sure enough, Dave swung his sledgehammer once for every two times Julio swung his. She felt her annoyance deflate.

"And here's a thing about guys: he won't quit if you don't."

"Cripes," Phoebe said. "He's an idiot."

"Yeah, and here's the other thing: if Dave doesn't quit, then *I* have to swing a hammer, and let me tell you, *cher*, I don't want to. It's heavy, dirty work, and I've got a bad knee. And I don't want Dave Greenaway making me look like a lazy, no-good bum. I have appearances to keep up around here."

Phoebe grinned. "I amend that. *Men* are idiots."

Chase grinned back. "What about the women who do

work that's too heavy for them just to keep up with the guys?"

Phoebe laughed. That one swing she'd taken really had been a shock.

"Okay, *fine*. You made your point. *People* are idiots. Happy now?"

"Yes. Kristin would like you to work on the stadium spectacular. Will Dave be okay with that?"

"The stadium spectacular needs security, too. Anyway, doing stuff for the company probably falls under security work, generally speaking, since you're our only client right now. Plus, he told me not to ask him about every blinking thing I do. But I'll ask him to make sure."

"Good. Now there's something I need from you."

"What's—" Phoebe started, but Chase pulled her into his arms and kissed her. A deep, throbbing, heartfelt, heart-stopping kiss.

For a second Phoebe pushed back against his chest. They were at work! They shouldn't—! But then his hands stroked her shoulders and back and his powerful thighs pressed against her legs and the energy that seemed always to pulse through him flowed through her, too. The sounds of the factory faded, and she felt cocooned by his size and strength, isolated from the outside world.

At some point—it could have been an hour, it could have been a second—Chase pulled back and rested his forehead against Phoebe's. Her heartbeat thundered in her ears, and she could see that he was breathing quickly, too. As they stood, his face so close to hers, his breath warm against her skin, she floated back down to earth. She heard the sounds of the factory again. She realized where they were.

"Don't think I didn't enjoy that, because I surely did," she said without moving. "But that was so inappropriate."

Even without seeing his face, she could feel his smile. He lifted his head and stroked a finger down her cheek.

"I apologize," he said. "And nobody saw us."

They started back to the demolition. Then Phoebe had a thought.

"Wait a second," she said, stopping. "Was that whole

'you could hurt yourself' business just a gambit? It was, wasn't it?"

"I wanted you to step away from Dave," he said. "I thought if you were riled up a little bit, that would be more likely to happen. I didn't want him to hear that none of us should be swinging sledgehammers."

Phoebe covered her face with her hands. "I am so predictable," she moaned.

"I'd hardly say that, *cher*." He put his arm around her. "But I do know you a little bit."

She put her hands down. "You know what else? I'm not even sorry not to be doing the demolition. One swing and I felt it all through my arms and back. That's very hard work."

Chase nodded. "It is. I used to do construction and demolition with my dad, and I know from experience, it takes a lot out of you."

Dave had put down his sledgehammer and walked to meet them. With a pang of contrition, Phoebe saw that sweat glistened on his forehead.

"Lover's quarrel?" he asked as he approached. "Or something you can share?"

"Yeah, Dave, let me run this by you," Chase said. "I'd like Phoebe to help Kristin on the plans for the stadium spectacular, and she informed me in rather strong terms that she works for you. We need security for it, but Kristin probably will want her to do other things, too."

Dave nodded. "Phoebe's got an inside track here at the plant because of your relationship with her, so it's fine if she puts in some hours here. I know she'll keep her ears open for anything that sounds off. If you have a few minutes now, let's sit down and talk about security for your expo events, and then I'll be okay letting her run with it."

"Sure, I've got some time now," Chase said. "Whatever you need."

Dave turned to Phoebe. "While you're here, you let me know if you see anything suspicious. But if you see anything immediately dangerous, like somebody pointing a gun, call the cops. Don't try to stop it, okay? Don't get in the way. I don't have to tell you that, right?"

"Nope, you don't have to tell me," Phoebe said, a little annoyed. "I hear you loud and clear."

Dave nodded. "I hope so."

"Sounds like a plan." Chase smiled, a slow, hot smile that made Phoebe's knees weak. He stood there, smiling at her, all heat and desire and some kind of lustful knowing that melted her bones and turned her all squishy right there on the factory floor. She wished she could do that to him. So dang unfair.

"So let's get started," Dave said, rolling his eyes. "*Jeez.*"

"One thing first," Chase said, the spell broken. "*Cher*, introduce me to your crew."

Shaking her head, she led him over to the men. They all grinned and nodded, wiping their hands on their pants before extending to shake.

"*Muchas gracias por su trabajo*," Chase said, shaking each man's hand. *Many thanks for your work.* "*Hice trabajos de construcción antes. Es muy difícil.*"

"You speak Spanish?" Phoebe said. "'I worked construction before, it's very difficult'—that's pretty advanced language skills you've got there."

"I googled what to say," Chase said, "although I'm sure the grammar is all screwed up. Tell them if they finish by six o'clock with no accidents and the building still standing, they'll be paid double."

Phoebe blinked and told them, and Mario curled one arm in a bodybuilder's move and squeezed his bicep. Everyone laughed.

"Message received," Dave said. "Yeah, I think we can let these guys get on with the work."

Phoebe followed Chase and Dave up the stairs to the offices, happy to leave the heavy work to those with the stronger muscles. But she feared that keeping the new cars corralled behind the factory walls wouldn't do Chase much good if their vandal was already inside.

She wouldn't do anything stupid. But while she was here, she'd keep her eyes and ears open—and do what she could to stop any trouble. She wanted their saboteur caught before he damaged more cars.

Or did something worse.

Chapter 5

Pavel Rao glanced at the expo materials that he'd spread out on the dining table of his suite. He'd googled all the companies listed in the brochure, searching for relevant facts, making notes as he went along. Several of these firms would be worth pursuing.

One company in particular, Venture Automotive, expected to quadruple its workforce in the next two months. So the electric-car-manufacturing concern was growing fast, and its participation in the conference demonstrated that it wanted to enter overseas markets, especially India. Even better, the company's CEO, Chase Bonaventure, was a faded sports star, no doubt holding his office because the banks thought his name could attract investment. He was bound to be both a glory hound and an ignoramus, because *Venture Automotive*. Hello. Named after himself.

So there would lots of hubris, lots of money, and no intelligence about how to spend it. Perfect. He knew how to persuade uninformed, lazy, and overconfident CEOs to invest in his country.

And that would be very good for him.

Pavel Rao highlighted Venture Automotive on his spreadsheet. That was where he'd begin. By the time the expo started, he'd know all there was to know about electric vehicles.

And by the time the conference ended, all of Venture

Automotive's secrets would be his for the selling.

The shift at the Venture Automotive plant ended at five thirty, and by the time six o'clock rolled around, the factory was dark and quiet. Cliff Frizell got up from his desk, stretched, and walked to the door of his shared office to see if anybody was still around.

He stepped out onto the factory floor, craning his neck to check for light. Only the safety and exit lights glowed in the dim interior, although some light from the setting sun still leaked through the frosted windows. He strolled down the aisle between the robots, liking the feeling of power he got when the factory was vulnerable and he was the only person in it.

He hated this job, and he hated Chase Bonaventure. Had always hated him, from the first day they'd suited up in the Snakes locker room and Cliff learned that Bonaventure, six years his junior, straight out of college, had won the starting quarterback spot. And now, ten years later, Bonaventure owned a car company while he owned nothing, and Cliff was once again working under the bastard.

The thought of it just about roasted his weenie. From the very first, Bonaventure had lorded it over him. Always thought he was better than everybody else. There'd never been any good reason why the younger man had started for the Snakes for ten years, and he himself had seen scarcely four quarters of playing time in that same ten-year period. And hadn't he worked just as hard? Learned the same plays? Attended as many practices? Suited up for every game? But Bonaventure had made the big bucks while he'd made peanuts.

Nothing had changed. Ten years later, he was still earning peanuts. A measly hundred grand! He was making maybe a twentieth of what Bonaventure made. Probably less than that.

How could he get by on a hundred thousand dollars a year? He used to earn more than that in a month! Nancy ran through money faster now than when they'd been married. She and the kids seemed to eat money for breakfast. He wouldn't even be able to pay rent after his ex and the kids sucked out one-third of his check and Uncle Sam sucked out another third. What was left wouldn't leave him enough for a Starbucks run, much less cover his gambling losses. While Chase Bonaventure probably pulled down his customary twenty-five mil.

He never would have taken this job if Nancy hadn't bitched endlessly at him about bringing some money in. He'd applied as a joke. But between her nagging and his waiting to hear what kind of broadcast or coaching offers he'd get, he'd thought he might as well be a pain in Bonaventure's butt if he could be.

But he hadn't heard back yet from any of the pro franchises, colleges, TV networks—or even the affiliates—so here he was, working for Chase Fucking Bonaventure with no end in sight. He kicked a trash can that got in his way, sending it skittering into the dusk, where it bounced off one of the robots and clanged to a halt someplace he couldn't see. *Shit.* This is what his life had become? Nine to five with an hour for lunch? He was no better off than a kid slinging burgers at Mickey D's.

He glanced around again, satisfied that all the offices that rimmed the production floor were dark, and turned on the empty coffeepot. Maybe it wouldn't melt down or catch fire by tomorrow, but maybe it would.

Walking down the aisle of the factory floor, he scoped out things he could do. Small things. Things that wouldn't draw unnecessary attention, because he didn't want to bring more cops onto the premises. But until he got a better job offer, he'd enjoy doing what he could to damage the prospects of the man who'd ruined his professional playing career.

Cliff pocketed a thumb drive in one office and shredded some documents from another. Opened a window in another. It rarely rained in Vegas, but the wind would blow things around. Maybe an animal would get in. Or a thief. He smiled at the thought. He found an open can of soda on someone's desk and tipped it over so it poured onto a keyboard, and then he rearranged a few things on the desk, trying to make the mess look like the fault of the cleaning service.

He headed out of the plant, leaving the exit unsecured, and went to the employee parking lot, where he'd parked the company car he'd been given to use. The car was loaded with diagnostics that Bonaventure's engineers used to make improvements, or so they said, but the HR hag had specifically said that they didn't gather data on *where* employees drove, but *how* they drove. Might as well test that theory out now. Not that he cared if Bonaventure knew he was going to a casino. Lots of people went to casinos.

One thing about this setup—only idiots could mess up a simple job like the one he had in R&D, but it was a way to pass the time until he landed something better. He'd check with his contacts for coaching and broadcasting again. Once he got back to football in a job that was commensurate with his experience and expertise, he could earn some real money. Because one thing was for sure: Bonaventure would never pay him what he was worth. And the day he couldn't outsmart, outthink, outperform, and outwit that pretty-boy has-been, he was finished for good.

He'd been second-string during his entire career with the Snakes—a loser quarterback as far as the world was concerned. Now that football was over for both of them, he'd show Chase Bonaventure what losing really felt like.

Up in the mezzanine conference room, Phoebe heard something—some kind of metal crash. Chase had left work early for a meeting with the accountants, and everybody else was supposed to have gone by now. But something was down there, and she wasn't a PI in training for nothing.

She jumped up and dashed to Chase's office only two doors away. It had windows so you could see down to the factory floor. The lights were off everywhere in the plant, but she could see movement. A shape—a person she couldn't identify—walking leisurely down the aisle. In the shadows.

She didn't have time to call the cops. And it might not be an intruder. It might be Rinsho, who'd already turned off the master light switch and knew his way to the door. But she had to find out who it was. Time enough to freak out if she bumped into their saboteur.

She ran down the stairs and burst into the production area, heading in the direction she'd seen movement. The master light switch was in the other direction, near Rinsho's office, and she didn't want to take the time to go there first. But when she tore around a corner, she collided with a large metal trash can that had tipped over. She sprawled across the polished concrete floor, sending the can spinning against a table.

Should have turned on the stupid light. Now she hadn't saved any time, and she'd alerted whoever was still in the building. If they even *were* still in the building.

But that's what she must have heard. The can going over.

Then the person wasn't Rinsho. If he'd kicked it over, he'd have picked it up.

At least she wasn't hurt. She got to her feet and ran—a little more slowly now—to the side door. She flung it open just in time to see a yellow Venture Automotive car pull out of the parking lot.

It could have been anybody. Even someone who didn't mean the company any harm.

But it definitely was an employee.

When all the banging and crashing and running finally ended, Aquintis Jones turned the brightness back up on the screen he'd been working on. He shouldn't be here. If anyone found out what he was really doing, he'd be fired for sure. His parole officer would be all over his ass, and he'd be back in the joint before he knew it.

But he had to take the risk. He'd been inside too long and he'd lost too much time, too much *life*. If he was ever going to catch up, forge a new way for himself, he had to start someplace.

And Venture Automotive was as good a place as any to do that. If he was careful, no one would ever notice what he was up to.

Phoebe went back upstairs to the conference room to collect her stuff and called Dave to tell him what had happened. Then she called Chase and told her story all over again. Dave said the incident was suspicious, but with no damage done, there wasn't much to follow up on. Chase thought it was probably somebody working late.

"Like you were," he told her.

"I wasn't kicking trash cans over in the dark."

"Even Rinsho doesn't know where all the trash cans are. Whoever it was didn't see it. They're not bolted to the floor, you know. But thanks for letting me know. I'll ask around tomorrow to find out if anything is missing or damaged."

She wasn't satisfied with that response, but she was ready to leave. When she got home—a brisk twenty-minute bike ride later—Trouble rushed to greet her at the door, prancing and hopping like a canine that desperately needed to smell some grass. Phoebe snapped a leash on him and they headed for the park, Phoebe pedaling her bike and Trouble trotting briskly alongside. Her phone rang just as they arrived.

She dug it out of her pocket. Her mother.

Phoebe hadn't heard from Brenda in a while, which meant that if she was calling now, she'd probably broken up with her latest boyfriend—or he'd broken up with her—and she needed a place to crash and a shoulder to cry on. Phoebe had a clear-eyed but not unsympathetic relationship with her mother, a cocktail waitress who worked hard and deserved better. But Brenda was an eternal optimist who thought that every man who gazed into her eyes from across the bar and swore he loved her would keep all his promises.

So far, that hadn't worked out for her. And in one misadventure twenty-five years ago, Phoebe had been conceived.

She stopped the bike, planted her feet on the pavement, and hit the green button. "Hi, Mom."

"Phoebe, honey," Brenda said, relief in her voice. "How are you, sugar? I am so sorry to bother you, but I have had such a rough day, you don't know. Listen, can I bunk with you tonight? Well, maybe for a little while. The thing is—"

Sharing her apartment wouldn't be comfortable for either of them. Somebody would have to sleep on the sofa, and

Brenda usually got home from work between two and three in the morning. Even Trouble was inconvenienced by those kinds of hours, and because Phoebe's lease depended on her dog's not barking, she didn't like to tempt fate.

But Phoebe owed her mom. Brenda had never been anyone's idea of an attentive parent, but her babysitting arrangements had led to Phoebe speaking eight languages fluently. When Phoebe's life at the CIA had crashed and burned and she needed a place to stay, Brenda had taken her in. So Phoebe had to reciprocate.

"Sure, Mom, that's okay," Phoebe said now. "Don't worry. Come on over. I'll leave the door unlocked for you."

"Thanks so much, sweetie! When do you get home? I could make something for dinner, or—"

Phoebe, who had a healthy fear of Brenda's cooking, shuddered just thinking about it. "Oh, don't worry about that. I'm at the park with Trouble. We'll be home in an hour or so, and then we can make spaghetti or something together. Okay? Are you off tonight?"

"Yes. That would be perfect! I always love catching up with my baby. Bye!"

Phoebe sighed and stashed her phone back in her pocket. If history was anything to go by, Brenda would pick up a new boyfriend relatively quickly and move out again within a few weeks. But the next few weeks would definitely be crowded *chez* Phoebe.

She'd chained her bike to the rack, dug out Trouble's ball, and unsnapped his leash when the phone rang again. What could Brenda want now? But when Phoebe checked the display, she saw the caller was Chase. She hoped he wasn't calling with bad news.

"Hey." When Trouble looked back at her with, she was sure, exasperation, she tossed the ball for him as far as she could. "What's up?"

"I thought we were getting together tonight, so I'm sittin' here like a lazy river rat, waitin' for something to happen, and I got tired of waitin'. Want to come over? I would enjoy your company, even that no-good eating machine you got on a leash. And Marta was here today, and whatever she's got cookin' would make a New Orleans four-star chef weep."

"You sweet talker," Phoebe said. Trouble had raced back with the ball, and she threw it out for him again. "I wish I could, but Mom called and she's coming to stay with me for a while. I said I'd meet her at my place in an hour and we'll make something. She'll need to tell me her latest tale of woe."

"I feel sure your momma can use your support, but I'll miss you. Where are you now?"

"At the park. I brought a ball for Trouble, and you know how he loves to chase that. No pun intended."

"What pun? You know, *cher*, you could throw the ball to him at my place. The yard's big enough to hold a Super Bowl ten times over. And you're only about a mile away. If you took up jogging, you'd get here real quick. Since you can't drive and all."

"Ha," Phoebe said. "I have my bike. But a real gentleman would offer to pick me up."

"A real *friend* would know how important a woman's exercise routine is to her. Bike on over here, why don't you?"

Phoebe snorted. "You *are* a lazy river rat. I take it all back about your being a sweet talker. Next you'll be giving me a gym membership for my birthday."

She heard Chase laugh as she disconnected.

Trouble had run down the ball and trotted back to her in triumph, dropping it, damp and drooly, at her feet. Now he waited impatiently, wanting her to throw it again. But Chase was right—she could toss the ball to Trouble at his place. The yard was huge, it was fenced, and she suspected that Trouble liked it better there anyway. And if they went there, she could see Chase, Trouble could get his playtime, and she could leave him there for the night while Brenda stayed over. Win-win-win.

She picked up the ball and ruffled his fur.

"Let's go see Chase, boy," she said, reaching for the leash. "We can play there. That'll be even more fun, right?"

Straightening, she turned. And there he was. All six foot

four of the most gorgeous hunk of man Phoebe had ever seen, leaning against his bright yellow Venture Automotive SUV, one foot resting against the door, a slow smile on his face, heat in his eyes. Chase Bonaventure. Waiting for her.

She gulped, the leash slipping forgotten to the ground. A sight like that stripped the thoughts right out of her head.

"Time to go," she told the dog. "There's Chase."

Trouble streaked ahead, and by the time Phoebe retrieved her bike and got to the car, Chase had patted the dog and let him into the back seat.

"How did you get here so fast?" she said, stashing her bike in the cargo hold. "I just talked to you on the phone one second ago."

His eyes crinkled with amusement. "Magic, *cher*." He reached for her. And then he pulled her into his arms and kissed her.

Lights out. When he kissed her like that, Phoebe floated—there was no other way to describe it. She lost all sense of where her feet were, because every nerve, every pulse, every synapse was focused on his lips on hers. The lips that made her forget her name. He really was magic.

"You were already in the car," she said breathlessly when she came up for air, holding on to him to steady herself. "Or even already at the park."

He pulled back, still holding her, a glint in his eye. "It doesn't exactly take a detective to figure out your routine." He walked her around to the passenger side of the car.

She wouldn't have needed to exercise at all today. Simply kissing him made her heart rate double. That alone was a cardio workout.

When they got to his place, he let Trouble into the back yard.

"How about this, *cher*," he said. "If we have only an hour, why don't you and I sit on the patio and enjoy ourselves for a bit, and I promise you I'll play catch with your dog after you leave."

"Sounds good to me. He's your dog, too, you know."

He grinned. "He's my dog whenever you need a babysitter for him. Come on in. Let's see what I have in the kitchen to tide us over until dinnertime."

Phoebe followed him in and opened the can of mixed nuts he pointed her to.

"Dave said to make my driving a priority," she said, pouring the nuts into a bowl. "He told me I could expense a class, so I signed up. At this rate, I'll get my license in no time."

"I'll take you out driving, too." Chase took out a corkscrew and opened a bottle of wine. "We can do such creative things in automobiles, not that I recommend any of it when you're actually on the road. Does Saturday work for you?"

"Saturday would be great. That way I get a little practice in with you before I go out with the teacher next week."

They carried the wine and snacks out to the patio by the pool, where Phoebe stretched out on a cushioned redwood lounge chair. In late summer, the days were still fairly long and the weather warm, although by now some early stars were twinkling at them.

"This is the life," she said, picking out a few cashews from the bowl. She held up her empty glass to him. "I'll take a little of that, thank you."

Chase grinned and poured her a glass of sparkling white wine and sat down on a chair next to her. "To driving." He lifted his glass.

"To driving," she said, toasting him. She watched him over the rim of her glass. Learning to drive was important to her, but it was nothing compared to what Chase was learning to do. Starting up an electric-automobile manufacturing company was a huge deal, and he was handling it like he'd been in the business forever instead of a year. She liked that about him, about his ability to start over in a new career. She was doing that, too—or at least thinking about it—so she knew how scary it could be.

But besides that, every time she looked at him, she shivered. He might not be playing football anymore, but he still had the broad shoulders, flat waist, narrow hips, and powerful thighs of an athlete or, say, a Greek god. Achilles, only with a bad knee.

"This is nice." Chase leaned back in his lounge chair.

"It really is. You have a beautiful place. It's too big, of course. Who needs fifteen bedrooms? You just rattle around in there by yourself. But it's incredible."

"I've been thinking." Chase turned his head to see her better. "If your mother is moving into your place, maybe you should bring your stuff over here. We don't get enough time together as it is, and I sure would enjoy having you here all the time."

"Bring my stuff here? Like moving in, you mean?"

"Yeah. Like moving in."

Phoebe took a deep breath. They'd talked about this before, but he hadn't sounded this serious before. She wanted to move in with him, she really did. Her heart yelled *yes, yes, yes*. Because being with Chase was like Christmas and the Fourth of July rolled into one—all lights and sparklers. When she was with him, the air fizzed and crackled with excitement.

But there was a lot more to a relationship than that, not that she had much experience with relationships. That was sort of the point. He was the hottest and smartest guy she'd ever met, but she knew from her mom's experience that making a long-term decision on a short-term acquaintance could lead to disaster.

Phoebe didn't want that. She loved Christmas when the tree was up with all its decorations and lights twinkling on the branches, but when the holidays were over, you still had a lot of winter ahead of you with plenty of snow to shovel. When she moved in with a guy, she wanted to be sure they'd both be ready and willing to face whatever the future held. She wanted forever.

"I—thank you—but it's too soon. I can't."

"Thank you? Did you say *thank you*?" Chase sounded amused. "I'm not aware that the suggestion calls for thanks, *cher*. We're good together. And there's advantages. Your place is so small, and now your mom will be there, too. And Trouble likes it here."

"I know," Phoebe said, hoping she wasn't being an idiot. "It's not about that. It's too soon. Mom—" She shook her head. "No. I can't. I'm sorry. *Really* sorry."

"Tell me something." Chase took a sip of his wine and gazed out at the pool. "Are we on the same page here? Do *you* think we're good together?"

"Yes! Yes, of course. Why? Does this change anything for us?"

"No, and that's what I'm a little worried about. If your leave is up in six months, don't you think we should try to step up our relationship? How will you decide if you want to stay or go if we don't live together? If we keep goin' along the way we are, what additional information will you have at the end of the six months that will help you make that choice?"

"I don't know." Phoebe chewed her lip. "But I think more time together in an unpressured environment is important. Is this a deal breaker?"

"Not for me. It's not the response I wanted to hear, but we're still good."

"Okay," she said, relieved but uncertain. "You know, I'm not saying not *ever*, just not *yet*. And didn't you plan to turn this place into a hotel?"

"That was the plan, but I haven't made any decisions yet. Okay, move over on that chair. If you're not staying tonight and you're not moving in, I have to take a little advantage here."

"This chair won't hold both of us!"

"Sure it will. It'll hold four hundred pounds, that's what the sales guy said. I had to get the biggest, strongest chairs for when the team comes over. Those linebackers are *big*. DeShaun Young alone weighs three seventy-five."

He nudged Phoebe's leg and she inched over, making room for him as he slid onto the low-slung lounge chair, stretching out and entwining his legs with hers. At least there was room on the chairs, especially if you didn't mind being a little squooshed close to the person next to you. Which she didn't mind in the slightest.

"This is better," he said, pulling her closer. "You know—"

Phoebe felt the chair quiver. "I think we're too much for the chair."

"Not a chance," Chase said as one of the chair legs groaned.

"Really? Because—"

"Do you weigh two hundred pounds? No. I weigh two-ten, so we have almost another hundred to spare."

"Are you *sure?* Because—"

Something cracked, and then the chair sagged and collapsed with a clatter onto the sandstone patio, Chase mostly on top of her. The thump was significant but not injury inducing. Phoebe bumped her head on the stone, but they hadn't had far to fall and she wasn't hurt.

"Well, that sure breaks the mood." Chase lifted his head to peer at her face. "Are you okay?"

"Yes, you? How's the knee?"

"Your thigh cushioned its fall. Everything is fine. Except for your thigh."

"My thigh is fine," she said, rubbing her scalp and mostly enjoying Chase's weight on her. Even getting stabbed by broken-chair debris while lying on the flagstone patio was heat inducing if Chase was touching her. "Good thing we weren't kissing. We'd both have chipped teeth about now."

"I'm sending these defective chairs back tomorrow." Chase untangled himself from the cushions and wooden slats, got to his feet with feline grace, and reached down a hand to help her to her feet. Phoebe brushed off the seat of her pants and surveyed the wreckage on the patio.

"Now that I've drunk your wine, eaten your cashews, and destroyed your patio furniture, I believe it's my cue to go," she said. "What else is there to do? Can't stay for dinner, can't make out on the lounge chair. And Mom's waiting for me, anyway."

"I'll give you a ride. Sure you're okay?"

Phoebe nodded. "I might have a bruise tomorrow somewhere, but I'm fine."

"Let me try to take your mind off it."

He pulled her in and kissed her. His mouth moved

against hers, and his hands roamed across her back. Her thoughts—her rational thoughts—skittered away. A little fall would never break the mood for her if he kept this up.

He wanted to spend more time together? *Kissing*, was all Phoebe could think. More kissing would be good.

When he let her go, he rested his head against hers. "I promise I'll get better lounge chairs," he said. "In the future, you'll be safe."

She smiled as she pulled away. She wasn't really "safe" when he was around—at least, her better sense wasn't. Practical, smart, handsome, a terrific kisser—and he could do unbelievable, incredible things in the front seat of a small SUV. What more could any woman want?

When he pulled the yellow car up to her apartment building, Chase got out with her and walked her and her bicycle to her door. He leaned the bicycle against the side of the building and slipped his arms around her and kissed her again, slow and deep, leaving Phoebe a little dizzy.

"Think about what I said," he said. "I'd love for you to move in. And you know there's plenty of room. Keep it in mind, *cher*." And, giving her a swift parting kiss, headed back to his car.

As if a kiss like that—and an offer like that—wouldn't be on her mind for, oh, say, the best part of forever.

When he got home, Chase called a real estate agent and listed his house for sale, asking her to notify him of smaller places in his price range. His conversation with Phoebe had convinced him that he needed to dump the house. He sure as hell didn't need fifteen bedrooms, and she didn't like the size of it.

And if she didn't like the house, she might never move in. With the factory ramping up, he didn't want to spend time renovating the place into a boutique hotel, as he'd planned to do when he bought it. Selling the place and buying something smaller that Phoebe did like was the easiest option. Maybe a better house would help persuade her to move into it.

He hoped so, anyway. Because nothing else seemed be doing the trick.

Chapter 6

The persistent, clamoring ring of her phone jolted Phoebe awake at six the next morning. Who would call at this hour? Was Chase having an emergency? Or Sanjay? Or Kristin? Or maybe it was her mother, off on one of her hairbrained escapades. In which case, it probably wasn't an emergency. She fumbled for the phone, squinting at the display.

Greg Peeling? Her boss at the CIA? What could he want? And at this hour of the morning, too?

"Greg?" she croaked, picking up the call.

"Phoebe. Sorry to call you so early." Greg sounded like he usually sounded, brisk and not at all sorry. "I have something to run by you."

Since when did Greg have things to "run by" her? Whatever it was, it probably wasn't good, and she'd need to be upright for it. She struggled to sit, thumping the pillow to give herself something to lean against.

"Okay," she said cautiously.

"Our directorate has received a mandate from the deputy director to form a new working subgroup."

And this was the thing that was so important that he had to call her at six in the morning? Since when did Greg feel compelled to inform Phoebe about organizational mandates from upper management? Since *never*.

"Okay…"

"This subgroup is tasked with identifying outlier threat potential."

"Um, what? Isn't threat potential what we already do?"

"This would be different. This working subgroup would be drawn from multiple directorates and would apply unconventional approaches to various threat scenarios."

The light bulb flashed. *Unconventional approaches.* That's why Greg was talking to her. Because she'd said that there was a plot at the Empire State Building—about which she'd been proven right, eventually—and then she, along with many others, had thwarted the kidnapping of the secretary of state, thanks to no help at all from the CIA or law enforcement. It sounded like now the agency wanted to isolate her. Maybe stick her in a windowless closet somewhere with the other misfits from around the agency so they could forget about them.

If that was the road he was barreling down, she had one thing to say to him: *Not so fast.*

"Are you in charge of this working subgroup?"

"No. Tamsin Dwyer is heading it up. Julian Garza signed on, too. And there are a couple of other people you might know."

Phoebe blinked. Tamsin Dwyer was higher than Greg on the CIA org chart. This wasn't a plan to derail her. This was a *promotion* he was talking about. Even better, Tamsin was the only boss who hadn't wanted to fire her for making that call on the Empire State Building that had gone sideways. And she knew Jules Garza a little, too, and liked him.

This offer, if it was an offer, could be incredible.

"This group is expected to approach language, data, and event analysis in new ways and potentially with new solutions," Greg said. "And because of the, ah, creative nature of this endeavor, the transition would come with a considerable raise in salary. Tamsin and I think that you might be interested in joining the group. Tamsin had a family emergency and is expected to be out until next week. She'll be in touch with you about specifics when she gets back."

"I look forward to talking to her. How does this affect

my leave of absence?"

"You can still take the full six months, if that's what you want to do after you talk to Tamsin," Greg said. "Of course, with this offer, and the details that will come up with starting a new group like this, we're hoping you'll come back sooner."

"I'll talk about that with Tamsin next week, then," Phoebe said. "Thanks for the call, Greg."

She disconnected, feeling joy bubble up. The CIA wanted her to join a special working group! For unconventional thinkers! With a *raise!*

How that would affect her life here in Vegas—and especially her relationship with Chase—well, she'd wait until next week and her talk with Tamsin.

That morning as Chase arrived at the office, he saw a truck bearing the logo of a security-camera company parked at the side of the building.

Dave and Daryl, his regular security guy, stood next to it, frowning up at a third guy installing a camera on the side of the building. Maybe that meant Phoebe was around here someplace, too. That was always fun.

He went inside and greeted Megan, the receptionist, then went straight to the production area to see what progress had been made on the vehicles for the Cars of the Future expo. Rinsho and a couple members of the design team were bunched up around a car off the production line, and he strode in that direction.

"Morning, guys," he said as he approached. "What have we got?"

The group parted for him to see. It was a new prototype. Something he'd never seen before. And it was gorgeous.

The car was sleek and low but big enough for a linebacker—or at least a wide receiver—to fit comfortably behind the wheel. There was a sunroof and wire rims. The fittings were first-class and gleamed in the sun that streamed through the factory windows.

"It's the NFL car," Rinsho said. "Before paint and interior trim. We're thinking silver exterior with the red logo and red leather seats. The Snakes colors. The silver finish will make it stand out from all the other expo cars."

"It's sharp." He walked around it slowly. It was a beautiful car, and it hadn't been on the planning boards at all. "You built us a new prototype? *In two days?* How did you do that?"

"Design-wise, we used the chassis from the sports car, so that gave us a big head start," Margo Bollingbrook, his head of R&D, said. "This is mostly Bill's work. Bill, tell Coach what you did."

"I've been thinking about the luxury line for a while, so I'd already worked up some design ideas," Bill Nettelhorst said. "But we all tweaked it. It was a group effort."

Chase nodded at Nettelhorst. The designer had gotten his start at Volkswagen and had moved west for the job at Venture Automotive. They'd been lucky to get him.

"You did an incredible job with it." He felt a rush of respect, responsibility, affection, and loyalty as strong for these men and women as he'd ever felt for his football teammates. Their faces shone with pride and determination, but in fact, everyone in the circle looked tired. He was embarrassed that he'd had a full night's sleep the night before. "You must have had to put in a lot of extra hours to get it done."

Rinsho nodded, smiling wanly. "We've been coming in pretty early. I authorized the overtime."

"You put it to good use," Chase said. "The car is incredible."

Margo beamed. "We're not letting the bastards get us down," she said. "That's all."

"Whatever success we have at the expo will be because of the hard work y'all put in this week," he said. "I've never worked with a better team."

"Thank you, Coach," Rinsho said. "We wanted to do it. Now, last thing—we finished the first of the show models. It's in the area that the labor crew built yesterday. The guy you hired for night security will take off whenever Daryl gets back in here from setting up the security cameras outside."

Chase went to meet the off-duty cop and see the finished car. They had decided all the expo vehicles would have fire-engine red exteriors with black leather seats. The SUV's wheels and trim sparkled in the early-morning light. The car was flawless. And Chase was determined to keep it that way.

"Any trouble last night?" Chase asked after he'd introduced himself. He was happy to see that the cop, Delmar Oates, looked strong and capable, and best of all, still seemed very alert, even after a twelve-hour late-night shift.

"Not while I was here," Delmar said. "Quiet as church."

"First good news we've had. Did Dave Greenaway have a chance to tell you that Phoebe Renfrew was here working past six when everyone should have left? Place was dark. She saw someone moving around. It seemed odd to her, but nothing seemed amiss."

"Dave called me," Delmar said. "I walked around, saw a trash can tipped over, that was it. Want to shift my hours around? Or add another guy for more coverage? The production crew came in at four this morning, so I could start earlier and leave when they come in, if you want that."

Four o'clock. No wonder the crew looked tired.

"I'll call Dave and work it out with him. He'll let you know. But thanks for being flexible. We definitely want these cars protected."

"So he said. Tough break about the vandalism. Shit like that makes me mad. Who wouldn't want you to succeed?"

Who indeed? That was the question. Sometimes aggressive fans whose teams lost to the Snakes took out their frustrations after the game on nearby people or objects, but Chase couldn't imagine any of them caring enough to come out to the factory during the off-season to damage cars. Who else would dislike him that much? It didn't make sense.

He headed up the stairs to his office on the mezzanine. Not too long ago, this trip up the stairs had just about killed his injured knee. No more. Ice, anti-inflammatories, and lots of physical therapy had mostly taken care of that. Now it only twinged when he did something to it—like when he'd banged it against the door handle having sex with Phoebe in the front seat of his car. With luck and a little more time, he'd be able to whack that knee against a door handle all he wanted and the knee wouldn't bother him a bit.

The woman certainly would bother him. But the knee would be fine.

"Morning, Coach," Kristin said when he got up to his office.

"Hi, Kristin. The guys are making great progress downstairs. Any disasters up here so far this morning?"

She grinned. "None so far, I'm happy to say. Coffee's ready. Reports are in your inbox. I filed the W-2s for one hundred and six new employees, and thank you, I will accept that raise. Don't forget to call the loan officer. We've got us a stadium spectacular to put on, and Phoebe and I need more money to pull it off. A *lot* more."

"Is she here?"

"She is. She and Dave were here with the security-camera guys when I got here at seven thirty, but Dave said, and I quote, she didn't need to watch guys screw crap into walls, so she's down in the conference room lining up NASCAR drivers. Or buying sod to redo the stadium after the NASCAR drivers tear up the old stuff. I'm not sure which."

"Okay. I'll say hello and then call the bank."

He poured a cup of coffee and carried it down to the conference room, tapping lightly on the door before he entered. Phoebe was on the phone, winding up an order it sounded like, but she glanced up when he knocked, her face brightening with a smile when she saw him.

He thought that might be the thing he liked best about her, that warm, open smile. She seemed radiant with energy, as corny as that sounded. Everything about her glowed, and when she turned that smile in your direction, you wanted to smile back and say yes to whatever she said. Whenever he was with her, the air felt ripe with possibility and adventure. He hadn't had as much fun with anybody since, well, ever.

He put the coffee down in front of her, next to the empty cup she already had, and she mouthed *thank you* to him. Then she said goodbye to whoever was on the phone and hung up.

"Do you have any idea how much it costs to resod a football field to professional standards?" she asked, reaching up for a kiss.

He leaned down to kiss her and smelled coffee on her breath and something light and citrusy about her generally. She seemed enthusiastic about the kissing, and that was another thing he liked about her.

"No, how much does it cost to resod a football field to professional standards?" he asked when he let her go.

"A *lot*." Phoebe sounded a little breathless but settled back into her seat. "Everything about this stadium spectacular costs a gazillion dollars."

"I'm calling the loan officer to authorize a few gazillion more on the credit line, so if we can come in with the estimates you and Kristin got, we're fine."

"Good to know," Phoebe said, tapping something into her computer. "Because guys who lay sod are strangely reluctant to negotiate on price. However, everybody in the entire country, as always, will do anything for you yesterday, if not sooner. Even the guy designing the actual show is working double-time to get the specs to the drivers so we can schedule some rehearsal time. It won't do you any good if guys are driving around like the Keystone Kops out there and hitting each other all over the place."

"Not unless we're staging a tragedy."

"The Red Wedding." Phoebe nodded. "Blood everywhere. We don't want that."

"We certainly don't. Okay, I'll leave you to it. Don't forget we have that lunch today for the Indian ambassador. And the meetings. And the cocktail party tonight."

"I haven't forgotten," Phoebe said. "Brought my stuff with me." She pointed to the back of the door where a garment bag hung.

"Okay. Let's leave here by eleven thirty."

Phoebe nodded again, already reaching for the phone, and he went back to his office to call his bank. In less than five minutes, he'd pushed his entire marketing budget into Venture's revolving credit line. That should give even

Phoebe and Kristin enough scope for their spectacular.

But he'd be lying to himself if he didn't acknowledge that authorizing so much money for a flashy marketing event worried him. He thought of the employees downstairs who'd given up sleep and family time to build the NFL car for him. Their welfare—and the welfare of 217 other employees—as well as the hundreds of millions of dollars the investment group and his bank had given him, weighed heavily. A lot was at stake, and most of the responsibility for success sat on his shoulders. He couldn't let these people down.

He was the newest CEO on the block in a fledgling industry, and lots of people, from economic soothsayers to Steelers fans, expected—even wanted—him to fail. The vandalism was proof of that. But failure was not an option. It hadn't been on the field, and it wasn't here in the factory. He was pouring everything he had into the operation—and then some—to make sure that Venture Automotive built the best cars possible and reached the broadest possible customer base.

He intended to get their cars into every international market. If all went well, by the time the week was out, he'd have trade agreements with Indian manufacturers. And if this stadium spectacular that Phoebe and Kristin were working on was successful, he'd make a big splash in the domestic market, too.

He'd find a way to get it done. Because everyone was counting on him to succeed.

"I'm a little nervous," Phoebe said as she got out of Chase's car at the convention hotel. She smoothed down her knee-length, blue silk dress covered in embroidery. "I've never been to a cocktail party. Do I look all right?"

Chase smiled, handing the keys to the valet. If he'd chosen her outfit, she'd be wearing something different. Nevertheless, she was lovely. "You look beautiful."

Phoebe rolled her eyes. "Thank you, but I wasn't fishing for compliments. I want to know if this dress is *appropriate*. And just so you know, I expensed the outfit. You'll be getting the bill for it, labeled Miscellaneous, from Western Private Investigations."

"In that case, if I'm paying for it, make it shorter and tighter next time."

He grinned as Phoebe punched him lightly on the arm. He wanted to suggest that they go back to her teeny place and stay there, doing whatever came to mind. Instead, they joined the security line, where beefy guys dressed in tuxedoes checked the invitations against a guest list.

"You look beautifully appropriate," Chase said. "I'll be the envy of all the men present."

Phoebe laughed. "More like, I'll be the envy of all the women. And all the men, too, for that matter. So what's our game plan?"

He shrugged. "I'll be talking shop. I want you to listen. Evaluate. See if anything sounds off. Or too good to be true. Whatever."

"Are you expecting some kind of trouble?"

They inched closer to security. "No. But it'll be a room full of sharp, international business types, all of whom will want to promote their companies. Me, too, for that matter. Having two pairs of eyes and ears on the competition has to be good."

"I was wondering—" She glanced at a Vegas Fun Fare taxi that pulled into the driveway. "Look!" she said, waving vigorously. "It's Sanjay!" His fare got out of the cab and gave him some money. As the stranger walked to the end of the security line, Sanjay gazed at the bills in his hand and shook his head. But then he saw Phoebe, lifted his hand, and walked to where she and Chase waited their turn to enter the building.

"Greetings, Mr. Bonaventure and Phoebe," he said as he joined them. "I understand from seeing you here that you have been invited to all these ambassador shenanigans sponsored by the Indian government. This party appears to be quite the occasion."

"Right," Phoebe said. "Are you invited, too?"

Sanjay shook his head. "Oh no. I am not nearly an

august enough personage to receive an invitation. My, ah, cousin—*distant* cousin, I should say—is attending. I had to give him a ride; that is why I am here. He has some position in the Indian Ministry of Commerce and Industry."

"Your *cousin*?" Phoebe asked. "You have a cousin in the Indian government?"

Sanjay wagged his hand. "For the sake of simplicity, let us agree that he is a cousin," he said. "A distant cousin. So distant that even a person with very sharp vision could not see him on the horizon if he were standing on the back of a very large elephant. That is how distant a cousin he is."

"Still," Phoebe said.

"It is not precisely an honor to know him."

"Why drive him around, then?"

"My Auntie Lupa blackmailed me. However, today at least he is paying the going rate for transportation services, although, I might add, not one penny more, not that I wish to fixate on the fiduciary nature of the taxicab business. I regret that I seem to be more involved in his plans than I'd intended."

"He might be a useful person to know," Chase said. Sanjay seemed to have a very large family, and all of them had varied interests. "And he's a relative of yours. You could introduce us."

Sanjay gazed at him with sad eyes. "Yes, or perhaps not," he said. "He is one of the lesser relations, if you'll pardon my saying so, Mr. Bonaventure."

Chase frowned. "Sanjay, how long have we known each other? Please call me Chase. All my friends do."

"Oh, thank you very much for suggesting it, but I could not possibly."

"If you can't call me Chase, I don't see how I can call you Sanjay. That's what wouldn't be right."

Sanjay's face fell. "Mr. Bonaventure, you don't understand. It would not be correct."

Chase shook his head. "You want to play hardball. Okay. I can play hardball, too. Here's what's going to happen. You call me Chase, or I'll tell all your relations that you ate barbecue beef at my house."

An expression of horror passed over Sanjay's face. "You wouldn't! Mr. Bonaventure! I mean—"

"You ate barbecue beef, and you *enjoyed* it."

"That is unfair! I am most— I didn't—"

"He's kidding, Sanjay." Phoebe patted his arm. "He wouldn't do that. Just call him Chase, okay? He really wants you to."

"I don't know," Sanjay said, looking flustered. "Doing so does not seem very respectful."

"Friends don't call me Mister," Chase said. "A little part of me dies every time you say that."

"Mr. Bonaventure! Chase, I mean. That is— Well. It would be my greatest honor to call you friend."

"Then it's done. Thank you."

"Blackmailed on all sides, Sanjay," Phoebe said, grinning at him.

Chase smiled, too. "Don't look now, Sanjay, but here comes your lesser relation."

Sanjay sighed. "Of course he is coming. He is speedier than a mongoose to spot an opportunity."

"Sanjay?" The lesser relation strode up and joined them. "You did not tell me you were invited to this party. You are poorly dressed for it. Although perhaps they are letting in all and sundry."

Chase was startled by the man's rudeness. No wonder Sanjay called him the lesser relation. Guy had the finesse of a four-hundred-pound linebacker with a bee in his helmet.

Sanjay sighed. "No, I did not receive an invitation, Pavel. I am saying hello to my friends here."

"Your friends?" He raised his eyebrows at Sanjay. "These are your friends? And yet you have not introduced us. Have your manners gone visiting?"

A second ago, Chase had been interested in meeting Sanjay's "lesser relation." But now that he saw the guy in action, he understood Sanjay's point.

"I have scarcely had the chance," Sanjay said. "Phoebe and, ah, Chase, let me introduce Pavel Rao of the Indian

Ministry of Commerce and Industry. Chase Bonaventure, CEO of Venture Automotive, formerly of the Las Vegas Rattlesnakes, our professional football team. And—"

"*Venture Automotive?*" Pavel Rao said, thrusting out his hand. "I have been wanting to find out more about your company! And I did not know that my little cousin Sanjay had such illustrious and distinguished friends! He has been keeping secrets from me."

Sanjay rolled his eyes.

"However, no major harm has been done!" Pavel enthused. "This is a most fortuitous circumstance! I have been greatly anticipating meeting the famous Chase Bonaventure!"

"Ah, thank you," Chase said, shaking hands. He was used to the raptures of fandom, but even so, this guy's enthusiasm was over the top. "Let me introduce—"

"Why did you not tell me that you were friends with Chase Bonaventure?" Pavel asked, turning to Sanjay. "Do you not understand my mission here?"

Sanjay furrowed his brow. "The question of my friendships did not arise. You also want to meet—"

"We in the Indian government are most anxious to expand the production and sale of alternative-fuel vehicles," Pavel said, turning back to Chase. "We're hoping to take the opportunity of this conference to form partnerships with more Western manufacturing concerns."

"Great," Chase said. Did this guy not see Phoebe standing right here? "In that case, you want to meet Phoebe Renfrew, our international trade liaison."

"Also with the CIA," Sanjay said.

Chase stifled a grin. Strictly speaking, Phoebe was on leave from the agency. But he couldn't blame Sanjay for wanting to take a little dig at Pavel, who had jumped at the mention of the CIA—there was no other way to describe it.

"CIA?" Pavel asked. "Is there an international security component to this event about which I also know nothing?"

"No, no," Phoebe said. "I'm not here in a governmental capacity. Strictly international trade liaison for Venture

Automotive."

Pavel pursed his lips, considering her. "I can see why you'd have trouble keeping your cover," he said. "The weaker sex! And the pretty ones always come under extra scrutiny, do they not?"

Phoebe's eyes narrowed, and she straightened her shoulders, ready for a fight. "I wasn't a field agent, so I didn't have to keep a cover, but I've never observed that female field agents are less reliable than men," she said, her voice tight. "Anyway, I'm not working for the government at the moment."

"And yet, is that not what the CIA says always?" Pavel asked. "However, do not worry. I understand completely about clandestine operations. Your secret is safe with me. Safer with me than with the female agents of which you speak. Never was a woman born who could keep a secret!"

"Not true," Phoebe said, gritting her teeth. "But in fact, *I'm not working for the CIA.*"

"I know." Pavel winked at her. "So you have said. Although no one can shred the truth faster than the CIA, am I not correct? Although, perhaps, a woman! How did you meet my cousin Sanjay?"

"He was my driver when I was, ah, working on a case."

Pavel whirled to Sanjay. "So you are one of those super drivers? One of those specially trained defensive drivers who protect dignitaries in bulletproof vehicles? Have you managed to accomplish that?"

"No," Sanjay said. "I drove my taxicab. I merely—"

"I understand!" Pavel said. "Of course you do not have these special skills. Or a special vehicle. Forget I said anything."

"Yes, indeed," Sanjay said. "Best to forget everything you say."

"Sanjay drives very well," Phoebe said. "He's teaching me."

"I can't imagine that my little cousin Sanjay has any skills that he could teach a CIA operative."

Chase was tired of the CIA conversation, and he could

tell that Phoebe was impatient with it, too. This Pavel Rao character sure could chew a bone until it was nothing but splinters and manage to offend just about everybody while he was at it.

"So, Pavel," he said, hoping to change the topic. "What are your thoughts on Las Vegas and Indian companies joining forces in business?"

"It's an excellent proposition," Pavel said. "Our ministry believes that India could play a significant role in the new manufacturing environment that has been launched here."

"Glad to hear it. Let me tell you about—"

"Next," droned the tuxedo-clad security guard, waving them forward.

Sanjay said goodbye, and Phoebe handed her invitation to the guard, surrendering her purse for inspection before she went through the metal detectors. Chase and Pavel followed.

"The executives at Mozo Motors would be thrilled to meet you," Pavel said when they got inside. "Their technology is not as advanced as yours, but their management team is very forward-thinking."

"I'll make sure to introduce myself."

"I can be the business agent for you, help you navigate the system, and simplify procedures," Pavel said. "That is what I'm here for."

Chase wanted to learn a lot more before he got too cozy with this guy or any company he was trying to promote. "Good to know," he said. "Ah, here are my colleagues." He nodded to Margo Bollingbrook, Cliff Frizell, and Bill Nettelhorst as they approached.

"Fantastic party, Coach!" Margo said after Chase introduced them.

"I have long been an admirer of Mr. Bonaventure's on the playing field, and now your company is finding great success!" Pavel said.

"Thanks, but we have a long way to go yet," Chase said.

Cliff's expression had soured ever so slightly. Was he still jealous of Chase's time with the Snakes? *Jesus*. Football was yesterday's news for both of them.

"I can help you expand into the Indian market," Pavel said. "Everything—patents, permits, expansions, import, export, parts, labor—goes through my ministry. Venture Automotive has been singularly astute with supply-chain management, but I can provide expertise when you need it. What issues are most pressing for you?"

"Right now we're having design complications." Chase avoided glancing at Phoebe, who, of course, would know exactly what kind of design complications they'd run into.

"Design?" Pavel said. "What about performance? For a company as far-reaching as yours, under your stellar leadership, I can only imagine the efforts you are making with performance."

"Performance is important, but I'm more worried about door handles," Chase said, keeping his voice bland.

Phoebe made sort of a strangled sound. It might have been a cough. But then, it might have been a laugh.

"Door handles?" Pavel said.

"Exactly. Each detail—"

Evidently Pavel had had enough. "Door handles, most interesting," he said. "It was a pleasure meeting you, Mr. Bonaventure, and, ah, everyone. For now, please excuse me. I see— Must attend to—"

"Of course," Chase said as Pavel Rao scurried away. He grinned at Margo. "And that's how you clear a room."

"Yeah, why did you do that?" Margo asked. "Door handles? I thought you wanted to build ties here. Make connections."

"I don't like that guy," Chase said. "And he's a middleman, a politician. Even if everything does have to go through the government there, I want to talk to the individual company executives first. And I want to choose which companies we do business with. I don't want some midlevel politician directing our partnership plans. Anyway, this is a party. It's more for meeting people and testing the waters than committing to a specific plan."

"Gotcha," Margo said. "Come on, guys. Let's find us some brains we can pick."

"Starting with our own," Cliff said, turning away.

Phoebe lowered her voice as Cliff headed toward the bar. "You can't tell me Cliff is working out. I just don't believe it."

"Too soon to tell," Chase said. "But yeah, okay. Margo says he's taking long lunches and acting bored. That's not a good sign for long-term success on the job."

Phoebe watched as Cliff nodded to Pavel at the bar.

"He seems to be hooking up with your favorite Indian politician. Do you have to worry about Cliff wandering around this event on his own?"

"Nah," Chase said. "He doesn't know enough about Venture Automotive at this point to give away any secrets. We can let him be."

"You'd think he'd be trying to make a good impression on you."

Chase watched the ex-second-string quarterback pull out a barstool and sit down next to the Indian underminister. "He'd be wasting his time. It's way too late for that."

Chapter 7

The waiter appeared in Cliff's peripheral vision as if by magic, and in one fluid movement, he pivoted and snagged himself a fresh drink as the server strolled by. The so-called signature cocktail was red, and it was potent. The first one had been excellent, and the second was even better. Bonaventure had said that this party would be good exposure for the company and for themselves personally. He didn't see it, but for free food and booze, not to mention a roomful of attractive women, he didn't mind raising the flag to trade and mutual friendship. What the hell. He'd drink to anything.

He turned back to the conversation with—he'd already forgotten the guy's name.

"When you meet so many people at one of these events, it is difficult to remember all the names, is it not?" the guy was saying now. "Pavel Rao. Indian Ministry of Commerce and Industry."

That's right, Pavel Rao. The government hack. A pudgy, fiftyish man with a smooth, unlined face, Pavel beamed at him, exuding cheer. Cliff refocused.

"Yes," Cliff said. "Right. Cliff Frizell. Recently retired from the Las Vegas Rattlesnakes—same outfit Bonaventure played with—and now I'm an executive in the R&D group at Venture Automotive. Just started, as a matter of fact."

"How do you enjoy your role there?" Pavel asked. "The challenges must be comprehensive for such a start-up. And

Mr. Bonaventure seems, if you'll pardon my saying so, unusually focused on details rather than the big picture."

"Got that right." Cliff rolled his eyes. This guy Pavel Rao was smart to see that right away. He hated the job at Venture Automotive, and being the bottom guy in the R&D group sucked big-time. And so far, the R&D group wasn't doing anything interesting. *Door handles.* That's what Bonaventure thought was important? Guy was an idiot.

And he'd always loathed that glory-hogging, know-it-all son of a bitch. So working with him again was a challenge. There was that.

"But a start-up must offer many opportunities?" Pavel asked.

"Not so far. Bonaventure sees to that. Suppresses talent. Old story." Cliff took a big swallow of his drink.

"It is a shame that a man of your skills goes unappreciated."

What was this guy driving at? Maybe he was planning to make him a job offer! Cliff perked up at the thought. He sure as hell wouldn't move to India, but maybe they needed a contact in the States. At the very least, he could leverage an offer from him to get a raise out of Bonaventure. He finished his drink. *Damn*, that was good. He snagged another from a passing waiter.

"Working with Chase Bonaventure is the biggest challenge—always was, even at the Snakes," Cliff said. "My way or the highway and all that."

Pavel nodded. "I can imagine that a competitive leader with vision such as yourself, when working in close proximity to a man so narrowly focused, would experience frustrations. And your current position does not provide you with enough scope. You think outside the box, I can see that."

This guy *was* going to make him an offer. Cliff took a sip of his fresh drink and focused on his companion. Pavel Rao, right. That was his name. A government bureaucrat.

"Mr. Rao—Pavel, can I call you that?—is your department expecting to expand manufacturing, ah, opportunities at home or abroad?"

Pavel beamed even more broadly, if that were possible. "I *knew* you were one to see the big picture! Absolutely. The Indian government is supporting domestic fast-track development of electric vehicles with concessions and subsidies. We have many international consultants in this endeavor."

Well, hot damn! He could be a consultant. That was more like it!

"Very progressive," Cliff said. Now for the job offer!

"Mozo Motors in India, for example, would be a good partner for Venture Automotive," Pavel said. "Mozo is experimenting with battery life and chassis construction, and—"

Cliff lost interest faster than a punctured balloon. He'd had enough blah, blah, blah about electric cars to last him a lifetime. If this bird wasn't going to offer him a job or a consultancy, he'd have one more drink and then hit the road. He surveyed the area for that hovering waiter.

And then he had an idea. Something way better than a job offer.

Bonaventure had been right when he'd said that the people they'd meet at this party would be good for their careers. Pavel Rao could be very good for his career. Maybe not for Bonaventure's, though. And wouldn't that be fun?

"Let me run something by you," he said to the Indian underminister.

Three hours later, Chase pocketed his last business card. "You had enough, *cher*?"

"Yes," Phoebe said in obvious relief. "Can you take me home? I want to change into something comfortable. I shouldn't have worn new heels to this party. My feet are killing me."

"You can take your shoes off in the car." He glanced down at her legs. The high heels did something for him, but getting her out of her clothes did something for him, too, so he drove her to her place, where she immediately disappeared into the bedroom.

"Is your mom working?" he called out. He took off his suit coat and draped it over a chair and then opened an upper cabinet, hoping she still had some of that bottle of scotch he'd left there. She did.

"She is. She'll be gone for hours yet." Hangers clinked in her closet. She was probably out of that dress by now. He was tempted to go back there and help her, but he wasn't brave enough to get in the way of a woman's wardrobe changes, especially when her feet hurt. "Did everything go tonight the way you wanted it to?"

"We made some good connections." He took down two juice glasses from the cupboard next to the sink. "I think we can establish some trade deals, although I've heard that Indian bureaucracy is slow. Well, in fairness, ours probably is, too."

He splashed some scotch into each glass just as she came into the tiny kitchen, wearing yoga pants and a stretchy top. She stood at the counter in her bare feet, flushed and relaxed, her hair a little messed up. She'd never looked so good.

He handed her the glass and she took it, reaching up on her tiptoes and leaning in to kiss him. He smiled against her mouth as he felt her warm breath, still faintly redolent of the exotic spices they'd eaten at the party. He supposed she noticed the same about him.

"The food at that party was awesome," she said against his mouth.

Chase laughed. "It sure was. The Taj Palace. We'll have to go there one night when we can be more relaxed about it. Let's sit down. We've earned it."

He settled onto her short, scratchy, and uncomfortable sofa, loosened his tie, and tossed back his drink. Phoebe sat down on the other end and put her feet up on the cushions, stretching out and wiggling her toes.

"Next time I'm going to wear a sari and some of those cute jeweled flat sandals that the Indian women wore," she said, sipping her scotch. "I should have known better than to wear new shoes to an event like that."

He picked up one of her feet and massaged the arch, pressing down in several places but carefully avoiding the

red spots that were blisters coming up. One thing about training with the Snakes—management never stinted on drug-
free pain relief, and he'd picked up a few pointers along the
way. He was glad he could make use of that knowledge now.

"Did you enjoy any of the party otherwise?"

"I enjoyed all of it, except—oh *yes*! Right *there*!—except for the excess of Chase Bonaventure hero worship. I
thought I was going to drown in all the treacle."

She had scrunched down so she was lying on her back
now, her head pillowed by her arms, her hair spread out
around her, her eyes closed and legs relaxed. She looked like
a boneless cat. A hot, sexy, boneless cat. With a glass of
scotch balanced on her stomach.

"Good thing Trouble's at my place or he'd have a nose
in your drink." He slid over and put her glass on the coffee
table and then lifted her feet so they rested on his thigh. He
resumed the massage, extending it past her foot and up her
leg, enjoying the feel of her skin under his fingers. "Just what
is treacle, anyway?" he asked. "I've always wondered about
that."

He slid his hand under the elastic cuff of her yoga pants
until he reached the back of her knee. She jerked a little—
maybe she was ticklish there, another good thing to know—
but then she settled back with a gentle sigh. He traced small
circles on her soft skin.

"You've wondered about treacle?" Her voice was soft
and a little breathy. Maybe he could make her lose her breath
altogether.

He slid his hand higher, to the inside of her thigh. Her
skin was very warm—all of her was very warm—and very
soft. He kept his touch light, tracing those small circles, the
barest of whispers against her skin.

"I've always wondered about treacle."

He wanted to touch more of her. He leaned over, his
hand reaching higher, pushing those damn pants out of the
way. Good thing they were so stretchy, or he wouldn't be
getting this far. She made a little noise in the back of her
throat and reached up one arm to curl around his neck and

bent one knee to rest against his chest.

"Treacle," she murmured, sounding distracted. "It's, um, something you drown in. *Oh.*"

"Like a lake of treacle? A treacle lake?"

She wasn't wearing any underwear, a miracle in itself. He scrunched farther down on the cushions, settling into what he hoped would be a good long time of discovering her sensitive spots that he didn't already know about. "Or more like a treacle puddle?"

"What? Oh sure," Phoebe murmured. "A treacle whatever. You have a thing about treacle?"

She grabbed his shirt and yanked on it, to no effect. He hoped she wanted it off, but she didn't have enough leverage; too much of him was either leaning against her or leaning against the couch. Getting naked was a great idea, but the couch wouldn't give them much more room than the front seat of his SUV. Maybe Phoebe just liked to have sex in small, cramped spaces.

He could work with that.

In fact, that was a pretty good idea. Maybe he really should move in here with her. The place was unbelievably small, but he'd do it if it overcame her objections to their living together.

"I'm loving the treacle so far," he said.

Getting rid of his shirt was a lot harder from the prone position on the sofa than getting rid of Phoebe's yoga pants proved to be, but it was a lot of fun making the effort. Phoebe was hot and determined, and she generated more electricity than Hoover Dam as she slid around on him, yanking on this and pulling on that while he teased her out of her own clothes.

At last she was naked, straddling him on the sofa, her cheeks flushed, her hair in disarray. He drank her in. She was the most beautiful woman he'd ever known.

"You're still wearing your shirt," she said, sounding disapproving.

"Too hard to get it off while I'm lying on my back," he said, grinning lazily, letting his hands roam over her from her knees to her thighs, up her back, then around to her breasts. His desire was thick in his throat—and elsewhere—and he was positive she was ready, too.

But fooling around with her was so much fun. Making her skin flush, seeing if he could make it even pinker. Her hair, all messed up—he'd done that—sort of sparkled in the dim light from the kitchen's over-the-sink bulb. Thwarting her when she was fooling around with him—all the touching and feeling and stroking and licking, the wanting and demanding and asking and succumbing—the more he got, the more he wanted. Every time he was with her, it was better than the last time. Hotter, hungrier, stronger. Incredible.

And then he heard a key in the door.

A key? Who in hell had a key to Phoebe's apartment?

He froze, locking eyes with Phoebe. She was shocked, too.

Shit! Brenda. Of course, her mother, the temporary roommate, would choose this moment to come home early from work.

"*Cher*," he said, grabbing the lap blanket from the back of the sofa and dragging it over them. "We have company."

"Crap!" she whispered. "That's gotta be Mom. What's she doing home?" And wasn't that the ten-thousand-dollar question?

"Would you like to come in for a quick drink?" Brenda said now, gazing behind her. From his position on the sofa with a direct line to the front door, Chase could see someone—a man—behind her in the hallway.

"I would be most pleased," he said. "For a short time only."

And then Brenda turned, stepped through the front door, and shrieked.

"Mom!" Phoebe called through the doorway. "You're home early."

No kidding. At eleven o'clock on a Wednesday night, Brenda should still be working, not coming home and catching her only daughter and daughter's boyfriend fooling around on the couch like a couple of randy teenagers.

"Oh, my goodness, you scared me, sweetie," Brenda said, dropping her purse and entering the living room. "Who's that with you?"

Great. A woman with no boundaries.

"Oh, *Chase*. Hello!" She peered down at them. They were covered but obviously naked. And if she couldn't tell by how small the blanket was, she sure could tell by all the clothes strewn around.

"Hi, Brenda." Getting off the sofa with Phoebe and not exposing themselves would be a challenge.

"Bikki, come in," Brenda called to the man, who was still invisible in the hallway. "It's my daughter and Chase Bonaventure."

"Chase Bonaventure? I am delighted—" A middle-aged Indian man bounded through the doorway. "It is so good— Ah," he said, spotting him and Phoebe on the sofa. "I apologize. This is most awkward."

"Chase, you remember Bikram Agarwal?" Brenda asked.

Of course, he did. Bikram Agarwal, known far and wide as Uncle Boo-Boo, was Sanjay's uncle. Phoebe's landlord. Chase—and Brenda—had met him a few weeks ago at a car rally that Phoebe and Kristin had pulled together for Venture Automotive. And now here he was with Brenda. Obviously on a date.

Awkward didn't begin to cover it.

"Of course," Chase said from his position on the sofa. "Nice to see you again."

"Bikki, can I get you a drink?" Brenda asked.

"Mom!" Phoebe said. "Do you think you could give us a moment here?"

"Of course, dear," Brenda said, turning her back and bustling over to the kitchen counter.

"I mean, *out of the apartment*," Phoebe said. "So we can have some privacy. For a couple of minutes."

"Oh! Of course. Come on, Bikki. Let's give the kids their minute."

Phoebe sighed while Uncle Boo-Boo and Brenda tiptoed out of the apartment. Chase could only be glad they hadn't tiptoed in, or he and Phoebe might be more embarrassed than they were now.

"Someday we'll look back on this night and laugh," he said, rolling off the couch when the front door closed behind the other couple. He grabbed his pants and pulled them on.

"No, we won't." Phoebe frowned as she got up and gathered her clothes. "What are they doing here? We should have had hours yet."

"Come on." He grinned at her, watching her dress. "We can be generous. It's their turn now."

"Ew! This is my couch. Don't even *think* it." Phoebe made a face as she shoved her feet into flip-flops. "There. I'm decent now."

"Grab your stuff and let's get out of here. The last thing I want to do is stick around with your mother and her new boyfriend." Chase put his arm around her shoulders and kissed her, regaining some of the heat he'd lost when Brenda had charged in on them.

"There's a silver lining: if he *is* her new boyfriend, she'll be moving out soon." Phoebe lowered her voice as she tossed things into her tote. "That could be good. At least then I'll have the whole apartment to myself again. Small as it is."

They bid their farewells to Brenda and Uncle Boo-Boo on the landing and headed out to Chase's car.

"You're being a good daughter by letting your mother stay at your place," Chase said as they buckled themselves in. "Especially since a flea hardly has room to jump sideways over here."

"She took me in when I got into trouble at the CIA, and her apartment was only a little bigger than mine," Phoebe said, tuning the radio to a soft jazz station. "I have to take her in now until she can find another place."

"I applaud you for makin' that choice, because you got to support family when they need you." Chase pulled away from the curb and headed for home. "But it's crowded in that apartment. And you got to admit, after tonight, maybe she cramps your style a little bit."

Phoebe scowled. "Yeah, tonight was a close encounter

of the parental kind. No, thanks."

He glanced over at her. He'd already asked her to move in once, and she'd said no. Maybe these recent events would change her mind. How could he get her to say yes?

"We talked about this before," he said, speeding through a yellow light. "Moving in together, I mean. No pressure, *cher*, but I gotta say that the timing feels right to me."

"Because Mom and Uncle Boo-Boo walked in on us?"

He could feel her swift gaze on him, and he risked a glance. Under the streetlights, her skin was pale, her eyes wide and dark. She didn't have quite the overjoyed expression he'd hoped for.

"That sure did put the damper on *my* movin' in with *you*," he said, reaching out for her hand and toying with her fingers. She flashed a swift smile at him. *Better*.

"Four people plus a dog is a lot to accommodate in a space that small, so I think it's gotta go the other way," he said. "You movin' into my place. The logistics are all for it."

"Mom staying at my place is not a good enough reason for us to live together."

He wanted to admire her caution, but her reluctance to take the next step was frustrating.

"The size of your place—with your mom and Uncle Boo-Boo also staying there—is one reason, but I wasn't finished. Yeah, your place is small, and there's too many people in it, especially tonight. But think about what we have going for us. We have more fun together than a Mardi Gras crowd at a zydeco speakeasy, and we work well together, too. Wouldn't you say?"

"Um, yes," Phoebe said cautiously. "Zydeco?"

"Sort of a foot-stompin', squeeze-box playin', rollicking good time music. That's us. And we want to see how far we can go with this thing, right?"

"Yes," Phoebe said again, without hesitation this time. *Good.*

"Okay. So the situation being that we want to explore all the nooks and crannies of this thing that is you and me, we need to test ourselves a little bit."

"Test. I'm not sure I'm ready for a test."

"More like an experiment. See how we feel with the nitty-gritty. The daily grind. Am I boring? Do I sit around in my underwear drinking beer and scratching myself every night?"

Phoebe smiled, looking evil. "That would last exactly until I posted a picture of you on Instagram," she said. "The treacle would be over."

Chase laughed. "You are tougher than a rattlesnake skin left out in the sun too long. So if that's the case—if I turn out to be a beer-drinkin', belly-scratchin', TV-watchin', no-good layabout, you chuck me over. Better you find out sooner rather than later, right? Because I have to warn you, it's not all fancy parties and custom-made suits every day."

Her smile widened. Much better.

"Custom-made suits?"

"Hell, yeah. What, you think I go to the mall and get a wash-and-wear off the rack? That kind hasn't fit since middle school. I'm not sure you're payin' attention here, sweetheart."

"I'm paying attention."

Excellent.

"So what do you say? Want to give this a try?"

"Chase," she said, biting her lip. "It's not anything against you. I love what we have, but we don't know each other well enough. I can't move in with you yet. It's too soon."

He let go of her fingers as he gunned his way through another yellow light. "I get that you're nervous about it, but I don't get why."

"And now you're mad."

"I'm not mad! Just explain it to me. In a way that makes sense."

Phoebe turned cool eyes his way. "I did explain it. I said, it's too soon."

"*Cher*, we've got four or five months *tops* to figure out this situation," he said. "It sounds like a lot of time, but it isn't. How do we know what works if we don't try out the options?"

"I'm doing the best I can. I'm sorry if that's not good enough for you."

He exhaled and ran his hand through his hair. "Okay. If you won't move in, can we at least get rid of your money troubles so that doesn't pressure you to move back to DC? You don't want me to give you or even lend you the money for your school loan. Fine. How about if I hire you away from Dave? I bet I pay a lot more than Dave does."

"You do," Phoebe said. "But I can't. Thank you, but no."

"See, that's confusing me. Two months ago when I hired you to translate, you asked me for ten thousand a *week*. And I paid it, too."

"Yes, but that was only for two weeks, and I wasn't a regular employee. Also, I was mad at you, so I fleeced you."

"I don't see what being an employee has to do with it."

Phoebe sighed.

"You really don't get it? Because you were standing right there when Pavel Rao ignored me. That's what my life would be if I worked for you *and* I lived with you. Nobody would take me seriously. Nobody would care what I think because they'd know that you gave me the job only because we're dating. I wouldn't have any authority."

"I don't care what other people think, and I don't see why it should matter so much to you, either. You can't change what strangers think."

"No, I know," Phoebe said, sounding sad.

Chase pulled up to a red light. She was right—he *was* mad. He felt stuck, too. How could he show her that they were the real deal if she wouldn't take their relationship to the next level?

"My boss at the CIA called this morning," she said. "They offered me a promotion. In a new group for unconventional thinkers, he said. It's a great opportunity. It basically legitimizes that call I made on the Empire State Building that got me into so much trouble."

And didn't that just about put the hot sauce in the gumbo. "Are you going to take it?"

"I have to talk to the woman who'll be running the group first."

He was proud of her, of course, and it was wonderful that they knew what a great employee they had in her. But *damn*. If she didn't trust him enough to want to move in, and she had a great offer from the CIA, why would she stay in Vegas?

She wouldn't.

"It sounds like it would be a fantastic chance," he said. "And I'm happy to hear that they understand what a terrific employee you are. But you have opportunities here, too. You don't have to work for me, but you could still earn more money than Dave's paying you. There must be lots of options for people who speak eight languages."

"There are," she said. "Banks. Insurance companies. Law enforcement. Import-export. The hospitality industry. But I don't see it. No. That's not for me."

So she didn't care enough about him to take a less-than-perfect but well-paying job so they could be in the same city. That *really* sucked.

"What *do* you want, Phoebe? What's your best-case scenario here?" He tried not to sound as frustrated as he felt, because he really wanted to know. If she could say what that was, they had a shot at getting there.

The light turned green, and he accelerated through the intersection.

"I want to go home," she said. "We're both tired. This isn't a conversation we should have right now."

She was probably right about that, because what had started out as a great night sure had skidded downhill pretty quick. But he might as well take her home. If Phoebe spent an unhappy evening avoiding Brenda and Uncle Boo-Boo, so much the better. The romantic mood was broken, anyway. And if there was one thing he didn't want, it was Phoebe sad and reluctant in his bedroom.

He checked the traffic in his rearview mirror and did a U-turn on the wide, empty street. He could only hope that this relationship wouldn't do the same. How could he persuade her that she'd be better off—happier—here in Las Vegas with him?

He'd better figure it out—and quick.

Chapter 8

On Thursday morning at precisely nine o'clock, Sanjay called his mother, Neeta, exactly as he'd done every Thursday for years, barring illness, earthquake, flood, fire, or tempest. Neeta ran a thriving restaurant in Las Vegas and had recently expanded to include two food trucks, and Sanjay saw her regularly if infrequently at the restaurant on his lunch break. However, he continued to call weekly, as he had done before she immigrated to America, because she expected it and so they could enjoy the kinds of conversations they could not have in the presence of customers and family members during busy mealtimes.

Neeta was a font of information about everyone and everything. However, getting the information that one desired often required skillful diplomacy.

"Amma," he said, offering her his customary affectionate greeting.

"Sanjay, my delight! It is such a long time since we have spoken," Neeta replied untruthfully. "Tell me how you are and how the taxicab business is faring without one of your elders to oversee its operation?"

"I am doing most excellently, and the taxicab business is flourishing." Some questions never changed.

"And when are you getting married? You know you are not young anymore."

"I'm twenty-nine, Amma. Not old yet."

"You know how I worry."

"There is no need for you to worry. You can trust me on this. I will let you know when it is time for you to worry. Amma, I have a question for you. About a family connection. Pavel Rao."

"Pavel Rao. That would be the first son of your Auntie Lupa, who is sister to my brother's second wife," Neeta said, outlining the genealogical thread precisely and succinctly. "The underminister."

"Yes. That is the one. I believe that Auntie Lupa has informed you that he is visiting here in Las Vegas?"

"Of course. Are you helping him as she requested?"

"I am driving him around town, yes. But he does not think that offering a gratuity for outstanding service is a necessary transaction between relatives, and in addition to the negative monetary aspects of the relationship, I am distressed to reveal to you, Amma, that he is boring."

"Ah, well," Neeta said tolerantly. "Boring."

"He is married, I understand, with two daughters? One of whom recently achieved her medical degree at Harvard?"

"Yes, indeed. That Lupa—although she is your auntie and I regret to say it, she cannot stop herself from boasting—talks about her all the time. So now it is widely known that the first daughter has not only the medical degree from Harvard University, but now also a fine and lucrative private practice and handsome fiancé, whom she will be marrying soon there in Boston. Lupa has already bought her plane ticket and sari for the occasion. A beautiful red silk with gold embroidery. I have seen it: very lustrous. Of course, your children, when you finally decide to please your mother and have them, will be as accomplished."

"Yes, Amma. And Pavel's wife doesn't work?"

"No, she has an ailing elderly mother living with them, and a younger daughter still in college. Why are you asking these questions? If you called more often—or came to visit your lonely mother, who misses you to the edges of the heavens—you would know the answers."

Sanjay failed to see how Neeta could be lonely, what

with running a restaurant and two food trucks staffed by many friends and relations. But he never contradicted his mother. Contradicting his mother could have unforeseen and possibly uncomfortable consequences.

"I am asking these questions because I have been wondering if I should solicit Pavel for financial advice," he said, although he'd wondered no such thing. "His position in the ministry cannot be richly remunerated, and in addition, he seems to have many expenses. Yet he has a large and beautiful house, and—"

"How do you know this? About Pavel Rao's house?"

"You forget, Amma. You took me there for Auntie Lupa's second son's marriage."

"Oh yes, of course. I remember. Three years ago now, was it not?"

"Yes, I think so, but my question is, how does he manage? It is Pavel of whom I am speaking. To have such a nice house and yet so many obligations and I think only average income, he must be very clever with money."

"Oh no, do not ask Pavel for financial advice," Neeta said. "Asking him anything like that would be most unwise."

"Really? Because I am thinking—"

"No, indeed. No, no, no. Do not do any asking. Avoid the asking."

"Why should I avoid the asking? If he could provide us with wise advice about the taxicab business?"

"Sanjay, do not trouble me with these questions. Listen to your mother: do not ask him to advise you on the taxicab business. You want advice? Ask one of your uncles."

"He must be clever, that is all I am saying. Unless…" Sanjay paused, hoping that he sounded like he'd just had an idea. "Pavel does not have a second job, does he? Or an inheritance or trust fund? He must have an additional source of funds. That is all I can think of."

Neeta sighed.

Sanjay recognized the signs. This was when his mother would reveal what she knew.

"I think perhaps it is possible that Pavel might be using

his authority in the functions of his government office to influence outcomes that could benefit himself."

"He takes bribes," Sanjay said. "Baksheesh. That is what you are saying?"

"Harshly stated," Neeta said. "But yes. That is something I suspect."

"Do we know this for sure?"

"We do, because of your father's cousin's second son, who wanted to open a small factory in Kerala making bicycles, you know."

"Yes, I remember," Sanjay said with feeling. "You made me buy one of the bicycles."

"How could I make you do anything you did not wish to do? Anyway, it was a sound investment. The bicycle still works, does it not? And the bicycle factory is doing well, so the family is pleased. He has a young wife, too, very pretty, and a son on the way."

"Yes, Amma, but my point—"

"Is this not what I am telling you? Always you want to be rushing ahead. This always rushing is not good for you."

"Yes, Amma, my apologies. So how do we know that Pavel requires baksheesh? Because of the bicycle factory."

"To get all the parts he needs to build the bicycles at the bicycle factory, your father's cousin's second son needs to import several critical pieces. And to get the import license, he had to pay Pavel baksheesh. And thereafter when the parts enter the country."

"So Pavel is still getting rich from father's cousin's second son? All these years later? Does Auntie Lupa know that?"

"She must suspect," Neeta said. "But we cannot tell her or even hint. It would be a terrible blow. And the scandal! If such facts came out, Pavel would quite possibly lose his position in the government, and then they really would have money troubles. And should they be unable to meet their financial obligations, the responsibility for the maintenance of their household would then fall to the rest of the family. May the benevolent gods save us from such a catastrophe."

Sanjay could feel his mother shudder across the phone connection.

"Is that what would happen, Amma? You would be responsible for them? If Pavel lost his job, you would have to support his family?"

"Not us alone. But yes. Unless we want to bring shame to our own family for letting them starve. Therefore, your Auntie Lupa must remain forever in ignorance, and the facts of Pavel's treachery must never be revealed."

"I will tell no one, but I am most interested to know more of how Pavel takes advantage of honest businessmen. Do you know of more cases than this one situation of father's cousin's second son and the bicycle factory?"

"Of course. There was your third cousin once removed, who received advance information of a new regulation after he paid Pavel baksheesh. And there was the neighbor to your father's esteemed teacher who needed to know the plans of a competitor. Why are you asking this? You do not plan to avail yourself of his methods?"

"Of course not, and I am shocked that you should think so," Sanjay said, truly shocked. "No. I am thinking of someone I must advise."

"Very well," Neeta said. "As long as nothing whatsoever comes back to harm his family, and, therefore, ours. I have facts at my fingertips. You think your own mother would trade in gossip and innuendo?"

"I think no such thing," Sanjay said mendaciously. "Will you help me with particulars?"

"Absolutely," Neeta said. "Your Auntie Lupa—may Krishna smile on her honest endeavors, few as they are—is no friend of mine."

On that Thursday morning, Cliff woke with a fuzzy head and a song in his heart. He was done with petty vandalism. Now, thanks to Bonaventure's ambition to rule the world and Cliff's introduction to Pavel Rao, he had a plan to destroy Venture Automotive.

He showered, dressed, and ate a hearty breakfast because,

after all, he had to keep up his strength for the rigors ahead. And then he drove to the factory, only one hour late. He entered the production department, ignoring the glances that Margo and Bill exchanged, and went to his own desk.

"Late night, Cliff?" Margo asked. The bitch. But she—and all of them—would get theirs soon enough.

"Yeah," he said. "That party was something else, right?"

Pavel Rao wanted features, specs, and schematics of any and all models of vehicle that Venture Automotive produced. It would have been a simple matter to send those to him, if only the specs were online. But of course Chase Fucking Bonaventure lived in the Stone Age. The manufacturing data was all kept on a separate network, not attached to the internet. And the email system didn't allow packets over a tiny size, anyway.

He supposed it would be possible to put the data in the cloud someplace and send Pavel a link to it, but he didn't want to take the risk if the system had some kind of alert or other kinds of restrictions he didn't know about. Still, getting Pavel the information he wanted should be easy enough. He'd just copy it to a thumb drive and hand it over. No fuss, no muss.

Cliff fired up his computer, stuck the thumb drive in the machine when Bonaventure's puppets were huddled over something, and started the download for the Snap model. Right from under their noses! He'd show them.

The download was expected to take almost sixty minutes, which worried him a little. So much time! What if they saw? But he relaxed when they went back to their desks and didn't say anything. He checked his email, accepted a mandatory scheduled meeting, declined an invitation to surrender his company vehicle for a few days for some stupid marketing stunt, and generally ignored as much work as he could get away with. When the download finished and Margo and Bill left for lunch, he pocketed the thumb drive and raced out of the building to make his call. He couldn't wait to tell Pavel what he had.

"I've got the schematics for one of the models on a

thumb drive," he told the Indian underminister. "The one they're calling the Snap. You wouldn't believe how easy it was to download."

"Excellent," Pavel said. "Meet me after you get off work, but do not come to the hotel. Where is a public place that would be convenient to you? Is there a park nearby?"

"Yeah, the municipal park isn't far. Pretty big, has a pond with some benches and paths. A couple of playing fields." Even more than the actual stealing itself, the secretive nature of the activity was a blast.

"I'll find it," Pavel said. "There's a pond? Let's meet there at, say, six o'clock this evening." He disconnected the call.

On his way to the nearest fast-food joint to get something to eat, Cliff felt buoyant. Stealing the data had been, well, a snap. Fun. He'd put Bonaventure out of business and, even better, he'd get paid doing it! You couldn't ask for more than that.

And after he got his money, he could enjoy much better lunches, too.

Well past lunchtime, Phoebe's stomach was still tied up in knots from her discussion with Chase the night before. Was she being stupid by not moving in with him? She was crazy about him, but they'd known each other such a short time. She didn't want to wreck anything one way or the other—either by moving in or by *not* moving in. And if her mother was anything to go by—well, she wasn't anything to go by. Brenda couldn't stick to a relationship if she were covered in flypaper and attached to the guy with Super Glue.

At three, Kristin poked her head in the door, holding a tray with two cups of coffee and a paper plate heaped with cookies. "Ready for a break?"

"More than ready." Phoebe pushed her laptop and papers to one side and took one of the cups from Kristin with a handful of cookies. "Oh, good, oatmeal raisin. The nutritious cookie choice. How are things on your end?"

"If you're referring to my progress on the Cars of the

Future expo, we're doing great," Kristin said, sitting down and taking a cookie for herself. "But if you're talking about office atmospheric conditions, it's kind of chilly out there. What happened with you and Coach? Not that it's any of my business."

Phoebe exhaled, putting down her cup. "We had a discussion about my moving in with him," she said. "Unless maybe it was an argument. And nothing can change our positions, and really, neither of us has anything to apologize for—we just have different opinions. Very strong and different opinions. So we haven't spoken yet today. I don't know what to say. Nothing has changed, at least not for me."

Kristin pushed her cup around on the conference room table. "Here's what I think, not that you asked. Not about your moving in with Coach—I'm not getting into that territory. *At all*."

Phoebe grinned. "Yeah, messing around in your boss's personal life couldn't be a good career move. I can't even begin to imagine poking around in Greg Peeling's life." She shuddered.

Kristin laughed. "Exactly. No, I was thinking about all your reasons for going back to the CIA. I get that your school debt is an albatross. But you have a lot of friends here, you know that? Everybody in the plant wants you to stay, not just me."

Easy for her to say. Kristin had a great job, a job she loved, and she wasn't in hock for three hundred thousand. A lifetime of staggering debt. A lifetime of fewer options and diminished financial stability.

"You know what?" Kristin said now, her eyes twinkling. "You and I are tossing around millions of dollars of Coach's money. We could borrow some of it to pay off your loan."

Phoebe laughed. Now that was a plan that would get her an all-expenses-paid, ten-year stretch in the slammer.

"Yeah, too bad that's out. He's already offered, too. I don't know. I just—" Phoebe stopped. Things had changed with Greg Peeling's call. The job at the CIA had become more than simply getting rid of her debt. She had that new job to consider, a position almost tailor-made for her. She wanted to be debt-free, of course, but she wanted that job, too, *and* she wanted to develop her relationship with Chase. Getting all those things on the same track was the problem. Right now she didn't see how she could do it.

She needed more time to figure things out. She and Chase had a good thing going, but it was still early days. Even if Chase wanted more with her now, that didn't mean he'd feel the same about her in a year. It wasn't like he had a great track record with marriage, after all. History had a way of repeating itself.

One thing was for certain: she didn't want to talk about it anymore.

"Okay, I won't pressure you, too," Kristin said. "What I really came in here for—want to come to dinner tonight? It won't be fancy, but Nick has a few questions he wants to ask you before he accepts the job offer. Not many. I think it's mostly along the lines of, when can he start."

Phoebe grinned. "Dinner would be great. Mom's staying at my place, and I could use some distraction."

Kristin reached over and gave Phoebe a hug. "Everything will work out. You'll see."

"I hope so," Phoebe said. But in her experience, difficult situations did not "work out." Nothing in her life had ever resolved all on its own and to her benefit. She'd had to plan and work and fight and sacrifice for everything she'd ever gotten. Things wouldn't be any different this time.

She had a lot of decisions she'd have to make soon. And some of them promised to be very painful.

By late afternoon, Chase was back in his office, looking at a screenful of data that he couldn't focus on, wondering what he could say to Phoebe. She was down the hall in the conference room, probably working like crazy, but he hadn't gone to see her yet. Yesterday, when he'd strolled in and gotten a welcoming reception, seemed like years ago. He was pretty sure that if he went in there today, he'd get a cold shoulder. He had to admit it: he'd pushed her too hard. He wouldn't get what he wanted by doing that. And really, when he thought about it, maybe she'd be as likely to stay in Vegas after six months if he *didn't* pressure her to move in with him.

He wasn't sure what to do. And that was a new and uncomfortable place to be.

His phone rang, and he checked the ID display, hoping it was Phoebe checking in. But instead, he saw that the call was from his youngest sibling, his sister Josette. He leaned back in his chair and put up his feet.

"Hey, Jo-Bob, what's going on?"

"Don't call me that!" Josette said. "I'm fantastic, except for the part that I'll never get a job. No *big* firm will hire me because I'm female or I went to the wrong school or took the wrong classes or my portfolio has the wrong things in it. And no *small* firm will hire me because I'm female or I went to the wrong school or took the wrong classes or my portfolio has the wrong things in it. You? How are you?"

Chase blinked. "I'm good. You know, you just got your masters in architecture this spring. You haven't given the job search enough time. How many résumés have you sent out?"

"Forty! And only five interviews! And none of them called back!"

"Then I'd say you're targeting the wrong places."

"Easy for you to say. What did you do to get your first job? Sat around and waited for the Snakes to call. Which they did, five minutes later. First round. What's so hard about that?"

Chase laughed. The NFL draft had been a bit more nerve-racking than Josie remembered, but Chase had to agree that getting picked in the first round did take a lot of pressure off the job search.

"Okay, you're right. I'm not the person you want for advice about the job hunt. What else is new?" He knew his sister. She had something on her mind.

He loved his large, noisy, generous family and went back to Louisiana to see them whenever he could. He was especially grateful that they had never traded on his celebrity. Despite all the tabloid offers they'd had to sell photos or stories about him, they never had and never would. That didn't mean that they wouldn't sometimes ask him for something that was within his power to give. In Josie's case, he was pretty sure that whatever she wanted, any big brother could provide. Not just a big brother who used to play professional football or owned a car company.

Although he'd give her a car if she wanted one.

"I have an idea," she said finally.

"That's good for an architect, isn't it?" he asked, teasing her. "Ideas."

"It involves you. And you won't like it."

"Officially scared. What's your idea, Jo-Bob?"

"Don't call me that. Okay. Here's my thinking. I can't get a job. Maybe I've targeted the wrong places. I'm certainly planning to target more. But in the meantime, I can't sit around twiddling my thumbs, right?"

"Right," Chase said cautiously, not sure about what he was agreeing with.

"So I'm exploring how to expand my portfolio. What jobs I can take on, even pro bono, to show what I can do. That way I have more projects to show when I interview, or maybe I could even get enough experience to start my own firm. Right?"

"You want to start your own firm?"

"No! Well, not necessarily. I want to build my portfolio."

"That sounds like a good step. Where's the part I don't like?"

He heard her take a deep breath.

"You've got that giant house, right?" she asked. "You've always wanted to turn it into a hotel. How about letting me do it?"

"No," Chase said.

"I have an architecture degree," she pressed. "And I passed my boards. So I'm qualified. The job itself won't be that hard. I mean, it's not like designing an entire hotel from scratch. It's basically a remodel, adding, what? Six bathrooms, right? As unobtrusively as possible. Paying attention to detail, conforming to existing style, and sparing no expense. Is there anything else?"

"Josie—"

"You know I can manage a construction crew. You wouldn't have to do a thing. Think if I had that on my résumé! It would be the biggest coup ever. And you wouldn't have to pay me a dime. I'll do it totally for free."

Chase took a deep breath. Turn over a multimillion-dollar house to a twenty-five-year-old architecture grad with no experience to let her run roughshod over the place in the attempt to turn it into a hotel? That was a crazy idea if he ever heard one.

"No," he said. "Anyway, you're too late. I put the place up for sale."

"I asked Dad if he'd do the work for you," Josette said, ignoring him. "He said yes. But if you don't want him to do it—but why you wouldn't, I have no idea—I found a contractor in Las Vegas who's won awards for upgrading and modernizing hotels all over the place. He said he'd do it, too. At a reduced fee."

"Dad said he'd do it?" Their parents had a construction business, and Chase's two younger brothers were partners in it. In fact, all the kids had worked for the business during summers and after school. Bonaventure Construction had a decent-sized crew, and they had a solid reputation. If Ancel Bonaventure did the job, the work would be done right, so he had nothing to worry about on that score. But Bonaventure Construction was located in New Orleans. And he was in Las Vegas. He got a sinking feeling. "And they'd stay here for the duration?"

"Well, yes, of course, to save expenses, and you have plenty of space, what with those fifteen bedrooms. That's even more bedrooms than we need. And you'd get immediate, round-the-clock service and dedicated and professional personnel. Dad said he could start pretty soon."

"Josie, I don't think—"

"Listen, I wasn't going to tell you this, but if you're

going to say no, you need to know everything. Dad laid off Billy."

"*What?*" Billy Burnette had worked for his father for twenty years. "Why? Is Dad in financial trouble?"

"Yes. Well, not exactly. But yes. Remember how he had that subcontracting job for that gigantic condo complex in Baton Rouge? The developer went belly-up and didn't pay. Insurance will take care of some of it, but Dad's in the hole for hundreds of thousands at least, he won't say how much. Everybody's working fast and hard, hoping to catch up and hire Billy back. And nobody's saying, but I think the rest of the crew is working at half pay. So it's tough. Dad said he's seen times worse than this, but yeah, he could use the gig. You're good for the money, right?"

"Sure. Why didn't he tell me any of this?"

"Well, you're there and I'm here, so I see it every day. Besides, he doesn't want to take anything from you."

"I'm his damn son! He paid for a million football camps! He came to all my games! I can sure as hell help him out now! What is he *thinking*?"

"Calm down, okay? He doesn't like asking you, precisely because you're rich and famous now. He thinks other people would see him as taking charity, leaning on you to solve problems of his own making. You know Dad."

"That's bullshit." But he did know his father. Dammit, Ancel sounded just like Phoebe. The two of them would get on like pigs in mud.

"So can we do it?" Josie asked. "The remodel?"

"Of course. But listen—" he added as Josie whooped. "I only need some bathrooms. Not a whole redo."

"Right, six full bathrooms," Josie said, her voice light and bubbly now. "One for each bedroom that doesn't already have a private bath, and maybe a couple more half baths in the public spaces, too. You know what's good about that?"

"Sure. Billy Burnette is a plumber. Dad can hire him back, at least for this job."

"Right, and he's got a kid in college. So this is great, bro. Thank you."

"You should have told me."

"I *did* tell you. So now, the bathrooms," she said. "I've worked up some sketches so you can see a couple of the directions I'm going in. I'm sending you a link to the drawings now."

Chase shook his head, both amused and annoyed. Josie had been awfully confident that he'd agree to this harebrained scheme. And now he was turning over his multimillion-dollar house to his fresh-out-of-architecture-school baby sister, and she had zero experience.

On the other hand, his father would do the work, and he'd trust his father with any building at all.

And on the third hand, he wouldn't have to deal with potential buyers trampling through his house. Instead, he'd have his family underfoot. Which would be nice, actually. If they didn't scare off Phoebe.

And if he had trouble finding a manager for the hotel when it was done, he'd put Kristin and Phoebe on it. Between them, they'd have the place managed, budgeted, advertised, and occupied in an hour or so.

He grinned at the thought.

"Did you draw up a budget?" he asked, getting back to business.

"I thought you'd never ask," she said. "I drew up a couple of options. Depending on the materials and which way you go, half a mil. Tops."

"Dad supplied the specs?"

"He did. I told you, I can do this."

Half a million dollars was a lot of money. But in the end he'd have an asset, something that would even create a few jobs and send some money back into the community. That would be better than selling the place to some jackass who thought he needed fifteen bedrooms.

"Okay. I'll check out the drawings and your budget. Let's schedule a phone meeting after I've had a chance to look things over, see what we think and make some decisions."

"How about Sunday night?" Josie asked.

"Sure, that works," Chase said, tapping into his computer

to check his calendar. "Thanks for telling me about Dad."

"I knew you'd want to know," Josie said. "Okay, talk soon."

When he hung up with his sister, Chase called his real estate agent, took his house off the market, and asked her to find a house that was smaller but with a big yard and a pool. That should please both Trouble and Phoebe. He hoped.

If she was still speaking to him.

Chapter 9

Shortly before six that evening, Phoebe got up from her seat in the conference room, grabbed her messenger bag, and called to Trouble, who was dozing under the conference table.

"Time to go," she told the dog. "Sanjay will be here soon to pick us up and drive us to Kristin's."

She headed down the stairs after the eager dog. By five thirty people should have punched out and gone home. But as she entered the darkened lobby, she saw that the production area still had light. Delmar, the off-duty cop Dave had hired for security, would be working, and there was no time like the present to meet him.

She entered the production area and waved to Rinsho as he headed toward the side exit.

"Hi," she said as she approached the guard. "I came to introduce myself. I'm Phoebe Renfrew, and this is Trouble. You must be Delmar Oates."

"Correct," he said, shaking hands. He reached down to let Trouble sniff him, and then he ruffled the dog's fur. Trouble closed his eyes in ecstasy, his tail sweeping the floor in a happy wag. "Pleased to meet you both. Dave told me you'd be around."

"How have things been going the past couple of nights?"

"No trouble yet," Delmar said. "Just the way I like it."

Phoebe lingered with Delmar for a few minutes, checking

out the new cars and discussing his security concerns. Behind her, darkness descended quickly as Rinsho turned off the bank of overhead lights, each switch thunking like a hammer on an anvil. But the floor wasn't completely dark when Phoebe, Trouble at her heels, headed for the lobby. The opaque glass roof vents let in some light, the exit signs were lit, and Delmar had light in his area. But at the far end of the factory floor, the darkness was impenetrable.

Phoebe gazed down the aisles of silent robots. It was amazing to think that—

What was that?

Way down there, had something moved? No. Wait— maybe that was Rinsho leaving. Or was it a trick of the light? No, it was something. Not Rinsho. And Trouble was focused on something down the aisle, his ears alert. He barked, a short warning.

"Phoebe?" Delmar called. "You okay?"

"Yes. But I thought I saw—I'm going to check out something down there."

"Do you want me to come with you?"

Just a few days ago, someone had trashed all the new cars that had been earmarked for the expo, and she didn't want to get on the wrong side of that kind of fury. But she didn't want to pull Delmar off his post, either. If vandals had gotten inside somehow, he might be diverted by one character only to have the cars damaged by another. The production crew wouldn't have a second chance to redo any damage before the expo.

"I'll yell if I need help," she said.

Phoebe walked swiftly down the aisle, glancing from side to side, Trouble trotting next to her. Maybe it was her imagination. She was probably being hypersensitive, because she didn't hear anything or see anyone. Still, Trouble had barked, and she needed to check. She was glad Delmar was behind her if she needed him.

As she approached the far end of the floor, she heard a voice—someone speaking on the phone.

"I have to make that six thirty, Pavel," the voice said.

Pavel? Could that be Pavel Rao? How many Pavels could there be who'd be getting calls from someone in the factory? And who *was* calling Pavel Rao? That wasn't Rinsho's voice. Certainly not Chase's voice, either. She moved forward and saw a shadow—more a dark outline—against a dark wall.

"I got something else for you. See you soon."

"Hello?" Phoebe said. "Who's there?"

"What?" A man stepped out into the aisle where Phoebe could see.

Trouble growled softly, his fur standing on end.

"Cliff?" Phoebe said, recognizing him. "Sorry. I didn't mean to intrude, but I saw something move down here and came to check. Can't be too careful these days. Everything okay? I thought the shift went home at five thirty."

"I had some work to finish up."

"Right."

Cliff didn't move, and she sure wasn't going to, either, not until he did. There was nothing wrong with making a phone call after hours—maybe Pavel had offered him a job, and wouldn't Chase be happy about that—but he could have made a phone call outside. The plant was supposed to be empty now.

"Delmar will lock up after us," Phoebe said, remembering Cliff's assault record. She didn't want to be alone with him, although she had Trouble with her. And Trouble was still on alert, so if anything happened, he'd bark.

"After you." Cliff gestured toward the exit.

"Delmar," Phoebe called out. "Cliff and I are leaving. Make sure the front door locks after us, okay?"

"Got it," Delmar said.

When they got outside, Cliff headed toward the employee parking lot around the side, and she unlocked her bicycle from the bike rack. To her relief, Sanjay was parked in the small visitors lot up front.

"How much time do you have?" she asked him as she put her bike in the taxi's trunk. "I want to follow the next car that comes out of the employee lot."

Sanjay got in and buckled his seat belt. "I am at your disposal," he said while Phoebe buckled herself in. "You know, since I met you, following vehicles of a suspicious nature has become an unexpected skill set. Depending on what avoidance mechanisms this miscreant employs, you will have the opportunity to witness my secret defensive driving skills and the strength of my fortified taxi."

"Really?" Phoebe said. "You're taking those bodyguard driving classes?"

"No," Sanjay said as he idled the taxi. "I was mocking my distant relation, Pavel Rao. But if you and I continue to engage in clandestine operations, I plan to investigate the opportunities."

"You could probably get a lot of high-paid work driving politicians or movie stars," Phoebe said. "Wait—there he is." She pointed to Cliff's car as it emerged from the employee lot.

Sanjay pulled out of the visitors lot and followed Cliff's SUV at a discreet distance. "We are a small cavalcade of brightly colored vehicles," Sanjay said. "Not noticeable at all. Do you know who this person is?"

"Cliff Frizell," Phoebe said. "Yeah, I'm hoping he won't pay any attention to a taxi."

"What? Cliff Frizell is driving that car? The third-string quarterback who couldn't put a shine on Mr. Bonaven—*Chase's* shoes if he rubbed them with stardust? I doubt very much that he would notice a brightly colored vehicle behind him even if it was a Barnum & Bailey circus wagon circumnavigated by clowns on unicycles beeping horns."

"No clowns," Phoebe said. "Just us."

Sanjay snorted. "Am I to understand that Mr. Frizell's emergence from the factory at this hour means that he now works for Venture Automotive?"

"He does," Phoebe said. "Against Dave's and my advice, I might add. We're following him now because I overheard him talking to someone who might have been your lesser relation. Cliff's probably just looking for a new job, but I want to see where he's going and what he's up to. If we can figure that out."

"Huh," Sanjay said. "You know, I spoke to my mother about that branch of the family. According to her, Pavel Rao does not enjoy the highest reputation with his closest friends and relations, among whom I do not number myself."

"Really?" Phoebe said. "Why not?"

Sanjay wagged his hand. "He is thought to be rather too opportunistic and self-serving in his business dealings. He demands baksheesh to execute the duties that should be part of his government position. These gratuities are making him rich. Or at least allowing him to maintain a lifestyle that would otherwise be beyond his means."

"Interesting," Phoebe said.

"And now Pavel is consorting with Mr. Frizell, a partnership that sounds at best unlikely and at worst insalubrious." Sanjay picked up speed as he turned right after the other vehicle. "Given Mr. Frizell's odious attitude in the locker room and the potential for him to harm Venture Automotive, we cannot lose him now. Even if his current errand is entirely blameless."

"He had a bad attitude in the locker room?"

Sanjay nodded. "Narcissistic, vainglorious, boastful, self-serving, and pompous. Also uncomplimentary to his fellow teammates."

"That's comprehensive. How did you find out?"

"I like American football," Sanjay said. "I read the newspaper. It is all there."

"Huh." Phoebe shook her head.

Fifteen minutes later, they pulled into the parking lot for the Las Vegas Municipal Recreation Area. Phoebe knew this park well, because she brought Trouble here to play.

"Houston, we have a problem," Sanjay said, watching Cliff get out of his car.

No kidding. On this side, the park was mostly an open expanse, with wide, treeless spaces and playing fields. If she followed Cliff, he'd see her within seconds.

"Are you ready to expand your sleuthing skills?" Phoebe asked. "Cliff doesn't know you. Can you follow him as closely as possible? If he meets up with Pavel or someone else, try to listen. Or if he makes a call maybe."

Sanjay popped the trunk. "This plan does not strike me as a sound one, and I make every allowance for its spontaneous nature. Mr. Frizell doesn't know me, but Pavel does. If he's there and he sees me, he will suspect something."

"It's not a great plan, I agree, but I don't see how else to handle it." Phoebe got out of the taxi and snapped on Trouble's leash.

"Where will you be?"

"I'll go around to the other side of the park and walk back toward you. Trouble gives me an excuse to be here. And if we all meet up, you and I can say that we'd planned to get together for a walk. Pavel knows we're friends, so that sounds normal. After all, Cliff's reasons for being here could be totally innocent. Maybe he's here for some exercise."

"Do you believe that could be the case?"

"Not in the slightest."

"I also think that is highly unlikely, even though he has clearly added some flesh to his physique since he stopped working out with the Rattlesnakes. However, he might say that he has undertaken a new training regimen, and we could pretend to believe it. Since he is a former professional athlete, although not a very good one, that would be a most reasonable assumption."

"So we've got our story."

"We do." He took a baseball cap out of the trunk and settled it low on his forehead. Then he grabbed a pink floral collapsible umbrella and popped it open.

"Part of the disguise, the further to conceal my face," he said, setting off after Cliff at a brisk pace. Phoebe dug Trouble's ball out of her bag and stuck it in her pocket.

"This walk is a ruse," she told the dog, who was prancing with impatience. "Don't think we're out here to have fun. We're working now."

She jogged out to the street, putting some distance between herself and Sanjay. He was trailing Cliff by about twenty yards, doing his best to look nonchalant, if a tall man carrying a pink floral umbrella at day's end could appear nonchalant. So far, Cliff was alone.

The ex-footballer was following a path that would take him to the pond and picnic area. Phoebe increased her pace, hoping to beat him there, and a few minutes after she got to the site, she saw Cliff and Pavel Rao strolling down the path toward her. Following them almost too closely came Sanjay, the pink umbrella doing a decent job of covering his face as well as keeping off what little sun lingered on the horizon.

The sight worried her. Hadn't Pavel seen Sanjay? Or didn't he recognize him with that umbrella and the baseball cap? It seemed unlikely. But he was acting like he and Cliff were alone in the park.

Pretending to tie her shoe, she ducked down behind a bench and angled her head to watch their approach. From this position, she could see the men's legs, and that was it. She hoped they'd talk in loud voices, because she couldn't see anything worthwhile.

"This is most impressive, what you've accomplished so far," Rao said.

"I can get more for you," Cliff responded. "A lot more."

Phoebe had dropped all pretense of the shoe, but Trouble strained to get off the leash. He yipped, whining to get free and run.

"Someone's there," Pavel said. "Hello?"

Busted. She stood up, gathering Trouble's leash.

"Hey," she said, trying to act surprised as she approached them. "Are you guys having a postconference meeting?"

Pavel smiled. "We're tossing around some ideas. Expanding on things we learned."

"Anything Cliff and I can share with Chase?"

"Not so far," Cliff said, sounding belligerent. "You made good time getting here. Since I saw you at the factory only a few minutes ago."

"I did make good time, didn't I? You did, too."

"Traffic these days," Pavel said. "Always so unpredictable. Mr. Frizell and I were just saying that Venture Automotive's research and development team seems well poised to make its mark in the industry."

"If you're interested in Venture Automotive's R&D, you might want to talk to the department head," Phoebe said. "Or you can call Chase directly."

"Of course." Pavel glanced to Cliff. "Thank you for your time."

Cliff nodded and headed back along the path he'd come. Sanjay had sheared off when he'd seen Phoebe, and Cliff passed him without glancing his way.

"It has been most—*refreshing*—to run into you," Pavel said. "Quite the coincidence."

"Not as great a coincidence as you'd think," Phoebe said. "I bring my dog here most days."

"Of course. The dog. Well, I must be off."

"Have a pleasant evening." Phoebe nodded at him as Pavel took another path out of the park. She watched him saunter off and then ran to catch up to Sanjay.

"Did you hear anything of note?" Sanjay asked as they headed toward his taxi.

"Not really. Cliff said that he could get Pavel 'a lot more.' But a lot more of *what*? Did you hear anything?"

"Snatches of conversation only, what with raucous bird-song and the shrieks of children playing in the field. And I did not wish to give myself away by following too closely. However, I was able to ascertain with absolute certainty that they were discussing automobiles and their various specifi-cations. Mr. Frizell handed Mr. Rao something, but I could not determine what the object was. Did you see that?"

"No," Phoebe said. "I hid until Trouble gave me away. I saw their legs; that was it. You couldn't tell what it was?"

"The item, whatever it was, was small." Sanjay held his fingers a few inches apart. "Maybe a small envelope. A phone. It could have been nothing more than a business card. Something small enough that it fit into Mr. Frizell's palm and Pavel could fit it into his suit coat pocket."

"That's useful," Phoebe said. But even together with the little she'd heard, it didn't put them very much ahead. She needed to report this to Chase and Dave, too.

"Hang on," she said to Sanjay. "I want to make a couple

of calls."

She took a deep breath and punched in Chase's number. After all, it wasn't as though she was scared to call Chase. They hadn't broken up. They hadn't spoken in almost twenty-four hours, either, which was weird only if you weren't working about fifteen feet from each other. Which, of course, they were.

The phone rang only once before Chase picked up.

"Hey," she said. "Listen—"

"Phoebe," he said on an exhale. "*Cher*. I'm glad you called. I—"

"Wait," she said. "I've got something you should know. Although I have no idea what it means."

She told him what she and Sanjay had seen and heard in the park.

"It's suggestive," Chase asked. "Without being incriminating."

"That's what I thought," Phoebe said. "Probably it's nothing. Maybe Cliff just gave him a résumé, you know? But if he were applying for a job, why wouldn't he simply email him a résumé? It seems weird that they were hanging out in a park. It seems so… clandestine."

"It does. Have you told Dave about this?"

"Not yet. I'm calling him next."

"Where are you now?"

"We're still at the park. I called you as soon as they left. But I'm supposed to have dinner with Kristin and Nick in thirty minutes or so. Kristin said that Nick has some questions about the job offer."

"I'll meet you at Kristin's. I want to talk to Nick, too. Bring Sanjay. Hell, if Dave wants to come, bring him, too. I'll pick up a couple of pizzas on the way."

"Okay," Phoebe said, amused. She hoped Kristin would be okay with an onslaught of dinner guests.

An hour later, Phoebe, Chase, Sanjay, and Dave all crowded around Kristin and Nick's kitchen table, helping themselves to the three pizzas and salads that Chase had brought.

"This is great," Dave said, spearing two slices of pepperoni and sausage pizza and sliding them onto his plate. "My wife had her bridge group tonight, so I was at loose ends. Free eats, every cop's dream."

Kristin laughed. "And no cooking. *Everyone's* dream."

Chase grabbed a slice of the mushroom pie. "So, Nick, Dave, as the security experts here, what do you think about what Phoebe saw?" he asked, sprinkling some hot-pepper flakes on his slice.

"Who knows what was—" Nick began.

"Excuse me very much for interrupting," Sanjay said. "But before we begin discussing the various security protocols, I have some information that I think might be relevant to our conversation."

"We need all the information we can get." Chase took a bite of his slice. "Go."

"I talked to my mother this morning, as I do every Thursday," Sanjay said, reaching for the mushroom pie. "Is there enough of this one to go around? Yes? My mother informs me that because of what she knows about my father's cousin's second son's bicycle factory, Pavel Rao is almost certainly demanding baksheesh from many honest businesspeople. My mother implies there are many more such occurrences."

"Baksheesh?" Nick raised an eyebrow.

"A gratuity," Sanjay said. "An obligatory, under-the-table payment, often in cash or sometimes goods. For thanks, information, help. For doing one's job or easing restrictions or otherwise simplifying a regulatory process. And because Pavel is here in Las Vegas at this moment, I have begun to wonder. Perhaps he is angling for business that could yield him such extraneous payments here, as well."

"So—" Nick said.

"With Mr. Frizell and Pavel talking today, and with Mr. Frizell handing something to him—well, there are two potential scenarios here that fit Pavel's propensity to extort baksheesh," Sanjay said. "First is that Mr. Frizell is giving something—information, perhaps—to Pavel that he can sell to someone else. And what we saw was the handoff."

Chase looked grim. "Information about our company."

Sanjay nodded. "Yes. Or Mr. Frizell could be giving money to Pavel for information that he will use in some way that we have not anticipated. However, my belief is that that is almost certainly not what is being done. I would find that unlikely in the extreme."

Chase grabbed a beer from the six-pack and popped it open with a sharp twist. "What's more likely is that Cliff is selling information, not buying it, because that would fit in with the vandalism that has already been committed."

Sanjay nodded. "Yes. One or more of the electric-car companies in India would pay Pavel richly for information that Mr. Frizell supplies, is my estimation, and Pavel would then pass a percentage of this payment back to Mr. Frizell. An incentive, if you will. That is one theory, anyway."

Chase nodded. "A damn good one."

Phoebe bit into her vegetarian slice. "So when Cliff gave Pavel something, that was a—"

"A data-storage device," Nick said, his voice muffled by cheese. "A thumb drive or something like it."

"Can we prove it, though?" Kristin asked. "That's he's stealing information?"

"Don't have to prove it," Dave said around his slice of pepperoni pie. "Fastest way out of this problem is to get rid of Cliff, even if he hasn't actually done anything. Your employment contract probably says you can fire him at will."

Chase nodded. "It does. But I'd like to catch him in the act. Maybe bring suit. Or an arrest. Can we do that?"

"Maybe." Dave shrugged. "Depends on what he does."

"Okay," Nick said. "We can watch Cliff like a hawk, see what he does. But the bigger question for the company is security. We still have to address that, because lots of other people besides Cliff would like your data, Chase. In general, you have to clamp down on information sharing at your plant."

"I agree," Chase said. "It's past time."

Nick nodded, pushing his plate away. "Because in the

end, maybe Cliff didn't steal any data. Maybe he handed over his résumé to this Pavel Rao. And if so, you've got big trouble somehow, somewhere, because *somebody* smashed up your cars in the lot. Somebody inside, right? So you've had damage to your physical assets, and you can't be too careful about what's on your computers—your designs, banking information, everything else. That information is the beating heart of your company. That'll be under attack next, if it isn't already."

"It bugs the hell out of me," Chase said. "That it's some-body inside."

"We'll find him," Phoebe said. If she had to, she'd be willing to stake out the factory every minute of every day to catch the guy. "If it's Cliff—or whoever it is—we'll find him and we'll make sure he goes to jail, too."

Dave raised his eyebrows at her. "Well—we'll do our best to stop him and everyone after him who tries to rip you off," he said. "Phoebe and I can take care of the physical side. We've got some guys for you to interview for in-house secu-rity when Delmar Oates gets too tired to be up all day and all night, too, or when this expo is over, whichever comes first. The badging and door readers are next on our agenda. If Nick could take care of the software side?"

"Do I have the job?" Nick asked.

"You do." Chase nodded.

"I'll start tomorrow," Nick said. "Tonight, if you can get me on the system."

Chase laughed. "I like your enthusiasm," he said. "To-morrow is fine."

Nick turned to Kristin. "Sweetie, darling, I'm changing jobs, starting tomorrow. I hope that's okay with you? I'm go-ing to work for *Chase Bonaventure*."

Everyone laughed, but Phoebe thought they seemed fired up, too. They were all determined to find out who wanted to damage Chase's company—whether it was Cliff or someone else.

She just hoped that they could do it before anything worse happened.

Chapter 10

Phoebe was a little nervous when the party broke up. Would Chase invite her back to his place? And if she went, would he assume that she'd changed her mind about moving in? She didn't want him to think that because she wanted to spend time with him, including time in his bed, that she was ready to make that kind of commitment.

But heck, yeah. If he asked, she'd go.

They all trooped out of Kristin and Nick's apartment. Dave got in his car and drove away.

"I'll give you a ride," Chase said.

Sanjay raised his eyebrows.

She nodded. "I'll just get my bike," she told Sanjay. "Thanks for your help today."

"You're entirely welcome." He lifted her bicycle out of the trunk, handed it to her, got into his Vegas Fun Fare taxi, waved, and drove off.

The night suddenly seemed very dark and quiet.

Chase took the bike from her and wheeled it over to his vehicle.

"*Cher*, I want to apologize," he said as he lifted it into the storage area of the SUV.

A wave of relief washed over her. "Me, too."

"What do you have to apologize for? I was out of line. You told me how you felt. I pressured you."

Phoebe hitched her bag over her shoulder, watching

him close the SUV's hatch door. "I get how my feelings don't make any sense to you," she said. "Or maybe to anyone. But I have to go slower with this relationship than you'd like."

"Okay. I don't much like that—well, you know I don't— and I'll still do my best to change your mind. But no more pressure, *cher*. No more overt pressure, anyway."

"Just covert pressure?"

"That's fair. I'll make the prospect so appealing that you'll be *begging* me to *let* you move in."

Phoebe grinned and climbed into the passenger seat. "I look forward to that."

"Come to my place tonight?"

"Let the pressure begin."

An hour later, Phoebe stepped out of the shower. As covert pressure, the bathroom alone could almost get her to change her mind. This one had sand-colored tile and aqua accents and—like the eight other bathrooms in his house— was spacious as well as beautiful. The towels were huge and fluffy, the soap was hand-milled and fragrant, the lotions rich and creamy. There were loofas if she wanted and foot-massage thingies and a sandalwood atomizer that almost made her want to take up yoga. She'd give up a lot for this bathroom.

She put on her standard nightwear when she was at Chase's: one of his old Snakes jerseys. It came down almost to her knees; it was soft and faded from too many washings, comfortable and roomy. She thought about his apology as she brushed her teeth. It was time—maybe past time—she explained about Brenda. Chase had met her mother, of course, but he didn't *know* her.

She came out of the bathroom, rubbing lotion into her hands, gearing up for the task. Explaining Brenda was not easy.

Chase was in bed watching the late-night television report on the economy. He glanced up and smiled when she opened the door, that smile that always went straight to her heart and tingled all the way down. Plus, that naked chest was pretty attractive, too.

"The shirt looks a lot better on you than it ever did on me," he said, turning off the TV.

"Millions of fans would disagree with you." She swallowed. "We have to talk."

"Damn," Chase said. "Bad talk or good talk? I was hoping for something a little more romantic."

"Informative talk." Phoebe watched the muscles in his back flex as he turned away to put the remote on the nightstand. Those muscles moving had always been her weakness, and she'd hoped for something romantic tonight, too. But this had to come first.

Chase turned back, sitting up a little farther in the bed. "You coming to bed?"

"I'm not lying there next to you, if that's what you mean. I don't want to be distracted." She sat down at the foot of the bed and crossed her legs, fiddling with the blanket and getting comfortable.

"It's good to know I can be distracting. What's on your mind?"

She took a deep breath. "Okay, it's like this. *My mom is a good person.*" Her voice sounded a lot more fierce than she'd intended. She needed to dial it back a little.

He blinked. "Well, sure, of course she is. I knew that."

"She works hard. Harder than many."

"I'm sure she does. Cocktail waitress, right? That's gotta be hard on the feet. And the back."

Phoebe nodded. "And she's doing it in short skirts and high heels. And for that she earns low wages. Uncertain tips. She's got poor job security. Zero financial security—no pension, no 401(k). No health insurance. Sometimes shitty customers and lousy bosses. All that."

"Okay, yeah. I get that. What—"

"Even as a kid I could see it was a tough job. When I asked her about why she did it, she said she likes the work. But she doesn't have any job skills and she doesn't have an education beyond high school. And she didn't have many options because she had me. So she took the best-paying job she could get."

"You can't blame yourself—"

"I don't. For one thing, if you're not ready to have kids, you use birth control, *hello*. My point is that she worked hard and did her best."

"She did a terrific job, too," Chase said. "Because you turned out great."

Phoebe smiled. "Flattery might get you somewhere, I'm not sure yet. The thing about my mom—she got no respect in the hood. One time, she and I went to the bodega—the little store—on the corner. The clerk was leaning on the counter, reading the paper. When we came in, he glanced up but he didn't move. Right behind us came a woman in a suit carrying a briefcase. And when he saw *her*, he stood up and folded the paper. Right then, I decided that when I grew up, I'd be the woman the guy stood up for."

"That's a powerful image," he said carefully. "I see why you thought he was bein' disrespectful to your mom. But we don't really know. Maybe he was done reading the article. Or maybe that guy knew your mom for a regular customer, knew she was safe. Maybe he thought that woman in the suit was going to shoplift from him. Or hassle him about something, and he had to prepare for it."

Huh. She hadn't thought of that.

"That's an interesting interpretation," she said, nodding. "I like it. But I don't think that was it."

"What do you think it was?"

"Mom dresses a little flashy. Well, she's a cocktail waitress, goes with the territory, I suppose. I think the clerk thought she was trampy. No good, no-account."

"That's his mistake, though, right?"

"Mom's not exactly trampy, but she doesn't have a shutoff valve where guys are concerned. She's had a whole lot of boyfriends, and she always thinks the one she's with is The One." Phoebe drew air quotes around *the one*. "So then she goes off with whoever it is and disappears for weeks, sometimes even months. She believes in true love and love at first sight and all of that, so while I admire her optimism, I won't emulate her behavior."

"Months, *cher*? Truly? *Months*?" He looked horrified. "When you were a *child*? A *young* child? *How* young?"

"Pretty young."

"An *infant*?"

That was the part that always got to everybody. That Brenda would leave a baby—her—for months at a time and not always tell anyone, or at least not immediately, where she was.

Or if she was ever coming back.

"Yeah," Phoebe said, nodding. "Somehow the rent always got paid, and when I was older, I had a key. And—"

"That's neglect," he said, his voice hard. "Probably abuse, too. Nobody called Child Protective Services?"

Phoebe shrugged. "Our building was occupied by recent immigrants, and they avoid officialdom. They took care of me. And it might have seemed normal to them—it certainly seemed normal to me. It was what I knew, right? I'd float around the building, staying with one family or another until she came back. I played with all the kids, did chores with them, all that kind of stuff. It's why I know so many languages. I learned them really young. I'm not even sure English was my first language. Until I was maybe four, I didn't hear that much of it."

She saw something in his eyes that she didn't like. *Pity*.

"Do not feel sorry for me," she said, feeling fierce again. "I am not asking for your sympathy."

He blinked. "I don't feel sorry for you. Well, maybe a little. I think that you're strong and brave and that you overcame a lot of hardship you shouldn't have had to face if your mother had understood her responsibilities. But her behavior—as well as her clothes—might have had something to do with why the neighborhood did not hold her in high regard if that was the case."

"Mom's involvement with me always was marginal, but she did her best with what she had and—and, I guess—with what her limitations were," Phoebe said, backing down again. "Eventually she always called. Somebody always took care of me. She paid the families something for babysitting and feeding me and all that. I wasn't abused. I didn't go hungry. I was always clean. I went to school. And because those wonderful immigrant families didn't speak English at home or at all, now I speak eight languages, which is my professional meal ticket. I'm grateful for that. So Brenda and I are good."

"You might want to see a shrink about that notion, but that's a discussion for later."

She had to smile. "I'm just saying, I don't bear her any ill will. But even so, *I will not be like her.*" There it was—that fierce voice again. She needed to remember that Chase was on her side.

"Sweetheart. *Cher.* Where is this going? In terms of you and me. You think if you move in with me, the neighbors will disrespect you? Like that clerk in the bodega disrespected your mom?"

She smiled wryly. "Mostly I think the neighbors would envy me. But they'll also say I'm out for your money or chasing celebrity or whatever stupid thing they come up with."

"Do you care that much about what other people think?" he asked. "People said a lot of crap about me during football, and take it from me, it's a lot easier to let bullshit roll off your back."

"What strangers say doesn't worry me too much. It's more about what *I* think I'm doing. Talking about moving in with you so soon after I met you makes me wonder if I'm more like Mom than I want to admit. I'm afraid that I don't have a shutoff valve about guys."

Chase shook his head. "You think that's an inherited characteristic? Like eye color? Did you move in with all your other boyfriends?"

"No. Not that I had that many boyfriends."

"What was wrong with those guys? But that illustrates my point. You have a shutoff valve. Not that I'm judging. I played professional football. Sometimes shutoff valves are hard to find."

"Not moving in with any of my past boyfriends is not a test of whether I have a shutoff valve. You don't know those guys. Trust me."

He laughed. "I trust you."

She eyed him speculatively, pursing her lips. "Do *you* have a shutoff valve?"

Chase shrugged, still grinning. "I do now. When I was young and single, it was probably open more often than it was closed, but I wouldn't say the valve was wide open all the time even back then. But I got older, I got married. I got boundaries. Now that shutoff valve is working fine. If that's what you're worried about."

Phoebe nodded. Now that she was talking about him, not Brenda, she felt more relaxed, not nearly as tense as she had been. "To tell you the truth, I was a little worried about that, because I know you married and divorced your ex-wife within a year."

"Has that been bothering you?" he asked. "Tracy and I got married too soon. She's a Snakes cheerleader, and they're prohibited from dating the players. She didn't want to get fired, and I didn't want to keep our relationship a secret, so we got married. Not the best of reasons. And some would say, not the best of outcomes. Except that we weren't a good fit, so I'm glad it's over. But that experience was a wake-up call for me."

"How's that?"

"Day-to-day routine cuts into the honeymoon pretty quick, and I saw how I'd been—let's say *hasty*—in my judgment." He shrugged. "We both decided we were incompatible and wanted out."

"Well, see, that's why I want more time before we move in together. So we have more day-to-day routine behind us. So we're sure."

"That's why living together would accelerate that," he said. "Get through the nitty-gritty first. Do I leave wet towels on the bathroom floor? Do you get hairspray all over the bathroom mirror? Moving in would tell us that pretty quick."

"I don't use hairspray. Do you spend a lot of time looking in the bathroom mirror?"

Chase laughed. "No more so than the average unbelievably

handsome, well-muscled, extremely popular ex-jock worries about time catching up with him."

Phoebe grinned. "Maybe I'm dodging a bullet here. Are we at an impasse?"

"Not at all. Covert pressure, remember? I'll win you over."

Phoebe's smile faded. "I *will not* become like my mother. I won't move in with you now and then move out in two months when the glow wears off, and then move in with some other guy someplace else, over and over. That would wreck me emotionally and destroy any chance I have of a decent career, too. And I can't do that. I want a guy who'll stick with me, and I want a good job and a nest egg and some security. I want to be *solid*. I want to *make* something of myself."

She shoved a loose tendril of hair behind her ear. She had to get a grip. *Chase was on her side.*

"I get it," he said, his voice mild. "It's good to know what you want, *cher*. Also, I like hearing that being with me has a glow."

"Well, let's face it. You're an unbelievably handsome, well-muscled, and extremely popular ex-jock. Glowing is bound to happen. It's no wonder Tracy wanted to marry you. You must have women falling at your feet."

"I don't want them falling at my feet," Chase said. "I want them standing up to me."

Phoebe felt her face warm. He meant her.

"How does the CIA fit into this?" he asked.

"After I decided in high school that I wouldn't be a cocktail waitress, I thought languages might be a career option somehow. Mom told me she couldn't pay for college and I didn't need it anyway, so if I wanted to go, I had to get a scholarship. And my best scholarship option was the CIA, because they offered a full four-year ride plus training and then a job if I kept my grades up. So I worked like crazy ever since tenth grade and here I am. Or was, anyway. But if I give all that up to move in with you two months after I met you, what does that say about me?"

"It says—"

"It says that I'll give up my goal after almost ten years of work to be with a guy I barely know," Phoebe said, suddenly depressed. "Just like my mom. And in six or eight or ten months if the—the spark dies, like it did with your ex-wife, then what? At that point I couldn't go back to the CIA. I wouldn't have *anything*."

Her bad options all seemed to leer at her from dark corners. Why did her choices have to come down to sacrificing her skills and hard work, or sacrificing Chase? She didn't want to do either of those things.

"*Cher*, don't worry. You have time, and things have a way of sorting themselves out."

"That's what Kristin said, but things *don't* sort themselves," she said. "Not in my universe. *You* have to sort them. Meaning me, that is."

"You do have difficult choices to make. *My* point is that your mom isn't all wrong in how she goes about things. Eventually in a relationship you have to take some risk."

"I know, but—"

"Here's a thought." He reached out, picked up her hand, and carried it to his lips. "What have you got for stuff? One suitcase, the bike, and the box of books, right? Same as when you moved in there."

"I got some dishes and stuff from the thrift store," she said. "Also a shower curtain."

"A shower curtain. Seriously? You own a bike and a shower curtain and a suitcase. No wonder you're worried that people will think you're after my money."

Phoebe smiled, but her heart wasn't in it.

"What about this?" he said. "Let's do a trial run. Let's say that for as long as your mom lives in your apartment, you live with me. When your mom moves out, we see how we're doing. If you're not happy, you can always move back to your place. Moving your gear around would be a snap. A ten-year-old could do it in fifteen minutes. No disruption at all."

Just to her heart. Her heart would be seriously disrupted.

"Did you not understand one thing of what I just said?"

"Sure," he said. "You like stability. Who doesn't? You want a permanent home and a guy you can count on and a job that pays the bills with something left over. You just want those things a lot more than most people. That's good, *cher*. I like that. Means you know what you want and you're willing to work for it and not settle for something less. Plus, those are good goals. I have those goals, too."

"You make it sound so easy."

He cradled her hand between his own. They were very warm.

"I'd be lyin' to you if I said it was," he said. "We both know better. But I think we got what it takes to make it work. At least, we know enough right now to give it a try."

One thing for sure—Chase knew what he wanted and was willing to fight for it, too. This was so *not* covert pressure. This was overt pressure of the strongest kind. But in her heart, Phoebe knew he had a point. Jumping into any relationship involved risk. And she liked Chase. She wanted to move in. Her heart said yes, yes, *yes*!

Her heart wanted her to live happily ever after with this great guy. So what did her brain want her to do? Go back to that tiny apartment and share it with her mother? That was the future she could look forward to because she didn't trust her emotions enough to take a leap with him?

Phoebe had sworn she'd never make the same choices her mother had made. To get something solid—*someone* solid—you needed a solid foundation. You had to build trust and share experiences with someone. She hadn't done that before with anybody. But she knew that's what she had to do to make sure she was with the right guy. The guy she meant to keep.

Chase was playing with her fingers again, stroking her palm, not rushing her.

"What do you say, *cher*?"

What if she moved in with him and it went horribly wrong? Would she ever recover?

She didn't think so.

She loved being with Chase, but she'd known him only

a few weeks, all of them pretty much action-packed. How would he feel when the adrenaline wore off? How would *she* feel?

Maybe differently than she felt right now.

But Chase. This was *Chase*.

She drew a deep, shuddering breath. "Six months," she said. By then she'd have had to make a decision about the CIA, anyway. If she stayed in Vegas because of Chase, she'd have her answer. "In six months from today, if we both still feel the same, I'll move in."

Chapter 11

Phoebe woke slowly as sunlight filtered across her face. Chase was spooned behind her, his arm around her, holding her close against his chest, and she felt comfortable and cuddled. She didn't want to check the time, because although it was still early, it probably was time to get up. Lying here all drowsy and relaxed, not moving at all for one more minute, would be a good way to start the day.

Except her leg itched.

She reached down carefully to scratch it, trying hard not to disturb Chase, who slept on, oblivious. Well, they'd had a late night, and he had too many worries about the plant's security situation—the unfinished cars, the money he was spending on the stadium spectacular—not to mention that his knee probably wasn't fully healed yet. He needed his rest.

So yeah, now that she'd gotten that itch on her leg taken care of, she'd settle back, close her eyes, and—

"*Cher?*" His voice was thick with sleep.

"Shhh. Go back to sleep. We still have a minute."

He exhaled against her shoulder, his breath a whisper on her skin.

"You awake already?" He kissed her shoulder, a flare of heat that warmed her bones.

"Mmm." She didn't really want to talk. He was so solid behind her, strong and sure, and she wanted to enjoy that feeling for as long as she could. She reached one arm up and behind to run her hand through his hair, enjoying the soft shagginess against her fingers.

He stirred, coming to life like a lion after a doze in the shade, stretching against her back. His erection pressed hard against her thigh, and the muscles in his legs, so strong and powerful, contracted when he entwined them with hers.

She was feeling a lot more awake now.

"You know, it's almost time to get up," she said. "We have a lot to do today, and—"

"Mmm." He touched her cheek gently, exhaling into her hair, and then ran his hand down her neck and chest, squeezing her breast through the T-shirt, then down her belly to—*hello!*—then down her hip to the inside of her thigh. And then all the way back up. This time under the T-shirt.

Okay then. That was a wake-up call. Her girls had perked right up and were ready to do a few push-ups. Not to mention the rest of her.

Phoebe stretched, arching back against his chest, her shoulders and butt pushing against his muscular frame. His hand stayed where it was. That felt good. *Way* better than good.

Chase leaned on one elbow and pressed against her. He slid his fingers into her hair, kissing her nape, her shoulder blades, her neck, behind her ears... his fingers, his tongue, and his teeth stroking, sliding, nipping her sensitive skin.

Okay, she was really awake now. Her breath quickened and she leaned back into him. His mouth was soft against her lobe and his breath was hot in her ear, warming her to her core. She loved feeling his lips on her skin, the heat he generated in her, the tingle that ignited her down to her toes. She stretched against him, rubbing her legs along his, wanting the friction. The heat.

We should get up, she thought, but then she lost all rational thought as his hands stroked and glided and squeezed. Her skin itched with anticipation. Every nerve ending in her body clamored for more, and her mind shorted out on every thought that wasn't about *yes* and *harder* and *immediately*.

"Hey," she said. She could feel his smile against her ear.

"It's a beautiful morning." His fingers, so long and capable, stroked her, tracing small circles on her skin, tugging gently on her nipples.

A low hum seemed to kick up deep inside her, igniting a new urgency. He still held her against his chest, his arm around her, holding her tight. Phoebe closed her eyes, feeling herself surrender to his magical fingers and the strength of his body.

His hand drifted lower, caressing her stomach, dipping into her belly button, and she smiled to herself, clutching his hair and leaning back into him.

"You like that?" he asked.

She could stay like this all day, she thought, with Chase's hands melting her will to get up, creating a tension she was finding hard to resist.

"We should get up," she whispered, concentrating on what his hands were doing. *Damn*, that felt good. If they never got up, that would be fine with her.

No, no, no! *Not* fine! They had work to do! Events to plan! Security to set up!

"Sure," Chase agreed. "Whatever you say."

Bastard.

He trailed his hand over her breast, around and into her belly button again, then lower, and Phoebe gasped with the sheer pleasure of it when he slid two fingers inside and found a friction point that set up the hallelujah chorus in her brain.

"That... that's really good," she gasped. They needed to get moving, but another few minutes couldn't hurt.

"Glad to hear it. That's what I'm going for." He edged away from her, leaving his hand at the critical juncture, but the cool air against Phoebe's back was not what she wanted.

"Um..."

"Trying something here." He eased down her body, kissing her arm, her ribs, her stomach, stroking her skin as he drifted lower.

And before she knew it, Phoebe was lying on her back and Chase's hair was tickling her thighs and his fingers were inside her and his mouth was—*Holy crap.*

Phoebe arched against the intensity of the pleasure as it built, heating her skin, sending her blood pounding through her veins. She was so close but not quite there yet, the urgency growing while his tongue stroked her and his fingers set up a cadence that sweetened and reinforced the pressure. Her heart beat harder and faster, the need expanding until her breath came in short gasps and she felt like a violin string ready to break.

And then the tension peaked and she was there, soaring through infinity, stars glittering behind her eyelids while she cascaded into a breathless stillness. For a second she reveled in the aftermath of an orgasm that was even better than the one she'd had in the front seat of the SUV.

"That—" she said into the silence, "that was *awesome*."

Chase lifted his head and laughed. "My work here is done." He grinned. "For this morning, anyway."

"But wait, there's more," Phoebe said.

"Well, I can't say I'd object to more." Chase edged back up to the headboard and reached into the night table for a condom.

"And you shall have it. Let me do that." She tore open the packet and rolled it down his length. "There," she said, eying her handiwork.

Chase grinned. "I don't even want to know what you're thinking. Come here."

He rolled onto his back, bringing Phoebe with him.

"I wasn't thinking anything," she objected, straddling him.

"You're still wearing that T-shirt," he said. "How did I miss that?" And then he lifted her hips and eased inside her.

"You were busy." She gasped a little as she felt the full length of him slide into her.

"And getting busier."

Phoebe pulled off the shirt and tossed it aside, and he smiled at her as he ran his hands over her hips, up to mold her breasts and down her back. Then he gripped her hips and moved into her with a rhythm she had started to learn.

"I like this," she said. "Nothing against your SUV, but—"

"It's too small," Chase said, his voice tight. "Working on it."

His eyes were closed, the tendons on his forearms standing out from the strength he used to hold her. His fingers bit into her hips as Phoebe leaned forward, rocking into him as he thrust into her, enjoying the friction. The pressure built from her core, mounting through her chest, enveloping her heart, warming her skin. And then somehow he found her sweet spot again, and she gasped with the sharp wave of pleasure it brought her.

"At least... you won't... hurt your knee," she said, feeling breathless all over again, enjoying the tension she felt in him, loving the feeling of him inside her.

"No. But I won't be able to—" And then his speed picked up and he gave one last, tremendous thrust and fell back against the pillows, bringing her down with him.

After a couple of seconds, he opened his eyes and shifted to hold her. "Didn't I hear someone use the term *awesome*?"

Phoebe smiled, tucking her head in his shoulder. "I know I thought so." She took a deep breath and let it out on a long sigh. "You won't be able to what?"

"What?"

"You said you won't be able to. Won't be able to what?"

The pause was so long, Phoebe wondered if he'd fallen asleep again.

"I have no idea," he said. "I'll start over. I won't be able to get you out of my head all day."

Phoebe lifted her head to smile at him. "You say the sweetest things." *What if he knew that she hadn't been able to get him out of her head for weeks already?* But she couldn't tell him that yet.

She put her head back on his chest, and some minutes later, she sighed again, this time in resignation. "We really have to get up, or at least I do. Kristin and I have a quick meeting at seven thirty every morning to check in on progress with the stadium spectacular. I don't want to be late."

"Yeah," he said. "I have to get going, too."

Neither of them moved.

Phoebe laughed. "Are we getting up?" she asked. "On three. One, two, three."

She swung her legs out over the side of the bed and sat there, missing the warmth of the bed but remembering the luxury of the bathroom.

"I'm taking another shower," she said, standing up.

"I'll join you." When she looked at him, he rolled his eyes. "What? There are about six showerheads in that bathroom. It's luxury incarnate. Not to mention, cleanliness. That's why I picked this bedroom."

She shook her head, but the shower with its six showerheads turned out to be a lot of fun with him in it. She wrapped herself in a big towel as she stepped out, flushed from the warm water and Chase's roaming hands.

"Don't get hairspray all over the mirror," he said when he returned to the bedroom to dress. "I hate that."

She laughed, shaking her head, and reached for her brush and the hair dryer. In a few minutes her hair was as good as it would ever be, so she put away her things, ready to see what she could do with her crumpled wardrobe. Kristin would notice the walk of shame, but maybe she could—

She stepped into the bedroom, where Chase, wearing only his boxers and a shirt, was searching for something on the dresser. And then a tall young woman wearing jeans and a T-shirt burst into the room.

"Chase!" she shrieked, rushing into his arms.

Who was that? And how had she gotten in here? Didn't Chase lock his doors anymore? Vaguely in the background she heard some noise. Maybe a lot of noise.

Chase and the woman were still clenched in an embrace. So the woman's arrival wasn't unwelcome. *Okay, then.*

"Um, hello," Phoebe said. She wished she were dressed, but at least the towel covered everything important.

"*Cher,*" Chase said, breaking away, looking rueful. "Sorry about this."

"Oh, hi." The young woman stepped away from Chase and stared at Phoebe with interest. "I didn't see you there.

Sorry to interrupt. Well, not sorry, exactly. More like happy." She grinned, unrepentant.

"Jo-Bob," Chase said. "Manners."

"My manners are impeccable. And don't call me Jo-Bob." The young woman strode forward, holding out her hand. "I'm Josette Bonaventure, this guy's younger sister. Call me Josette, or Josie, but never Jo-Bob. If you do, I'll have to kill you. Chase is on borrowed time, although he doesn't seem to know it."

"Phoebe Renfrew." Phoebe shook Josette's hand, struggling a little to hold her towel in place. How was she supposed to identify herself to this young woman? She didn't want to say, *Chase's girlfriend.* Although from her attire, or lack thereof, that seemed to be self-evident.

"Phoebe Renfrew!" Josette said. "I hoped I'd have a chance to meet you! You foiled that kidnapping attempt against the secretary of state! I read about you in the newspaper."

"Well, your brother helped," Phoebe said. "And a lot of other people, too."

"Yeah, but it was mainly you. That was so cool. I want to hear all about it. Maybe tonight! So did Chase tell you that we're remodeling his house? That's why we're here."

"Ah, no. He didn't mention it. Listen—"

Chase glanced at her. "But you knew I wanted to turn it into a hotel."

"Yes, I knew that. So if I could just—"

"We're adding eight bathrooms," Josie said, "starting today, and—"

"Today?" Chase said. "*Eight?* I thought it was six."

"Eight," Josie said. "Two more half baths in the public space. And an elevator. That's why we're here. And—"

"I didn't okay an elevator," Chase said as an older man entered the room. He was only a couple of inches shorter than Chase and almost as muscular. Definitely a relation.

"Josie, where the hell—" he started, and then he saw Chase. His face broke into a beaming smile. "Son."

"Dad." Chase covered the room in two strides and

clasped his father in a big hug.

Really? Did they have to do the big family reunion thing right here in the bedroom? It was embarrassing, wearing only this towel.

The older guy and Chase broke apart, and the older guy glanced over and saw her. "Oh," he said, looking more embarrassed than she felt. "I didn't realize—I'm sorry, ma'am. We shouldn't have—"

"This is Phoebe Renfrew!" Josie said, and Chase's father smiled at her, still uneasy.

"Miz Renfrew," he said, nodding. "A pleasure. Josie's been wantin' to make your acquaintance. You probably figured out I'm the father of these two hopeless nitwits. Ancel Bonaventure."

"Pleased to meet you," Phoebe said politely. "Call me Phoebe." Because, after all, she was wearing a towel. Formality seemed unnecessary.

"I thought you had a job in New Orleans for a while," Chase said, turning to his father.

Because a little warning here would have been good, Phoebe thought, shifting on her bare feet, pulling the towel more securely around her.

"We should get out of here and let y'all get dressed," Ancel said as another big, tall guy came through the door. Unmistakably Chase's brother—just as tall, just as broad. The Bonaventures, family of giants. No wonder Chase had made it to the pros. She thought all of them could have.

"Dad, where the hell—Oh, hey," the newcomer said, seeing Chase. "If it isn't the guy who's afraid of a little hard work." He grinned, Chase grinned—obviously that was a family joke—and Chase socked him in the stomach before enveloping the other guy in a huge hug. These people were huggers.

"Don't worry," Josie said to her. "If you weren't in that towel, you'd get hugged, too."

"I'm not worried," Phoebe said as the new guy saw her. "But I wouldn't mind getting—"

"Hello." The new guy raised his eyebrows and glanced

at Chase.

"Phoebe, let me introduce my lazy brother, Max Bonaventure," Chase said. "Max, say hello to Phoebe Renfrew."

"Phoebe Renfrew?" Max said, his brow furrowed. "Why do I—Let me think."

"She's the one who rescued the secretary of state!" Josie said.

Max snapped his fingers. "That's right! Congratulations, ma'am. It's an honor. What you're doing with my brother, though, is somewhat mysterious."

I'm wearing a towel, Phoebe thought. *It's not that mysterious.*

"Don't be rude," Josie said.

"Just sayin,'" Max said. "He's a layabout. Clearly Miz Renfrew has it all going on. What does she see in him?"

"Shut up, Max," Chase said. "Everybody, excuse us. We'll talk later, but now we have to get to work."

"Yeah, we have to get to work, too," Ancel said as yet another tall, muscular man barged through the doorway.

"Max, where the hell—Oh, Chase, there you are," the newcomer said, making room for himself in the entryway. "Good to see you, man!"

Phoebe almost groaned. How many of them were there? She couldn't remember exactly what Chase had told her about his siblings. Wasn't there another sister? Had she come, too?

"When did you get a dog?" the newest guy asked, slapping Chase on the back. "And who's the lady in the towel?"

"Hello," Phoebe said. It wasn't like she *wanted* to wear the towel. The towel wasn't a fashion *choice*. If everybody would simply get out of here, she'd be happy to put some clothes on. Even yesterday's tired, crumpled outfit was pretty appealing right about now.

"Christ," Chase said. "Phoebe, this is my other brother, Leo. Leo, Phoebe Renfrew. She foiled the secretary of state kidnapping. Now that everyone's met, can you get out of here so we can get dressed?"

"Sure, Son, sure," Ancel said, looking like he'd have

been ready to leave some time ago. "But we need a quick word before you head out for the day."

"It has to be quick," Chase said. "Phoebe has a seven thirty meeting."

"That's early." Ancel glanced at Phoebe with approval.

"We have a lot to do by next week Saturday," Phoebe said. "Maybe Chase told you. We're renting a football field and then tearing it up."

"Seems counterproductive," Ancel said.

"You'd think so, but really it's a great marketing stunt." Phoebe shifted her feet. "Chase is going to sell a million cars."

"That's an exaggeration," Chase said. "I hope."

"Ancel, where in hell—" came another voice from the hallway.

Not another one, Phoebe thought, almost in despair. At this rate, she'd never get out of the towel.

"Is that Billy?" Chase asked.

"Needed a plumber," Ancel said. "Eight bathrooms. The other guys are here, too. Everybody but your mother. She's coming on the weekend. We're starting work today."

And isn't that just great. Although it explained the noise.

"That's just great," Chase said, echoing Phoebe's thought. "How did you get the permits so fast? I'd have thought—"

"I pulled them weeks ago!" Josie said. "I knew you'd go for it."

Ancel shook his head. "I had no idea, Son, I promise you."

"It's fine, Dad. No harm done. Glad to see everybody and get the work started, too. Now, everybody—out. We've got offices to get to and marketing stunts to plan."

The crowd shuffled out, laughing and poking each other as they filed into the hallway. Ancel was the last to leave.

"Sorry for the intrusion, ma'am," he said apologetically as he headed for the door. "It's a bit chaotic, I know. And a surprise, too, I see. Josie should have warned you."

"Please call me Phoebe." No one was sorrier for the intrusion than she was. She would have much preferred meeting his family in conventional circumstances—like when she was dressed and standing in a living room, for example. She hoped Ancel especially didn't think she was a cheap floozy. "And don't worry. I grew up in a lot of rowdy households."

"You'll be all right, then," he said, nodding, and closed the door.

When everyone had gone, the room seemed unnaturally quiet. And unusually large. Chase rubbed his hands over his face. What on earth would Phoebe think of all that?

"So, that's the fam," he started, taking a pair of pants out of his closet. "Most of it, anyway."

Phoebe nodded. "Unmistakable. You all look a lot alike."

She went back into the bathroom, came out again without the towel, and started scouting around for her clothes. She found her panties, turned them inside out, and put them on. Now that was an interesting laundry technique. Her black pants were next. She picked up her shirt, sniffed it, and wrinkled her nose. Maybe she wasn't ready to move in, but she could at least leave a change of clothes here. If she owned enough. One suitcase. *Christ.*

"If there's anything in my closet you can wear," he said, "you're welcome to it."

"Everything will be way too big," she said, but she went over to the closet and peered inside. "I hate putting on dirty stuff after that nice shower." She took a white shirt off the hanger. "Can I try this?"

Chase glanced up from tying his shoes. She had good taste, anyway. That was his best shirt. "Sure. Anything that's in there."

She put on his shirt. It was hopelessly large, but she rolled up the sleeves and rummaged in the closet again.

"Your belts are too big to go around once, but not big enough to go around twice." She tried one on and gazed critically at herself in the mirror before taking it off. "Can I use this bungee cord that's wrapped around your sleeping bag?"

"Sure, take it." He watched in fascination as she twitched

his shirt and wrapped the bungee cord around her waist a few times. It wouldn't pass as a designer outfit, but she looked damn cute anyway.

"Ready," she said.

The crew had been busy. Piles of lumber, toolboxes, saws, and boxes of unknown supplies were already stacked in hallways and the foyer. Ancel pulled him over for that quick talk with Josie, but Phoebe ambled into the kitchen. When she reappeared, she was carrying the lid to a cardboard box like a tray, from which a wisp of steam drifted. Gratitude rumbled through his brain just as his stomach growled.

Ancel grinned. "I think your sweetheart fixed you breakfast."

"She *is* a sweetheart," Chase said. "But in all fairness, there's at least some self-interest going on there, because she eats like a truck driver."

"Be nice to her," Josie said. "You don't want her to go away."

"No, I sure don't."

Phoebe picked her way through the chaos, dodging guys and piles of stuff. "All set?" she asked as she joined them.

Chase nodded, taking the tray from her and checking out what she'd brought. Coffee and square packets wrapped in wax paper. Sandwiches. Excellent.

They said goodbye and headed outside to Chase's SUV. He handed her the tray while he fished in his pockets for the keys. He could feel her thinking and was pretty sure he knew what was coming.

"Let me get this straight," she said, gazing at the construction vehicles. "You wanted me to move into your place so we could have more privacy from my mother, right? Who is one person. But now here at your place, you'll be supervised by your father and two brothers. Plus four other guys on the crew. Do I have that right?"

"And my sister." Chase pressed the key fob, unlocking the car doors. "And my mother is coming this weekend, evidently. Don't forget her. And I wouldn't be surprised if my brothers' wives and their kids showed up pretty soon, too."

"Right."

He came around to her side of the truck. "Just to be clear, though—I want you to move in because I want to be closer to you. Privacy would be more of a benefit than a goal. But fifteen bedrooms here, so there's plenty of room for everybody."

"Nothing against your family," Phoebe said. "They seem like really nice people. But I'm giving notice right now that I'm never moving in as long as all your family plus a bunch of other big, burly guys are living here. Just saying."

What if we were married? he thought, shocked when the thought entered his mind. Now that it had, though, it didn't bother him at all. In fact, it seemed like a damn fine idea.

It was probably having to wear that towel through all the introductions that had upset her a little.

"The construction should take only a few weeks." He took the box lid back from her. "They'll be out of our hair soon."

"Oh yeah, because nothing ever goes wrong on construction projects."

"Nothing will go wrong with this one," Chase said, although he could see her point about the house. Things *did* go wrong on construction projects, even projects that Ancel Bonaventure managed. "The remodel will be done in one month tops, *cher*, I swear on the quarterback oath."

"There's a quarterback oath? I learn something new every day."

"See? I knew you'd find a reason to move in here." He dropped the key fob into her hand and climbed into the passenger seat. "You drive."

Chapter 12

At six o'clock the following morning, the persistent clamoring ring of her phone jolted Phoebe awake. Was it the CIA again? Were these people planning to make a habit of calling her before the sun came up? Because if they were, she'd have to think twice about going back to work there.

She fumbled for her phone and checked the display. Unknown caller, it said. That had to be the CIA. Of course. How very CIA of them.

"Phoebe Renfrew," she said when she connected.

"Phoebe." The woman's crisp voice came through as though she were standing next to the bed, and Phoebe struggled to sit up. No way was she having this conversation while flat on her back. Her caller could probably see her lying there. Who knew what the CIA could do?

"This is Tamsin Dwyer," the woman continued. "I'm sorry to be calling you at this awful hour"—well, she had *that* right, anyway—"but I won't be in the office for another week, and I wanted to follow up as soon as possible on Greg's call about the working group I'm heading up. I want you to join the team. Do you have any questions for me?"

"Well, yeah." Phoebe cleared her throat. How could a person be professional when the CI-*freaking*-A kept calling you at six and you were still in bed? *It. Was. Not. Possible.* "Why me? I mean, after—"

"The Empire State Building, yes. That was a mess, for

sure."

Right again. It had been a mess.

"I never thanked you for arguing my side," Phoebe said. "I really appreciate that."

"I wasn't going to let them railroad you when there were plenty of points of failure on that one," Tamsin said. "Anyway, you weren't wrong. Just a bit ahead on the time-line. And that's why I want you on this group."

Phoebe stifled a laugh. "So I can move too quickly on some other threat?"

"That won't happen on my watch. No. Your thinking was creative, and then you trusted your instincts. You're good on Greg's team, but you'd be a better asset on mine. Your language skills are incredible, and your instincts are excellent. And you can stick to your guns. I like those qualities. I want them on my team, and I intend to give the officers who work for me the scope they need to find the anomalous threats that others might not."

Phoebe's head almost swam. She'd said her skills were incredible! Her instincts were excellent!

"And I think you'll like some of the other folks I've lined up, too."

"Julian Garza, Greg said."

"Yes, and Natasha Wilkinson."

"Nattie's joining your group?"

"I debriefed her after the secretary of state business that she helped you with. I was impressed with the teamwork that the two of you showed and how she went out on a limb to support you when doing so could have been a career-limiting move for her."

"I know. And she was a huge help."

"That kind of mutual support is another quality I like. Now, how soon can you start? I know you're on this long-term leave. That was fine when you were going back to Greg's office, but frankly, I want you a lot sooner. Next week would not be too soon. We have a lot to set up, and I want everyone to get comfortable working with each other as soon as possible."

"Next *week*?"

"Is that a problem?"

"Well, you probably know"—because the CIA seemed to know every dang thing about everything—"that I'm working with a private detective here, and we're providing security for a big event next weekend. I really have to be here for that. And I have some other, ah, obligations, too." *Chase*. Not that he was an obligation.

"Okay. Well, if I like you because you stick to your guns, I can't get mad because you want to fulfill an obligation to your boss for this event. But I need you here a lot sooner than six months. You'll be behind the eight ball if you don't start with the others, and I want to see this group up and running in a month. If you want in, get here by then."

And then she disconnected.

Phoebe felt a little stunned. Tamsin wanted her; that was good. But she wanted her back at Langley in a *month*. That was way, way too soon.

It was a great opportunity. Tamsin thought she had excellent instincts! People would believe her when she said something. Or at least they'd *listen*.

But what about her instincts for Chase? So far, she'd been nothing but confused. She liked him a lot. But if she stayed in Vegas with him, she'd be reenacting her mother's life, the thing that she'd promised herself she'd never do. And she'd be rejecting this great opportunity at the CIA—the job that she'd worked toward since high school. The job of a lifetime.

If she took the job, she'd have to say goodbye to Chase. Even the thought of it made her a little sick.

Could she find the strength to leave him? Did she want to?

When lunchtime rolled around, Chase unpacked his sandwich just as Kristin stuck her head in the door.

"Mail call, Coach." She brought in a stack of envelopes and magazines and, laying it on his desk, eyed his sandwich. "Are you planning to eat that?"

"Well, yeah. But I'm willing to share. Phoebe packed a couple for me. I've got enough to feed a construction crew."

"Thank you," Kristin said. "If you're sure? Because I bet Marta made that roast beef." Chase's housekeeper was a legendary cook.

"She did, and you're welcome to it."

"You don't have to tell me twice." She picked up the sandwich and took a bite. "Yum," she said around a mouthful of roast beef. "There's nothing in the snail mail, but the online *Oscillate* has an interesting article. Not that I read your business email. I get that newsletter myself."

"Feel free," he said as she departed. "My email is your email. Why don't you answer it while you're at it?" He flipped through the stack of mail, tossed most of the envelopes in the recycling, and opened his web browser to the article Kristin had pointed out.

CATCH THE BUZZ, the headline read. ELECTRIC CARS PAVE THE WAY TO THE FUTURE.

The feature was long, covering the design and manufacture of electric cars by several companies around the world, including a well-known company in California, another in Denmark, and Mozo Motors in India.

Not Venture Automotive in Las Vegas.

Why would the magazine interview Mozo Motors? According to Pavel Rao, if you could trust him, Mozo wasn't very far along in its development cycle.

Irritated, he read to the end of the article. Of course, the author probably didn't have time to interview every company around the world that manufactured electric cars, but Venture Automotive was a well-known start-up in the industry, run by a guy—him—that everyone seemed to want either to succeed because he was a former American sports figure, or to fail because he was a former American sports figure.

Something struck him about that section on Mozo Motors. He read it again. Then he picked up the phone and called down to production.

"Rinsho," he said when his foreman picked up. "Are Tony and Matt down there with you? Grab them and come up here right away, all right? Meet me in the conference room. I want y'all to see something."

"On our way," Rinsho said.

Chase put down the phone. "Kristin!"

She swiveled in her chair, tossing the wax paper from her sandwich into the trash. "Coach?"

"You were right. This article in *Oscillate* is interesting. Make five copies of it for me, will you? And I'd like you to sit in on a meeting in the conference room."

"Conference room? Right now? You know Phoebe's working in there."

"She should come to the meeting. Dave, too. See if you can get him on the phone. And Nick. And Andrew West."

"Our *attorney*? Okay."

Kristin sent the article to the printer, and Chase picked up his laptop and carried it to the conference room. His office was large enough to hold a small meeting, but his space on the mezzanine didn't have a door that closed. He liked the informality of it, but the lack of privacy was occasionally inconvenient. For now he didn't want to take a chance that someone would overhear what they talked about.

He knocked once on the conference room door and went in. "We have to have a meeting in here."

"No problem." Phoebe shoved back her chair and stood.

"No, no." He waved her back. "You, too. Production and security. You should stay."

She settled in again as Kristin, carrying the stack of articles, entered the conference room with Rinsho, Tony, Matt, and Nick in tow.

"I'm getting Dave and Andrew on the phone," Kristin said as the others pulled out chairs and sat down.

"Who's Andrew?" Phoebe asked.

"Our lawyer." Kristin consulted the directory and punched in the number.

"*Lawyer?* What's this about?" Phoebe asked.

"Coach thinks we have a sitch."

Chase frowned. "We *do* have a sitch."

When Dave and Andrew West were both on the line,

Kristin said, "Guys, you're on speaker. You got the article I emailed you?"

"Yes," they said.

"Kristin, give everybody a copy," Chase said, closing the door. "I'd like you all to read it and tell me what you think. Kristin, you too."

"What's going on?" Tony asked, nodding at the closed door.

"Read the article first, then we'll talk about it."

At that, each department head took a copy and started to read. For several minutes the only sound in the conference room was the sound of rustling paper and turning pages. A few minutes later, Rinsho looked up, a troubled expression on his face.

"That company in India," he said. "Mozo Motors."

Matt nodded. "That battery technology they're talking about—the article doesn't go into a lot of detail. But what they're saying here sounds a lot like the technology we developed. We've got a patent on that."

"So we're talking about intellectual property theft here," Andrew said. "Potentially."

Tony jabbed a finger at the article. "Yeah. And the software. What they're working with sounds like the algorithms I wrote."

"I thought so, too," Chase said. "And at that trade conference the Indian embassy sponsored, I met a guy from Mozo Motors, and he said that they weren't far along with their electric designs. Even Pavel Rao said that."

"How can they have tech that's so close to ours, then?" Kristin said. "We're cutting edge, right?"

"Yeah." Rinsho scowled. "We are."

"*Could* they have stolen it?" Andrew asked.

"I don't see how," Tony said. "We've never had any contact with Indian manufacturers. Until recently we've been really small. Hell, we're *still* really small in the car-manufacturing world."

"I don't think I'm exactly going out on a limb here," Phoebe said. "But I think Cliff Frizell probably stole it."

Chase nodded as all heads swiveled to stare at her, and he realized that although he and the security team—Nick, Dave, Kristin, even Sanjay—had discussed their deep suspicions about Cliff, he hadn't informed his department heads about their thoughts. Big mistake there.

But when he saw their shock and disbelief, the anger he'd tamped down flared up again. The possibility that one of his former teammates had stolen from him when he'd been trying to help the guy out really galled him. And he wasn't the only one Cliff had duped—he'd betrayed everybody else he worked with, too.

"Cliff Frizell?" Andrew West asked from the phone. "That fifth-string ex-quarterback? Why do you think that?"

"He works here now," she said. "The evidence is all circumstantial. But it fits."

"Better explain for those of us who are just joining the conversation," Andrew said.

"He's not happy in his job and he's got a grudge against Chase, so he's got motive," Phoebe ticked off on her fingers. "He has access to important company information. And he gave something to Pavel Rao, an Indian bureaucrat who likes Mozo. And according to the mother of my friend Sanjay, this Pavel Rao is on the take."

"Does she—or he—have any evidence of that?"

"Sanjay says yes. Because of the bicycle factory."

"Bicycle factory," the lawyer said. "Okay. I'll go with that for now. What did Cliff give this guy who's on the take?"

"Sanjay saw the transfer but couldn't see the object. Something small, he said. Maybe an envelope or a little container, something like that. Or a thumb drive."

Rinsho thumped his hand on the table. "Let's fire him right now."

"If he stole data, I'd like to catch him in the act, if we can," Chase said.

"That might be a job for the police," Dave said on the phone.

"I'm happy to bring the police into it," Chase said. "But

I don't want anything hitting the scandal sheets."

"That lets the police out," Phoebe said. "Police records are open to the public, right?"

"Some are, yeah," Dave said. "In any event, the police are more likely to take an interest if a crime has occurred. So far, that's not been determined."

"Are you current with your NDAs?" Andrew asked. "I hope we didn't set those up for nothing. All the employees signed one, right? Vendors, too? Contractors?"

"Yes," Phoebe, Dave, and Kristin said together.

The nondisclosure agreement, common in the industry, prohibited employees or anyone doing business with the company from discussing or leaking information about Venture Automotive's research, technology, or manufacturing methods to anyone else. That didn't mean that someone wouldn't violate the agreement, although doing so would incur penalties. A lawsuit, for starters. Which he didn't want, because he didn't want legal difficulties broadcasted in the press, which they likely would be if it came to that.

"What now?" Rinsho asked.

"Our first priority has to be finding out what this Indian company has or is doing," Chase said. "If someone *is* stealing our corporate data, we have to stop that quickly or we'll be ruined."

"I'll check the activity logs," Nick said. "See if I can find out who downloaded what that might be suspicious."

"That's a great place to start," Chase said.

"In the meantime, do we halt production?" Rinsho asked. "What about R&D?"

"I hate to do that with the expo coming up," Chase said.

"I think you can operate more or less as normal," Andrew said. "Your production data's on a closed circuit, right? You can't access it with an internet connection. Just be sure that all the cars stay under wraps so none of them can be stolen and reverse engineered."

"Our workstations," Nick said. "Nobody gets access to data who shouldn't. Not Cliff and not the Russians or Chinese, either. We'll change the passwords every day. I'll set that up."

"That'll be tough," Rinsho said. "We're short-staffed, and people trade off assignments. Work across departments. If we implement a bunch of security measures that show we don't trust anyone, the guys won't like that."

"We've already had to incorporate new measures to satisfy investors," Chase said. "Background checks, for example. We can say whatever we're doing now is part of that."

"The idea is to take away opportunities for theft," Dave said. "Make sure that nobody can access anything they're not entitled to by job description, down to basics like keeping doors locked and monitoring delivery guys."

"Nobody takes work home," Nick said. "If it doesn't leave the building, it can't get lost, stolen, or copied."

"We're installing badge readers on Monday, so after that, only people who need to go someplace in the building will be able to get there," Dave said. "Until then, we should shut down the plant over the weekend. Nobody comes in to work. Change the security code on the doors to make sure."

"I hate to do that," Chase said. "It'll kill the revamped production schedule we initiated for the expo."

"If it keeps our data safe, it's worth it," Tony said. "We'll work thirty-six hours a day afterwards to make up for it."

"Heck, yeah," Matt said. "We'll get it done, Coach."

"Absolutely," Rinsho said.

Chase gazed at each man in turn. He was more than touched by their determination and loyalty. Not even on the football field, when pride and honor—not to mention, millions in bonuses and incentives—were at stake, had he seen this kind of resolve.

"Thank you," he said. "I appreciate that."

"We're all in this together," Matt said.

"That's settled then," Andrew said. "What about metal detectors?"

"We can install those, too, if you want them," Dave said. "And since we can't be positive how the data is getting stolen—or *if* it's getting stolen—we can also look for hidden cameras, audio bugs, that kind of thing."

"Oh yeah," Phoebe said. "Recording devices, USB gadgets, surveillance gadgets, key loggers, monitor loggers. Detection techniques, for sure. Maybe we should install noise generators."

All the men turned and stared at her.

"What?" Phoebe said. "CIA, remember?"

"I'm not hearing this," Andrew, the lawyer, said.

"You were a *language analyst*." Chase raised a brow. "For three months. You aren't supposed to know surveillance techniques."

"I picked up a few things."

"*The point is*," Dave said, "whatever's there, we'll find it."

"Without metal detectors," Chase said. "If Cliff or anybody else is sneaking something out, it's probably not on a laptop or other metal device. I don't want to be flagging everybody's car keys every day. And a metal detector—that really does convey an attitude of distrust. The other stuff—okay."

"I have an idea," Phoebe said. "It might not be a good one, though. And it'll be difficult to implement."

"Way to sell it, Phoebs," Kristin said with a grin.

Chase realized that he'd underestimated Phoebe's security experience, which was just plain nuts. She might have worked there for only three months, but she was *CIA*. Former CIA, anyway. The mother of all secret spying operations. She probably knew a lot more about this stuff than she was letting on.

Phoebe flashed a quick smile in Kristin's direction. "What I was thinking—this week leading up to the expo is the critical week, right? This isn't a long-term solution, but if we want to be sure that nobody steals any data this week, can we move it to a different server altogether, someplace secure and off-site? One of those bunker places for data storage? We could even alter the data that's on the servers here at the plant to make it inaccurate or outdated. If the thief manages to copy anything, the data will be wrong. Would that work?"

"Two sets of data?" Nick asked.

Phoebe nodded. "Right."

"Like a disinformation campaign," Chase said.

"Yes," Phoebe said.

"I'm not objecting, but I have to point out that we wouldn't be able to access our real data at all," Nick said. "We couldn't do updates."

"I didn't think it would be easy," Phoebe said.

"If we needed to make changes, one of us sitting here at this table would have to go to the bunker to do it," Nick said.

"If that would keep the data safe, though—" Rinsho said. "We're heads down on building the expo cars. Not really doing any new development."

"It might work, then," Nick said. "Short term, anyway. I could set that up today."

"Great," Chase said. "Let's go ahead with that. And for now, keep this among ourselves. *Nobody* else knows. Is that it for ideas?"

"I'll put out a memo this afternoon telling people about the changes," Kristin said. "Except for the data bunker, I mean."

"Thanks, Kristin," Chase said, feeling grateful to his staff for their quick willingness to respond. "One more thing. Andrew, what happens if Mozo *did* steal the data and is making cars already, like the article suggests? What are our options going forward?"

"You can sue. You'd probably win. What you'd get for damages is less clear. Maybe nothing. The cost could be astronomical. That's the nuclear option."

Chase sighed. "Shit."

"But that would force them to stop."

"Well, that's something," Chase said. "It would be a lot of R&D down the drain, though. You said that's the nuclear option. There are others?"

"We can send them a cease and desist letter," he said.

"Really?" Phoebe asked. "That sounds too simple to work."

"It lets them know that a lawsuit is being prepared,"

Andrew said. "Sometimes it works, if the target company doesn't have deep pockets. They get scared."

Chase turned to Phoebe. "If the CIA found out that a foreign government or person had stolen something vital, what would the agency do?"

"We'd waterboard the bastards."

"I'm *really* not hearing this," the lawyer said.

"No, really, what would you do?" Chase asked.

"Really." Phoebe looked uncomfortable. "That's what we'd do. Or something equivalent. I mean, not me personally. I was a language analyst. But yeah. Bad guys? Stealing state secrets? That could undermine and destabilize legitimate governments? Do your worst and keep it out of the press."

"We're not going to waterboard anybody," Chase said with a grimace.

"No," Phoebe said. "Just kidding. Dave doesn't like it."

"None of my employees or clients will get involved with waterboarding," Dave said from the phone. "Or anything like it. Now or ever."

"Good to know," the lawyer said. "Hold that thought."

"So," Chase said, "waterboarding is off the table. In the meantime, is there anything else we can do to find out if Mozo has been getting our data?"

"Oh, sure," Phoebe said. "That's the easy part."

"Really?" Chase asked. "And what's that?"

"I'll just call them up and ask."

Chapter 13

In shock and disbelief, Cliff read the memo from Chase Fucking Bonaventure at the end of Friday. It said that the company was closed for the weekend and the security team would be installing badge readers on Monday, which would restrict employee access to areas of the building where they had responsibilities. All done to ensure safety, accountability, smooth workflow, blah, blah, blah.

That meant he wouldn't be able to get into the production department. How could he steal data for Pavel? His plan to get rich and bring down Bonaventure at the same time evaporated before his eyes.

Were they on to him? Why would they install those badge readers unless they'd realized that they were missing something?

With a shitty end to a shitty day after a shitty week, what he needed was a drink. A tall, stiff one.

So when he got home, he had one. The second drink was better than the first, and the third better still. He tossed down the fourth and fifth almost unnoticed, but by the sixth, as angry as he was, he'd started to think. Bonaventure wanted to limit access in the building? Then he better get in there now while he still could.

Shortly before ten, he changed into black pants and a black jacket and drove to the nearest big box store, where he used cash to buy a black ski mask and gloves. Then he drove to the factory. New surveillance cameras had been installed everywhere outside, but with his dark clothes and the mask, he wouldn't be recognized going in.

He parked in the farthest corner of the lot, in an area where the cameras weren't installed yet, and walked unsteadily to the rear door. The production area was dark, but faint light glowed from the far end of the building. Was that the security cop? Cliff peered through the window and didn't see anyone. Clear sailing!

Keying in his access code turned the lock display red, and the door wouldn't open. Maybe he'd made a mistake. He punched the numbers in again. Still red. Tried again. Still red.

The access code didn't work.

What the hell? Now was not the time for a computer malfunction!

The building had exits on all four sides, so he moved to the east side and tried that door. The damn access code didn't work there, either.

They'd changed the code. That had to be it. *Chase Fucking Bonaventure had changed the code.*

Impotent rage froze him to his spot in the shadows. The king always thought he was better than everybody else. Always one step ahead. This was just another example of how he stuck it to you every single damn time.

How was he supposed to get in now? He couldn't go home yet. His opportunity to copy data would never be better than it was right now.

What the hell.

He stepped over to the window, tested it, found it locked, and smashed his gloved fist through the heavy industrial glass. A hot flash of pain shot through his hand and up his arm, and somewhere an alarm siren began a loud, rhythmic honk.

Dammit to fucking hell! His hand hurt like crap, and the noise was enough to deafen the entire state of Nevada. What was Bonaventure trying to do? Put everyone around here on disability?

But he was here now. Might as well get what he came

for. He reached through the broken glass, unlocked the window, and pushed the casement open as far as it would go. Most of the window glass had cascaded onto the factory floor, but some came back with him when he pulled his hand back. He brushed the splinters off his gloves and jacket, then squeezed through the window, almost toppling over when he hit the factory floor.

The alarm was louder inside, but unless the siren was hooked up to the police department—and why should it be?—he'd have enough time to get the data he'd come for. Except for that dumpy diner down the road, this stupid factory was a million miles from no place. Nobody would ever hear that stupid siren. Well, except for him, of course.

He staggered into R&D, stuck the thumb drive into the port on his machine, and started downloading the specs for the new NFL car. Losing the data for that one would be a special blow to the king.

So what could he do here for sixty minutes or more until the download finished? Besides go deaf. He should have brought his old friend Johnnie Walker. Johnnie knew how to spend quality time *and* throw a party.

Maybe he could wreck the finished cars again! That would be fun.

He crouched as low as he could and creeped as stealthily as possible down to the area where they'd parked the finished cars. But damn! That rent-a-cop was sitting there, calling somebody. Maybe the cops.

So that idea was out. And now he wouldn't have as much time as he wanted, either.

He backed away from the guard. What else could he do? Then he had an idea.

Maybe he could download every damn thing in the company at the same time! That would show those bastards.

He felt his way through the darkened factory into the production area and booted up Tony's machine. *Damn.* It was password protected. Matt's, too. All the machines he tried had passwords he couldn't get around.

After a few minutes—he wasn't sure how long—he

heard a siren in the distance over the honking alarm. A chill slithered down his spine. That had to be the cops or even a security detail coming to the plant. Who else could it be?

Better safe than sorry. And maybe by now the data that he'd collected was enough to sell to Pavel.

He staggered back to R&D and grabbed the thumb drive from his machine. Stuffing it in his pocket, he wobbled down the darkened aisle, shoved open the rear exit, and stumbled to the edge of the parking lot, where his car was all but hidden in the darkness.

By then the factory siren had turned off and the cops were pounding on the front door of the building. Cliff had never been so happy to be driving an electric vehicle, which made almost no noise at all. Feeling his heart race, he watched as the front door opened and that security guard let the police in. Then, headlights off, Cliff drove out of the parking lot and onto the street, heading for his downtown condo.

Nothing simpler.

He'd gotten the data, and he'd gotten clean away. He was so elated that he rolled down the window and yelled into the night sky. He'd just masterminded a huge data rip-off, and no one would be able to pin it on him.

Pavel Rao would pay big for this.

And so, in a different way, would Chase Bonaventure.

Chase sat at his dining room table on Friday night with the rest of his family, nursing a beer and holding the worst poker hand in the history of the game. The Bonaventure Construction crew had cleaned up and gone to the Strip to check out the bright lights, but his dad and siblings had opted for a quiet evening at his place.

He wondered what Phoebe was up to. She'd slipped out of the office before he'd had a chance to talk to her, and after that towel scene this morning, she might be reluctant to come over. How could they find any privacy with Brenda and Uncle Boo-Boo at her place and his family in his? The chances of her moving in with him—or even staying past the time the

CIA had given her to decide—were fading faster than a gator's hopes in a handbag factory.

"Hey, bro," Max said, kicking his chair. "Mind on the game."

Chase came back to earth and folded his hand, and then, thank God, his phone rang. Maybe that was Phoebe.

But no. It was Delmar Oates. The cop doing security work at the plant. A call from Delmar Oates late on a Friday night could not be good news. He surged to his feet, leaving the table.

"Yeah," he said into the phone, pacing into the foyer. "Delmar. What's up?"

"Bad news, Chief," Delmar said. "We've had a break-in. They came through a window on the east side. The cops—the on-duty cops, I mean—are here now."

"What did they get? Or do?"

"I don't know. Nothing obvious. They weren't in here long. I heard the glass break, the alarm went off, and I called 911. Dave said your orders are never to leave the finished cars unguarded, so I didn't. But they had maybe ten minutes in here." He sounded frustrated.

"You did the right thing, Delmar. We need those cars in perfect condition. Okay, I'm coming down, and I'll ask Nick Balasco, our data security guy, to come, too. Just so you know if he gets there before I do."

"The cops will wait for you. They want to ask you a few questions."

When Chase disconnected, he turned around to see his family standing in the doorway. Even Trouble was there, his head tilted, one ear up, alert and ready for action.

"Bad news?" his father asked.

"Break-in at the plant," he said. "I have to go down there. Cops are waiting. And it sounds like we have to get the window patched up, too."

"I'll go with you," Leo said. "I've always wanted to see that place."

"We'll all go," Ancel said. "We can fix that window for you."

"That's not necessary, Dad," Chase said, touched. "But thanks."

Ancel shrugged. "Game was lousy, anyway," he said. "You were losing your shirt, probably because you were thinking about something else."

"Towel Lady is my guess." Leo grinned.

"Yeah, but I was taking him for a bundle," Josie objected. "I could use the money. Don't have a job, you know. Plus, working for free here."

"If I'd wanted to beat you, I could have," Chase said. "But it's not right to cheat family."

Everyone hooted with derision. Chase grinned.

"Okay, I'm leaving now." He called Nick while he went to get his jacket, and by the time he got back to the foyer, everyone was standing at the front door, jackets on, looking impatient.

"We're all going," Max said. "We don't want to play four-handed poker. We want to see the factory. Let's get a move on."

They packed into Chase's SUV—they definitely had to investigate the possibilities of building a big-and-tall model—and Chase drove to the factory as fast as possible, running every yellow. Even so, Nick had beat them to it.

"They were definitely looking for data," he said as they entered the production area.

"Check out the robots!" Josie said, staring at them open-mouthed.

"I'm happy they didn't smash them," Chase said. "What did they get, Nick?"

"I won't know for sure until I examine the security dashboard," Nick said. "But every computer in R&D and some in production are turned on. Most of the screens are stalled at the password prompt, so whoever was in here either wasn't knowledgeable about what the passwords are or not adept enough to get past them."

"That's good news," Chase said.

"Here's the kicker," Nick said. "Our thief got into the schematics files only from Cliff Frizell's computer."

"*Damn.*" Chase rubbed his face. "That settles it for me. He's our guy."

Nick nodded. "I'll be able to see on the dashboard if and when he last tried to enter the building with his badge. That might be another bit of evidence right there."

"*Cliff Frizell?*" Max said. "Cliff *Frizell* works here? That washed-up ex-quarterback who sat on the bench for so long they named it after him? *That* Cliff Frizell? He *works* here?"

Chase shrugged. "Yeah. Bad hire there."

"Sounds like," Max said. "Why would you make a bad hire?"

Chase sighed. "I was trying to do the right thing."

"Well, you shouldn't do that if the guy's a crook," Max said.

"Son," Ancel said.

"On the up side, you can't download entire schematics files in ten minutes," Nick said. "And that's how long Delmar said the thief was in here. And all he got was altered data. I got all the real stuff moved to the bunker already."

"That's a break," Chase said. "Good work, Nick."

Nick nodded. "If you don't need me here, I'll go to my office and see what I can see."

"You got a bunker?" Max asked as Nick jogged off.

"Yeah," Chase said, grinning ruefully. "A data bunker. Can't be too careful. Don't tell anybody, okay?"

The cops came over, and they all shook hands.

"Can you tell if anything's missing?" one of them asked as they strolled past the robots, examined the workstations, and peered into offices. "Anything physical, I mean. Your IT guy said data might be missing."

"Yeah," Chase said. "He's investigating that now. I might notice if any big physical assets are gone, but I won't know if anything small or personal's been stolen until Monday, when people return to work."

"Okay," the cop said. "You can always call and update the report then. One question—if the guy wants to steal something, why doesn't he take these laptops? They'd be easy to carry. Once he had them, he'd have all the time in the world to figure out the passwords, see what data he could get, if any. And then he could sell them for cash value, too."

"I can't say what our thief is thinking, but we let all the employees know that we can shut down an off-site machine from here, making it inoperable," Chase said. "So a laptop thief couldn't access our data. And we think this is an inside job."

"Inside job?" the cop asked.

"We think it's Cliff Frizell," Chase said.

"The seat-warming ex-quarterback Cliff Frizell? *He* works here?"

Max shook his head. "If you can call a guy who never threw a football a quarterback, ex or otherwise."

"He always had the cleanest uniform on the squad," the cop said. "Always looked brand-new."

"Anyway…" Chase couldn't argue with any of that, but they needed to move it along.

"Right." The cop nodded. "You want to file the report to get the break-in on record, but if nothing's been stolen and without any evidence, there's not much we can do. I'm sure you'll take steps to protect your property. Call us if anything else happens."

When the cops left, Chase called an emergency-window-replacement place and then gave his family a short tour.

"Y'all don't have to hang around and wait for the window guy," he said back in the lobby. "Take my car. I'll drive one of our spares home when I'm done here. I'm just sorry I won't be seeing much of you until we get past this expo. Well, you see what it's like around here."

"Do what you have to do," Max said. "We'll be hunkered down in your mansion, eating your food, watching your cable, and working out in your gym. You know, tough job, but somebody's gotta do it."

Chase grinned. "Glad you're willing to make the hard sacrifices."

Ancel lingered in the door as the others piled out into the visitors parking lot. "That burglar is stealing data now," he said. "But the way I see it, he's escalating. First he committed some vandalism outside your building. Now he's breaking glass to get in. I'm worried about what he'll do the next time."

Chase felt grim as he closed and locked the front door behind them. What his dad didn't know was that Cliff had a gun, and he might be more than willing to use it.

So there couldn't be a next time.

It wasn't just about data anymore. The lives of everyone who worked here could be at stake.

Phoebe hung around after the Friday meeting for a little while, waiting for Chase, but he was busy talking first to Dave and then Tony and Matt, so she took off. He'd get in touch when he finished and they'd make a plan. And for sure she'd see him on Sunday when they called Mozo Motors in Kolkata. Kolkata was about twelve hours later than Las Vegas, so the best time to call Mozo and ask them about their technology would be eight or nine o'clock on Sunday evening.

Chase called when he got home and said he had construction business to go over with Josie and his dad and he'd be staying in. She had stuff to do for the spectacular, so she worked for a while and then went to bed early, if camping out on the living room sofa could be called "going to bed." She woke early on Saturday morning after a surprisingly sound sleep and saw that the door to her bedroom was closed. Evidently Brenda had come home last night and been quiet about it, so Phoebe tried to reciprocate. She put on her new black jeans and her nice black top, pulled her hair in a ponytail, and ate some cereal. But as she washed her bowl and spoon, Brenda stumbled out of the bedroom and headed into the kitchen.

"Hi, baby," she said, eying Phoebe's outfit. "You going to work?"

"I have an appointment," Phoebe said, nodding. "Mom, you know I'm happy to put you up for a while, but I didn't count on Uncle Boo-Boo and losing my bedroom every night, too. I don't mean to rush you or anything, but are you guys making other arrangements? This place isn't really big enough for all of us."

Brenda leaned in. "The truth of it is," she said, keeping her voice low, "I hadn't really expected Bikki to stick around so long, and I'm between jobs right now. We're—"

"I don't need details," Phoebe said quickly. "I just—"

"No, I understand," Brenda said. "I'll speak to Bikki. We'll work something out."

"I'd appreciate that," Phoebe said. "And now, if I don't want to be late, I have to go."

She carried her bike downstairs and set off down the street. Most of the work for the stadium spectacular was complete. More than seventy NASCAR drivers had committed to drive in the spectacular, and their security checks were complete. They'd be arriving in town soon to begin practice. She had reserved hotel rooms and set up expense vouchers for them. Venture Automotive employees had volunteered their cars and would deliver them on the first day of rehearsal. The ticket takers, snack food and merchandise vendors, and security personnel for the stadium were contracted and backgrounded. Publicity people were lined up. The television stations had been notified, and several had expressed interest in filming a segment. The confetti was purchased, the T-shirts were printed and delivered, the T-shirt guns were rented, the bobbleheads had shipped. Only one piece of the spectacular remained to be settled.

She needed cheerleaders to fire up the crowd. And she was hoping to sign up a few today.

The Las Vegas Rattlesnake cheerleading squad practiced in a gym near the university. When she got there, forty or more young women in snug Lycra shorts or exercise pants and racer-back tops sat on the floor and stretched to music. Several of them had their legs spread wide, their foreheads resting on the polished planks of the gym floor. *Good grief.* She'd never be able to do that if she stretched all day.

And it wasn't just their athleticism. All the cheerleaders were gorgeous, with long hair curled and coifed, makeup— false eyelashes!—in place, nail polish perfect. For practice! Their legs and arms were tanned and lean, their stomachs flat.

Their outfits were sleek and color-coordinated. It was like watching an Olympic team. A cheerleading Olympic team.

None of them stopped to look at her, but another woman, an older version of the women stretching, stood at the side of the gym with a clipboard and a whistle. She had to be the coach. Phoebe walked over to her.

"Ms. Brautigan?" she asked. "I'm Phoebe Renfrew. I'm here to talk to the cheerleaders about the gig I discussed with you."

"The girls are just finishing up their practice," Brautigan said. "I'll get them together for you."

She blew on her whistle, and all the cheerleaders stopped what they were doing and concentrated on her.

"Girls, gather around," she called.

The young women got up from the floor, arched their backs, rolled their shoulders, shook out their hair, and approached. *They're like racehorses*, Phoebe thought. Beautiful. Strong. Well taken care of. Vain.

"All right," Brautigan said in a lower voice when the cheerleaders were standing around them. "This is Phoebe Renfrew. She wants to propose a non-NFL appearance for you. Management has approved your participation. It's a business event for Venture Automotive, which is owned by Chase Bonaventure, whom of course most of you know. The event is next Saturday. And don't forget—practice on Tuesday at one o'clock."

All the women turned to Phoebe. She felt as if forty or fifty pairs of eyes were assessing her for a makeover.

"What's the fee?" called out one young woman.

"Five thousand dollars," Phoebe said, hoping that would be enough money to draw them in. That was what she was paying the NASCAR drivers, the rock-bottom fee they could command for personal appearances. The cheerleaders, of course, had had a lot more television exposure, and they worked for a richer organization. If five thousand wasn't enough for the women, she'd go higher. She wanted the cheerleaders there.

"Will Chase be there?" asked another.

Several of the young women laughed.

"Yes," Phoebe said, trying not to feel annoyed. "He'll be working, though."

"My boyfriend would be pissed if Chase is there," one of them said. "I better not."

What kind of boyfriend did this woman have? Phoebe almost felt sorry for her.

"Okay," she said. "Participation is up to you."

"Don't listen to your boyfriend, Raven," someone else said. "Chase settled down after he married Tracy. Or so she says."

"The problem was, *he* wanted *me* to settle down," a stunning blonde said.

All the other cheerleaders laughed.

So that was Tracy. Chase's ex.

Phoebe tried not to stare at her, although Tracy was unbelievably, perfectly beautiful. She had long, thick, wavy hair that was streaked from almost white to dark amber, a rainbow of blond that flowed like a river of honey down her back. Her big blue eyes were accented with smoky shadow and long, dark lashes. She was tall and curvy. Very curvy.

This was the woman that Chase had divorced. This perfect creature.

Phoebe didn't feel insecure about her looks, but she didn't harbor any illusions about her appearance, either. She had a good complexion and regular features, but her hair was an undistinguished light brown and anybody would call her "strong" before they described her as "curvy."

But Chase was with her now—and not just "with" her. He wanted to *live* with her. Wanted to grow their relationship. Wanted more time with *her*, Phoebe Renfrew.

Because Tracy, even though she was gorgeous, was not the right person for him.

As she watched these beautiful, graceful, athletic women chat around her, Phoebe felt stronger, more sure. More confident of herself and Chase and what they had together. More confident of him and his decisions. It was like the tendrils of their connection grew and wound around her heart and each other, strengthening their bond.

She hadn't been sure what to expect when she met Tracy, but it wasn't this increasing certainty.

"Maybe after his divorce, he *un*settled again," one of the women said.

"You still wouldn't stand a chance, Alanna," another said.

They all laughed again.

He isn't unsettled, Phoebe thought fiercely. He's *settled*. He settled with *me*. *I* settled him.

"Chase Bonaventure is in an exclusive relationship," she said, hanging on to her temper. "Now, *about this appearance*. Do you have any questions?"

"I'm in." Another woman, this one with long russet hair—were they *required* to have long hair?—spoke up from the edge of the crowd. "For the gig, I mean. What do you need?"

"Great," Phoebe said. She told them about the event— where it was, what she wanted them to do, how long it would last.

"If you're interested, I have a short contract for you to sign." She dug into her messenger bag, then handed out contracts and pens for the women who came forward.

"Wait a second," Alanna said, looking up from the form with a frown. "How do we know what we'll get paid? This section just says five thousand dollars."

"Right," Phoebe said, confused. "Five thousand. What's the question?"

"Well, what we get depends on how many of us appear, right?" she said. "Five thousand divided by X number of cheerleaders."

Phoebe blinked. "Uh, no. That's five thousand each. For the appearance. Same as the NASCAR guys get."

"Five thousand *each*?" The woman with the bad boyfriend whirled around. "To hell with Jason. Give me a contract. And a pen."

Phoebe handed them over as all the rest of the cheerleaders, some of whom had already grabbed their stuff to go, turned back.

"Five thousand *each*?" one of them said. "You're *sure*?"

"Yes," Phoebe said. "I set the rate. Five thousand each." She watched as every cheerleader signed a contract. "How much do you normally get paid for an appearance?"

"We earn minimum wage," Tracy said. "About three thousand a year. That's for all the home games, three practices a week, and mandatory public appearances."

Phoebe couldn't believe it.

"*Minimum wage?* How many appearances do you make?"

"Depends," Tracy said. "Sometimes two a month. Sometimes two hundred a year."

Incredible. And for all that they earned about three thousand in a *year*? No wonder everybody had jumped at five thousand. No wonder they'd thought they'd all have to share it.

Tracy handed back her signed contract, and Phoebe stuffed it in her messenger bag.

"Let me get this straight," she said. "Minimum wage for cheerleading. For the NFL. I mean, I'm not a football fan, but the NFL is huge, right? Like billion-dollars-a-year huge?"

"Crazy, isn't it?" Tracy nodded as she changed into street shoes, jamming her sneakers into a duffel bag. "And that's about three times as much as we used to get a couple of years ago. But somebody sued for labor law violations, so three thousand a year is a big improvement."

Phoebe still couldn't believe it. The minimum wage for a rookie football player was about four hundred thousand a year. Chase had made top dollar when he played, maybe twenty-five million a year. For rookies, four hundred thousand came to twenty-five thousand per game. Chase had earned about a million and a half for a *single game*—and that wasn't counting the off-season. And the cheerleaders made minimum wage?

Tracy smiled at Phoebe's astonishment. "Yeah," she said as they headed for the door. "Nine bucks an hour. Sixty or so bucks a game for a seven-hour day. And there's a handbook, too. Rules. How we should behave in public. What color nail polish we can wear. We can't change our hairstyle without permission from management. We can't date players at all. Our pay is docked if we're late to practice. In the old days, sometimes *girls* owed the *team* at the end of the year."

Phoebe felt shocked now. "That's *medieval*. Is it worth it?" Tracy was so gorgeous, and she seemed smart, too. She could probably do anything. Why would she want to submit to those kinds of working conditions?

"Is it *worth* it?" Tracy looked incredulous. "*Hell*, yeah, it's worth it. You ever hear of Paula Abdul, Teri Hatcher, Megan Fox? All former cheerleaders. All huge now in television. That's what I want. That's what we all want, if we're honest about it. A career in TV."

But that's only three people, Phoebe almost said. Three examples. You had a better chance of hitting it big in television if you'd lived during the age of radio.

"But the *rules*, and the *pay*."

"There's always plan B," Tracy said, an easy smile on her face.

"What's plan B?"

"Marry the quarterback."

"But that didn't last." Phoebe felt a little sick as they headed toward the parking lot. If Tracy's plan had been to use Chase somehow to get ahead in her TV career—well, no wonder they'd divorced.

"Maybe next time it *will* last." Tracy gazed at Phoebe, speculation in her eyes. "You're dating him now, right?"

"Venture Automotive contracts with the company I work for. That said—"

Tracy smiled, eyeing her up and down. "You're a lot different. I guess I'm surprised. Or maybe he's changed."

Phoebe smiled back. "I don't think he changed. He just figured out what he really wants."

Chapter 14

After Tracy took off, Phoebe called Kristin.

"Got any plans for the rest of the day?" she asked. "I could use a strong dose of normal person."

"Want to go to that nice discount mall?" Kristin said. "You could use a lot more clothes."

If she wanted to spend more nights at Chase's, she should get an outfit to leave over there. Not counting her CIA suits, she had exactly five outfits for work—one of which was the jeans outfit she had on. For every reason in the book, she didn't like wearing Chase's shirts to work.

So they went shopping and Phoebe got two cute new outfits. Then they went out for dinner, which included a bottle of wine. She had a message from Chase to call him when she got home, but when she did, she went straight to voice mail.

On Sunday, she went for a late brunch with Brenda and Uncle Boo-Boo. In the early afternoon, Dave rang to tell her that Venture Automotive had had a break-in on Friday night but nothing seemed stolen. She called Chase again but didn't get him. Well, he was busy with the break-in. And his family. And his house. And the construction crew. She had a great book and the classic-movie channel on cable. And of course she'd see him at the meeting that night when they called Mozo Motors.

They'd decided to call Mozo from the Western office

rather than the plant on the off chance that the Indian company would try calling back, thus blowing their cover. They'd planned to say that Phoebe was writing a magazine article and she wanted to interview a technical person for it. Rinsho and Chase would provide technical expertise. Sanjay would supply language support in Bengali if they needed it, because Phoebe spoke only Hindi.

She rode over on her bike, and when she got there, Chase, Rinsho, Sanjay, and Dave were already crowded around Western's picnic table, barely leaving enough room for her. They *had* to replace that thing, not that it was bad to be smooshed up against Chase.

Dave had come, as he said, to make sure that nobody trashed the office.

"Divorce cases," he grumbled now. "That's what I wanted when I set up this little shop. I thought, retire from the PD, get a little divorce work, missing persons, what have you, make some easy money, do some fishing. And instead, I get late-night calls to Calcutta. Kolkata. Wherever the hell."

Phoebe checked her notes. "Divorce cases are messy, and they can be dangerous. You told me that domestics are the hardest and most unpredictable calls."

"You shouldn't listen to every damn thing I say." Dave sighed. "Are we ready yet?"

"Yes," Phoebe rolled her shoulders and dialed the number, nodding at them when someone at the other end picked up.

"Hello, good morning," she said. "I'm a researcher for Western, ah, Publishing Company in the United States. I'm writing an article for a large automotive magazine, and I'd like to speak with Ram Kumar." Ram Kumar had been the interview subject in the *Oscillate* article.

"Hold, please," the pleasant voice said. "I'll transfer you."

She nodded at the men hunched over the shabby table. "Transferring."

They all glanced at each other. Rinsho looked nervous. Chase looked grim. Sanjay looked excited. Dave looked skeptical.

Her posse.

"Ram Kumar," Phoebe heard.

"Mr. Kumar." She repeated the false background she'd given the receptionist. "The interview you did for *Oscillate* magazine was—let me say—tantalizing. The magazine I'm working for wants to do a deep dive on Mozo Motors for the cover of our annual special issue." That was supposed to flatter him into accepting.

"Intriguing," Ram Kumar said. "Tell me what you need."

"Details. Specifics. We want our readers to understand how revolutionary your technology is." She mimed sticking her finger down her throat, pretending to barf, for the benefit of the others.

Dave grinned. Even Chase had lost that grim look.

"Does now work?" Kumar said. "I have a meeting in an hour. But you understand that anything I say must be approved by our legal department before it can be published."

"Yes, of course," Phoebe said. "I have the technical staff of the magazine right here. I'd like to put us all on speaker. Can we record?"

"Sure," Kumar said. "Let's roll."

For the next hour, Phoebe, Chase, and Rinsho asked questions. Phoebe didn't understand the more technical elements, but as time went on, both Rinsho and Chase appeared increasingly incensed.

Ram Kumar seemed surprised at their depth of interest. "You plan to put all that in the magazine article?"

Rinsho shot a finger gun at Phoebe.

"I'm not sure," she said. "But we want enough detail that our readers can see what makes Mozo different. Tell me—how are your cars performing? What do your customers tell you? Or what do your diagnostics show?"

"We do not yet have enough data yet to do a significant analysis," Ram said. "But we are very confident of our technology. You'll be seeing great things from us."

"Will we be able to photograph a prototype? That would

be fantastic."

"I'm afraid that is proprietary information," Ram Kumar said. "Perhaps we could make available a design drawing. I'll check with our legal department."

Shortly after that, they said goodbye and hung up. Phoebe turned to Chase.

"He'll hear from legal all right," Chase said, sounding furious.

Rinsho nodded. "There's no question that's our technology they're using."

"Is it possible that they developed the same technology on their own?" Dave asked. "Before you or at the same time as you?"

"No," Chase said. "Everybody knows what other companies are doing. We build and test prototypes. Results are published. Patent applications are filed. Articles get written. We put out proposals to attract investors. We even hire each other's people. If they were developing technology similar to ours, we'd know about it."

"The idea that the prototypes are proprietary is most suspicious," Sanjay said. "I believe that they cannot show anything because they have yet to build something. They only recently obtained the specifications, did they not? That car that Mr. Kumar was just now so hasty to brag about—so far, it is nothing but an illustration on a drawing board."

"Sanjay's right," Rinsho said. "What do we do to stop them from going forward? And can they face any penalties?"

"You'll have to speak to your lawyers about that," Dave said. "Maybe you could sue."

"Suing them would take years and cost more than I want to pay," Chase said. "That is, if it's even possible to sue a company halfway across the world."

"But of course, there *could* be repercussions, no matter what your lawyer says," Phoebe said.

All the men stared at her.

"What? Just saying." She waved her hand in Chase's direction. "You're an internationally recognized sports star. You could find a way to make them suffer."

"*Former* sports star," Chase said.

"Interesting idea," Rinsho said.

"No, it isn't." Dave closed his eyes. "I'll never be able to go fishing," he said to no one in particular. "I'll be in jail. Swear to God."

"I have been thinking," Sanjay said. "An idea has occurred to me. It does not involve, I am sorry to say, punishment. But in the immediate future, for the cessation of the thievery, I believe it might work."

Everyone looked up.

"I'm all for ideas," Chase said. "We could use a couple right about now. Shoot."

"Well, I could call my mother."

"Your *mother*," Chase said after a painful pause.

Phoebe didn't blame him. She felt confused herself.

"Your *mother*?" Rinsho asked.

"What does your mother have to do with it?" Dave asked.

"Better explain it to us," Phoebe said.

Sanjay nodded. "I was thinking that perhaps we could be examining this problem from another angle," he said. "We have been thinking, Cliff is stealing data and selling it to Mozo Motors. Therefore, how can we stop Cliff? And tonight we are thinking, Mozo is buying data, so how can we stop Mozo? But maybe we could be thinking, how can we stop Pavel Rao? If we are assuming that it is he who is brokering the data sale from Mr. Frizell to Mozo Motors."

"I'd say that's a sound assumption," Dave said.

"I'm not seeing how we can stop Pavel Rao," Chase said. "He's a government official. How do we get any leverage there?"

Sanjay nodded. "That is where the mothers come in."

"There's more than one mother now?" Dave asked.

"I don't care how many mothers there are if we can end the theft by stopping Pavel Rao," Chase said. "That's the only piece of the puzzle we haven't considered."

"I can see why," Phoebe said. "Nobody would ever call *my* mother to fix something."

"Your mother is a piece of work," Chase agreed.

Sanjay looked pained. "I believe it would be most clarifying if I started at the beginning."

"Please do," Phoebe said. "How can your mother stop Pavel Rao? That's the question."

"Like this. My mother and the mother of Pavel Rao, my Auntie Lupa, speak on the telephone every week. My Auntie Lupa is the sister to my mother's brother's second wife, so it is a distant connection, and moreover, my mother dislikes Auntie Lupa intensely, but speak they must because that is the way of my family."

"Family first, thick or thin," Chase said. "I get that."

"Yes. The two of them are very competitive. Always comparing their purchases, their investment decisions, their children. My mother frequently makes polite requests of me that I cannot possibly turn down so that she can demonstrate to Auntie Lupa that I am an exemplary son."

"Like giving free rides to Pavel," Phoebe said.

"Yes, that is a prime example. And that behavior goes in reverse also."

"Like how?" Dave asked.

Phoebe grinned. "I see a glimmer."

"If I were to reveal to my mother that Pavel has been acting in an, shall we say, unsavory manner while he is here in Las Vegas, she would be delighted to suggest to Auntie Lupa that *her* son is not the exemplary son that she pretends he is. Auntie Lupa would deny this, of course, but she would make inquiries to Pavel, who most certainly would take steps to demonstrate that he is every bit as exemplary as Auntie Lupa always says he is."

"I'm still not following how this helps us," Dave said.

"I am not surprised," Sanjay said. "My family's connections are as tangled as a New Delhi roundabout in rush hour traffic."

"Take us step by step," Chase said.

Sanjay nodded. "I will tell my mother that Pavel is paying baksheesh to Mr. Frizell for proprietary data about Venture Automotive's manufacturing methods."

"Baksheesh," Dave said.

"The illegal exchange of cash or services for the rendering of services that should not be bartered." Sanjay shook his head. "A person gives baksheesh to get something from someone. And he accepts baksheesh when someone wants something from him."

"Bribes," Dave said.

"Yes," Sanjay said. "Corruption. Naturally, he is not the only government minister to engage in such payments, but doing so is officially frowned upon and can result in dismissal from the service, depending on the scale of the transgression. Most leaders will look the other way with infrequent or small transactions. It is when the situation becomes too big to ignore that action is taken."

"And this baksheesh business—it carries a social stigma?" Rinsho asked.

"Oh yes," Sanjay said. "If it is done in a big way. Losing one's position through corruption is almost always trumpeted in the newspapers, and the scandal causes much shame to the families. So to make sure that scandal does not fall upon him, Pavel would sever his connection to Mr. Frizell, who would then lose the incentive to steal data from you."

"Pardon my saying so, but that seems rather, ah, convoluted," Rinsho asked. "Would it work?"

"Yes," Sanjay said. "Because of the bicycle factory and the baksheesh that my father's cousin's second son continuously pays Pavel, we already know for a fact that he is not the exemplary son Auntie Lupa thinks he is. And my mother says many more examples abound. That's where the scale of the corruption comes into the picture. Pavel would find it impossible to deny or defend such practices, were he to be questioned about them."

"What bicycle factory?" Dave asked.

Sanjay told them about the bicycle factory and the baksheesh that Pavel demanded.

"So your mother would be willing to talk to Auntie Lupa?" Phoebe asked.

Sanjay shrugged. "Amma would be not so much *willing*

to talk to Auntie Lupa as *eager*."

"So what will you say exactly?" Phoebe asked.

Sanjay smiled. "I will be telling Amma that Venture Automotive is experiencing data theft and that Chase is knowing that Mr. Frizell is behind it and also that Mr. Frizell and Pavel are good friends. Is it possible that such a thing could be coincidence, I shall say. But my mother will know, as anyone would, that this friendship cannot be a coincidence. And so my mother will tell these facts to my Auntie Lupa and ask, what light can Pavel throw on this situation? My mother will say that Pavel is of course utterly blameless, but nonetheless the Venture Automotive CEO plans to take drastic action. Something along those lines."

"That's *diabolical*." Phoebe grinned. "I *love* that."

"Let me get this straight," Dave said. "Sanjay will tell his mother, who will tell Pavel Rao's mother, that we know Cliff is selling data to Pavel. And then Pavel's mother will pressure Pavel to stop."

"In a nutshell," Sanjay said. "Additionally, that Chase will ruin Pavel's life if he does not."

"How will I do that?" Chase asked, looking interested.

"I will remind my mother that you are a titan of industry with many friends high in government, much more highly placed than the friends Pavel can command—"

"Wait," Phoebe said. "Chase, is that actually true?"

He shrugged. "I know a few people."

Phoebe shook her head. "Sports heroes. *Honestly*."

"What? You know the secretary of state."

"Fair enough," Phoebe said. "*Anyway*. Sanjay, go on."

"I will tell my mother in the *strictest* confidence that Chase is so angry about the data theft and the danger that Mr. Frizell and Pavel pose to his company and the American automobile industry in general that, to keep Pavel out of the way, he plans to make sure that Pavel and his wife and his wife's mother and his other daughter do not get visas for the first daughter's upcoming wedding. Which I know because I am a close friend of Chase Bonaventure, and I frequently go to his house and in fact am privy to many of his business secrets. Which is, of course, not true, but my mother and especially Auntie Lupa have no need to know this."

"It's mostly true, though," Chase said.

"Could you actually do that?" Rinsho asked Chase. "Could you stop those people from getting visas?"

"Almost certainly not," Chase said. "Phoebe probably could, though."

"Yeah, I probably could," Phoebe agreed.

Sanjay nodded. "I thought so. And this would be a crushing blow to Pavel's family as well as a deep embarrassment. Pavel's daughter is a doctor now, very up-and-coming, and she is planning to marry a fellow doctor specialist in the fall. Auntie Lupa already has her grandmother-of-the-bride sari purchased—a lustrous red silk with gold thread, my mother says."

"Sounds pretty. I loved the saris I saw at that reception party a few weeks ago. Such beautiful colors."

"The wedding will be a very grand and expensive affair," Sanjay said. "And when my mother reports to Auntie Lupa that Chase is pulling Pavel's family's visas for it, my Auntie Lupa will report this to Pavel. Pavel would believe these repercussions because he knows that I am friends with you. He has seen us together. So he would believe that I am reporting truthfully. And the idea of not being able to go his daughter's wedding and thereby incurring the wrath of his mother, my Auntie Lupa? As well as his wife, two daughters, and mother-in-law? Pavel would no more do this thing than eat beef on a holy day. And I have just now had another thought."

"What's that?" Chase asked. "You're on a roll here, Sanjay. Don't hold back now."

"I could mention to my mother that Phoebe, as a highly placed officer in the CIA, could put Pavel on an international no-fly list. He does travel a great deal, going to conferences such as this one. If he could not fly, his extracurricular finances would face a serious deficit."

"Would your mother believe you?" Phoebe asked.

"She would be delighted to believe me, but it doesn't

matter if she believes me. The issue here is whether she would tell my Auntie Lupa, which she absolutely would. And then my Auntie Lupa would repeat it, with embellishments, to her son Pavel, who would then, I am sure, panic."

"And clinch his determination to cut off Cliff," Chase said.

"Yes. I see no other route open to him in the matter of Venture Automotive. Let us consider his options. He has plenty of avenues for gaining illegal financial boons. He does not need Cliff Frizell for that. No. In fact, if he still wants data from an electric-car company, he can simply go elsewhere, away from the two of you who have the potential to ruin his life."

There was a stunned silence.

"That's brilliant, Sanjay," Phoebe said. "I vote we let Sanjay's mother do her worst and cut Pavel—and Cliff—off at the knees."

"By all means," Chase said. "Sanjay, go for it, please. When do you next speak with your mother?"

"Thursday next," Sanjay said. "Perhaps sooner, since this is an emergency."

Chase nodded. "From my point of view, tomorrow is not too soon."

"Consider it done."

"Just one problem," Rinsho said. "Back to Mozo. According to this Ram Kumar, they've already got one of our models on their drawing board. How can we stop them from using the data they already have?"

"Good question," Dave said.

"No worries on that front," Sanjay said. "Pavel will take care of that for us, because he will fear what Chase and Phoebe can do to him. So he himself will cut off Mozo."

"Say again," Dave said. "Why does that happen?"

"Do not forget that Pavel is baksheeshing all over India. To operate, Mozo still needs favors from Pavel. If he tells Mozo not to use what they have on pain of never getting an export license or passing other regulatory hurdles, they will erase that data faster than a comet travels in the night sky."

"I have underestimated the power of informal net-works," Rinsho said.

"Thank you, Sanjay." Phoebe beamed. "You're genius."

"I am most happy to help. Also to thrust a spoke in my Auntie Lupa's wheel."

Dave shook his head. "Okay, then it's settled. Sanjay will call his mother, and all our problems will be solved. This is the weirdest security setup I've ever seen, but if it works, I have no complaints. I just got one thing to say."

"What's that?" Phoebe asked.

"My job with the cops would have been a lot simpler if we'd hired Sanjay's mother."

The meeting broke up. Chase waited in his car for Phoebe and watched Rinsho drive off to his wife and a warm meal. Next, Sanjay took off in his Vegas Fun Fare taxi. Ten minutes later, Phoebe came out of the office with Dave, pushing her bicycle. They said good night and Phoebe headed over to his car.

He got out and leaned against the car door, waiting for her. When she got close enough, he reached out and wrapped his arms around her.

Phoebe sighed and then melted into him. He couldn't believe how good that felt. Holding her like this—this felt right.

"I'm sorry we didn't connect this weekend," he said. "I missed you."

"Likewise," she said against his shoulder. "I met Tracy yesterday."

Shit. He'd called but never reached her. And between the cops and the break-in, getting the window repaired and security bars installed, meeting the insurance adjuster and fil-ing the claim, and meeting with Nick all day yesterday, he hadn't had a minute to follow up. But this didn't seem like the time to bring up how her moving in with him would give them more time together.

"How did that go?"

Phoebe broke away to lean against his shoulder, and he

put his arm around her. Talking about work like this every day could be fun as long as they wouldn't always have to talk about his ex-wife.

"Every single cheerleader signed the appearance contract, so that'll cost us a little bit more than I expected, althhough we're still within budget."

"Okay. As for you and Tracy—?"

Phoebe shrugged. "Nothing, really. I kind of liked her, although she seems obsessed about cheerleading as a career path."

"She is that."

"I understand having professional goals, so I sympathize with her. But you'd think there'd be better ways to get on TV."

"You'd think."

"And she has really nice hair," Phoebe said. "*Really* nice."

"It should be nice. She goes to an incredibly expensive hairdresser." He ran a hand through Phoebe's hair, feeling its soft weight and gentle waves in his fingers. "Do you know why I like to play with your hair?"

"Um, because you can?"

"Because it's like corn silk. Soft but strong. And it sort of sparkles when the light catches it right. When we get home, I'll show you. Tracy's hair is all extensions. All the cheerleaders depend on hair extensions."

"I don't know what those are."

"Seriously?" He pulled back, gazing at her in surprise. "It's when you glue extra strands of fake hair to your real hair. It's supposed to make your own hair look thicker."

"Really? They glue fake hair to their real hair?"

"Yes. Well, a hairdresser has to do it."

"I didn't know. Interesting."

"So you're okay? After meeting the ex?"

Phoebe glanced up in surprise. "Sure. Why wouldn't I be? For one thing, she wanted you, so I can't fault her taste in men. I can't say she and I would ever be best friends, but... I don't know. I sort of *get* her."

"Good to know." He still toyed with her hair, feeling it ripple soft and fluid against his hand, and then reached down to kiss her, her lips warm and soft against his. *Tracy and Phoebe*. He almost laughed. He knew other women whose self-esteem hadn't survived fully intact after a meeting with the Rattlesnake cheerleaders. Phoebe seemed to have come through it completely unfazed.

He relaxed into her and she nipped his bottom lip, the jolt sending a surge of heat everywhere. He'd really meant for the kiss to be just a *hey, glad to see you, I missed you, I'm so sorry, it won't happen again* kind of welcome, but Phoebe always grabbed the gusto. Who was he kidding? They combusted. Forget heat. They created fire all the way.

He boosted her onto the hood of his car while Phoebe grappled with his shirt. She was wearing those ridiculous bike shorts, and getting her out of them would be something of a challenge. However, the back seat was down, and he had some nice cushions back there. They could—

Then Phoebe eased away, her hands fisted in his shirt, holding him close, her forehead resting against his chest. She was breathing too quickly, he was pleased to see. Of course, he was, too. He bent to kiss her cheek, her hair, whatever he could reach, and gently tucked some stray tendrils of hair behind her ear.

"Is anything wrong?"

Phoebe shook her head, her hair gaining static as she rubbed it against his shirt. In the dry evening air, it floated around her head like a nimbus.

"I don't want anybody to report us for indecent exposure, or whatever," she said. "And I'm thinking we could spend some quality time together at home, right? If I got something to eat first. I missed dinner, and I'm really hungry."

Chase took a deep breath, trying to get his head back in the game. Quality time, *right*. And *home*. Whose home did she mean? He was having trouble staying on top of the conversation. And she'd said she was hungry. First things first.

"I've got food at my place. But also my family. You

want to stop somewhere?" He didn't want to push too hard, too fast, but he wanted her to think that his place was the norm, even if his family was there. Her place was too small, and her mother lived there, too. He didn't relish Brenda hanging around as a roommate or chaperone.

"I feel inundated by relatives," she said. "And relatives of relatives."

"Let's go to the diner," Chase decided. "And then my place. Everyone will be in bed by the time we get there. You won't have to deal with them." He hoped.

"I bought a new outfit yesterday to leave at your place," Phoebe said. "But it's at my place, and Mom's off tonight, so she and Uncle Boo-Boo will be at my apartment now."

Chase tilted his head back and laughed. "What are we doin' here, *cher*? Between us, we've got ourselves two domiciles, sixteen bedrooms, and a football field's worth of square footage, but when it comes to having some alone time, we have more logistical problems than a buzzard in a bounce house."

Phoebe grinned. "That doesn't even make sense. No self-respecting buzzard gets within a hundred miles of a bounce house. Or wants to. I fear you might be losing your grip."

He laughed as he popped the rear door and lifted her bicycle into the storage space. "One thing I'm wondering. If your mom's dating Uncle Boo-Boo, why don't they ever go to *his* place? *Any* place has to be bigger than your place."

Phoebe grinned. "You'll enjoy this. He said he's got too much family living with him."

Chapter 15

The next morning, Phoebe hitched a ride with Chase to her office. When he stopped at the front door of Western Private Investigations, she pulled her bike from the SUV's cargo area and wheeled it over to the driver-side window.

"You could get a bike rack for this thing." She leaned in to kiss him goodbye. He smelled terrific—sort of a subtle sandalwood. His nine, soon-to-be-seventeen, bathrooms had some incredible toiletries. His pheromones were off the charts. She nearly swooned.

"Or you could get a driver's license." He pulled her in and kissed her back.

"I'm *working* on it," she said, coming up for air, "which is more than you can say about a bike rack."

He tugged her closer, breathing into her ear. "I'm never getting a bike rack. How would that look? The CEO of a car company with a bike rack. Totally the wrong message."

"It's an *electric*-car company." Phoebe pulled away to scowl at him, knowing how lame she sounded. "Everybody knows that's good for the environment. Like bicycles. You're into saving energy."

"Yeah, except I know how to spend energy when I want to." He raised his eyebrows at her.

Phoebe rolled her eyes, but she grinned and put a little extra swing to her hips as she pushed her bike toward the office. That'd give him something to think about besides her dumb driver's license.

Dave was inside waiting for her. "Park that thing some-place and let's go," he said. "We're going downtown to buy some camera equipment. You're driving."

After a harrowing trip to the store, Phoebe got them out to the factory without smashing into anything.

"That was easy," she said, wiping her sweaty palms on her jeans.

Dave snorted, but she just grabbed the badge printer and laptop and headed inside. Kristin was in the lobby, supervis-ing the badge-installation firm, and she helped them lug eve-rything upstairs to the conference room.

"We'll set up over here, use the blank wall for a back-drop," Dave said, checking out the facilities.

They pushed the conference table to the side and rear-ranged the chairs. Phoebe set up the camera the way he told her.

He squinted into it. "This'll work."

"I sent you all the names," Kristin said. "We assigned everybody an employee number with a job description and permissions, like you told us to. Holler when you're ready, and we'll start the ball rolling."

"Thanks, Kristin. Give us about ten," Dave said. "Phoebe, sit in the chair for a minute. Got to get the lighting right."

Kristin took off and Phoebe sat in the chair while Dave fiddled with the portable lights, reflective umbrellas, and camera. When she heard someone at the door, she whirled around to see Cliff Frizell.

"I wondered what was going on." He frowned. "This the photoshoot?"

Phoebe jumped up. "Cliff! You're our first customer?"

"Have a seat," Dave said. "We need another minute."

Cliff didn't move. "I don't see why we have to do this. Get the badges and all that. It seems unnecessary."

Phoebe shrugged. She wasn't about to say that company data had been stolen, not if Chase hadn't already done so. Especially since they all thought Cliff had done it.

"All I know is that the banks and investors have asked for more security controls," she said. "You'll have to talk to the bosses about specifics."

"I don't like having my picture taken."

Dave straightened from where he'd been setting up the badge printer and gazed at the former football player. Always relaxed in the office, now he was a cop on full alert. His body was perfectly still, his face expressionless, his dark eyes unblinking. Phoebe almost shivered.

She'd met Dave when she tracked down the terrorists who'd threatened to kidnap the secretary of state, and she'd liked him. She'd seen him determined and exasperated—even ruthless—but never really threatening. Still, he'd been a cop for twenty-five years, and he must have seen some heavy stuff. Right now he was evaluating Cliff, looking at him like an eagle would look at a mouse, as if he were wondering if crushing him in his talons and eating him for lunch would be worth his time.

"The photo isn't going public," Dave said, his voice mild. "It's for internal use only."

"I'm in R&D! I should be able to go anywhere I need to go in this building."

"Your boss feels differently. Should I tell him that you're refusing to have your ID made?" Dave's voice was quiet, but the threat was implied. She was going to practice that tone of voice. Because crap! Cliff was sitting down, and they weren't even the boss of him.

"No, of course not. I'm not *refusing*." Cliff settled into the chair. "I simply don't see why we have to do it. One thing I liked about the place is how informal it was. That's all over now. Bonaventure made sure of that."

"Hold, please." Dave touched a button on the camera, catching Cliff in a pose with his mouth open and scowling.

That'll show him, Phoebe thought.

"We're just bringing corporate security up to standard," she said, trying to sound soothing. "All the high-tech companies have badge readers to improve security and simplify operations."

"That's crap!" Cliff said. "Hell, even *you* know—"

"Phoebe, let me show you how this works."

Phoebe read a warning in Dave's eye, so with a strong sense of resolve, she ignored Cliff and sat down at the laptop. Following Dave's directions, she pasted in Cliff's name and ID number, assigned the security clearance, and pressed another button to save the changes.

"The badge prints over here, we laminate it like this, attach the clip and lanyard, and"—Dave handed the badge to Cliff—"you're good to go. Those guys downstairs are installing the badge readers now, so by the end of the day tomorrow, you'll need to swipe your badge to pass from one part of the building to another."

Cliff took the badge and stared at it. "Shit," he said and left the room.

"Fun guy," Dave said. "Word of advice—when you've got somebody belligerent like that, don't engage. Or don't engage more than you must to get the job done, because when you start with an angry guy, it doesn't take much to set him off."

"Noted. I liked how you got him to sit down. That glare! I want to be able to do that."

Dave grinned. "That look comes naturally to cops. I think it's mostly heartburn. Ah, here's our next customer."

A tall, middle-aged woman with wavy, red-gold hair stood uncertainly in the door. "I'm Margo Bollingbrook," she said to Dave. "Are you ready for me?"

"Hi, Margo. You're just in time." Phoebe patted the chair and checked off the name. "Sit right here. This won't hurt a bit."

Cliff left the conference room, the photo ID badge burning like a hot coal in his palm. Who did Chase Fucking Bonaventure think he was? He was still lording it over everybody else, the way he used to on the football field. Photo IDs. *Simplify operations*, my ass. *Improve security*, bullshit. He was R&D! He should be able to go wherever he wanted to in this damn company. It was only right. He'd played second fiddle to Bonaventure for ten years on the football field. The ass-hole *owed* him.

He had to tell Pavel about these developments. The data he'd stolen Friday night during his break-in was incomplete. Well, he hadn't had enough time, had he? Pavel had bitched about that, so he'd promised that he'd get the rest of the data this week. But how could he if his badge wouldn't let him into those areas? Pavel had told him to call only when something was urgent. This was urgent.

"Cliff," Pavel said when he picked up. "Do you have more data for us?"

"No, but it's an emergency. There's a security company here right now—two security companies, in fact. We're getting photo ID badges with readers on every department door. After tomorrow I won't have access to all the departments."

"ID badges," Pavel said. "You think this is an emergency?"

"They're limiting what data I have access to." *Duh.* That much should be obvious.

"Do you know why these ID protocols are being established at this time? Do they suspect you of anything?"

"They said that the venture capitalists and bankers want more security now that Bonaventure is hiring so many people to expand."

"That's probably true," Pavel said. "They have to protect their investment. They wouldn't want to be victims of corporate espionage!" He chuckled at his own joke.

Cliff felt a wave of irritation. He was the one taking all the risk, and Pavel wanted to laugh about it? Cliff didn't know what the laws were about corporate data theft, but if anybody got jail time, it would be he, not Pavel. Pavel could afford to laugh. Himself, not so much.

"So what do you want me to do?"

"If the IDs are activated tomorrow, then you have not much time," Pavel said. "You must find a way to finish those downloads."

Cliff thought about it. He was as smart as Bonaventure, for sure. Pavel was right to trust him. "I'll get it. I'll have something for you soon."

"Try for battery technology," Pavel said. "They'd really like to know more about the battery technology."

Cliff knew that he'd have to steal that data tonight. By tomorrow it would be too late. And he'd have to stay inside the building after his shift ended, because now he knew from brutal experience that if he broke in, the siren would sound and the cops would come before he could get a full download. If he wanted to see any payment—and put the screws to Bonaventure at the same time—he'd have to find a way to get that data.

The rewards were too great not to.

Chase spent a long day reviewing budgets and projections. The company was growing so fast that soon he'd have to hire more management, and the first person he wanted was somebody to do the financials. He'd rather be working on the big picture than sweating the spreadsheets.

He'd think about that tonight when he got home. Unless Phoebe distracted him.

Of course, his family was there, and they'd be distracting, too. He enjoyed having them, though. He'd missed his parents and siblings, all of whom lived in or near New Orleans, and envied their closeness. He'd resisted joining the family business—the only son not to—and first the Snakes and now Venture Automotive kept him away from Louisiana. Having everybody under one roof periodically helped to cement the bonds.

He took out the can of cashews he kept in his bottom drawer, scooped out a handful, and took them to the window overlooking the shop floor. He ate the nuts, Phoebe's favorite, while he gazed down onto the production area, dark now that it was early evening, the robots motionless. Dave had said that the new ID badges and badge readers would be operational by tomorrow, and not a minute too soon. He felt a constant, simmering fury about Cliff and the data theft he'd engineered. *Probably* engineered.

The light was on in one of the offices that took up one

wall of the shop floor. No reason why somebody shouldn't be down there doing something—working late, like he was—but he had to check it out. They had to be careful about every way that data could leak out of the company.

He ran down the mezzanine steps to the lobby, turned right, went through the door with its as-yet-unconnected badge reader, and entered the production area. Down here he could hear something, too—a quiet, repetitive hum. He approached the office as quietly as he could.

Aquintis Jones, the ex-con new employee, was looking into a laptop screen and making photocopies, and he leaped a mile, closing the computer, when he saw Chase. What the hell was a production worker doing in an office using a computer and making photocopies? Not that he intended to accuse him of anything until he found out.

"Hey, sorry," he said. "Didn't mean to sneak up on you, but I saw the light on and wanted to check it out."

"I'll pay you for the copies," Aquintis said, jumping up and shuffling the paper into a neat stack.

Chase shrugged. "Not necessary. What are you working on?"

Aquintis stiffened, looking defensive. *Damn it to hell.* He didn't want to find out the guy was stealing. But if he was—

"I was using the CAD system."

"You know how to use the CAD system?" That software was complicated. Where had a guy who'd spent however many years in the joint learned CAD?

"I was in a computer program," Aquintis said. "When I was inside. I got a certificate."

Chase blinked. He didn't know the prison system had such sophisticated education programs. "You did? Shit, man, you're wasted on the line. So what are you working on?"

"I talked to Rinsho about it, like you said."

"It's okay, Aquintis. If it's too personal, you don't have to tell me. I'm just curious."

"Nah, I'm just— My little girl—well, she ain't so little anymore, you know? I hardly seen her growing up. I can't make up for all that lost time. But I want to step up my game where I can."

"So you're helping your daughter?"

"She's in the school play. Only a freshman in high school, but she got a part in the play. I told her I could help with the sets. They're doing something with castles and shit."

Chase grinned. "Set design. I like that. Will you show me?"

Aquintis opened the laptop and brought up the drawings. "This is what I got so far. I'm not sure how I'm going to do this bit for a drawbridge. But I'm working on it."

"Looks good to me. You know, we have a fund set up for employees who do volunteer work. Ask HR for the form. The money isn't a lot, but it'll help cover the cost of materials. In case you want to go hog wild and, I don't know, import a drawbridge from England or something."

Aquintis laughed. "Yeah, I'm not doin' that. But I'll talk to the lady in HR. Thanks, Coach."

Chase said good night and headed down to talk to Delmar Oates, who'd be guarding the finished cars at the other end of the enormous building. Had he seen or heard Aquintis working? They'd need to hire more security guards if Delmar was unaware that someone was on the floor.

But a few steps later, he heard the faint sound of something crashing.

Aquintis poked his head out of the office. "What was that? I thought I was alone down here."

"I'll check. Something might be broken." *Or a vandal might be hiding out in here someplace.*

"I'll come with you." Aquintis said. "I'm ready to go, anyway."

They headed for the electrical engineering area where they'd heard the crash, flipping on the overhead lights as they walked. The noise had sounded like the wind catching one of the old, loose windows or vents, but everything they checked was intact. When they got to the electrical engineering department, Cliff Frizell was leaning out an open window.

"Cliff?" Chase said. "What's going on? What are you

doing here?"

"I thought I heard something," Cliff said, turning back into the room. "I came in here and the window was open, but I don't see anyone out there. Maybe it was just the wind."

And didn't that sound like a lie. But you never knew. Maybe. Chase walked over to the window and peered out into the dusk, looking for—well, probably nothing. What had Cliff been doing in the electrical engineering department? His work was in R&D, at the other end of the building. When the badge readers were installed, he wouldn't be able to get over here.

"It's not that windy tonight." He shut the window and latched it.

"Maybe it was some kind of wild animal," Cliff said.

"Want me to go outside and look around, Coach?" Aquintis asked.

"Nah. Whatever it was, it's gone now. Come on. Let's get out of here."

He watched the other two men leave the building and then went to talk to Delmar Oates.

"There wasn't anybody out there," Chase said. "He lied about that."

"Nobody comes out this far except people who work here," Delmar said. "I always check the outside perimeter before I leave in the morning, and there's never anything to see except sometimes the paw prints of a critter."

"Did those guys let you know they'd be working?

"The Black guy did. He checked in with me when I came on. But you know I wouldn't be able to tell if anybody was emailing data to the Russians, or whatever. If somebody tries to cart out a laptop or damage a car, that's what I can stop."

Chase grinned. "Nobody's emailing data to the Russians—that's the good news. And we're working on a plan that should stop any more data thefts."

"You think it's one of those two guys?"

"We think it's Cliff Frizell."

"That waste of bench space? Can't you fire him?"

"I can, but I'd like to get enough on him that he could be charged with a crime. Dave is staying on top of that. But yeah. If we can't catch Frizell doing whatever he's doing in the next couple of days or so, he's gone."

"If he's your guy, that'd make everything simpler."

"It sure would," Chase said. "Because even if he doesn't get our data, he could damage us in other ways. And I won't let that happen."

Chapter 16

The badge reader installation was complete by Wednesday, so Phoebe rode her bike over to the Drive Well Driving School for her first driving lesson. She filled out some paperwork, and then the manager introduced her to Brandon, her teacher. Her very young teacher.

But she was here to learn, and presumably Brandon had his license, so Phoebe got into the car, adjusted her seat, and buckled her seat belt. She realigned the rear and side windows. She checked for her lights and blinkers.

"Ready," she said.

Brandon glanced over from his phone, from which he'd been texting. "Start the engine."

She started the motor. "Now what?"

"Head down the street."

Mr. Talkative he wasn't.

"Is there anything you want to tell me before we get started?" Phoebe looked over her shoulder, put on her turn signal, and pulled carefully away from the curb.

"Like what?" Brandon's thumbs flew so quickly over the phone keypad they were practically a blur. The CIA could probably use that skill somehow.

"Like anything," Phoebe said. "Like how to drive a car."

"You're driving a car." Brandon glanced out the window. "Just go a little faster. Turn left at the next corner."

Left. She didn't much care for left. Left was turning in

front of oncoming traffic.

"How about right?"

"We can go right first," Brandon agreed. "But you might as well get used to it. You have to turn left for the test."

Yes, she did.

Phoebe took a deep breath, trying to calm her rapid heartbeat. Was she a woman, or was she a wuss? Was she an up-and-coming private detective with three months of CIA experience who'd brought down a ring of conspirators that wanted to kidnap the secretary of state? Or was she a timid loser who couldn't learn a basic life skill that would enhance her daily existence and let her join the ranks of millions of people who already commuted to work on the strength of a state-issued photo ID?

She would turn left at the corner.

"I'm going left."

"Okay." Brandon didn't even glace up.

She was at the corner. The light was green. She had her turn signal on. The cars whizzed past.

Brandon looked up. "Now."

Phoebe yanked the wheel left and stomped on the gas. The car screeched around the corner. She didn't hit anything! Nobody hit her! They were safe!

But then the car kept going left in a circle, right into the oncoming traffic.

"Turn back," Brandon said.

Turn back?

"Let the wheel go," Brandon said more urgently.

Let the wheel go.

"*Turn the wheel back to the right,*" Brandon said again, louder this time.

Right. Turn back before she crashed into traffic.

Phoebe turned the wheel back, straightened out the car, and scowled at the driver of the oncoming car, who'd flipped her off. What did he expect? The giant STUDENT DRIVER sign anchored on the top of the car should have been a tipoff. He could cut her some slack.

"Okay," Brandon said, lapsing back into his phone.

"That was good. Stay on this road for a while."

"What happened back there?" Phoebe demanded, her heart pounding, her hands slick with sweat, her armpits damp.

"You did fine," Brandon said. "You didn't hit anything."

"I almost did, though."

"Almost doesn't count."

"But *technique*. What did I do?"

"You forgot to release the wheel," Brandon said. "Next time? Remember."

Phoebe rolled her eyes.

"Really, you were fine," Brandon said. "I've seen a lot worse. From licensed drivers."

Phoebe drove down the street. The weather was beautiful, with a soft, early-morning sun beaming down from a cloudless deep blue sky. Weirdly shaped cacti dominated retail landscaping, and occasional pots of annual flowers brightened doorways. At a red light she powered open the windows and turned down the air-conditioning.

She was getting the hang of this! She was *driving*!

A wasp flew in through the open window.

"A wasp!" she said. "Can you get it out?"

"Leave it alone," Brandon said. "It won't bother you."

"It's a *wasp*. Bothering people is what they *do*."

The wasp hovered near the edge of the windshield, smacking against the glass in its futile effort to escape, diving sometimes perilously close to Phoebe's head.

"Don't you have something to push it out of the car?" Phoebe said. "An old newspaper? Anything?"

"Newspaper?"

Kids today.

Phoebe swept her arm gently through the air, trying not to threaten the wasp, just push it toward the open window. It buzzed furiously around her arm.

"Crap," Phoebe said, ducking away from the attacking wasp.

"You got the green."

Phoebe looked up and saw that the light was, indeed,

green. The car behind her honked.

"Shut up," Phoebe said, and then to Brandon, "Not you. Sorry."

The wasp bombed her head, and for a nasty moment, Phoebe thought it would get caught in her hair. She shook her head, trying to become an unattractive landing spot for a wasp.

"I have to pull over and get this thing out of the car," she said, realizing that the next block was solidly parked with cars.

"Okay. Next block, pull into the driveway for that hamburger place. Don't forget to signal."

But before she got there, the wasp dived for her face. Phoebe yelped and, too late, ducked. The wasp stung her on her cheek, and Phoebe involuntarily yanked on the steering wheel.

The Drive Well Driving School car plowed into a parked Mercedes with a sickening crunch as metal scraped on metal. Phoebe and Brandon were thrown against their seat belts. Brakes screeched around them as other drivers tried to avoid them. Except for the clink of glass when broken bits fell to the pavement, the sudden silence was startling in its completeness.

The wasp flew out the window.

Brandon picked up his phone from where it had fallen on the floor. "You hurt?"

"I don't think so," Phoebe said, her mouth dry. Her insides felt all trembly, like unsupported Jell-O. "You?"

"Nah," Brandon said. "Happens all the time."

"I can't believe I did that."

Brandon shrugged, pressing a number on his phone. "Not all your fault. You got stung by a bee. But then you want to try not to hit anything. If you can."

Phoebe scowled at the rearview mirror, the mirror she'd adjusted so carefully just minutes before. Lot of good that had done. You adjust the rearview mirror, and you hit something looking forward. Pointless.

Now that they were blocking the street, people were

getting out of their cars, trying to tell the drivers behind them to back up so they could get back to the main thoroughfare. One aggressive driver gunned his motor and bounced over the curb, driving around them on the sidewalk, scattering pedestrians.

That couldn't be the right response.

And now her cheek was throbbing.

She needed to get out of the car. She opened the door, metal screeching as the crumpled hood partially blocked the doorframe, and climbed out on shaky legs. She surveyed the damage. The red convertible that had been following them had not rear-ended them, but the car following the convertible—a white Lexus SUV—had smashed into the convertible. Both the convertible and the Lexus would need bodywork.

She dug out her phone and called Chase.

"*Cher!*" he said when he picked up. "What a nice surprise. What's up?"

"Don't laugh," Phoebe said. "I'm out driving, and I was in an accident. I hit a car." Suddenly her legs wouldn't hold her anymore, and she sank to the curb. *She'd hit a car.*

"I'm not laughing," Chase said. "Are you hurt? Where are you?"

"I'm okay, except I got stung by a wasp," Phoebe said, her outrage taking over. "Dumb thing flew in the window and *stung* me! And I jerked on the wheel and hit a parked car. A Mercedes. We're blocking traffic at the corner of Hacienda and Edmond, waiting for the cops. Brandon—that's my teacher—is calling someone."

"Do you need an ambulance? Are you allergic to stings? Is anything broken?"

"I feel a little shaky, but I'm fine. Two cars behind us are damaged. So there's that, but those drivers don't seem hurt, either." Phoebe glanced over at the other cars. "They're talking to each other."

Brandon got out of the car and leaned against the trunk of the Drive Well vehicle.

"I gotta go," she said. "Brandon's here; I think there are

developments. I'll call you later." She disconnected and turned to Brandon.

"Cops'll be here soon," he said. "Insurance adjusters, too. A tow truck. And another Drive Well car."

"A Drive Well car? You want me to keep driving?"

"If you want to." Brandon shrugged. "Or else to get back to the office."

"Oh, right, good point." Phoebe glanced at the driver of the convertible talking to the Lexus SUV driver, both of whom looked exasperated. "I'm going over there to talk to those people for a minute before the cops come. Make sure everybody's all right."

He shrugged, taking out his phone. "Just don't say you're in the wrong."

"Right, because that parked Mercedes jumped into the road and hit me."

"You were stung by a bee. I think that's a medical emergency. Or something."

"It was a *wasp*."

Phoebe strolled over to where the other two drivers were exchanging information.

"Hi," she said. "Listen, I'm sorry for the mess." She waved her hand at the damaged cars.

"This is your fault," the convertible driver said, his voice aggressive.

Phoebe bit her lip. "A wasp got in and stung me on my face," she said. "I jumped."

"You shouldn't—" he started. And then he looked at her face. "Oh."

"The reason I came over here," she said. "I saw that your cars got damaged. If your insurance won't give you a loaner, Venture Automotive sometimes gives cars to people so they can collect data from actual driving conditions. They might help you out."

"Oh, I'd love to test-drive one of those cars," the Lexus driver, a young woman, said. "I mean, *Chase Bonaventure*. What I wouldn't do to get in *that* guy's car. Am I right?" She raised her eyebrows and grinned at Phoebe conspiratorially.

Phoebe's eyes narrowed. "He's really too tall for that kind of thing. Venture's cars aren't built for guys that size. Not yet, anyway."

The woman shook her head in disbelief, her blond curls bouncing. "I *meant*, test-drive *Chase Bonaventure*."

"I know what you meant."

"What kind of cars?" the belligerent convertible driver asked. "I'd want a convertible."

"Electric cars," Phoebe said. "I don't know what models they have in the program. I'm not sure they make convertibles."

"Chase Bonaventure can rev my motor anytime," the Lexus driver said.

"Electric motors don't rev," Phoebe said, who'd had a reason to learn this. "They don't go louder, just faster."

"It's an *expression*. I meant—"

"I know what you meant."

"Sounds like a hassle," the convertible driver said. "That program. Paperwork, the monitoring. Probably all kinds of liability."

"Don't call, then," Phoebe said, losing patience.

"Would I get to meet Chase Bonaventure?" the Lexus driver asked, but Phoebe stomped back to the Drive Well car and pretended not to hear. People could be so annoying.

The cops, insurance adjustors, tow truck, and Drive Well backup vehicle had not yet materialized when Phoebe saw a bright yellow SUV pull into the street a little too quickly and jerk to a stop.

A Venture Automotive vehicle.

She straightened from where she'd been leaning against the Drive Well car and started toward it as Chase emerged from the vehicle. And then she ran over and he pulled her in for a hug.

Phoebe leaned into him. He was so big and strong and warm. Brandon was calm, but not very comforting.

He rested his head against hers. "How you doin', *cher*?"

"Fine," Phoebe said, her voice muffled. "You got here awfully fast. You must have flown."

"I was home talking to Dad, so I was close."

She leaned back and looked up at him. "Listen, I should tell you, that Lexus driver over there is a big fan of yours. I mean, a really, *really* big fan. You might want to get a restraining order."

"I see her," Chase said. "But I don't need a restraining order. I've got my security person right here providing bodyguard services, so I'm safe."

"Mr. Bonaventure? Chase Bonaventure?" The Lexus driver approached.

Phoebe sighed, resting against him. "This is what I was talking about."

"Fans," he said. "At least when the season starts they'll focus on a new quarterback." He raised his voice. "Excuse me, ma'am. I need a few minutes here."

"I'm sorry to interrupt, but I wanted to say—"

He raised his head. "As soon as we get this injury taken care of."

"Of course. But as a longtime fan—"

"*In a few minutes.*"

Phoebe was surprised at the irritation in his voice. Of course, he'd been bothered by fans for more than a decade now. No wonder he got exasperated. The Lexus driver had stopped in her tracks, disappointment etched across her features. Well, tough. A wasp hadn't just stung her on the face.

Chase kissed her and leaned back. "Okay, where were we? Sorry this driving thing is being so uncooperative. Let's take a look at that cheek."

She turned her head so he could see. "It's throbbing. I know it looks bad because the convertible driver stopped arguing with me when he saw it."

"You look like a giant puffer fish, but I think we can do a little something about that." He reached into his pocket and pulled out his wallet, extracting a credit card.

"A *puffer fish*? I want you to know—"

"Don't move." He scraped the card across her cheek.

"Ow!" Phoebe yanked back. "What are you *doing*?"

"Getting the stinger out." Chase examined her face again.

"You pull it straight out, it leaves venom behind. You scrape it out at an angle, it doesn't. That's what my mama always told us when we kids got stung by wasps, and we always believed her. Don't know if it's true. Stinger's out now, anyway."

He reached into his car and pulled out a cold pack, some tablets, and a bottle of water.

"More first aid," He watched as she swallowed the pill and then handed her a cold pack. "The antihistamine should take down the swelling, but you won't be able to operate heavy machinery for a couple of hours. Driving's out for the rest of the day."

Phoebe gently laid the cold pack against her cheek. "You always travel with medical supplies? Not that I'm not grateful."

"I grabbed the first aid kit from the house. We've got construction going on over there. Comes in handy."

The cold pack was making her face feel a lot better already.

"You know, you'd recover a lot faster if we went home," Chase said. "You could sack out in the guest house, or I think nobody's working on the third floor yet. You could lie down, and I could comfort you."

Phoebe grinned, adjusting the cold pack. "Is that what they're calling it now? That Lexus driver wants you to comfort her, I know for a fact."

"Forget about her," Chase said, not looking at the Lexus driver.

Phoebe sighed. The coolness on her cheek felt good, and the heat of the car's metal fender through her clothes as she leaned against it was relaxing. Chase's arm around her felt secure. She was a little drowsy. The antihistamine must be kicking in.

"As much as I'd like to go home and lie down, we have to wait for the cops and a tow truck and the Drive Well car," she said. "Brandon and I, I mean."

"And as much as I'd like to take you home with me, my house is full of my dad and my siblings plus a construction crew. It's not exactly quiet over there."

A cop car pulled around the corner and parked, and the Lexus driver abandoned her scruples and approached Chase again.

"Just so you know," Phoebe said in a low voice as she straightened up to join Brandon. "The Lexus driver wants to, ah, rev your engine, she said."

Chase smiled, his eyes warm. "Just so *you* know, you're the only one who has the key to my ignition."

Dave pulled into the street right behind the cop, so Chase took off. Dave looked unhappy as he got out of his car, but then, he probably didn't like it that she'd smashed up the driving-school car on her first outing. Maybe his insurance would get dinged.

"Phoebe," he said as he approached. "You okay? Your face is pretty swollen."

Phoebe shrugged, taking off the ice pack Chase had left with her. "A wasp stung me. That's what caused this whole mess. Otherwise I'm basically fine. How did you get here so fast? I haven't even had time to call you."

"Police scanner. When I heard that there was an accident involving a parked car and a driving-school vehicle, I thought it had to be you."

That seemed a little harsh.

"It was a *wasp*. I wouldn't have crashed otherwise."

"At least you're not hurt. Let's go talk to the cop."

They approached the uniform who was interviewing Brandon.

"LVPD detective Dave Greenaway, retired," Dave said, pulling out some kind of police identification and handing it to the young guy in uniform. "And you are?"

The young cop took the ID, his eyes widening. "Marcus Platt, sir."

"What are your observations so far, Platt?"

The young officer blinked. "Well, it appears to be reckless driving, sir."

Dave nodded. "Operating a vehicle with a willful or

wanton disregard of the safety of persons or property. Nevada law NRS 484B.653. You've got a solid understanding of the code."

"I wasn't willful or wanton!" Phoebe objected. "I was trying to get the wasp out of the car! I was doing fine until it stung me!"

"In which case, was it a gross misdemeanor, sir?" Officer Platt said. "Traffic is slowed or detoured to perform a stunt?"

"Let's ask." Dave turned to Brandon. "Was Phoebe committing a stunt when she hit the parked car?"

"No stunt," Brandon said. "She waved her arm around a bit, like she said, but the other hand was always on the wheel. Traffic wasn't slowed or detoured."

Dave nodded. "So not a gross misdemeanor then."

"The wasp flew at my face and stung me, and I jerked the wheel," Phoebe said. "Anybody would have reacted the same."

"That's true," Brandon said.

"So then maybe it wasn't willful or wanton," Dave said.

The cop looked thoughtful. "You think so, sir?"

"Let's think about it. She was in a supervised setting. Her driving instructor would have objected to any reckless driving as part of the training course."

"Right," Brandon said. "Anyway, beginning drivers aren't reckless. If anything, they're overcautious. They make mistakes sometimes, though."

Phoebe could have kissed him. Brandon to the rescue!

"So maybe it was an accident," the cop said. "Not reckless driving."

"I think I agree with you," Dave said.

"Thank you, sir." Officer Platt turned to Phoebe and Brandon. "Everyone okay here? Need an ambulance? I'll just write up the accident report and you can cite it for your insurance."

"The company would appreciate that," Brandon said.

The cop finished the paperwork, tore it off with a flourish, handed it to Dave, shook his hand, and got back in his squad car and drove away.

"Thank you, both of you," Phoebe said. "I appreciate that. Getting me off like that."

"Most cops would see an accident for what it was, but Officer Platt seems to have both ambition and inexperience," Dave said. "Is Phoebe free to go?"

"Sure." Brandon pulled his phone back out of his pocket. "I'm waiting for the tow truck and the pickup car, but she doesn't have to be here for that."

"Great," Dave said. "Phoebe, let's go back to the office, where I can explain to you how I got you out of a fine, points on a driver's license you don't even have yet, and hundreds of hours of community service if not jail time."

"Really? Jail time?"

"No, don't be ridiculous. You don't go to jail for something like that. What did I say in the beginning about no scratches? I said *no scratches*!"

"I know, and I'm sorry, Dave," Phoebe said, getting into his car. "And the good thing is, nobody got scratched!" Except for a couple of cars, which were, okay, smashed up pretty bad, but none of the people had scratches. Except for her wasp sting.

"I don't like it," Dave said, starting the motor. "I have a bad feeling, and when I have a bad feeling—"

"Don't worry." Phoebe settled back in the seat as fatigue overcame her. "The worst is behind us now. What else could possibly happen?"

Sanjay's phone dragged him out of a sound sleep on Thursday morning just before eight. He forced his eyes open at the annoying sound. From now on, after the shifts when he drove his taxicab until the wee hours of the morning, he must remember to turn off his phone's ringer when he retired for the evening. He must either remember to do this or caution Phoebe never again to call at this hour. He thought he had mentioned once that he was not a morning person. But evidently he had not been sufficiently forceful.

Or perhaps it was an emergency. The thought made him

sit up with a jerk.

But when he picked up the phone, he saw on the display that his too-early caller was his cousin Pavel. His heart sank. No doubt his lesser relation wanted yet again to go somewhere for free. Sanjay wished with all his heart he could let the call go to voice mail or tell Pavel that he was too busy, too sick, too tired, or too annoyed to pick him up and deliver him somewhere, anywhere at no cost. But there was his mother and his Auntie Lupa. So of course, he could not do this thing that he wanted.

He wondered what the result had been of the phone call he'd placed to his mother on Monday.

"Pavel," he said, connecting the call.

"I need a ride to the municipal park in fifteen minutes," Pavel said. "I am at the hotel."

"Yes, I am free, thank you for asking, always happy to be of service," Sanjay said. The ironic delivery, he knew, would be lost on Pavel. He wasn't the lesser relation for nothing.

"Don't be late." And then Pavel disconnected.

Sanjay looked at the dead phone in disbelief. How did men such as he succeed in government? Although, of course, Pavel was just an underminister. At his age, to be truly successful, he should no doubt have been a regular minister by now, or perhaps even an overminister. Sanjay wasn't quite sure about the pecking order of ministers. Especially since Pavel was abusing his position. With all the graft his lesser relation was engaging in, how could he not be elevated to overminister by now?

Perhaps he was as inefficient at grifting as he was at governing.

Sanjay pulled on a clean shirt and pair of trousers, slid his feet into his rubber flip-flops, and headed out to the garage and his taxicab. He would drop Pavel at the park—and what respectable Indian underminister wanted to go to the municipal park at eight fifteen on a Thursday morning?—and afterward he would go to his mother's food cart for a sustaining breakfast. By then he would need it, and perhaps also Amma would reveal to him the success of her phone call to Auntie Lupa.

But when Sanjay dropped Pavel at his destination, he saw that his lesser relation was meeting Cliff Frizell, who, even in his playing days, had had the arm strength of a pea-hen, if a peahen had arms. Why the Snakes had wanted to keep this poor specimen on the roster for more than a week—much less ten years—was a mystery greater than the habits of the Himalayan yeti.

But the bigger question was why Pavel wanted to meet Cliff Frizell.

Maybe the grapevine had already worked its magic.

Cliff strode toward Pavel Rao as the Indian undermin-ister got out of the taxi. Finally! That lazy shyster politician was finally here with his money. This was the moment he'd been waiting for, because not only could he stick it to that asshole Chase Bonaventure, he could get rich doing it. Some-times dreams really did come true.

Pavel shook his head, motioning for Cliff to follow him, and they stepped away from the taxi. Probably wise.

"Do you have my money?" Cliff asked, trying to curb his impatience.

"It is over," Pavel Rao said.

Cliff jerked his head in disbelief. Was this guy *kidding?* "What do you mean, *over*? I got your data! I want to be paid for it!"

Pavel shrugged. "There will be no payment. It is over. Our, ah, collaboration is over."

"But I stole data for you! Full specs to the Snap model! I risked my job! You said—"

Pavel scowled. "Anything I said from which you con-strued more than I meant was said before Mr. Bonaventure and his security team discovered that you were stealing data."

"What are you talking about? They don't know that! I was careful!"

"Not careful enough. They *do* know. And now threats

have been made against my family and my government position."

"Bonaventure *threatened* you?" This could be good! Even better than stealing from him. Once the press found out—

"Don't be ridiculous. Of course, Mr. Bonaventure has not threatened me. No. He has conducted an investigation, discovered somehow that you are the source of the data thefts, and reported his findings to, ah, various channels. And now these people are asking questions in quarters where I cannot have any questions asked."

Shit. But even if all this were true, if this Pavel Rao guy gave the data to Mozo Motors, surely they could use it. Build their own cars. Steal his thunder. Damage Bonaventure that way.

"But the data is all good! And you *said*—"

"You are not understanding the problem. The problem is that *Mr. Bonaventure knows*. He has taken steps that could ruin me. I must avert this threat. So we are finished. And now I must go."

"Wait!"

But the Indian underminister didn't wait. He walked back to the waiting taxi and got in. The driver started the engine, and the cab pulled out of the parking space into the street. Furious, Cliff watched it leave.

Shit, shit, shit. How could this Pavel Rao guy just welsh on a deal like that? A government official? These days you couldn't count on anybody.

Well, he wasn't beaten yet. He might be down, but he wasn't out. There were other ways to get what he wanted. Better ways.

And the best way would put Bonaventure and his company out of business for good.

Chapter 17

By the end of Friday when the expo's exhibit hall closed, Phoebe was more than ready to call it a day. Her feet hurt. Her back hurt. Her throat was raw from talking to visitors. She wanted nothing more than to have a hot bath and a good night's sleep.

However, the time at the expo had gone by faster than she'd thought possible. Thousands of people had come to see the beautiful red cars that the production team had rushed to complete. They'd asked questions and gotten Chase's autograph. At two o'clock the Victory model—the NFL car—was rolled out, full of Snakes players. The crowd loved it. They signed up for appointments to test-drive all the models, and even better, as far as Phoebe was concerned, they filled out slips for raffle tickets, hoping to win a free car.

"Great effort, everyone," Chase said at the end of the day, looking buoyant from the day's success. "Thank you all. Back here at ten tomorrow. Is anyone up for pizza? Or Chinese?"

"I'm fried," Phoebe said, her voice croaking a little.

Chase smiled. "You do look a little crispy around the edges," he said, giving her a quick kiss. "I'll catch up with you later, then."

Others, though, were ready to eat, so they headed out for a neighborhood spot, and Phoebe rode her bike back to her apartment, stretching her legs in the warm evening air.

She soaked in the tub and, when the water cooled, put on her pajamas and made a cup of mint tea and honey for her raw throat. By nine she was tucking the sheets into the sofa when she heard a knock on her door. *Chase.* And when she flung it open, there he was, tall, broad-shouldered, handsome, looking tired, but somehow conveying energy, too. Just seeing him sent a low-key hum through her blood. He slouched against the doorjamb, looking lazy but alert, his eyes warm as he gazed at her.

"*Cher*," he said with a slow smile. "Can I come in?"

Like she'd ever turn him away.

"The place is all ours," she said. "For now, anyway."

"Can't ask for anything more." He handed her a bottle of champagne and stepped into her tiny living room. "I wanted to bring you a token something for all your work for us—for me. I'll think of something better later. That raffle idea—did you know we've given out fifty thousand tickets? And we've got names and contact info for every name, so we have a great start for that marketing team I want to put together."

She'd talked to her share of fifty thousand people. No wonder she was hoarse. "That's fantastic. Let's open the bubbly. This calls for a celebration."

"I'll second that motion." He opened her cupboard and took out two of the juice glasses.

Phoebe opened the wine, poured it out, and led the way over to the sofa. "It'll be a big day tomorrow."

"For you, too."

She shrugged, settling down and crossing her legs. "I'm glad everything's turning out so well, but when the expo's over…" She took a sip of her wine. "I'm worried about the future. Like next week, the future."

Chase joined her on the sofa. "Because of the CIA offer."

Phoebe nodded. "I have to decide on that. If I don't go back—"

"We can figure it out. Between me and everybody else you know, we'll come up with something. You won't starve in a ditch."

"Does Vegas even have ditches? I suppose it must." Phoebe took another sip of wine.

"I know you've been frettin' about how you have to decide sooner than you'd expected. And I know that new CIA job is everything you wanted. What are your thoughts?"

Phoebe shrugged, feeling a little sick. She didn't want to leave him to go back to the CIA, but she didn't see how she could stay in Vegas, either.

Chase toyed with his glass. "Do you like working for Dave?"

Phoebe nodded. "So far. But I think that's because I'm working with you for Venture Automotive. Otherwise, I'm not sure that I'm cut out to be a PI. I don't use my language skills at all, so that's a disappointment. And would I want to do background checks forever? Divorce work? Surveillance? That doesn't sound like much fun. And I don't really want to get proficient with weapons. Which is required."

"Have you thought about other work you might do here in Vegas?"

"There's not that much scope for my skill set," she said. "At least, not doing the kind of work I'd like to do."

"You know that I'd be happy—more than happy—to give you a job. With what you did for the expo—with all the work you've done for me so far—you'd be an asset either in security or in marketing."

Phoebe took a deep breath, closing her eyes. This was the rub. Turning down a job offer from Chase—it was like turning down the man personally. Not the job. The man. She didn't want Chase to think that's what she was doing.

"I wish I could, Chase, I really do. But I can't."

"So am I understanding you correctly, *cher*? There's not one job here in Las Vegas you'd be willing to do so you can stay here. You won't work for me, even in a job you'd be good at and that would pay well, and you won't take a loan or a gift of the money to get the CIA off your back."

Phoebe's breath shortened. That was it, pretty much. Except it didn't sound very good when he said it.

"I appreciate your willingness to hire me more than you

know." She reached out and took his hand in both of hers. "An offer like that goes above and beyond. But I have to make choices that are right for *me*, so that I can stand tall and be the friend and—and the sweetheart to you that I want to be. So that you can be proud of me. I can't be true to myself if I accept your charity. I can't be an extension of you. I have to pay my own debts."

"You wouldn't be a charity case, as you call it, if you're *working*."

"Nobody would believe I was working," Phoebe said, her stomach in knots. "Or that I had any talent. They'd think I was taking you for a ride."

"What do you care what other people think? They'd be wrong."

"Remember how Pavel Rao behaved when we met? How he discounted me? It would always be like that."

"Your mom in the bodega," he said. "That's what it would feel like to you."

"Yes, exactly. And here's another thing. I know we talked about it, but what happens if we break up in six weeks? Or six months? I'd be stranded."

"That wouldn't happen."

"You can't know that for sure. You married and divorced Tracy within a year."

Chase clenched his jaw. "You and I are not the same. You and she are not the same."

"I know. What I'm saying is, your relationship with her didn't work out. And—for different reasons—maybe this one with me won't, either. It happens. And if our relationship does end, my working for you would be awkward in the extreme."

"Tell me something." Chase set his empty glass on the coffee table. "What would it take for you to commit to our relationship? For you to stay here with me? You're a language analyst. What words do you need to hear from me, or what actions do you need to see, that would make you feel confident about us and our future together?"

Phoebe shook her head, feeling miserable. "I don't

know. I really, truly don't. I think I'll know it when I see it. I hope so, anyway."

"So, lacking that tangible evidence, you've decided to go back to the CIA. To Langley."

"I don't see any choice, really. I owe them a lot of money. And the opportunity—I couldn't have written a better job description for myself."

"And where does that leave us?"

Phoebe took a deep breath. "I want to make the relationship work long distance," she said tentatively. "I think we could do it, if we're committed to it."

"So how do we make that happen? For six years, as you say. Plus a little more."

Phoebe swallowed, hearing the sarcasm. "Six years is a long time, but it's not impossible. We can be together for vacations and holidays, even long weekends. We could meet halfway, maybe Chicago or Saint Louis, someplace like that. Denver!"

"Every holiday a different port of call," Chase said. "Booty call, that is."

Okay, that was just rude. He wasn't taking this well at all.

"It wouldn't be any different than couples where both people have to travel a lot," she said doggedly. Long distance could work. She *knew* it could. "We can *communicate*. We can call. Video chat. Text. Email. We can see each other, or talk, every day. Maybe several times a day. As much as we want."

Chase shook his head and leaned forward, resting his forearms on his knees. He turned his head to look at her. "And after six years, then what?"

That was the good news.

"After six years, I'm free of the CIA," she said. "The loan's paid off."

"So you move back to Las Vegas and you still don't have a job you like? What then?"

She hadn't really thought that far ahead. True, she'd be free of the CIA. But if she wanted a career using her skills, she still wouldn't have many, if *any*, options in Las Vegas.

Chase shrugged. "Or maybe your plan is that you stay at the CIA permanently, because that's the job that's best for you, and you think we'll have a long-distance relationship for the rest of our lives?"

She felt herself tighten, shrink somehow. "No—I don't know," she said. "By then everything will have changed. We'll have more options."

"What kind of options? What will have changed? Besides our ages, I mean."

"The slate will be wiped clean," she said. "We can see where we go from there. Without obligations. Except to each other, I mean."

"How would we have obligations to each other? We wouldn't have had any for six years. Six years *plus* of not needing to be there for each other when we're happy or sad, succeeding or failing. We'd have a relationship by appointment only, taking a plane to Denver for Thanksgiving or the Fourth of July. I have family, Phoebe. Parents. Brothers and sisters. Nieces and nephews. I like to spend time with them, too."

"I could meet you when you visited family," Phoebe said. "I like them, too. I want to spend time with them, too. I mean, if that would be okay with you."

"Don't you get it? I want to *build* something with you. I don't want to spend sixteen hours of forty-eight on a flight to meet you in a hotel room on the occasional weekend. That just sounds crappy. I want to *live* with you."

"Okay, so—"

"And here's something else. Maybe you'd come to resent me for all the plane trips to Denver that you couldn't afford. Because you wouldn't let me pay for those, right?"

Every word he said felt like a hammer.

"It wouldn't be like that," Phoebe said. But maybe it would.

"Sure, it would," Chase said. "And what about those weekends when you have to work during a national security alert? How much time would we really have?"

She'd run out of arguments. What had felt like a challenge now seemed an impossibility.

"We should try," she said, rubbing her arms. "I want to try. Other people make it work. We can, too. You want to give up?"

Chase sighed, looking tired. "You're shutting me out. You want to take care of yourself, great. Admirable goal. But your way doesn't let us be together. We won't be able to take care of each other."

"It isn't like that."

"It's *exactly* like that. And you know what? It's been like that from the start. You've been here three or four months, and you still don't own anything. You live in a furnished apartment on a month-to-month lease. Everything you own fits in one suitcase. You never intended to stay. You weren't ever serious about me. Or anything."

"That's not true!" Phoebe said, but she didn't have any more words to argue with him. And he was sort of right about one thing. When she'd arrived in Las Vegas, she *had* intended to return to Langley as soon as possible. She hadn't realized how much could happen in a few short months. How much her feelings could change.

Chase shook his head. "I'm sorry, *real* sorry, believe me, but your plan doesn't work for me. I can't do it. *Won't* do it."

Phoebe's heart and blood and breathing seemed to stop, waiting for the final blow that was coming. "What are you saying?"

"There's no point. We won't be together enough. We won't *share* enough. You won't stay here, and you don't have an exit strategy on this CIA deal. I don't see what the end game is."

"So you won't even *try*?"

"Occasional weekend visits for six years?" He paced across the teeny living room. "Felons have better visitation hours than that! I've thought of everything I can to help you to stay. But you have some bug about not duplicating the behavior of your mother. I don't get that. You're 180 degrees different from your mother."

"If I make the same choices, I'm *not* different! I have to make *different* choices. I *want* to make different choices."

"You don't think that having a long-term serious relationship with one guy makes you different from your mother? You don't think that the two of us staying together for the long haul could be the ultimate proof of how different you are from her?"

"I don't know," she said. "If I give up after a couple of months what I've worked toward for so many years, how is that behavior different from hers?"

"I guess that's all there is to say, then. Have fun back at the CIA. All the best, and all that." He headed toward the door.

"Wait a second!" Phoebe said. "Are you breaking up with me? That whole speech you gave me that time about wanting a woman to stand up to you, not fall at your feet—that applies only if the woman who stands up does what you want? And then if she doesn't, you're gone?"

He stared at her, disbelief on his face. "Phoebe. We've got nowhere to go here. We're out of options. You chose your path, and it doesn't include me. I know you see it, too. I'm sorry as hell, because I thought we had something special. But if what we have isn't enough to keep you here, it isn't enough to survive your departure. It's not me breaking up with you, *cher*—it's *you* breaking up with *me*. I'm just the one who's calling it out."

He shook his head and went out the door, closing it softly behind him.

Phoebe stared after him in disbelief. Chase had left her, and now he was gone, gone for good. She was alone. Truly alone.

She felt empty from her head to her feet. She couldn't think. She couldn't breathe. She stared blindly at the closed door.

Her eyes filled with tears. When the tears spilled over and kept coming, she crumpled on the sofa.

Chase was gone, gone forever. And he'd taken her heart with him.

Chase avoided his family when he got home. He was too upset to have casual conversation or make approving noises about whatever the hell they were doing to his house. The guest quarters weren't much of a sanctuary, though. The hair dryer was out on the sink where Phoebe had left it. His junky old Snakes jersey was on the bed where she'd tossed it. The flip-flops she used were sitting under the chair.

He poured a brandy, remembering how her face had drained of color—boom, turned white, just like that—as he'd left. He'd thought she might pass out, she looked so stricken. What the hell did she think would happen to them if she went back east? He remembered how distant Tracy had felt when he'd been on the road even for a couple of weeks. He and Tracy hadn't had much in common to begin with, but still— six years! And then what? What was the point of making plans to call or visit? Phoebe would never leave the CIA. They wouldn't make it. *Couldn't* make it.

His phone pinged, and his hope leaped. Phoebe! Maybe she'd changed her mind. But no, it was his father texting him. Wanting to know why he wasn't at the house.

Chase sighed. The thought that he could hide out from his family had probably been optimistic on his part, anyway. He called.

"Dad," he said. "I'm not much for company tonight. Can it wait?"

"Not really," Ancel said. "We have a few questions about the work before we can move forward, and tomorrow's another long day for you. I don't want the crew sitting around for twenty-four hours until you're free. Come on over. This won't take long. Bring Phoebe. I'd like her opinion, too."

"She isn't here," Chase said. "I'll be right there."

He disconnected. Damn. Now he'd face a gauntlet of *where's Phoebe* from a bunch of well-meaning family who didn't know enough to leave things be. He took a deep breath, girding himself for explanations he didn't want to make, and headed over to the big house.

Ancel walked him through the construction, and Chase admired the work the crew had done so far.

"Everything looks good," he said. "If you didn't know before that not every bedroom had its own bath, you couldn't tell it now."

Ancel pointed to a door that had been framed in. "This closet will be awkwardly placed. No way around it."

"It's a hotel," Chase said. "A boutique hotel. I think people will accept a slightly awkward floor plan. They'd much rather have a convenient bathroom."

"So where's Phoebe?" Ancel asked as they headed down the stairs. "Is everything okay with you two?"

Chase sighed. He'd known this was coming. "We broke up tonight."

"Damn." Ancel stopped on the stairs. "I liked that girl. Did you do something stupid?"

"No," Chase said, irritated. He didn't owe his father, or the rest of his family, any explanation. He had nothing to reproach himself for. Phoebe was going back to the CIA. She'd chosen her job over him. Simple as that.

So that's what he told his father. Briefly.

"Well, that's lousy," Ancel said. "Can you find a way around it?"

"I don't see one. We've gone over it a bunch of times."

"Have a beer with me," Ancel said as he headed into the kitchen. "Everybody's either out tonight or they went to bed early. It's lonely in this big place when nobody else is around."

They each grabbed a beer and headed into the living room, which so far had escaped the ravages of the construction crew.

"I'm sorry about Phoebe," Ancel said as he settled into one of the overstuffed chairs. "You two seem to get along so well."

"Yeah, we do. Or we did, anyway. That's why it's so lousy that she's going back to the CIA. Although I can't blame her. She's got a great opportunity there now. They're inviting her to join some special group, and it sounds like she'd be crazy not to take it."

Ancel nodded, staring at the floor, fiddling with his bottle. "It wouldn't do the two of you any good if she was unhappy," he said. "Anybody can see she's a hard worker, so she needs work she likes. She can't sit around your house all day and wait for you to come home."

And who was asking her to do that? No one.

"No. But she could work for me. I've got plenty of jobs she'd be good at."

"You said she wouldn't like that."

"That's what she said."

"Yeah." Ancel said. "And she'd be the one to know."

Chase stared at his father. "What are you saying, Dad? Just come out with it."

"Nothing, son. I was thinking about how I always knew you'd never go into the business like your brothers did. You always wanted to go your own way, lead your own crew. You found a way to do that. First with football and now with your company."

"I know that was a disappointment—"

"Nah. You're a natural-born leader. This business— working with me—wasn't your thing. No. But it seems to me that Phoebe is pretty independent, too. I'm wondering if there was a way she could have what she wants. If she's important enough to you. Which I don't know, of course."

"She's very important. Essential. But she doesn't seem to feel the same about me."

"Maybe. Maybe not. You said one time that she's here on a leave of absence. That whole secretary of state rescue that Josie so admires, where everybody pointed a gun at everybody else—your mother was very upset about that, by the way—that was all about Phoebe trying to get that job back, right? And then she *did* get the job back, but now she's here in Vegas anyway. She put it all on hold. Sounds to me that she likes you quite a bit."

Chase nodded. "Yeah, that's true. When we talked tonight, she was pretty torn up about leaving."

"She's got backbone. Not every woman would pick a hard job like the CIA over a pampered life with a handsome and rich captain of industry like you."

Chase snorted, catching his father's eye. They both

grinned ruefully.

"Phoebe didn't know who I was when we met," Chase said. "The whole football thing. She's a total novice about sports."

"Must have been refreshing."

"It was. It really was." Chase took a long pull from his bottle and finished the beer.

"In one way you're lucky," Ancel said. "You found out what her bottom line is early on. And if your bottom line can't go there—well." He shrugged. "Saves you bigger heartache down the road. Nothing to do about it."

That's exactly what he'd been saying all along.

Ancel shook his head. "It's too bad. I just *liked* her."

"Me, too," Chase said, feeling the loss for himself and for Ancel, too. His father had never liked Tracy very much.

"She reminds me of your mother."

"What? Phoebe? How does she remind you of Mom?"

"Thwarted by some guy," Ancel said with a swift smile. "Claire wanted to be a veterinarian. She was going great guns in all her science classes. But then she got pregnant—that was you—and we got married. I started the business, and she ran the office. She never went to vet school. I've always felt a little bad about it. Not about you. No regrets there. Only that she didn't get her dream."

"You're happy, though, right? She's happy."

Ancel shrugged. "Sure. Just saying. I got everything I wanted. She didn't."

"This job they offered Phoebe—she has to be back there to take it. I don't see how that can work for us."

"You're a smart guy," Ancel said. "Maybe an idea will come to you in the morning."

Sure. And I'll find buried treasure in the bayou, too.

"Maybe," Chase said to placate his father, getting to his feet. "I hope so."

But if an answer was lurking there somewhere, he sure didn't see it.

Chapter 18

Dawn finally broke on Saturday morning, but the fresh day didn't make Phoebe feel any better. She'd lain awake most of the night, heavy with grief, her stomach in knots, her eyes dry and scratchy from crying, thinking about what Chase had said. She'd heard Brenda and Uncle Boo-Boo come in, but she'd pretended to be asleep. She didn't want to talk to them. But tossing and turning hadn't revealed any new ideas. She was who she was. Chase, too. They were stuck.

But she still had an expo to work and a stadium spectacular to put on, so she'd muster her strength and do her best.

She dressed in the yellow Venture Automotive T-shirt and black pants they were all wearing for the expo and brewed and drank an entire pot of coffee. That wouldn't keep her from being a tired, miserable, and brokenhearted ex-girl-friend, but maybe she'd stay awake for the duration. That had to be worth something.

She called Sanjay for a ride to the expo, and when she got into the taxi, she handed him a mug of the cardamom-scented sweet tea he liked. Sanjay sighed in appreciation, but he halted, the cup in midair, when he heard her news.

"No," he said with touching certainty, settling the mug in his taxi's cup holder. "You and Chase are *suited*. There must be a way. You will find it. Of this, I am sure."

The only thing she was sure of was that this event had to go off without a hitch. It would be crucial for Chase's future—and the future of Venture Automotive.

"I hope so," she said mournfully.

"And thank you very much for the passes to the expo stadium spectacular. Both my mother and I are looking forward to it with acute interest."

"My pleasure, Sanjay—and thanks for all your help with it. That goes for your mom, too."

When Sanjay dropped her off at the expo, the crowd was, if anything, even larger than it had been the day before, which made it easy for Phoebe to avoid Chase. She didn't see him for hours, and then when she did, he was busy signing autographs and selling cars. By two, when it was time to go to the stadium for the car giveaway and spectacular, she was more than ready to head out. The sooner the day was over, the better, as far as she was concerned.

Kristin hustled over to where Phoebe was consolidating the raffle ticket buckets.

"Phoebs, Coach says you ride with me or Tony, and we'll all meet up over there. What happened with you guys? He's all ornery and distracted. Not making a good impression on the customers. *At. All.*"

"We broke up," Phoebe said, miserable all over again.

"*What?*" Kristin wrapped her arms around her in a big hug and didn't let go. "I don't believe it. You ride with me and tell me everything. We'll figure it out."

Phoebe sniffed, breathing in Kristin's affection, the sympathy soaking into her bones and easing her grief for the first time in twenty-four hours. She held on for a long minute.

"All set?" Kristin asked.

"Ready," Phoebe said. "Let's go."

Phoebe filled her in on the way to the stadium, but the ten-minute ride didn't give her much time to discuss details.

"I'd say come over tonight, but we've got Coach's barbecue to go to," Kristin said as she parked the giveaway car in front of the entrance gates. "Maybe you guys will patch things up there. I don't believe it's over for you."

"What barbecue?" Phoebe said. "I'm not invited to a barbecue. And that's if I'm still standing after this thing is over."

"Of course you're invited to the barbecue. Everybody's invited."

"Not me."

"That's a mistake, then. Coach wouldn't not invite you. Listen, just come along. He'll be disappointed if you don't show."

Phoebe shook her head and got out of the car. It was time to get to work. People were already trickling into the stadium, and she waved to Delmar, who was working one of the gates, checking the expo badges people needed to get in. All the gates were staffed by men and women wearing the bright yellow Venture T-shirts—off-duty cops that Dave had lined up earlier. With security in place, at least one thing was going right today.

She checked out the belowground medical facilities first, saying hello to the nurse in the first aid station and then looking into the maintenance area to make sure that the two ambulances that were required for their insurance had arrived. They had. They were sort of jammed between the injury carts and other small vehicles useful for athletic circumstances she could only imagine. She introduced herself to the paramedics and moved on. She hadn't seen Dave yet, but no doubt he was here, checking things out somewhere.

So far, so good.

She was meeting the NASCAR drivers and the cheerleaders in the VIP parking lot and time was running short now, so she hustled outside find them. She was relieved to see the sea of yellow cars and people standing around talking to each other.

"Hi!" she called, trotting over to them. The cheerleaders' skimpy, spangly red outfits and white pom-poms contrasted with the yellow cars and T-shirts the drivers wore. The spectacular would be colorful, that was for sure. "Everybody accounted for?"

"Yup," one of the men said, stepping forward. "We're

good to go."

"Us, too," Tracy said, stepping out of the crowd and linking her arm with the driver. Phoebe felt a stab near her heart as she considered that she had something in common with the cheerleader now: she was as ex to Chase as Tracy was. But it looked like Tracy had set her sights on this guy now.

She wondered when—*if*—she'd get over Chase. She smiled at the cheerleader. "Hi, Tracy."

"Hi." Tracy leaned into the driver and smiled up at him. He shifted a little under Tracy's weight.

"Hey," he said to Phoebe. "Listen. Chase Bonaventure called me last night and invited all of us out to his place for a barbecue when this thing is over. Can we drive these loaners over there? It would make everything a lot simpler."

"He called me, too!" Tracy said. "He invited all us girls. He said we should have a big party to celebrate."

He didn't call me, Phoebe thought, the stab of pain so sharp now she had to catch her breath. *He didn't invite me to a barbecue.* She concentrated on keeping her face neutral. She would get through the afternoon or die trying.

"Um," Phoebe said. "Did he talk to you about parking? There's not a lot of street parking over there."

"He said he arranged for a valet."

"Okay, then, sure. Drive the loaners over there. You got the address?"

"Yup, I got it." He stuck out his hand. "Kenny Childers."

"Phoebe Renfrew," Phoebe said, shaking his hand.

"I know where his place is." Tracy bumped her head on Kenny's shoulder. "I can show you."

Phoebe's heartache swam up to her head, which pounded dully.

"He told me the big place on Ephraim Court." Kenny put his arm around Tracy.

"That's the place," Phoebe said. "All right, then. Any last-minute questions?"

"Nope," Kenny said. "We got this. It'll be a blast, besides having a barbecue with Chase Bonaventure. And the drivers have been practicing their routine really hard. I think the audience will go for it, seeing us do a little fancy driving." He grinned, nudging Tracy.

She frowned. "This event isn't just about driving, you know. We'll be there, too."

"Right." Kenny looked startled. "And I'm sure you'll do a fine job."

Tracy glared at him. "Dancing might look easy, but it's hard work. Especially in these damn high-heeled boots! You should see what they do to my feet! I have calluses! And it's *sandal season*!"

"Sure, but I don't—"

"We're just as important to the event as you are," Tracy said. "We fire up the crowd. People *like* us. And we earned as much money as you did, too!"

Kenny's look of surprise had morphed into something more beleaguered. "Okay," he said. "And you look great, too."

"Of *course* I look great. I *always* look great. *Great* is my *average*." Tracy stomped off, her teeny skirt twitching with the sway of her hips, her pom-poms shivering in her wake.

Phoebe admired Tracy's exit even though she could see why Chase might be happy that he wasn't married to her any more.

"What did *I* do?" Kenny sounded beleaguered.

"That's just Tracy, I think," Phoebe said. "She's sensitive about the cheerleaders' role."

Kenny shook his head. "I guess so. Anyway. I'm just saying that it'll be a great show. Wait until you see the marching band. You'll like what they're doing."

"Marching band?" Phoebe hadn't asked for a marching band. But okay. Whatever. As long as one of the NASCAR drivers didn't run over a piccolo player, she'd be happy. Well, maybe not *happy*. She wouldn't be happy again for a long time. But at least she'd be satisfied with the outcome.

And if one of the NASCAR drivers *did* run over a piccolo player, at least they had the ambulances on standby.

Cliff Frizell woke late on Saturday morning, hungover but looking forward to the day. Hair of the dog, that's what he needed.

He helped himself to a breakfast beer and then had another. Those and a couple of aspirin did a lot to smooth the edges of the headache that pounded at the back of his skull, and after he swallowed one of those little pink tablets he kept for emergencies, he felt strong and ready for what lay ahead.

He'd figured it out. What he needed to do.

Hurting the company wasn't enough. Venture Automotive was important, but damaging the company—or even destroying it—didn't do squat against its CEO.

He needed to stop Chase Fucking Bonaventure. One way or another. The man who'd stolen his chances, obliterated his dreams, destroyed his career, and ruined his life.

Only when he demolished Bonaventure would he be able to show the world what he was capable of.

He checked his watch. That amateur-hour show they were putting on today would start soon. Where better to put an end to Bonaventure's career? For the second and *final* time.

He loaded his firearm and tucked it into the waistband of his pants. Then he left his apartment, climbed into his bright yellow Venture Automotive car, and headed for the stadium.

Time to make things right.

Chase headed up to the stadium's skybox, hoping that Phoebe would be there. But what would he say to her if she was? He had only a few minutes before he had to go down to the field and give away some cars, but he wanted to tell her and Kristin now what a good job they'd done. If somebody had asked him a week ago, he'd have said that this event would never work. But Phoebe and Kristin were pulling it off without a hitch, and now they had the names of thousands of people who were interested in buying Venture Automotive cars.

But if Phoebe left him, it would all be meaningless.

He entered the skybox and saw Kristin, alone, slumped in a seat, staring out at the field. He knew just how she felt. He took a mineral water from the cooler, popped the cap, and joined her, looking out at the green field where he'd spent a lot of Sundays—and plenty of other days, too, for that matter—for the past ten years or so.

"You did a great job," he said. "You and Phoebe. This spectacular is running like clockwork. It really is spectacular."

She turned a wan smile on him. "Thanks. I think everybody's having a good time. But Phoebe! She said you broke up with her. Because of logistics, sort of? That's dumb, Coach."

Since when did a breakup become the business of just about everybody he knew?

"Sort of, but about that—while we're here, I wanted to mention an idea I have that affects you." He outlined his plans. "We can talk later, but give it some thought."

"Sure thing." Kristin looked intrigued, which was positive. "Did you invite Phoebe to the barbecue? She says you didn't."

"Of course I invited her," he said. "I don't know if she'll come, though."

"Her invitation must have gone into the spam filter," Kristin said. "She swears she didn't get it."

"*Damn.* I wanted to talk to her before things got into full swing."

Kristin visibly brightened, and he realized how much his breakup with Phoebe and her departure for Langley would affect others.

"Email her again, Coach," she said. "I think she'll come. Even though she's miserable."

That was something, anyway. He didn't want Phoebe to be miserable, but if she was unhappy about leaving him, so much the better.

He took out his phone and thumbed in a message. "Done. Now I have to get going. Cars to give away and all that."

"Break a leg, Coach."

Chase laughed as he headed for the door. "Let's hope not. That'd be all we'd need."

He charged down the ramp to the stadium entrance, where Tony, Matt, Rinsho, and Margo Bollingbrook were waiting by the giveaway cars. He heard the roar of the crowd and knew they had another couple of minutes.

"I'm firing Cliff on Monday," he told them. "I've been holding out, waiting for him to do something we could arrest him for, but I'm done waiting. I think he's been escalating his attacks, and I don't want him to go off the rails at anyone's expense."

"I can't say I'll be sorry, even though his loss leaves us short one systems designer," Margo said. "I know we made the best hire we could at the time, but we should try to get somebody really top-notch. Do a nationwide search."

Chase nodded. "Way ahead of you. And while I'm thinking about it, talk to Aquintis Jones. We've got him on the assembly line right now. He'd need training, but he knows CAD and he seems to have a knack for design."

"Aquintis Jones," she said. "Okay. He might be able to replace Cliff straight up. He certainly didn't do much for the department."

"Something else. I'm sorry to spring it on everyone so suddenly, but I need quick feedback on an idea I've had."

"Whatever you need, Coach," Rinsho said. "After this week—I'd say anything is possible."

Tony nodded. "Me, too."

"And me," Matt added.

"Absolutely," Margo said.

Chase nodded, feeling more connected to these people—and more appreciative of their efforts—than to most of the men he'd played football with. And that was saying something.

"Thank you. Y'all have been terrific the past few weeks. We wouldn't have been able to make this happen if you hadn't worked so hard. So here's what I have in mind." He laid out his idea.

"I think I speak for us all when I say, we can do it. I mean, we are the champions." Tony grinned, tossing him the football he'd been holding, a prop they'd planned to use, thinking it might help to rev up the crowd.

Right now the crowd didn't sound like it needed much revving. People were streaming for the entrance gates, talking and laughing, looking excited and happy. Just what he wanted to see.

"Great," he said. "And now I think the fans are waiting."

They were driving the four raffle cars out onto the field after the NASCAR drivers had executed their performance, so they got in their vehicles and edged to the side of the service doors so that the NASCAR drivers could get past them into the maintenance tunnel and out onto the field. He could tell when the first cars drove onto the turf because the crowd roared again and confetti streamed down, even out here in the lot where they were parked. *Almost like game day*, he thought, only without getting smacked around and ruining his knee. And this was better—he was creating jobs and sustainable vehicles as well as challenges for himself and his crew.

And he'd never forget that the spark of this success was due to Phoebe. But way more than success, she added a spark to his happiness.

He could not let her go.

Phoebe checked her watch as the NASCAR drivers and the cheerleaders got in their borrowed Venture Automotive cars, fired up the engines, and maneuvered slowly through the gathering crowd to the stadium's service doors. Once inside, they'd drive through the vast maintenance area and enter the playing field promptly at three. Drivers, check. Cheerleaders, check.

Then a vehicle horn blasted behind her, and Phoebe whirled around as two huge buses lumbered into the parking area and lurched to a stop. The doors whooshed open, and a guy with a clipboard and a harassed expression bounced down the steps, looked around, and trotted over.

"I'm looking for Phoebe Renfrew," he said. "Are you she?"

"Yes," Phoebe said. "And you are?"

"John Hackbarth. I brought the marching band."

"Okay," Phoebe said. "The thing is, I didn't ask for a marching band."

"You didn't? We've been rehearsing all week. The band's really excited. Chase Bonaventure, you know. Hero worship. We all got invited to a barbecue at his place afterward. The kids'll be disappointed if they're not wanted."

"They're wanted," Phoebe said, regrouping. Evidently Chase had invited all of Las Vegas to his house for a barbecue, everybody except for her. Who would he invite next? The Las Vegas All-Elvis Revue?

"If you've been rehearsing all week, you must know where you should line up," she said. "The drivers and cheerleaders are already in place."

"Good to know. And where do we pick up the free T-shirts?"

"T-shirts?"

"Yeah, like the one you're wearing." He checked his clipboard. "We were told the kids would each get a Venture Automotive T-shirt."

"Oh. You must have talked to Kristin about that. Yeah, I'll get that squared away. Maybe at the barbecue. But I'll let you know. Give me your number." She jotted it down in her notes.

"Okay, we'll get going now," John said. "Thanks."

He went back to the bus and stepped in. Seconds later, dozens of young people wearing bright purple military-style band uniforms and carrying instruments and tall hats poured out of the vehicles. Chatting and laughing, they adjusted their headgear and formed tight, even rows, trombones first, drums in the middle, wind instruments in the back.

A young woman in an even taller hat, wearing a whistle and carrying a tall silver stick with tassels, went to the front of the formation. She swung the tasseled stick, pointed it forward, and blasted two short tweets. The band members snapped to attention, their instruments ready. Two shorts and a long later, the snare drum beat out a tattoo and the marching band stepped out, heading to the stadium's first gate.

Okay, then. One marching band, coming right up.

She called Kristin.

"Hey," she said. "The marching band is here. The band director wants to know where the kids can pick up their T-shirts."

"At the barbecue," Kristin said. "Matt's taking them over in his other car."

"I'll let him know," Phoebe said. "My life is out of control, you know that? I didn't even know there *was* a marching band. You'll have to handle the T-shirts at the barbecue, since I won't be there."

"Of course you'll be there."

"Really not." Phoebe almost couldn't get the words out, her throat felt so thick as she said them. "No invitation. Broke up, remember?"

"You aren't broken up, that is stupid, but even if you were, it wouldn't matter," Kristin said, sounding brisk. "You put in the effort, you get the invite. That's how it works. *Tracy* got an invite. Why wouldn't you?"

Because Chase really, really doesn't want me there.

"Gotta go," Phoebe said, her voice thick with tears.

She disconnected, dashing her hand across her eyes, and thought for a second what she needed to do next. Maybe after she checked on the T-shirt guns, the confetti cannons, and the fireworks guys, she could join Kristin in the skybox. Unless Chase was there. If he was, she'd have to find someplace else to sit. She couldn't trust herself to stay up there with him and not snivel the whole time.

She entered the stadium and ran up the ramp to where the guys working the T-shirt guns sat with crates of confetti and logo apparel. They lounged back on the seats, chatting or checking their phones.

"All set?" she asked them.

"We're ready," one guy said.

"You got the sequence, right? At three o'clock *exactly*,

the T-shirts go out. Then when the cars drive out, the confetti shoots out. And when winners are announced, the fireworks go off. Where are the fireworks guys?"

Another guy pointed. "There's a concrete bunker-type thing over there," he said. "In section FF, behind the stairs. I saw them come in, so they should be ready."

"Thanks, I'll check. Any questions?"

"Yeah, everybody went to the stadium and got a free car; how come all I get is this lousy T-shirt?" the first guy said, and everyone laughed.

No doubt the T-shirt shooter's idea of a professional joke.

She left the T-shirt guys and checked in on the fireworks crew, all of whom seemed ready and more than competent. Then she climbed the stairs to the skybox. She wasn't sure where Chase would be until he ran out onto the playing field, but he was probably hobnobbing somewhere.

Kristin was on the phone and Chase was nowhere in sight when Phoebe entered the glass VIP seating area high in the stands. As she hesitated in the doorway, Kristin saw her and patted the empty chair next to her. Phoebe poured herself a glass of water and sat down, looking out at the crowd. The stadium was packed on one side—the side Chase would face when he was giving away the cars—and from what she could see, everybody was having a good time.

"You just missed Coach," Kristin whispered, clearly on hold. "How are you doing?"

Phoebe shrugged. Kristin reached out and squeezed her hand. Phoebe squeezed back.

Then it was three o'clock. Showtime. The T-shirts boomed out over the crowd. People roared. Many pulled the bright shirts on over their street clothes, creating a sea of red and yellow.

So far, so good.

Cliff jerked to a stop in the stadium parking lot and saw the Venture Automotive vehicles bunched up, ready to enter the stadium. The drivers and the cheerleaders were standing around talking, obviously waiting for the signal to begin whatever the hell they were planning to do.

It was perfect camouflage. He drove his car to the edge of the group and turned off the engine, but he stayed in the car. Somebody might recognize him, or simply realize that he hadn't been there before. This was not the time to be challenged.

He glanced around at the setup, tapping his fingers on the wheel impatiently. The security people monitoring activity behind barricades didn't glance twice at the late arrival, and his own Venture hunk of junk blended perfectly with all the rest. Nobody, not even the NASCAR drivers, suspected a thing.

Finally everything was going his way. Soon he'd be on the field with the rest of these clowns, and then he'd show Bonaventure who ruled the stadium and the playing field.

Just then one of the drivers, looking around, spotted him and began walking his way. *Shit.*

"Hey," the guy said as he got nearer. "Hold up."

This was a wrinkle he hadn't anticipated. Cliff eased his gun out of his pants and held it loosely in his lap, ready for anything. One guy wouldn't stop him. He'd do what he came here to do.

The NASCAR driver was almost at his car. Cliff buzzed down the window and raised the gun enough to be ready, but below the line of the window. This guy wouldn't be able to see it until he got right up to the car, and if he stayed back, nobody had to get hurt.

"I didn't see you at rehearsals," the driver said, at the window now. "Listen, I'm sorry, but—"

The guy glanced down. Unless he was blind, he must have seen the weapon.

He probably wasn't blind.

In one fluid movement, Cliff raised the gun and smashed the butt into the driver's face. The driver staggered back and sat down hard on the asphalt, blood streaming from his nose and a cut on his forehead.

Just then the marching band played a fanfare. The other

drivers hustled into their cars and started the engines. Cliff joined the end of the queue as the cars inched into the stadium.

From where she sat in the skybox, Phoebe couldn't see the marching band, but their fanfare quieted the crowd. Seconds later, they high-stepped out onto the field, playing a bouncy tune that she recognized but couldn't name. They pranced across the grass, regrouping to form a car, then marched out of that and into the word VENTURE. Then they strutted out of that, forming the Venture Automotive logo. Finally they lined up on the twenty-yard line, still playing.

Then the bright yellow Venture Automotive electric vehicles poured out onto the field and the confetti guns went off, showering the fans, cars, and band with glittery gold and red confetti. The cars drove through the glitter, speeding single file along the sideline, and then turned sharply so they faced the crowd.

The cheerleaders hopped out, shaking their pom-poms, and formed a long line in front. The cars reversed, spun around, and headed to the center of the field, executing a spiral and separating into wide columns. The marching band regrouped, high-stepping their way between the cars, playing a rousing show tune that the cheerleaders danced to, their pom-poms shaking and their sequins sparkling. The cars turned and circled, forming tighter and then looser spirals, stars, and collapsing squares—even a giant rattlesnake — with the marching band weaving in and out.

It really was spectacular. And so far, none of the drivers had run over any of the musicians. Big thumbs-up for that.

"The marching band was a terrific idea," she told Kristin.

"Wasn't it?" Kristin agreed. "The guy we hired to choreograph the cars thought of it." She turned back to the phone.

After ten or fifteen minutes, the NASCAR drivers sped to one side of the field, the band lined up on the other side, and the cheerleaders paused on the sideline, pom-poms on their hips. Matt, Tony, Rinsho, and Margo drove the giveaway cars, all of them painted an eye-catching, fire-engine red, out onto the field and parked. Then Chase ran out onto the field and waved. He looked strong and powerful and beautiful, still a conditioned athlete. The crowd roared.

Not exactly a tough audience.

A Venture Automotive SUV in the new, signature fire-engine red towed out a flatbed trailer on which was mounted a wire cage spinner filled with the raffle tickets. When everything was safely parked, Chase leaped onto the trailer. The crowd roared again.

Well, why wouldn't they yell, Phoebe thought miserably. Everybody loved him. He looked like a Greek god, and for more than a decade, he'd won football games and a few Super Bowls for these people. Now he was giving cars away. What wasn't to like?

"I have to go," she told Kristin, jumping up.

"Phoebe, wait!" Kristin said, but Phoebe was already out the door.

As she walked down the ramp to the main entrance—no need to rush at this point—she heard the murmur of Chase's voice on the speakers followed by the applause of the crowd. Evidently the car giveaway was going off without a hitch. Good. When the spectacular was over, she could go home. And soon, back to Langley.

Today might be the last time she ever saw Chase.

The first burst of fireworks went off. So the first winner had been announced.

She was about halfway down the ramp when her text ring trilled. Probably Kristin. But whatever her friend wanted, it was too late.

The message was from Kenny Childers. What was that about? He should be sitting in his car in the middle of the football field. She opened the message.

URGENT! It read.

What could be urgent? A problem at the barbecue she hadn't been invited to? Call somebody else.

Guy has a gun! she read. *In a car. Gone rogue! Security?*

What on earth? Phoebe punched in his number.

"Kenny, tell me! What happened?"

"There was an extra—*ow!*—car in the lineup. Out in the parking lot. I went to check it out, and the guy hit me with a gun. I think maybe he went out onto the field. I'm not sure. I was pretty woozy."

"He *shot* you? I'll call the ambulance crew! We've got one right here."

"He didn't shoot me, he just hit me with the end of it. I'm at the first aid station getting stitches. I'll be fine."

"Okay, but go to the hospital if the nurse says, all right? And I'm sorry, Kenny. This event was supposed to be fun."

"Who says I'm not having fun?"

Phoebe snorted as she disconnected. Those NASCAR drivers. But how could she find the guy with the gun? The stadium was enormous and now packed almost to capacity with forty or fifty thousand people. How could anybody find one guy in a place that huge? But somehow they had to find him and disarm him before he hurt anyone else or—unthinkably—shot someone. Or many people.

She punched in 911.

"I'm at the stadium show that Chase Bonaventure is putting on today," she told the dispatcher. "We have forty or fifty thousand people here. One of the participants has been attacked by an unknown assailant with a gun. No reports of shots fired, but we think the gunman is inside the stadium now. Some off-duty police officers are here providing security. Dave Greenaway is in charge of that. I called you first."

"On our way," the dispatcher said.

Phoebe hoped so. She punched in Dave's number as she continued down the ramp to medical. She would check on Kenny and then go out to meet the cops. Also warn Kristin. *But how could she find the gunman?*

"Dave," she said when he picked up. "Somebody attacked one of the drivers with a gun. He's been injured but not shot. The gunman's got a Venture Automotive car. Or maybe is on the field in a car, we're not sure. I called the cops. They said they're coming."

"I'll let the rest of security know," Dave said. "Good work. And Phoebe? Stay down. If you see this guy, remember that he's armed and dangerous. Stay away from him."

"Okay. What do you want me to do?"

But he'd disconnected.

Phoebe frowned. What did "stay down" mean? She couldn't stand around like a still life with fruit. She had to do everything she could to stop this guy.

But first she had to find him.

Chapter 19

Cliff hunkered down in the Venture Automotive car that he'd parked in an underground repair bay as the fleet of Venture Automotive cars paraded onto the field, followed fifteen minutes later by four bright red giveaway cars, driven by Chase Fucking Bonaventure's jolly band of suck-ups. The time for the king's comeuppance would be soon, and then a stadium full of fans—and the whole world—would see who was really king. Who had been the best all along.

What was funny was how the security goons were racing around, looking for somebody with a gun. The nosy driver getting stitches in medical hadn't recognized him, but one of these security rent-a-cops had come up to him, greeted him by name, and even asked if he'd seen a guy with a weapon! That was a laugh. Cliff had said no, offered him an autograph, not that the rent-a-cop had taken him up on it—which just shows you how soon people forget—and then he'd sent the guy on his way. Let them look for some un-named assailant. He was right under their bloody noses.

He took the gun out of the glove box, put it on the seat next to him, and hit the ignition button. It was go time.

And that was when Bonaventure's moocher girlfriend showed up.

"Cliff," she called, jogging up to the window. "What are you doing down here in the repair bay?"

"Waiting. Not that it's any of your business."

"If your car needs repair, it should be towed it back to the plant," she said. "You won't be able to leave it here. You weren't in the driver show, were you?"

"A cop told me there'd been assault. You know anything about that?"

"No." She backed away from the car. "Okay, gotta go. Things to do. Catch you later."

She'd seen the weapon.

She must have. She'd looked through the window, and the gun was sitting right here on the seat. The light was dim in the repair bay, and the gun sort of blended into the upholstery, but she must have seen it. And now she was out of range to slug.

But not to shoot.

She was moving pretty fast, out of the repair bay now and around the corner into the maintenance tunnel, where he couldn't see her.

He peeled out of the bay and into the tunnel. She was maybe thirty yards ahead of him.

And there was more than one way he could hurt Bonaventure.

He picked up the gun and leaned out of the open window, angling to get a decent shot. But then ahead of them a guy came out from an intersecting hallway.

"Dave!" she screamed. "Gun!"

Dammit. He popped off a shot in the guy's direction and then stomped on the accelerator. The car's wheels screeched on the polished concrete surface as they fought for traction. In seconds he'd have her.

She'd looked over her shoulder; knew how close he was. She was running now, with no place to hide.

Wherever she thought she was going, she'd never make it.

Phoebe glanced over her shoulder to see how much time she had, but she'd been calculating her best options ever since she'd seen the handgun sitting on Cliff's passenger-side seat. *He* was the gunman! And probably if any of the security personnel had seen him down here, they'd never have suspected him because of that whole football thing, even though he evidently was the worst second-string quarterback in the history of the NFL.

She had seconds—or fractions of seconds—to find a way to save herself down here. In a maintenance hallway lined with equipment. Lawn mowers, pushing and riding. Groundskeeper-type machines for whatever groundskeepers did. Tools she didn't recognize and various pieces of machinery for painting and whatever. Injury carts. Wheelbarrow-type carts. Carts and wagons for doing things she couldn't guess at. How could these things help her?

It would have been nice if the CIA had taught people how to do something besides write a report.

Was Dave hurt? He hadn't cried out when Cliff fired, so maybe Cliff had missed. If the ex-Rattlesnake wasn't more accurate with a pistol than he was with a football, they had a fighting chance.

She sprinted down the hall. She could almost feel the heat of Cliff's vehicle against her back. One more step and then—there was that flatbed cart with room underneath. Her goal.

Cliff was almost upon her, and his car was a lot bigger and heavier than the cart. But the cart was what she had. She dived headlong for it, flinging herself under the flatbed's overhang, sliding as far forward as she could go. She pulled up her knees, curling into a tight ball underneath the flimsy vehicle, awaiting the worst.

One second later, Cliff crashed his car into the cart.

The impact was tremendous. The back end of the cart crumpled like an accordion. The front tires of Cliff's car were about one inch from her leg, that's how close he'd come to crushing her. Broken, splintered pieces of wood, metal, and plastic scraped and stabbed her. Her arm hurt from contact with something. Maybe her leg, too. She'd have cuts and bruises.

But she didn't think anything was broken. She wasn't seriously hurt.

As long as Cliff didn't back up and hit her again.

Damn! He hadn't gotten her. He knew it, although she'd slid under that damn cart and rolled up tighter than a church sidewalk on a Saturday night. One more smash should do it, though.

He pushed the car into reverse and felt metal scrape against the tire. He'd damaged the car crashing into that cart, but it would still drive, which was the most important thing. Glancing at the rearview mirror, he saw the guy he'd shot at edging around the corner of the intersecting hallway. He had a gun. He was pointing it, getting a bead on him.

He couldn't waste any more time on the girlfriend. He had to keep his eye on the prize—Chase Bonaventure and what he could do to him out there on the field. First things first.

But he'd scared her enough—and maybe injured her enough—to keep her busy for a while, anyway. She wouldn't interfere now.

He pushed the car into drive again, steering away from the dented injury cart, and sped down the maintenance hall-way toward the open field, tires screeching.

Now he'd show Bonaventure once and for all who ruled the field.

When Cliff's car pulled away and sped down the maintenance tunnel, Phoebe couldn't believe her luck. And then Dave ran up, shouldering his weapon. Which explained the luck. She had never been more grateful.

"Phoebe! Are you hurt?" he asked, leaning down to peer at her.

"No." She scrambled out from underneath the cart. "I'm fine. How about you?"

"Unhurt, but unhappy." He ran both his hands through his close-cropped hair. "That Cliff Frizell is a serious nutjob."

"Totally off the rails," Phoebe agreed. "Come on! He's going to shoot Chase, bet you any money. We have to stop him!"

"He'll try. But stopping him is not your job. The cops are minutes out. I'll alert them. They'll stop him."

"That'll be too late! He's out on the field! We have to stop him *now*!"

"Not *you*! Listen to me! You're *bleeding*. Medical's right around the corner. Go there. Go *now*. I'm *ordering* you."

She couldn't go to medical when Cliff was driving out onto the field to hurt Chase and who knew how many others. Tens of thousands of spectators were out there. The drivers. Cheerleaders. The marching band. How many bullets did a gun like that hold? How much damage could he do?

She couldn't let that happen.

Dave turned away to make his call, and Phoebe looked into the crushed cart. The keys dangled from the ignition. *Yes!*

Glancing at Dave's back, she slipped into the driver's seat. She might not have a driver's license, but if this thing started, she was pretty sure she could get it out onto the field. After that, she'd have to see.

The engine fired right up. Dave whirled around.

"Phoebe! Stop right now!" he yelled.

But she couldn't stop. She'd wasted precious seconds already, and she couldn't waste one second more. Not when Chase's life was in danger.

She floored the accelerator and peeled out of the space, tearing through the maintenance tunnel and out onto the football field.

Chase was ready to pull the second winning raffle ticket from the drum when a Venture Automotive car with a damaged front fender and bent grill sped out onto the field behind the marching band. What on earth was that? *Who* was that? All the drivers and cars that had taken part in the driving show were lined up on the twenty-yard line. Had this guy missed the show somehow? Or was it some deranged fan?

"Well, folks, it looks like we've got a mystery guest today," he said into the microphone that was clipped to his shirt. He wanted to stall for a bit of time until he could see who this guy was or what he did next.

And then another vehicle—a maintenance cart of some sort—careened out onto the field, evidently pursuing the Venture Automotive car. The maintenance cart was also damaged—the back end was crushed—but the engine was evidently fine, because it was barreling at top speed for a maintenance cart and closing the gap to the Venture Automotive car in a surprising show of staying power.

In about two seconds as the vehicles sped closer, he saw that Phoebe was driving the open maintenance cart, bent over the wheel, concentrating on the car ahead of her.

What was she doing? What was going on out here?

And then, five seconds behind Phoebe and traveling at a much-reduced rate of speed, Dave Greenaway lumbered out onto the field behind the wheel of a riding lawn mower. The huge machine spewed a thick plume of chopped grass and discarded confetti into the air and left a swath of precisely trimmed turf behind him. The members of the marching band broke ranks, scattering on the field to avoid the whirlwind of airborne vegetation.

This was his crack security team? And what on earth were they doing out here?

And then Cliff Frizell leaned out through the open window of the car, looked backward, and pointed a gun at Phoebe.

Phoebe, who was utterly unprotected in the open maintenance cart. And who was following too close for Cliff to miss.

A cold, hard knot of fear tightened in his stomach and rage filled his brain.

This ended now. Cliff Frizell was finished.

"Give me the football *now*," Chase said, turning to Tony, who'd been tossing it lightly in the air.

The crowd murmured, hearing the command and the urgency but not yet understanding the danger.

Even though Cliff had slowed the vehicle to lean out and look back, hitting the ex-quarterback with a football through the window at this range and the speed at which he was driving would take a miracle, Chase knew. But he'd have no trouble hitting the car itself, which should redirect Cliff's focus away from Phoebe and toward himself. He had to be the real cause of Cliff's bitterness.

Tony tossed him the ball, still grinning, not seeing the danger.

"Get down," he told the men on the platform with him, gripping the football, feeling the laces between his fingers. "Call the cops. Cliff has a gun."

He'd forgotten for a second that he was mic'd up. The crowd gasped. Several people shrieked.

Showtime.

"Cliff!" he bellowed, trying to draw his attention. "Over here!"

It worked, too. At the sound of his amplified voice, Cliff looked his way, swung the gun around. Fired.

The shot went wide and low, the bullet embedding in the turf at least ten yards to the right.

Well, there was a reason the guy hadn't made the starting lineup for any team.

But he couldn't afford to let him get much closer, have a better shot. If he got close and stopped the car, he might hit him. Or worse, someone else.

Phoebe.

He had one chance to make this work. And it wasn't a good one. He wasn't in training. He hadn't practiced a throw like this since the last Super Bowl ruined his knee. And the car was moving at a pretty good clip.

The distance would be maybe forty or fifty yards. In a perfect world, he'd hit the car, startle Cliff, and make him drop the gun.

In a really lousy world, he'd hit the car and Cliff would drive straight at him. In which case, he—and Margo, Tony, Matt, and Rinsho—would be defenseless.

The car was almost at the goalpost now and was angling toward him. Phoebe, unbelievably, was closing the gap, maybe trying to cut him off. What did she think she was doing? When this was over, they'd be having words.

He sized up the field, the angle, the car, the window, the

gun. He'd have one shot. He had to make it work.

He waited until the car got a little closer and the angle improved.

The warm leather of the football in his hand felt like an old friend. And just like in his playing days when they were deep in the red zone, time slowed to a crawl. His mind crystalized and his eye focused. He waited for the perfect moment.

And then he drew back his arm and threw the ball. It flew low and fast, the kind of missile his fans had come to expect in his playing days. The ball sliced the air like a rocket and incredibly went right through the car window, threading the needle as cleanly as it ever had, and smacked Cliff in the jaw.

Cliff's head jerked back; his arms flew up. The gun— all praise to the football gods—fell to the ground.

In the moment, Cliff must have taken his foot off the accelerator, too, because the car slowed.

And then Phoebe, who had not slackened her pace one bit, smashed into the car's rear corner, sending it spinning into a standstill. But her lighter-weight cart ricocheted into the goalpost, hitting it with a sickening thud.

For a second no one moved. Then the crowd roared as a stunned Cliff struggled out of the car and Chase leaped off the platform. He had to stop Cliff from reaching that gun.

Cliff was shaky on his feet, but he was a lot closer to the weapon. Chase stopped abruptly when Cliff grabbed the weapon and pointed it at him.

"Don't do it, Cliff," Chase said. "I know you hate my guts, but you want a lifetime of prison for this? Put down the gun."

"You ruined my life," Cliff snarled. "Now I'm going to ruin yours."

"Hey, Cliff," Dave Greenaway yelled, churning up on the riding lawn mower. "What the hell are you doing?"

In the split second that Cliff glanced at Dave, Chase dove for the retired quarterback. Cliff fired at him, but Chase was already low and parallel to the ground, going for Cliff's knees, and the shot again went wide and long.

Chase wrapped his arms around Cliff's legs, and the momentum drove them to the ground. Cliff hit the turf with a solid whump and Chase grabbed Cliff's right hand, banging it on the ground, hoping to dislodge the weapon, hoping that Cliff's finger was off the trigger. Who did this creep think he was, bringing a loaded gun into a stadium crowded with people? What kind of person did that?

And he'd hurt Phoebe, who from what he'd seen was probably knocked unconscious—or worse—over by the goalposts. A white-hot fury overcame him.

"Get off me!" Cliff croaked, his voice sounding strangled. "Get off!"

Dave charged up and grabbed Cliff's arm, wrestling the gun away.

"Good job," he said to Chase. "I got this now. And you know what? You want to take off that microphone."

Unbelievably, the wireless mic was still clipped to his shirt. Chase ripped it off and jammed it in his pocket.

Now that the danger was over, people streamed onto the field. The marching band, the cheerleaders, and the drivers all milled around, looking shell-shocked or excited, mingling with fans who'd poured over the stands and onto the grass.

"You got this, Dave? I have to find Phoebe."

"EMTs are with her now. Help me turn this guy over first, okay? I want to put the cuffs on him."

They rolled Cliff, and Chase was glad to see the redness on the guy's neck. Cliff would have a pretty big bruise from that football. Maybe trouble swallowing, too. Good.

"Cliff Frizell, you're under arrest," Dave said as they struggled to help him stand.

"Jeez, Cliff, you've packed on a few pounds since they cut you from the squad," Chase said. "Gotta lay off the chips and beer a little bit. But prison will take care of that for you."

Dave glared at him. "I'm talking now, hotshot. *You have the right to remain silent.* Can I get a car from somebody? I can't take this guy out of here on the lawn mower. *Anything you say can be used against you in a court of law.*

You have the right to…"

By now Dave's security detail, the off-duty cops, had arrived and swarmed the scene, separating him from Dave. Uniforms were coming through the west gates, too. He started through the mass of bodies, heading toward the goalpost where Phoebe had crashed her cart. He had to find her, see how bad she was hurt. Yell at her for pulling that stupid stunt.

"Coach! Coach, are you all right?" Tony and the rest of his crew had scrambled off the platform and run after him.

"I'm fine. Listen, I have to find Phoebe. Can you take it from here?"

"Yeah, Coach, but the cops will want to talk to you before you go." Tony looked over to where the uniforms were pushing through the crowd toward them.

"I'll join you as soon as I can." He'd seen his dad, Josie, two brothers, and the construction crew approaching, all looking like they were going to war. They'd be as mad as hornets at Cliff.

The crew took off to talk to the police, and his family charged up, looking like they'd be ready to take on the Steelers in a playoff game themselves.

"Son, are you all right?" Ancel asked. "And Phoebe? How's she?"

"Dave said the EMTs are with her. I'm fine."

"That damn fool Cliff Frizell could have *killed* you," Ancel fumed.

"Not with his accuracy on the field," Max said. "He has a lifetime thirty-seven quarterback passer rating, that's it."

"Sucks to be him," Leo said.

"He should have gotten a job doing something more commensurate with his abilities," Josie said. "Like picking up trash on the highway."

"Josie," Ancel said.

Chase looked around the field. The ambulance that had treated Phoebe was driving off the field. It was probably going to the medical facility inside the stadium. If so, that would be good news. And if they took her to the hospital, the medical facility would know which one.

But before he could look for her, he had to get the stadium situation under control. The spectacular had turned into a spectacular mess. The marching band had lost all pretense of a formation, and now the musicians, hats and instruments on the ground, were brushing grass off each other's uniforms and chatting. The cheerleaders, pom-poms and sequins flashing, tumbled like human ping-pong balls over the field and built pyramids for the fans, who recorded everything with their phones. No doubt the videos would show up all over the internet in a few minutes. The NASCAR drivers were posing for selfies. News crews were interviewing anybody who'd stop to chat. Cops swarmed everywhere, talking to employees and observers, taking notes.

And he still had those new, shiny red cars to give away.

"Dad, guys, help me out here." He pulled the microphone out of his pocket and handed it to Ancel. "I have to find Phoebe. Will you finish up this raffle? Draw three names from the spinner. Give it a little razzle-dazzle if you can. Kristin is up in the skybox; she'll finalize the paperwork with the winners. Okay? I gotta go."

He trotted over to the marching band and spoke to the drum major, who blasted two shorts and a long on her whistle. The band picked up their instruments, snapped to attention, and blew a fanfare.

He looked back. Thirty yards away, his dad clipped the microphone to his shirt and stepped onto the mobile platform.

"Folks, if I could have your attention," he started.

Chase didn't wait to hear any more. And he sure wasn't going to talk to the cops now. They could find him later. Right now he had more important things to do.

He ran along the sidelines, through the gates, and out of the stadium.

Time to find Phoebe.

Chapter 20

The paramedics had given her a shot of something, so the ride to the hospital seemed to pass in a warm and pleasant five seconds or less. The hospital wasn't nearly as mellow. Phoebe winced when they plunked her on a cold metal table for X-rays on her foot, which did not feel good at all, and then a resident inspected her nose.

"Not broken," he said cheerfully as he probed it, feeling for a fracture. "You'll have a nice shiner though."

"Ouch," Phoebe said. Maybe a black eye would give her some street cred in the PI world. That might help to make up for how battered, bruised, cold, and abandoned she felt. It seemed like she'd been here for hours, and Chase hadn't come. Well, he didn't know where she was, and he had his barbecue. And, of course, they'd broken up. That might shift a guy's priorities.

"Somebody will be in here pretty soon with your X-rays," the resident said. "Maybe even me." And then he left her alone again.

Being alone in this cold and sterile place gave her a lot of time to think, and none of those thoughts were cheerful ones. She had to get used to the idea that Chase was out of her life, and by her own decisions. She hadn't fully realized how much she'd miss him. How much she'd come to count on him. How much fun she had with him.

How much she loved him.

She took a deep breath.

How much she loved him.

At one time she'd wondered if she'd ever know for sure the right guy when she met him—the one she wanted to stay with forever. She'd feared that she wouldn't. Her mother thought every guy was the right one, so she wasn't any help in the guideline department.

She had the answer to that question now. When Cliff had roared out of that maintenance tunnel onto the field, planning to hurt Chase—planning to *shoot* him—her fear and anger had blazed to life. At that moment, she'd been terrified for Chase's safety and would have done anything to protect him.

Because she couldn't bear to lose him.

Going back to Langley and the CIA would be the hardest thing she'd ever done. If she even could.

A heavy weight settled on her chest, squeezing her heart. Tears welled up behind her eyelids, making her sinuses ache, her nose throb, and her head pound. She felt utterly lousy, from her head to her toes and everything in between.

And now she couldn't even have a decent cry without *some damn thing hurting.*

It could have been minutes, or it could have been hours, when a hand pushed back the curtain and Dave poked his head in.

"Phoebe," he said. "How you doin'? It's like a rathole in here. I thought I'd never find you."

"Hey," she said, glad to see a friendly face. "I'm okay, just waiting for X-rays. How are you? How did things turn out at the stadium?"

"*Jesus*, Phoebe, that was some stunt you pulled. Where did you learn that PIT maneuver?" He pulled out the rolling chair in the curtained alcove and sat down, crossing his arms.

"The *what* maneuver?"

"Shit, you don't even know what you did? I thought you must have learned that in the CIA. Because you sure didn't learn it from me."

"I got in a cart and went after Cliff. Is that what you mean?"

Dave closed his eyes. "Lord, help me." He opened his eyes and glared at Phoebe. "When you came up and hit his back bumper like that. Cops practice that technique to stop cars trying to make a getaway. If you do it right, the car you're pursuing spins out."

"And I did that."

"Yes. Except you also bounced into the goalpost and landed in the hospital."

"That wouldn't have happened if the goalpost hadn't been there," Phoebe said, feeling pretty lame as she said it.

"You were on a *football field*. There's *always* a goalpost on a football field."

"I'm sorry, Dave."

"No need to be sorry. You stopped the guy. Well, you and Bonaventure. But here's the thing, Phoebe."

He uncrossed his arms, putting his hands on his knees. He looked, well, regretful.

Phoebe took a deep breath. She knew what was coming.

"When you started with me, I told you what kind of agency I wanted to run," he said. "We talked about it. You've got guts and smarts, and I'd hoped—against my better judgment, I gotta say—that we could make this partnership work."

"You don't think it's working?"

"Hell, Phoebe, you *know* it isn't working. Somebody *shot* at us today. I want a quiet life. My *wife* wants me to have a quiet life. I don't want to spend my retirement chasing more crooks and dodging more bullets than I did when I was with the cops. And my dignity, not to mention my backside, won't survive another chase on a riding lawn mower."

Phoebe grinned. "Dave, your dignity could survive anything. Trust me on that."

Dave snorted. "If I were twenty-five years younger or we were cops together on a beat, we'd be tellin' a different story here. But I gotta let you go. You'll be happier at the CIA anyway."

He rolled over to her bedside and held out a hand. She

shook it, and he stood to leave.

"It's been a pleasure knowing you," he said. "Good luck with everything."

Phoebe grinned. "I'll miss you, Dave. If I can ever do anything for you at the CIA…"

"I'll know who to call. Although I hope I never have the occasion to."

Getting fired put a period to a really bad day, and now she felt more tired than ever and the doctor still hadn't come back. She lay down again, the painkillers mostly doing their work, and drifted in and out of sleep. Eventually she became aware that the constant, low-key buzz of the emergency room had intensified outside her curtained cubicle. Maybe the doctor was finally coming. And then a male voice rose above the chatter.

"Phoebe? *Cher?* Where are you?"

Phoebe's heart leaped, joy obliterating the low, throbbing pain she felt everywhere. She almost couldn't believe it. *He'd come after all.*

"In here," she said, so happy and relieved to hear Chase's voice that she almost forgot they'd broken up.

A big hand reached in and swept aside the privacy curtain, and there he was, looking worried and confident and strong and *so fantastically good*, and she was so glad to see him that she started to cry even though it was murder on her head.

"*Cher!*" He pulled up the rolling stool as close to her bed as possible and picked up her hand, holding it between his own, leaned forward, and kissed her wet cheek. "Don't cry. Everything's going to be fine. Your hand is cold. Are you cold?"

Chase had come to the hospital to see her. They were broken up, and he'd worked a stadium spectacular, and now he had a barbecue to host and many other things to do. And yet here he was, sitting with her in the hospital, noticing that she was cold.

She loved him for that. And for everything else, too.

She'd never find another man like this one. And even if it was too late for them, she was going to tell him right now what was in her heart.

"*Cher*?" he said, looking worried now. "Did you hear me? Are you all right? Should I get the doctor?"

She shook her head, tears pouring down her face, her sinuses pounding.

He pulled the thin blanket up over her shoulders and handed her the box of tissues. "Tell me what's wrong. Why are you crying? I just got here. You *can't* be mad at me yet."

She struggled to sit up. She yanked out a handful of tissues and mopped her face, tried to blow her nose.

That was a bad idea. The pounding in her head increased to the volume of a bass drum in a bathroom.

She had to get on with it. No matter how hard it would be.

"Here's the thing," she said between sniffles. "I love you. I mean, I *really* love you. I love you a *lot*."

He blinked in surprise. "But *cher*, that's *good* news! Isn't it?"

She nodded, feeling tears well up again. "Yes," she said, hiccupping as she wiped her eyes. "Well, sort of. I didn't— I mean, I *thought*, but— I wasn't— And then at the stadium, I couldn't— But since I've been in the hospital— And you know, I didn't— But now— I mean, I *really* know it."

"Sweetheart, that's fantastic. What's wrong with that? Why are you crying?"

She tried to take a deep breath, but it came out as a huge, choking hiccup. This was not easy. Her future was a mess. She hated the idea of that. But she could not leave this man. Not while she felt how she felt about him. If he still had feelings for her, too. If he didn't send her away.

"Have you changed your mind?" she asked. "Are you here because you think you could try something long distance? Even for a little while?"

"*Cher*." His voice was very gentle. "I care about you too much to put us through that and watch our feelings turn to resentments."

She nodded. "Okay." His words felt like a boulder in her belly. "I thought that's what you'd probably say." She had one more option, and it was a lousy one. But it was the only idea she had. And she wasn't sure if they could survive it—if *she* could survive it.

But she had to try *something*. Any alternative would be worse.

"If long distance is out, that leaves us only one alternative that I see," she said. "I mean, if it's not too late."

"Let's hear it, *cher*."

She nodded, a massive lump in her throat as she said the words. "You're more important than any job. I'll quit the CIA and stay here in Vegas with you. I'll find something else to do."

Chase leaned forward, tenderly brushing a strand of hair off her damp cheek, smoothing her hair back. His eyes were warm, his voice soft. "Phoebe, sweetheart. *Cher*. I understand what you're willing to give up for me, and I appreciate your offer more than you know. But that is just about the dumbest-ass idea you've ever had."

Chase watched as Phoebe went from looking defeated to looking both hurt and outraged, if that were possible. Which was a lot better than how she'd looked when she'd said she'd quit the CIA for him. That sag in her shoulders, that slump in her posture. That look in her eyes. He *never* wanted to see that again. He never wanted her to trade her dreams for his. That was not the kind of partnership he wanted. That kind of deal totally sucked.

"Hey, buster, I offered to make a huge sacrifice for you." Phoebe scowled. "And you call it a dumb-ass idea?"

"Not just any dumb-ass idea," Chase said. "*Dumbest*-ass. The *most* dumb. Dumber than dumb-ass. *Way* dumber."

Phoebe's mouth quirked a little bit. He hoped that was because she was trying not to smile, not because she was feeling a twinge of pain.

"And it's not too late," he added.

Phoebe's tentative smile widened.

"I love you, too, *cher*, pretty much to the end of earth and back. I'm surprised you didn't cotton on to that sooner. Of course, you've been occupied with some real dumb-ass ideas lately. I, on the other hand, have been brilliant."

Phoebe settled back against her pillows. "So it's a competition now?" she said, her voice prim. "I didn't realize your penchant for winning had carried into civilian life. It's a very unattractive quality."

He grinned at her. Her color was a lot better, so that was good.

"And yet, you love me," he said. "I feel secure in my competitiveness. You want to hear my idea?"

"Please."

"You go back to the CIA. I move to DC with you and work remotely for six months. Like you did for me. We'll be together. No long-distance relationship. And if everything pans out, and you're still with the CIA and you haven't shown me the door, I move the factory to the East Coast or expand there permanently. Does that work for you?"

Phoebe blinked. The air seemed to have gone out of her lungs. And, evidently, her brain, too. She hadn't heard him correctly.

"Excuse me? What did you say?"

"I talked to all the department heads. We have a lot of details to sort out, but everyone's on board. We're all committed to making it work. I'll probably have to travel a fair amount, going back and forth. And then in six months, we'll see if and how it makes sense to move more operations to the DC area."

Her ears were playing a trick on her. And it was a really mean trick, too. Did Chase say that he'd move to DC? For *her*? Maybe even move the company?

Her whole body cramped. A tsunami of relief and gratitude, joy and pain and disbelief, formed in her stomach and swelled, choking her voice. The churning sea of emotion pushed a huge wall of tears up her chest, blocking her lungs, squeezing out her air.

"*Cher?* Can you say something? What do you think?"

Phoebe gulped, trying to create a space to force out some words. The tears flooded her throat. They might suffocate her if she wasn't careful.

This man, standing right here in front of her, this man whom she loved, had said he'd uproot himself for her.

Move across the country. Maybe move his *factory*. For *her*. So he could be with her.

She forced some air past her throat, past the tears, into her lungs.

"You'd do that? Move all that way?" She could hardly believe that he meant it. Or that it was possible.

He nodded. "Yes. You're the most important person in my life. You need to be in DC, but I don't need to be in Vegas. Why should you have to make all the big changes?"

The wall of tears rose past her throat, choking her, flooding her eyes, and poured over her cheeks.

No one had ever done anything like this for her.

No one had ever put her first.

Not her mother, who'd left her behind for much of her life to pursue her own desires. Not the father she'd never met, whose name she'd never heard.

Her needs or wants had never come first. With anyone. Ever.

Until today. Right now. With Chase.

A sob rose up from a place deep within her and broke from her lips, and then another, and then another. Great, harsh, hiccupping sobs that she'd never heard before and couldn't stop. She hunched over on the side of the bed, unable to regain control, wincing when she wiped her nose, almost unable to breathe, her foot and head throbbing.

"*Cher*! What's wrong? I thought you'd be happy. Don't cry. Your sinus passages will swell up and fill with mucus, and then you'll want to blow your nose, and that will hurt like crazy."

A nurse stuck her head in around the privacy curtain. "What's going on in here? Is everything all right?"

"I gave Phoebe some good news," Chase said. "I caught

her by surprise."

"Really? That's what good news looks like?"

Phoebe looked up and nodded, sniffing, wiping her nose. She couldn't let Chase get into trouble for her crying.

"If you say so, hon." The nurse frowned. "It would be better for your head, though, if you could stop crying."

Phoebe nodded again, mopping her face.

"Okay. Well. The doctor will be here soon, and then you can go home," the nurse said. "You'll feel better there." She ducked out again.

Phoebe became aware that Chase was sitting on the roller chair just inches from her, his arms and hands on either side of her legs, trying to comfort her.

She sniffled. The storm of tears was subsiding. Chase ripped some tissues out of a box and handed them to her.

She wiped her eyes and then her nose. She winced. Her head *hurt.*

"You're moving for me," she said, clearing her throat. "That's what you said."

He nodded. "Yeah. You need more time to feel certain about us, and you need to go back to the CIA. Okay. I can live with that. The thing I can't live without is you. So I won't. At first I had trouble wrapping my head around how relocating would work, but it makes sense."

"Nobody's ever done that for me before."

"I wouldn't think so," Chase said. "How many boy-friends with car companies have you had?"

She loved him. Here she was, making a muck of things in the hospital, and he was trying to cheer her up. She reached out to put her hand against his face. "I'm never leaving you."

Chase turned his head into her hand and kissed her palm. "That's the plan. I'm holding you to it."

He got up from the rolling chair and sat next to her on the edge of the bed, putting his arm around her. She leaned into him. He was so solid. And he was here for her. *And he was moving to Washington, DC!*

For *her.* To be with *her.*

"Are you sure?" she asked. "Sure you want to do that?"

"Yes, I'm sure. Don't take a job with the CIA in Antarctica, okay? That would be harder to pull off."

She gave a little sigh, relishing his comfort. "If… if the six months works out, won't moving the company be awfully disruptive? Or stretch your resources too far? I mean, right now, when it's just getting on its feet."

"Nope." Chase kissed her. "It's a great idea. In fact, I'm ready to do it right now, and I'm not sure why I didn't think of it sooner. We need to expand, and we have the investment to do it now. From the East Coast, we'll have access to more talent. We'll be closer to European markets. We can join the lobby for cleaner air. We can open a second production facility back there, maybe in West Virginia, I'm not sure about that yet. We'll have to research that some more."

"Maybe I could help with that."

"I would appreciate that very much if you're not too busy catching bad guys," he said. "Of course, you're an idiot for not letting me pay off the CIA loan for you. I'm loaded, in case you didn't know."

Phoebe rolled her eyes, and Chase grinned.

"And one more thing—in DC, I won't be nearly as famous. They've got their own handsome and talented ex-quarterback. I'm looking forward to going to a restaurant and not spending half my time signing autographs."

"That *is* a plus."

"But there's a catch to all this, *cher*. I've got conditions."

Worry stabbed her. *Of course he did.* But shoot. He was moving across the country for her! That's what he'd said. She could compromise.

"Okay," she said cautiously. "What are your conditions?"

"I've got a real estate agent looking for property in the area right now," he said. "I'm not worried about office space. Evidently, that's plentiful and my requirements aren't complicated. I could even work from home, at least for a while. But housing is another matter. I'm not familiar with any of the neighborhoods she talked about—she said Maryland, Virginia, whatever—but you probably are. I'd like you to check out the possibilities and choose a place you like.

Because the first condition is that we move in together."

Phoebe's head jerked.

"Yeah," he said, serious now. "I know you'd like more time, but my life passed before my eyes today when Cliff pointed that gun at you. I want you in my life, Phoebe, so if I'm moving to DC, we're living together."

She'd felt her life flash before her eyes, too. In that split second when the car crumpled against the goalpost and she saw stars, Phoebe thought of Chase and all the time she might have spent with him. Time she wouldn't have if she lost him. A great swell of *rightness* started in her belly and surged to the ends of her fingers and toes and up into her brain. She didn't regret the past, but going forward, starting right now— yeah, she wanted to be with Chase.

Because she knew now without a shadow of a doubt that she loved him.

"Okay," she whispered.

"What? I didn't hear that."

Bastard. But she grinned, clearing her throat.

"Okay," she said. "I'll find us a house. And we'll live in it. Together."

"That's more like it. Next. The second condition is that you marry me."

Phoebe blinked, the air sucked right out of her lungs. *What was he talking about?*

"No, that's impossible," she said. "*Way* too soon. We haven't even moved in together yet, and—"

"That's the condition," Chase said. "Marry me. It doesn't have to be soon. We can have a long engagement. You can have all the time you want to get used to the idea. But we'll live together and we'll be officially engaged, because we love each other. And we'll get married when you're ready."

Phoebe frowned, looking at him. His face was serious, but his eyes were dancing.

Oh, for Pete's sake. He was *enjoying* this.

So, okay. She was beyond thrilled with everything. Chase was moving to DC. She could work off her school loan. They weren't breaking up! He loved her and she loved him!

But *marriage*.

Well, why not? He'd just said she could have a long engagement. He hadn't put a date on it. He'd said, when she
was ready.

She might not be ready for a while. *Quite* a while.

"On one condition," she said.

Chapter 21

Chase looked at the woman he didn't want to live without. She was sort of a mess right now. She was developing one hell of a black eye, and her face and nose had traces of blood and snot. Her clothes were dirty and bloody, too. But she'd gone after Cliff even when she thought they were broken up, and by doing so, maybe saved his life. Or at least given him a decent shot at stopping Cliff with that football. And now, here she was, in the emergency room, bargaining with him about a marriage proposal.

Who did that?

Nobody but Phoebe.

"I understand," he said, smiling. "You want some token that I'm sincere. You're wondering where your ring is." He reached into his pocket and pulled out a Super Bowl ring. He hadn't had time to get to a jeweler to buy her a ring she might really like—he'd barely taken the time to dash home to get this one—and it was way too big for her hand, as well as outrageously gaudy. But if she wanted it, she could have it. He never wore the thing himself—his three championship rings just sat at home in his wall safe.

But he'd hoped that the ring showed her that she could have anything of his. Nothing was too big or too much. To protect him, she'd gone after a man with a gun. He wanted her to know—and feel in her heart—that he would do anything for her.

And they were making commitments to each other today, right now. She deserved a killer ring.

"It won't fit," he said as he held it out to her. "If you want to wear it, you'll need to have it resized."

Her eyes widened as she gazed at the huge cluster of gold and diamonds. "I can't take that. It's…" Words seem to have failed her.

He slipped it on her finger. It slid around and nearly fell off.

"We could put some tape on it," he said. "There's probably some in here somewhere."

"We're not putting tape on it! It's obviously worth a fortune. Where did you get it? *Why* did you get it?"

He grinned. She sure knew squat-all about football. "What's your condition?"

"Condition." She stared at him, uncomprehending. That had to be a first. He'd stripped the thought right from her head.

Chase laughed, wrapping his arms around her and kissing her. They hadn't known each other long—she'd always been right about that—but he'd known from the first that she was right for him. As he held her, he felt all the pieces of his life—pieces he hadn't known he kept separate—click into place. Family, home, work, leisure. Phoebe made it all come together. Phoebe bound every part of his life into one cohesive whole.

He loved her for that.

He savored the moment, breathing in the smells of sweat, blood, and disinfectant, knowing he'd never smelled anything so sweet. He held her for a long time, not hearing or seeing anything that wasn't Phoebe, but eventually the sounds and sights of the emergency room came back to him.

"Dr. Ostrand, please report to obstetrics," the PA system blared. "Dr. Ostrand, to obstetrics."

"Our song," he said, and Phoebe laughed.

"Yeah, we'll have to change that tune when we get out of here."

Just then a hand pushed back the privacy curtain, and a

man in a white coat entered. "Hi, Phoebe? I'm Dr. Maloof. Good news about your foot."

Phoebe beamed. "It's not broken?"

"Just a sprain. I'll tape it up for you, and you'll be good to go."

"Great! And that's not the only good news! We're engaged!" She flashed her ring.

"Congratulations!" the doctor said, taking out an elastic bandage. "We don't see that every day in the emergency room."

"It'll be great." Phoebe took Chase's hand. "We'll have fun, and we'll be together, through thick and thin. That's what matters."

Dr. Maloof started to wrap Phoebe's foot. "You're right," he said. "In sickness and in health."

Chase nodded. "For richer or for poorer."

Phoebe grinned. "Although so far, it's been mostly for richer."

Chase laughed. "You can't always count on that. Nobody knows what the future brings."

"I don't count on it," Phoebe said. "I'm counting on *you*. Because no matter what, you'll always be there for me."

"Like you'll always be there for me. No matter what."

Phoebe nodded and squeezed his hand. "There's just one small thing. The condition. I remembered it."

Chase frowned. "You did? What's that?"

Phoebe shook her head. "Are you kidding me? Our house. What did you have? *Fifteen bedrooms*. I'm telling you right now, fifteen bedrooms is *out*."

ABOUT THE AUTHOR

Kay Keppler abandoned the freezing climes of Wisconsin, where she was raised, for northern California, where she lives in a drafty old house with wonky plumbing. Now if the duct tape holds, everything will be perfect.